# Yellow Death: Arrival

Book 1 of the Yellow Death Chronicles

Peter R Hall

Yellow Death: Arrival

Book 1 of the Yellow Death Chronicles

Copyright © 2021 to 2024 by Peter R Hall

First published 2021

All rights reserved.

ISBN: 9798642771532

No part of this publication may be reproduced, distributed, or transmitted in any form or by any means, including photocopying, recording, or other electronic or mechanical methods, without the author's prior written permission, except as permitted by U.S. and U.K. copyright law. For permission requests, contact peter@peterhallauthor.com.

Use of this publication for training of generative artificial intelligence software is strictly prohibited without the author's prior written permission.

The story, all names, characters, and incidents portrayed in this production are fictitious. No identification with actual persons (living or deceased), places, buildings, and products is intended or should be inferred.

Paperback 2nd edition 2024

For more information, please email the author at: peter@peterhallauthor.com.

Website: https://peterhallauthor.com

# Content Warning

Dear reader,

This story is intended for an adult audience. The setting is a post-apocalyptic world and aims to be realistic about the behaviour of people when all semblance of law and order has disappeared.

Thus, it deals with mature themes including violence and sexual abuse—although none of this is intended to be gratuitous. There is also swearing, including the f-word. If this is likely to offend or upset you, please do not read on.

Please also note, the story is set in Britain and written by a British author so—not surprisingly—it is written in UK English and uses UK terminology.

I hope you enjoy the story and I hope it makes you think.

# Contents

| | |
|---|---|
| Prologue | VII |
| 1. Cal & The Pheasant | 1 |
| 2. Final Thoughts | 5 |
| 3. Cal & the Red Minibus | 9 |
| 4. Diagnosis | 27 |
| 5. Cal & The Raiders | 39 |
| 6. John Grows Up | 47 |
| 7. Cal & The Invitation | 55 |
| 8. John Goes To School | 63 |
| 9. Cal Meets Gibson | 69 |
| 10. John's Teenage Years | 83 |
| 11. Cal & Sabine Alone | 93 |
| 12. John Gets His Gun | 115 |
| 13. Cal Meets Juliet | 127 |
| 14. John & the Interrogation | 141 |

| | | |
|---|---|---|
| 15. | Cal Makes A Decision | 157 |
| 16. | John & Aarika | 177 |
| 17. | Cal & Juliet | 189 |
| 18. | John & Britney | 199 |
| 19. | Cal's Perfect Life | 217 |
| 20. | John's Exploding Disc | 239 |
| 21. | Kim & The Outbreak | 249 |
| 22. | John & The Outbreak | 271 |
| 23. | Cal Meets Ken & Sue | 283 |
| 24. | Kim Makes A Choice | 293 |
| 25. | Cal & The Ultimatum | 305 |
| 26. | John & The Yellow Death | 315 |
| 27. | Cal Meets the C.U.G. | 325 |
| 28. | John & Cal | 345 |
| 29. | Kim & The Yellow Death | 355 |
| Afterword | | 361 |
| Acknowledgements | | 363 |

# Prologue

ON THE 20TH ANNIVERSARY OF FREEDOM DAY

I tried so hard to forget about Freedom Day. To pretend it didn't exist.

That idea disappeared when I entered the Tavern.

I'd walked to the hamlet of Fresh Hope, intending to barter for salt and a few other provisions. It was unusually quiet. The only sound was raucous singing coming from the pub. The locals had decorated it with colourful bunting. Even the horses tied up outside had ribbons and flowers adorning their bridles.

I assumed there was a wedding no one told me about. It wouldn't be the first time. Everyone knows I'm not a party animal. I nearly turned back for home. Except that I'd walked for five miles and really needed that salt.

So, I took a deep breath and plucked up the courage to enter. The place was crammed. Where had all these people come from? I scanned for a friendly face and met eyes with Fred behind the bar.

He beamed at me. "Happy Freedom Day! Come, get a drink."

Others chorused, "Happy Freedom Day." One young lad added, "Death to the oppressors."

This was crazy. How did they know about Freedom Day?

Fred passed me a tankard of dark frothy beer. I sat down with the rest of them to listen to old Tom tell the Freedom Day story. It turns out they'd heard it many times before, but the retelling was part of their annual celebration. Between gulps of ale, Tom's gravelly voice related the tale of the stranger who appeared out of nowhere to lead the rebellion.

None of them realised I was the stranger they celebrated. It felt weird to hear Tom refer to me as a hero. According to his version of the story, I had superhuman powers and performed miraculous acts. It's easy to see how folk tales such as Robin Hood became popular. People need heroes, so invent them.

In reality, I did so little. I was only a catalyst. The right person in the right place at the right time. Perhaps the fightback wouldn't have happened without me, but that's true of so many others, especially Kim. She sacrificed much more than me.

My wonderful Kim. I think of you every day. I wonder what would have happened if we'd met before the Yellow Death? But who am I kidding? Before the plague, I was a very different person and not somebody you would have given a second glance to.

I changed so much after the Death. Looking back, it was like a metamorphosis. All the decades of therapy through my childhood barely scratched the surface of my nerdiness. Yet—somehow—the few years following the plague altered me at a fundamental level. In the maelstrom of death, brutality, and desperate sadness, I learnt to be a half-decent person. At least I hope so.

When Tom finished his rambling tale, one kid asked where the stranger lived now. Tom smiled. "Nobody knows for sure. Some say he wandered off into the wilderness, heartbroken.

But, he waits for the time when freedom is threatened once again. Then he'll return to lead us to victory once more!"

The crowd cheered.

Ha! Don't hold your breath, Tom.

## Chapter One

# CAL & THE PHEASANT

TIMELINE: MARCH 15TH 2030: 6 MONTHS FOLLOWING THE YELLOW DEATH

*"A single death is a tragedy; a million deaths is a statistic."*

Josef Stalin (1879-1953)

The melody and lyrics of Mad World entered Cal's consciousness. His mouth was dry and tasted of old leather. Warm sunlight fell on his face. Why was he in the open air and not in his tent? He blinked a few times before clamping his eyes shut against the brightness. His phone continued to play the song, gradually increasing in volume.

Keeping his eyes shut, he fumbled around before cancelling the alarm, leaving only birdsong to disturb the silence. The cool, fresh, morning air caressed his bare arm and contrasted with the sticky heat inside the sleeping bag.

Cal fumbled with the zipper of his padded cocoon. His regular sleeping companion—a Glock automatic pistol—jabbed into his thigh.

"Ow! Sodding hell."

Now he was wide awake. He recalled last evening—cloudless and still. The stars had been diamonds set against jet-black velvet. Uncharacteristically, he had slept in the open air. Perhaps risky with no weather forecast, but the decision turned out well—only a few streaks of high cirrus cloud disturbed the canvas of blue sky. It promised to be a beautiful spring day.

Slowly, he stretched and twisted, easing the stiffness out of his back, before rolling over and clambering out.

"Welcome to another day in post-apocalyptic paradise. Your schedule today is...well, the same as yesterday and the day before."

Talking to himself had become a habit.

Cal picked up the phone and checked for a signal. Of course, there would be no signal. There had been none for 186 days. There would never be a signal. Nevertheless, he scanned the screen. Checking was part of his routine, and the routine was important.

He stood and stretched. Out of habit, he checked his surroundings, confirming all was exactly the same as last night.

The site had been a picnic spot before the Yellow Death. One of many scattered throughout the Devon countryside to cater for the summer tourists. A dirt track lead from the highway to a small patch of asphalt, providing parking for several cars and motorhomes. Mature oak and ash trees surrounded the clearing. The seclusion meant Cal had not needed to camouflage his SUV last night. On the edge of the car park stood a public toilet built to look like a log cabin. However, the stench inside was so rank that Cal kept well away from it.

After slipping on his boots and shouldering his combat shotgun, he walked over to the tree line to relieve himself, carefully stepping over the tripwire surrounding the campsite.

The steaming jet splashed against the side of an ancient oak tree, making bizarre patterns as it raced to the ground.

*Why do I feel the need to pee up against something? Must be instinct. Like a dog. At least that's one thing I share with most men.*

The unmistakable 'kok-kok-kok' of a nearby pheasant brought his reverie to an end. Cal crouched and slid the combat shotgun off his shoulder before scanning the undergrowth. The bird sounded once again. Cal smiled as he spotted it strutting through the long grass.

Cal lifted his shotgun and took careful aim.

*Not very sporting, but this is about getting food. Survival. Filling my belly.*

At a distance of twenty metres and standing twice the height of surrounding vegetation, the bird would be an easy kill. It looked in Cal's direction, and he frowned as a wave of guilt flowed through him. This was a magnificent specimen, with scarlet wattles contrasting against its iridescent bottle-green head. No blending into the background for this creature—the bird was hell-bent on attracting a female.

The thought of fresh meat made Cal's mouth water. Then he remembered the supplies crammed into his SUV, and the many food caches hidden throughout Devon.

Cal couldn't bring himself to pull the trigger, so lowered his shotgun. "Okay, Mr Pheasant, this is your lucky day. Just don't cross my path when I'm starving."

The bird strutted on, blissfully ignorant of its brush with death.

*I've really got to learn to toughen up.*

An hour later, Cal was nearing the completion of his daily run. His body was like a machine, moving smoothly and in perfect rhythm. On warm sunny days, this was his favourite time, and today he wanted to run further—but this was a Wednesday and he always ran five miles on Wednesdays. No more and no less. That was the routine. The routine was important. When the music track in his earphones changed to Bonnie Tyler's '*I Need A Hero*', Cal broke into a final sprint down the dirt track leading to his campsite.

He stopped and wiped the sweat from his brow before checking his wristwatch. Yes! Under forty-eight minutes. Pretty damn good, considering he ran with a rifle and ammo belt.

From habit, Cal scanned the surroundings and, finding nothing hostile, allowed himself to relax slightly. Lifting his foot over the tripwire, he walked into his campsite and loosened up a little more. The daily run was risky, so he always felt relieved to return to his base.

Cal's stomach felt hollow. Thoughts of breakfast came to him. First, he must complete the rest of his daily routine. He lit a fire with wood selected to burn with almost no smoke. Then he collected his food rucksack from the back of the SUV. Neatly labelled bags contained everything needed for today's meals. Cal opened the breakfast bag and tipped out the portion of porridge oats to soak. There were four heaped spoonfuls—always four.

Now was the time for exercises and a wash in the stream.

Cal liked the morning routine. The ritual made a satisfying start to the day. Without the routine, nothing felt quite right.

Besides, this had been his routine before the Yellow Death. Why should the end of civilisation change it?

## Chapter Two

## FINAL THOUGHTS

TIMELINE: AT THE TIME OF THE YELLOW DEATH.

"Often when you think you're at the end of something, you're at the beginning of something else."

Fred Rogers (1928-2003)

**The following is the last log entry of Dr Fiona Chirivino, Clinical Research Centre, Addenbrooke's Hospital, Cambridge, England.**

I expect this to be my last journal entry. My laptop battery is down to 10% and when that's gone, I'm back to the Stone Age. God knows why I'm bothering to write this, since no one will ever read it.

Perhaps, as a research scientist, recording everything in detail is a tough habit to break. More likely, I need to share my thoughts, and there's nobody left alive to talk to. Maybe I'm more of an optimist than I would give myself credit for, and I cling to the hope someone in the future may benefit from my ramblings. Before succumbing to the disease, I'll print out my recent log entries.

There has been no time for research these past few days. Anybody with a medical qualification—and many without—were recalled to the wards when the front-line medical staff started dropping. However, before the internet crashed, I contacted my colleagues around the world and so have an inkling of what hit us.

There's so much we still don't know and never will. But here's what we're reasonably certain of:

The enemy is a mutation of the Yersinia Pestis bacterium. Ironic that billions will die without knowing the name of their killer. This microscopic organism is accepted as being the 'Black Death', which halved Europe's population in the 1300s, returning many times later until it disappeared in the 19th century. This variation of the bacterium has significant and deadly differences to its predecessor.

The Black Death was spread, at least in part, by fleas and lice living on humans and rodents. This limited the rate of infection. The Yellow Death variant has no such limitation. Two or three days after infecting a human, it becomes resident in the sinuses, trachea and lungs. Sometimes it causes the victim to cough, although usually there are no symptoms. Yet from that point on, whenever the victim sneezes or coughs, they spew the bacteria into the air, to be inhaled by someone else. A kiss from an infected person might be a kiss of death.

Of course, if a sick person touches their mouth, the bacteria will be on their hands and transferred to everything they touch, to be picked up by the next victim.

The early stages are often asymptomatic and, by the time a sufferer shows obvious signs of illness, they might have passed on the disease to many others, who themselves have already infected still more. It's a sad fact that when somebody finds out they are ill, they might already have killed everyone they love.

Modern living contributed to the rapid escalation. When the Black Death ravaged Europe, the fastest transport was a horse and cart, and most people rarely left their town or village. In twenty-first-century society, the mass transport systems and high population density provided a perfect medium for the transmission of this disease.

I remember how COVID-19 caught us out. It took us months to realise infected people with no symptoms were spreading the disease. "Never again," we all said. How soon we dropped our guard. In truth, we never stood a chance against this new foe. The spread was too fast and deadly. By the time we put a name to it, every country was already contaminated.

The New Variant Yersinia Pestis combines the worst aspects of bubonic, pneumonic, and septicaemic plagues. This led to speculation that this strain must have been created in a laboratory—perhaps a biological warfare experiment released by mistake? I am not of this view. Viruses and bacteria mutate readily, so it was only a matter of time before a variant appeared, which was both highly infectious and virulent. There are hundreds of such viruses circulating within the animal kingdom, just waiting to jump to a new species.

Besides, surely the most insane government would not deliberately create a disease which killed almost everyone—would they? It is unlikely we will ever know for sure. Either way, our preparations should have been more thorough.

The Yellow Death proved resistant to our normal antibiotics, such as streptomycin and tetracycline. In the early days, a massive intervention with multiple antibiotics reduced the mortality rate to under 90%—still alarmingly high. Usually, our best efforts only had the effect of deferring death for a few days—long enough for liver failure to turn the skin a yellow pallor—hence the name coined by the media.

Unfortunately, our stocks of drugs soon ran out and, when they were gone, we had nothing. Our medical facilities were so overwhelmed that many died from dehydration and the lack of basic care.

The attempts to stall the advance of the disease proved useless. The images of the RAF bombing the motorways were spectacular, but I suspect the exercise was the classic example of shutting the stable door after the horse has bolted.

It's getting light outside. The start of a beautiful day. Usually, the hospital would be buzzing, but the only sounds are birds singing outside the window. Their cheerful tweets are like taunts, given our situation. I doubt I'll see the end of this day. My head started pounding half an hour ago and my armpits are swollen and tender. As a researcher, I'd love to know why it took so long to take hold of me.

I think I'm the last person in the hospital to fall ill. Addenbrooke's is a gigantic morgue with the bodies of doctors and nurses lying side-by-side with their patients in the corridors.

I've watched everyone I know die, and said my final goodbye to my fiancé, Jean, only this morning. Not everyone is dead yet. A few hardy souls cling to life, but whether they will eventually pull through is uncertain. We ran out of IV drips two days ago, so I've been trying to get the few patients left surviving to sip water. However, it appears I shall soon be unable to perform even that small service to them.

I have no intention of suffering the same horrific death I've witnessed in many others. I've put something aside to speed my journey when the time comes. My laptop is now telling me it has less than 5% power and I'm starting to feel feverish. Perhaps there's time for just one more visit to my patients?

## Chapter Three

# Cal & the Red Minibus

TIMELINE: 6 MONTHS FOLLOWING THE
YELLOW DEATH

"A person with autism lives in his own world, while a person with Asperger's lives in our world, in a way of his own choosing"
       Nicholas Sparks (1965– )

Cal sat cross-legged next to his campfire, eating his breakfast porridge. A year ago, it would have been served with fresh milk, topped with berries, chopped nuts and Greek yoghurt. Today, he used powdered milk, which turned it into a grey unappealing stodge. Cal mechanically shovelled it into his mouth as he studied the road map laid out before him. A cloud passed in front of the sun, and he shivered. It was early enough in the year for the morning air to be chilly with no direct sunlight.

Today, he planned to raid an army base on Salisbury Plain. This meant travelling outside his familiar territory, but there was no alternative. Where possible, Cal avoided driving long distances because of potential hostiles, plus the scarcity of fuel. However, in the six months since the Yellow Death, he had raided every military base in Devon. Unfortunately, his caches of weaponry still lacked certain specialist items he wanted to lay his hands on. Thus, a trip further afield was called for. Cal's SUV and trailer had been emptied in readiness for the scavenging journey.

His finger traced the roads on the map. In moments such as this, he missed the internet. Prior to the Death, he would have located all the military bases with their units and had his route planned within minutes. Now he was forced to driving around Salisbury Plain hoping to spot a helpful signpost. Still, he recognised things might be worse. He was only a two-hour drive from the greatest concentration of army training grounds in the UK. By taking his time, he would find everything on his wish list.

He turned his attention to an Ordnance Survey map of North Devon. It was covered with symbols and notations. These were a code showing the locations of caches he had created since the Death. This was only one of several similar maps hidden in his vehicle. Just looking at the various symbols gave him a sense of satisfaction.

After surviving the terrible fever, Cal was so weak he could do little more than think. So he thought and thought. Not about the past and what had been lost, but the possibilities for the future. Everything had changed. Having studied military history for most of his life, he knew how fast society would turn nasty since the mechanisms of the law were gone.

Most folk would be reasonable, friendly and cooperative—at least whilst food remained plentiful. Yet some would see this as an excuse to live out their violent dreams. It would be great if only decent people survived the plague, but surely psychopaths, rapists and other lowlifes would wake up to this shiny new world?

Law and order would be enforced by the barrel of a gun, so best to make sure the good guys owned the guns. Unfortunately, the low-lives would be the first to arm themselves. Cal saw the opportunity to swing the balance. He knew about weaponry—perhaps more than any other survivor. His mission became to find and hide as many armaments as possible. When respectable people were threatened, he could give them weapons and the training to use them.

Cal wasted no time beginning his self-appointed task. Whilst most survivors spent the early weeks wallowing in grief, or shocked into inactivity, he had been busy. As soon as he regained strength to stand for more than a few minutes, he visited his first army base.

Finding suitable hiding places proved to be the toughest part. They had to be secret and protected from the weather—the same locations survivors might seek refuge—so he chose them carefully. One of his largest caches was in the basement of a village church. The stench from the decaying corpses of those who had sheltered to pray and die would deter anyone stumbling upon the building.

After a few weeks, he changed tack. He noted most travellers formed small groups, which scavenged from shops and houses, taking what they needed for now, with no thought for the years ahead. Often, he found stores broken into with only a few items taken. After the looters had smashed the windows, the remaining stock became exposed to the elements and roaming animals. A shocking waste of an irreplaceable resource. Eventually, most people would settle down and make new permanent homes. When that happened, they would need reserves of supplies until they became self-sufficient. Yet it seemed nobody was preparing for this.

On the occasions Cal met with others on the road, he hinted they should also store and conserve. Yet most people showed little enthusiasm for his ideas. Most survivors existed in a depressive fug with barely enough energy to get out of bed in the morning.

Thus, he began gathering and storing irreplaceable supplies, such as petrol, medicine, army ration packs and toothpaste. These would be shared when times became hard—something he felt sure would happen sooner than anyone imagined.

Perhaps today he might seem like an obsessive, pessimistic jerk, but he hoped that before long, others would wake up to reality and praise his foresight.

By mid-morning, Cal was driving east along the A303 towards Salisbury Plain. He had made good progress so far. The sun was high in the sky. The dry roads meant no potholes hidden under puddles. He even allowed himself to relax a little and enjoy the views. The flat countryside with endless fields separated by hedgerows and copses still appeared neat and well-tended—remarkably unchanged in the six months since the Yellow Death. Of course, that would soon change. Spring had arrived, so the hedges and verges were about to burst forth with new vegetation. This year, there would be no farmers or council workers to hold back nature's fecundity.

The road was a wide and straight single carriageway stretching out before him. Except for a few abandoned vehicles and pot-holes, the way was clear. He kept his speed under fifty to conserve fuel and give him plenty of time to react to others coming from the opposite direction—his biggest concern.

Normally, Cal focussed forwards, keeping his eyes on the road, but his attention became drawn to the ancient stone circle of Stonehenge passing by on his left. The road passed within a hundred metres of the iconic landmark, with the massive silcrete and bluestone pillars standing proudly above the flat grassy plain.

Cal had seen Stonehenge many times on television, but never in reality. The thought of it gave him a buzz. Five thousand years ago, primitives had lifted rocks weighing hundreds of tons and placed them with extreme precision, using nothing more than stone tools and timber lifting gear. Some stones had been transported for 180 miles over land and water. But what was the purpose?

Stonehenge had permanence and solidity, which he sensed. They appeared to stand in judgement—mocking the upstart humans who had placed them here.

When his eyes returned to the road, his worst fear materialised. In the distance, coming straight at him, was another vehicle. A red mini-bus strained under a massively overloaded roof rack.

Cal panicked and braked hard as he pulled over to the side of the road. He grabbed his rifle and combat shotgun, jumped out of the car and went around the rear, stepping over the trailer's tow bar. The mini-bus was a couple of hundred metres away now. He crawled along the verge until the vegetation was dense enough to give cover, then scrambled through it, scratching the backs of his hands with brambles. He lay flat, giving him a clear view of the road through the bottom of the hedgerow.

Cal took a few seconds to catch his breath and assess the situation while watching the mini-bus come closer. If he was lucky, they would not have seen his car moving, so would pass by, thinking the SUV was just another abandoned vehicle. He hoped so. They could not see him hiding behind the hedgerow, but bushes would not stop bullets.

*Dammit! This is exactly why I hate travelling.*

He checked his weapons and made sure they were ready to fire.

The mini-bus slowed and finally stopped a few yards from his SUV. It had sliding doors and could carry about fifteen people, although the rear two-thirds were stuffed to the roof with supplies. The bus sported a collection of dents and rusty patches, which was incongruous with the brightly painted 'Rainbow Tours' logo on the side. The roof rack was a poor fit, with ropes tied to the back door handles helping to secure it. Cal saw four people inside, but since the vehicle was packed with belongings, perhaps others might be hidden.

The engine died. A man in his forties, sporting a bushy beard and noticeable paunch, climbed out, then walked to Cal's Lexus. Cal noted he carried a double-barrelled shotgun. If that was the extent of their weapons, he had little to fear. The bearded man peered into the SUV, then strode around it suspiciously. He put his hand on the bonnet.

"Engine's warm," he shouted to the mini-bus. "You were right, Mia. It was moving. But there's nobody here now. It doesn't look damaged. The tyres are okay. I don't reckon anyone would have just left it here." He shielded his eyes from the sun and looked around, pausing for a moment at the bushes where Cal hid. Cal gripped his rifle and reminded himself he was invisible to them.

A woman's voice called from the bus. "Let's move on, George. Whoever it is, obviously doesn't want to meet us."

*That's excellent advice. Listen to her, George.*

Somebody inside the bus had other ideas. The sliding side door opened and a young woman nimbly jumped out. She could not have been a bigger contrast to George. Cal reckoned she was in her mid-twenties and had short blonde hair. She wore faded jeans and a white T-shirt which sported the slogan *'In Training For The Zombie Apocalypse'*.

"Get back on the bus," George shouted. "It might be dangerous."

"For God's sake, George, you're not my dad," she said. "I wish you and Mia would stop telling me what to do."

"Look, you agreed to do what we told you if we brought you along."

"Yeah, yeah, yeah."

"Sharon! Do as George says," a hysterical voice shouted from the bus. That must have been Mia.

Sharon ignored her two older companions, her eyes scanning the surroundings. "Hey, you out there. Why not come out and meet us? We don't bite."

Cal felt foolish lurking behind the bushes. Was he over-cautious? This might be a trick. Who else was in the mini-bus, and were they armed? He should go ahead with discretion and take no chances.

"Okay," Cal shouted. "Listen carefully. I want everyone on the bus to come out with their hands on their head. No sudden moves. You, with the beard, lay down your shotgun, very, very slowly."

"Why should I?" George said, the tremor in his voice giving away his false bravado.

"Because you're standing out in the open and I'm hidden with an assault rifle."

"H-How do I know you're telling the truth?"

Cal fired a burst from his rifle into the air. The staccato shots caused George to flinch, and he promptly knelt down, placing his shotgun on the ground. Sharon casually placed her hands on her head, seemingly unconcerned by the gunfire. A middle-aged woman with a wild explosion of ginger hair came out first. An older man who gripped a walking stick followed her. His free hand was placed on his head.

"Don't shoot, don't shoot," Mia said, holding her arms up high.

Cal forced his way through the hedgerow. Keeping his assault rifle trained on the small group, walked past the bus, glancing inside. He saw no one else, so shouldered his rifle.

"Relax everyone, I'm friendly," he said, then bent to pick up George's shotgun and break it open.

"This is empty, you've got no cartridges," Cal said to George.

"I—I ran out a couple of weeks ago. I only carry it for show."

"I see. Well, I can give you some shells." Cal resisted the urge to point out that by carrying a gun, George was likely to get himself shot on sight. George may as well have been wearing a sign saying 'shoot me' around his neck.

"Okay, everyone, you can lower your hands. Sorry if I scared you. I needed to make sure of your intentions. I get jittery when people wave shotguns around." He handed the shotgun back to George. "Here you go. My name's Cal. Pleased to meet you."

☣☣☣☣

"Oh, Lord," Cal said. "This bread is absolutely gorgeous. I didn't realise how much I missed proper fresh-baked bread. How do you manage to make it?"

Mia beamed at Cal's exuberant compliments. "It's quite easy, really. I've rigged a bread-maker to run off the bus power point. We've got plenty of flour. The problem is yeast has a short shelf life. I don't know where I'll get some more."

"Me neither, but I suggest you make it a priority."

Once they had got past the stage of pointing guns at each other, they relaxed and introduced themselves. George suggested they shared lunch and exchanged news. Cal agreed, but didn't want to stay on the road. Stonehenge was a stone's throw away—an opportunity too good to miss. The five of them sat in a circle on the grass, eating and drinking. The food included cold beer, canned meat, fruit, and the pièce de résistance was Mia's crusty, malty bread.

The impromptu picnic felt surreal since they were surrounded by immense bluestone pillars looking down upon them. Stonehenge sat on a slight rise above the flat landscape, so they enjoyed a panoramic view of the Wiltshire countryside.

Under an almost cloudless sky, the warmth from the March sun encouraged a relaxed atmosphere. Cal sat back against one of the massive standing stones while George and Mia related their story.

All four travellers had lived and worked in London before the Yellow Death.

"The plague decimated the population," George said. "But there were enough alive in the city for groups to form up quickly. Government buildings and some big corporations had generators, so became popular as bases. Some folk raided hospitals to steal their generators. As long as fuel was available, people lived comfortably." George swigged from a bottle. "That's an excellent beer. Wonder how long it'll be before somebody makes stuff like this again?" He belched.

"Get on with the story, George," Mia said.

"Sorry. Anyway, the biggest problem was the bodies. Bodies everywhere. For a couple of months, a foul stench hung over the city. There were no escaping it" He chuckled under his breath. "Before the plague, some people used to nickname London 'The Big Stink'. They had no idea how true that became. Strangely, after a while, we sort of got used to it. I guess you can get used to almost anything. When the cold weather came, it disappeared."

"Or we just stopped noticing it," Mia said.

"Yeah, possibly," George said, nodding thoughtfully. "Anyway, there were vast supplies all around London. Not only in shops and supermarkets, but in restaurants and people's houses. Fresh and frozen food spoiled straight away, but there was plenty of other stuff which would last ages...at least we thought it would." He sipped his beer before continuing.

"It was the same with fuel. When the petrol stations ran dry, we started syphoning the tanks of the thousands of cars left in the streets. So it seemed we'd be okay for a long time."

Mia huffed. "We should've known better. After a few months, supplies became short and things turned nasty. By then, most people had joined groups with established territories. Some gangs had nicer patches than others. Disputes started up over where one territory ended and another began. Fights broke out—especially at night. Most nights after dark, we heard gunfire and saw the sky glowing with flames."

Sharon laughed. "Bloody typical. Ninety-nine percent of the population gets killed by a plague and, within months, those left alive are fighting each other."

George continued. "Mia and I were in a group of twenty, living in what used to be a private clinic. It was a great place—once we'd cleared out the bodies. There was a working well for drinking water, and gardens, which we planted out with veggies. We tried to keep a low profile. No lights after dark, no fires before dark. But it was no good. One night, we were raided. The bastards were quick and brutal. They had no plans to take prisoners, and they shot anyone who resisted. Mia and I ran for our lives. I thought my lungs would burst. The next day we went back, only to find it was burnt to the ground. We saw nobody from our group again."

Mia put down her food and held her head in her hands. "It was terrible. We'd lost everyone we loved in the plague and just when we started making friends again..."

George put his arm around her and continued. "Next day we were cold, hungry and homeless. It pissed down all day. I'll tell you we were ready to give up. To throw in the towel. Both of us had enough. If it wasn't for James..."

James was the fourth member of the group. He smiled. "I saw them opposite my house, crouched in a doorway. And a sorry sight they were. I'm not sure why I took them in. Since the plague, I'd been living on my own and doing very well——existing in the shadows, not attracting attention."

"Oh, come on now," George said. "You helped us because you wanted out of London."

"Yeah, well, maybe," James said. "It was getting obvious there was no future staying in the capital. I'd stored up plenty of food and stuff, but it was only a stopgap. Thing is, I couldn't drive. I was in a terrible car crash a few years ago. Hence the walking stick. I never felt the need for a car in London—not before the plague, anyway. Of course, everything's different now."

"James took us both in," George said. "Convinced us to leave the capital with him for the West Country. We needed a big vehicle for all of James' supplies. After a bit of a search, we found the mini-bus. We were fitting the roof-rack when we met Sharon."

George glanced at Sharon, giving her the chance to take over the story. She was chewing a chocolate bar and motioned with her hand for George to continue.

"Sharon was leading a foraging team sent out to scavenge and loot. Luckily, the mini-bus was empty, so we had nothing to steal, and they left us alone. No doubt if we had some supplies, they'd have thieved everything. Anyway, half an hour later, Sharon appeared again. She'd doubled back and asked if she could join us. Like us, she realised living in London was not feasible and it was best to get out sooner rather than later. She was charming and promised to do what she was told—hah!—so we agreed to take her along. The next day we left London and, after a few hours of driving, we ran into you."

"That's not quite how I see things," Sharon said, licking chocolate off her fingers. "When my scrounge team found them, it was obvious they were fitting out the van to carry supplies. Standard procedure was to rough 'em up 'till they blabbed where they'd hidden their stash. But I saw these folks as a way to get out of London. So I ordered my team to move on, then slipped back later. My crew were suspicious, but knew better than to disobey my orders."

During the uncomfortable silence which followed, Cal noted the friction between Sharon and the others.

"That's quite a story," he said. "I find it hard to believe you all stayed in London for so long."

"The city was our home," Mia said. "It was all we had left. At the start, it had everything we needed. We would've been crazy leaving early on, with food around everywhere for the taking. Things became worse so slowly we didn't notice. Honestly, I shudder now when I think of how we lived towards the end."

"Bit by bit we turned into animals," George said. "Every day, a little more of our humanity got eaten away. Nobody cared. We became used to the stench of death. We moved around corpses without a second thought. Rat stew became a delicacy. When I look at all this beautiful countryside, I reckon we were mad to stay there. But there are still hundreds, maybe thousands, too scared to leave. I guess if you've spent your entire life in a metropolis, the great outdoors is like another planet. Most city folk wouldn't have the faintest idea how to survive out here."

The group became quiet for a few moments, each lost in their own thoughts.

Sharon broke the silence. "What about you, Cal? What've you been up to since the Dying?"

"The Dying?"

"Yeah, that's what most people in London are calling the plague."

"That's the first time I've heard it called The Dying. In fact, I'm not even sure why it's called the Yellow Death."

"Well, I know that," George said, clearly pleased to impart his superior knowledge. "When it first appeared, they tried pumping the victims with loads of antibiotics. Mostly, they only kept them alive for a few days. Long enough for liver failure, so their skin and eyes turned yellow. Of course, when things got terrible, people died too quick for that to happen, but by then the name had stuck. The media love a catchy name."

Cal was barely listening. He already knew why the plague was nicknamed the Yellow Death. He played dumb to deflect the question about himself.

Sharon was not to be put off so easily. "Well, whatever you want to call it, you still haven't said what you've been doing for the past six months."

"Oh right, yeah. Nothing much, really. Same as most people. Travelling around, scavenging. Seeing what develops. I'm looking for a good place to start a settlement."

Cal kept the knowledge of his weapon and food caches a secret. The mini-bus crew were no threat—they were friendly and harmless—but he would not want them spreading stories about invaluable hidden stockpiles all over Devon.

"What did you do before the Dying?" Sharon said.

Cal swallowed. "I was in the Army. An officer in the infantry. When the plague hit, I was on leave. Pretty lucky in a way——I might have been stranded in some God-forsaken hell hole."

"Really!" Mia said. "That's amazing. What was it like in the army? Did you see any action?"

Mia's questions prompted a barrage of queries. They wanted to know every detail of his army life and combat experience. Cal answered with as little detail as possible. Most of what he said was exaggeration or fabrication. As the questioning continued, Cal's chest tightened and his mouth dried up. During the interrogation, Sharon stared at him silently, like a predator observing its prey.

"Did you work out a lot before the Dying, Cal?" she said. "You've got a well-toned body."

Cal flushed. "Really? Do you think so? Er, well...I guess that just comes from being a soldier. And I go running most days."

"Well, whatever you do, it looks good on you. It's nice that you still bother to shave, too. It's rare to see a man without a beard these days and, let's be honest, they don't suit everyone."

George scowled and rubbed his own beard.

"Er...thanks," Cal said. "Shaving is just part of my routine."

Answering questions about his invented past was bad, but worse was being flirted at by an attractive woman. Cal coughed to clear his throat and began rubbing his thumb and forefinger together nervously.

"What are your plans, James?" Cal said, hoping to move the subject of conversation away from himself.

"Oh, I'll be looking for a home somewhere. Preferably an established settlement."

"Interesting. I don't mean to be rude, but won't that be difficult—what with your disability?"

George and Mia exchanged glances, but James did not appear to take offence. "Don't you worry about me, Cal," he said. "I'm a dentist. I might be the only surviving dentist in the country. Wait until somebody gets toothache and then we'll see whether they regard me as a liability."

Cal considered this for a moment. "Will you be able to work without your drills and other tools?"

James beamed. "Hopefully, I'll find a settlement in a central location and set up a practice. There's a lot of equipment on the bus, and I'm sure I can get whatever else I need from abandoned dental surgeries in Devon. There's no reason anyone would have looted a dentist. Over the last six months, while I've been on my own, I've researched traditional dental methods. I even have an old drill worked by pumping a foot pedal. So, I reckon I'll make a good living from pulling teeth. Dentists existed a hundred years ago, you know."

"I suppose so," Cal said. "Well, I wish you luck. It'll be interesting to see how you get on. No doubt I'll have need of your services sometime."

*Let's hope that's not anytime soon. I don't fancy having my teeth attacked with a pedal powered drill by a man with only one good leg.*

☣☣☣☣

The meal within the standing stones gradually wound up. George and Mia would have chatted all afternoon, but Cal wanted to move on. He liked the group, but this was the most socialising he had experienced for months, and the chatter caused him agitation. He desperately needed solitude.

Cal advised George to be more cautious when approaching strangers and gave him a box of shotgun cartridges.

As they re-packed their vehicles, Cal noticed Sharon pull a mirror from her bag, check her face and plump up her hair, frowning as she did so. She saw him watching and smiled.

"It's a mess, isn't it? What I'd give for a decent hairdresser and I hate these fucking brown roots growing out."

"Oh, I think it looks fine... great, it does, really."

"You're very sweet, Cal."

Cal picked up his map and began checking the rest of the route. The sound of a rifle cocking startled him. He turned and swung the shotgun off his shoulder, ready to defend himself. Sharon stood at the back of the vehicle, casually holding his assault rifle. She had removed the magazine filled with live rounds.

"Careful!" he said. "That's a dangerous weapon."

"No shit," she replied, then grinned. "It wouldn't be much use if it wasn't."

Without hesitation, she slammed the magazine back into the gun, cocked it and tossed it to Cal, who caught it clumsily.

"Don't worry, the safety's on."

Cal looked at the rifle. She was right. "Where'd you learn to handle one of these?"

"Back in London, my squad was well armed. You'd be surprised how much stuff we found in T.A. centres and police stations."

"Actually, I wouldn't. Why didn't you take some weapons when you left your gang, or whatever it was called?"

"I would've liked to, but if I stole any guns, my crew would've never given up looking for me. Besides, why would I need a gun when George the hero is protecting me?"

Cal laughed. "Tell me, earlier on—when we first met—you jumped out of the bus. What was the idea? You could've got shot."

"Naah! If you were unarmed, you were harmless. If you had guns, you could've already shot George and raked our bus with bullets. I was unarmed, and didn't look threatening."

"I suppose not."

"While I was stuck in that bus with George waving his stupid empty shotgun around, we were all in danger. He was making us look hostile. But as soon as I jumped out, the situation totally changed. Am I right?"

"Yeah. I guess so."

"Believe me, I've been in far riskier situations than that. To survive in London like it is now, you develop an instinct for when there's real danger."

Sharon peered into the rear of the Lexus.

"Wow, you've got some serious hardware. Grenades. Machine gun. Cool. Bet nobody messes with you."

Cal cleared his throat and put down the rifles he cradled. "Well, I mostly try to avoid people."

"You must get rather lonely? A young, healthy man like yourself. All on your own, like."

Sharon moved in close. They almost touched. Cal stiffened as he felt his personal space invaded.

She lowered her voice. "Take me with you."

"What?"

"It's not safe travelling with George and the dragon over there. They've got no instinct for survival. If you weren't such a nice guy, George could've got us all killed this afternoon. If I was with you, I'd feel a hell of a lot safer. Don't be fooled by my looks. I'm tough as old leather and I know how to use guns. We'd be great together."

Cal hesitated and his eyes flicked up and down Sharon's body reflexively.

"Don't get the wrong idea," Sharon said. "I'm not asking you to marry me. This is purely business—mutual survival—at least for a start."

If Cal had an hour to consider the proposal logically, he might have agreed. It made a lot of sense.

Yet, with Sharon almost pressing against him and her musky perfume wafting up his nose, adrenaline kicked in, causing his face to flush and his guts to tighten.

He had been alone for so long that living with somebody was difficult to imagine. And in such primitive conditions. And a young woman.

A million questions crowded into his brain. What would be the sleeping and toilet and washing arrangements? How would they decide where to travel? How could he keep his real past secret? Would she go along with all his security measures? How would he respond if she wanted sex? How would he get privacy? What if they argued? How would they share future caches? What about those already completed? What if they met others on the road? Would she want to join with them? They might disagree over...over...almost anything! How? Why? What if? What if? What if? Argh!

Cal realised he had stopped breathing and inhaled deeply. "Er...Actually, no thanks. I really do prefer to travel alone."

"Just for a short time, please, until I meet somebody else?"

"NO!" He spoke with more force than intended. The others looked in his direction.

He whispered. "Listen, Sharon. You're a lovely girl and, yes, I've no doubt you're able to take care of yourself but, please understand that I—I travel alone. I hope you can accept that. You know nothing about me and, believe me, it just wouldn't work out. I'm sorry, but that's it." He summoned a tone of finality in the last words.

She moved back, clearly surprised. "You're fucking crazy, you know that, don't you?"

"It's not the first time that's been said."

"Okay. It's your loss. You have a nice life. A nice, long, boring, lonely life. I think we'd have made a kick-ass team."

She swivelled around.

Cal watched her stride back to the mini-bus.

*I don't do teams.*

Watching her walk away brought a moment of regret.

"Er... Sharon?"

She stopped and turned.

"Just hang on a minute, will you?"

Cal rummaged in the back of his car, then pulled out an assault rifle; boxes of ammo; magazines, and a cleaning kit.

"Here, take these."

Sharon smiled as she took them. "Thanks. George'll be green with envy. Perhaps you're not such a toss-pot after all."

## Chapter Four

# DIAGNOSIS

TIMELINE: 29 YEARS BEFORE THE
YELLOW DEATH

"Education commences at the mother's knee, and every word spoken within earshot of little children tends toward the formation of character."

Hosea Ballou (1771–1852)

"I'm sure Dr Kendall won't be much longer," said the receptionist, giving Sarah a practised smile, lacking any genuine warmth.

Sarah smiled back and nodded, then returned to her seat in the waiting room. She resisted the impulse to nibble her top lip, but rotated her wedding ring over and over. The walls of the small windowless room closed in on her. Sarah guessed it used to be a storage cupboard. A faint whiff of antiseptic hung in the air. Somebody had attempted to cheer up the room with pastel-coloured walls and generic artwork, but to Sarah's mind, they were not proper paintings. They were the sort of modern art which a monkey might have made with a paint roller.

Earlier, she had left her three-year-old son, John, with Doctor Kendall for a psychological assessment and now anxiously awaited the results.

In the corner, a small radio broadcasted a phone-in show. The public gave their advice on how the Government should resolve the latest Afghanistan dilemma. The discourse was passionate, with one caller asking why her husband's death was worth propping up a corrupt regime on the other side of the world. "Haven't we learned anything from the last time?" she screamed from the radio microphone.

Sarah shook her head.

*No, my friend. I don't think we ever do.*

The radio programme made Sarah think of her own husband—Charles—a colonel in the army. She believed he might be in Afghanistan, or nearby—but could never be sure. Charles was in a hush-hush intelligence role. Not that it mattered exactly where he was. What counted was his absence at yet another critical moment for John. She understood her husband's work was important to national security and the war against terrorism—anyhow, that's what he kept telling her. Still, it would be nice if he showed up once in a while.

Thinking about Charles increased her anxiety. She realised she was nibbling her lip after all. *Dammit!*

She snatched a mirror out of her handbag and studied her face. An attractive visage stared back at her—thin, with high cheekbones and a sharp nose, which some said gave her an aristocratic appearance. She tried to make the best of what nature had given her. Even though Charles was never around to appreciate her, she enjoyed the admiring glances in her direction from the soldiers on the army base where she worked. They were too disciplined to comment, but she sensed it—their eyes said it all.

She picked up one of the dog-eared magazines from the low table and flicked through the pages without registering their contents. Anxiety gnawed inside her guts. Maybe the doctor would find nothing amiss with her son and declare John was perfectly normal. That could not be right. John was so solitary and uncommunicative—much of the time he acted as if he was on another planet. He loved playing with Lego and was making models intended for much older children, yet he was incapable of catching a ball. Something was odd about John. Surely somebody else saw that?

Eventually, Dr Kendall put his head around the waiting room door and gave one of his best welcoming smiles.

"Mrs Callaghan-Bryant, you can come in now. I'm so sorry to keep you waiting."

The doctor led Sarah along a cramped corridor into his office, where the bright sunlight made her squint. Kendall angled the blinds to reduce the glare. "Sorry about that. How did you get on in town?"

"Oh, fine," she said. "I did some window shopping while you were assessing John. I got him a new book. Where is he, by the way?"

"He's in the next room playing. I wanted to speak to you alone before bringing him in."

The doctor swivelled his computer screen so Sarah could view it. "Look, there he is."

The bottom right corner showed a CCTV image of her three-year-old son sitting at a table and drawing. A bored-looking nurse sat next to him, staring out of the window.

Dr Kendall sat behind his desk, leaving Sarah to take the much smaller chair proffered on the other side. The room was nondescript and might have been any medical consulting room anywhere. The furniture comprised an imposing wooden desk with a computer, three chairs, and a bank of mismatched filing cabinets. On the walls were the doctor's certificates and more of the monkey paintings. An imposing scale model of the human brain stood on the cabinets, looking far too realistic in Sarah's opinion. The only evidence the office belonged to a child psychologist was the box of toys in the corner.

"Would you like a cup of tea or coffee?" Kendall asked.

She would have loved a coffee, but was more eager to hear about the assessment. "No, thanks, I'm fine."

*Just get on with it.*

Doctor Kendall steepled his fingers, which Sarah recognised as a signal he was about to speak with the utmost authority.

"As you know, I've spent the last couple of hours analysing John to assess his physical, mental, and social capabilities. The results of the tests require time to fully interpret what they might show. I'll study them at length and in due course will write a detailed report for you."

"Yes, but surely you have an idea—"

"However, as I was about to say, I expect you're eager to get some idea of the findings, so I'll give you my initial impressions of John."

*At these prices, I should bloody well think so.*

Sarah smiled politely, then slid forward in her chair, ready to absorb every word Dr Kendall spoke.

"Please understand you should not see these investigations as passing or failing. There's no right or wrong. The tests measure certain characteristics and traits. Each one is just a piece of the puzzle. Nevertheless, when taken as a whole and compared to population norms, they can show where a person may have difficulties...or issues."

He paused and turned over a few pages in front of him, glancing briefly at them. Sarah nibbled at her top lip.

"John is highly intelligent, and he has an excellent memory. I'm sure you're aware of that."

She nodded. "Yes, he learns rapidly."

The doctor stared at his notes. "Yes...yes," he mumbled, flicking the pages back and forth. "John's results do show up certain anomalies with his personality."

Sarah exhaled. At last, her suspicions were confirmed.

"Mrs Callaghan-Bryant...May I call you Sarah?" Dr Kendall said.

"Er, yes, yes, of course. I know my surname's a bit of a monster."

*A bit like my marriage.*

"Great. Well, Sarah, how much do you know about Autistic Spectrum Disorder, or ASD?"

Sarah had done her research. However, she wanted to hear it direct from the doctor. "I've heard of autism, of course. But I don't know anyone who has it."

Kendall smiled in that condescending, all-knowing, superior way doctors must spend months practising to get just right. "Oh, I think you have met people with autism, but you probably aren't aware of it. They rarely wear a label."

Sarah remained silent, so Kendall cleared his throat and referred to his notes again. "Yes, well, I still have to review the test results thoroughly, but I believe John is on the Autistic Spectrum. Unfortunately, he also appears to be highly introverted. Not the best combination."

☣☣☣☣

Sarah smiled as she drove home from Dr Kendall's office. The sky was crowded with fluffy white cumulus clouds, matching her mood. She knew something was not quite right with John. Nobody believed her—not her sister, nor John's doctor and, most galling of all, not even Charles. They said she was being overly concerned, that John was just a quiet lad. "Stop fussing, he'll grow out of it."

Now she felt vindicated. She had secretly recorded her meeting with Doctor Kendall on her phone. She had listened to the recording once already, yet could not resist listening again, so pulled over into a layby and pressed the 'Play' button. The doctor's voice came out of the car speakers...

*"Yes, well, as I said, I still have to review the test results thoroughly, but I believe John is on the Autistic Spectrum."*

*"He's autistic?"*

*"Er, well technically, yes, but that's such a broad term. It's more complicated than that.*

*"Please go on. Decomplicate it for me."*

On the recording, Sarah heard Kendall shuffling through his notes and mumbling to himself. She realised with hindsight she had been somewhat impatient and aggressive. Fighting for John had become a habit.

*"In my view, John has what we call higher-functioning autism. I shouldn't really say this, but it used to be categorised as a distinct condition known as Asperger's Syndrome. These days, we prefer to regard it as part of the Autistic Spectrum."*

*"Oh, right. So what are the symptoms? What can we do about it?"*

*"Well, Sarah. I'm sure you've noticed the signs yourself, which is why you brought John here. The key indicators are; impairment in social interaction; restricted and repetitive behaviour patterns; clumsiness and obsessive tendencies. Also, there are characteristics which are less obvious. People with autism struggle with social niceties. They tend to be very direct and... well, honest. John might say something crass or hurtful without meaning to."*

*"Oh dear! That sounds bad."*

*"Well, having autism manifest in this form isn't so bad, and certainly not in John's case. John is highly intelligent and that can be a significant compensation. There are other things you should know about the condition to understand it fully."*

*"Go on, please."*

*"This is a very individual condition. It's different for every sufferer. There's an old saying amongst psychologists: Once you've met one person with Asperger's, you've met one person with Asperger's."*

The doctor chuckled at his own joke, but stopped abruptly when Sarah did not join in.

*"Yes, well. Although this form of autism presents difficulties, it often comes with positive personality traits."*

*"Oh, good."*

*"Individuals with this presentation of autism are typically trustworthy, reliable and conscientious. They can show great physical and mental endurance when following subjects they are interested in. Curiously, they do not tend to be followers—they form their own opinions and do their own thing. They prefer to work on their own and find teamwork particularly challenging."*

Sarah pressed the 'Pause' button.

Kendall's description of the symptoms did indeed fit John well. She knew how he often acted alone, even when he was in a group of children. But another idea occurred to her. It sounded like Kendall was describing her husband, Charles. It had never struck her before. In fact, it seemed outrageous, since he was a colonel in the Army. Maybe that was why he had branched into intelligence?

Charles hated social functions and idle chit-chat. He was indeed clumsy—once he literally shot himself in the foot. Now she thought about it, John was a more extreme version of his father.

She pressed 'Play' again:

*"This form of autism is not all bad. It's accepted some of our greatest scientists had the condition—Isaac Newton and Einstein, to name but two. There's a lot of speculation that some titans in the tech industry have Asper—I mean, are autistic. Working in isolation for years with a passion in a single narrow subject is typical of a person with autism. In fact, some people argue that rather than thinking of it as a disadvantage or disability, we should treat it merely as a difference."*

*"That's fine, but in our society, being different is enough to be a disadvantage."*

*"Yes, well, quite. Let me be clear from the start, there's no cure for it. No pills or surgical procedures will take it away. It's a condition for life—part of John's personality."*

*"There must be things we can do. Treatments? Therapies?"*

*"Oh, yes, yes, of course. At three years old, John's very young and his brain is quite adaptable. You've done well to get this far so early. There's a great opportunity to influence John's behaviour before it becomes set."*

*"Good. Go on."*

*"Well, there are three options. You can wait for aid from the State, which might eventually lead to some sort of classroom help for John at his school. Regrettably, the waiting lists are so long and budgets so tight. Alternatively, you could send John to a private specialist school, but they are few and far between, and heavily oversubscribed. Thus, my preferred solution is intensive interventions at home."*

*"Okay."*

*"I can provide a plan which includes physical exercises to improve coordination, applied behaviour analysis, structured teaching, speech and language therapy and social skills therapy. Personal tutors would do this at home, with occasional visits here for monitoring and specialist work."*

Sarah remembered the doctor pausing at this point and giving her a serious look.

*"However, the burden of the task would fall on you and your husband. For John to reach his full potential, requires several hours of one-to-one activity every day and it will be quite intense. Bringing up any child is hard work. An intelligent child with autism even more so. Are you up for the challenge?"*

Sarah pressed the 'Stop' button.

Was she up for the challenge? If Kendall had known her, he would not have needed to ask. It only encouraged her further. Truth be told, she felt life lacked any proper direction or purpose. Now she had something to get her teeth into. Within the week, she intended to be an expert on autism.

Only one more hurdle remained. Kendall's plans called for personal tutors, specialist equipment, bespoke education programs, and regular psychological assessments. That would be costly, and she was not entirely in control of the purse strings. She would have to secure the funding for John's future.

☣☣☣☣

"Charles... Charles. Can you hear me?" Sarah saw her husband's face on her laptop screen. His mouth moved, but no sound came out. She checked the volume control, but everything was fine with her device. She shrugged towards the screen to show Charles something was wrong. He appeared to be inside a green tent. Only his head and shoulders were visible, with a bland canvas backdrop behind him moving as if being blown by the wind. He wore desert combat fatigues and sported a golden suntan.

*"—rah. Hello Sarah. Yes. Good. I can hear you now. Much better. So how are you? You look great."*

"I'm fine Charles, so is John. How are you?"

*"Good, very good. Lost a few pounds. One of the lads here has been getting me out running. I'm really enjoying it. Can't think why I stopped. Are you running these days?"*

The sound was a couple of seconds ahead of the video, so his lips were not moving in sync with his speech. Sarah hated these video calls. It was impossible to have a proper conversation.

*"Not so much. I try to go out once or twice a week with Cath. It's difficult to find time with John around. Where are you, Charles?"*

His expression changed when her question arrived a few seconds later. He paused, which always meant he was about to lie.

*"I'm in Afghanistan and it's hot as hell—in more ways than one. How is John doing?"*

A vague answer and quick change of subject. After eight years of marriage, she knew wherever he was, it was unlikely to be Afghanistan. Their video calls were so one-sided and superficial. Sometimes, it felt like he couldn't tell her what he had for dinner without breaching security. She pushed it to the back of her mind. This call was not about her and Charles or the bloody MoD. It was about John.

*"John's doing fine, Charles. Listen, I took him to a psychologist yesterday, like we agreed."*

This was not something Charles had willingly agreed to. Sarah pushed for it, with Charles conceding to keep the peace.

*"John saw a Doctor Kendall who is an expert child psychologist. The doctor gave him a thorough assessment. It took several hours."*

*"Sounds expensive."*

Sarah bridled. Was that his only reaction? The cost. Never mind. Now was not the time to argue.

She held up the written report to the camera. "There's a hundred-and-twenty-page document on the results of the tests. Shall I email you a copy?"

*"Can you just give me the short version? I'm a little pressed for time."*

*"Okay. Basically, John has a type of autism called Asperger's Syndrome—although we're not supposed to call it that any longer. Do you know what that is?"*

*"Of course, I'm aware of it. Let me just..."*

Sarah watched him typing and staring at his screen, no doubt looking the term up on Wikipedia. How typical. Charles would rather read about it than have her talk to him.

*"Are you sure?"* Charles said, still typing.

"Doctor Kendall's sure. If you read the report, the signs are all present."

*"Ah, here we are, Asperger's... yes, just a moment... interesting. I suppose it fits what you've been saying. I'd love to read the report, darling, but we're up to our eyeballs over here."*

*Not too busy to go running with his mates, though.*

*"The thing is, Charles, to a large extent, it's fixable. With interventions, therapies, personal tutors and the like, the effects can be mitigated. There's no reason John can't be very successful. But the therapy's not cheap. John needs a lot of expert help and equipment to reach his full potential."*

"Oh, I see."

Sarah noticed something distracted him out of her view. His mind had already moved onto another subject. He smiled at whatever he was looking at. *"Listen, I'm happy to leave that side of it up to you, Sarah. I'm sure you know what's best. Looks like you were right about John. Jolly well done. Good girl."*

*Good girl. Ugh!*

A young woman in uniform appeared and whispered into Charles's ear.

Charles nodded in response to her.

*"Sorry, Sarah, I must go now. Are we straight?"*

"Yes, Charles. Will you be back for John's birthday?"

His eyebrows shot up.

*Has he forgotten John's birthday—again?*

*"Well, I can't promise anything, but I'll try. It's a bit out of my hands. Anyway, got to go. Love you. Bye."*

Sarah went to say goodbye, but the connection was already cut.

*That was easier than expected. He sounded perky. I wonder if that woman has anything to do with his mood. Best not to think about it. I've got carte blanche to get John the help he needs, and that was the point of the call. Now it's full steam ahead. Time for a coffee and another reading of Kendall's report.*

## Chapter Five

# Cal & The Raiders

TIMELINE: 6 MONTHS FOLLOWING THE
YELLOW DEATH

"The human failing I would most like to correct is aggression. It may have had a survival advantage in caveman days, to get more food, territory, or a partner with whom to reproduce, but now it threatens to destroy us all."
Professor Stephen Hawking (1942–2018)

Cal drove along the A303 again, this time heading west, away from Salisbury Plain and back to familiar Devon. The setting sun shone directly in front, causing him to squint. He travelled towards ribbons of deep orange stretching from one horizon to the other, but had no appreciation of the sunset's beauty. His chief concern was finding a suitable campsite before darkness.

The journey to Salisbury Plain exceeded his expectations. He had stumbled upon Bulford Camp, which used to be the home of both mechanised and infantry battalions. The armoury was an Aladdin's Cave, containing weapons he had been hunting for months. Of course, the good stuff was secured in reinforced concrete bunkers, but the judicious application of a military excavator punched a hole in the wall big enough to crawl through.

His SUV's roof rack and trailer strained from the weight, and the interior was packed to the roof lining. He kept his speed down, since the vehicle sat low on its suspension. Even so, many more journeys would be required to strip the barracks of everything useful. This treasure trove might well bring an end to the need to stockpile weapons.

A cloud momentarily passed in front of the orange ball of the sun, casting a pall of darkness over the landscape. It reminded Cal he needed to stop soon. He would usually camp near a river, check out the area, camouflage his vehicle, and plant booby traps before darkness fell. Unfortunately, loading his SUV had taken longer than expected. His back ached, so lifting the last of the heavy crates on the roof rack was agony.

He was behind schedule and might need to alter his routine. Tendrils of anxiety crept into his guts, so he made a conscious effort to breathe deeply. Hell and damnation! He should have started back earlier, even if it meant leaving with his SUV half-full.

With the sun in his eyes and his attention directed towards finding a place to camp, he never noticed the pothole. The overloaded SUV jerked and the steering wheel wrenched out of his hand. Cal slammed his foot on the brake and, for the second time that day, boxes and equipment flew forward, striking the dashboard.

"Bollocks, bollocks, bollocks!"

The SUV stopped rocking, and the engine cut out, leaving his heavy breathing as the only sound.

*Stupid, stupid, stupid! You weren't paying attention to the road, you idiot. You might have taken out a wheel. Now get a grip and stop panicking. The world won't end if you don't get to set a few tripwires.*

Cal laughed at the thought—the world won't end—a bit late to worry about that.

A quick check on the tyres confirmed they were still intact. Feeling chastened and grateful no actual damage was done, he started off again, slower this time.

A few minutes later, Cal approached a stationary vehicle on the opposite carriageway. This was not uncommon, since many people ran out of fuel or broke down—yet something spawned a sense of menace. He couldn't remember this vehicle from his earlier journey, and it sat at an odd angle. The light was fading, so Cal came quite close before recognition dawned, causing him to jolt upright. The red mini-bus!

He braked hard and came to a halt about seventy metres from it. Grabbing his weapons, he jumped out of the SUV and took cover behind it. He could now see a Ford Transit van and Landrover Defender parked in front of the mini-bus. Several figures carried goods from the bus. They noticed him and shouted at each other. Two positioned themselves behind the bus and aimed rifles in his direction, whilst the others continued loading their vehicles—with greater urgency.

The roof rack on the mini-bus was already empty. The thieves now worked on the interior. Boxes and clothing were strewn across the road. Cal moved around his vehicle to get a different viewing angle. None of the mini-bus quartet could be seen.

This was tricky. A Mexican standoff. Except he counted at least five of the buggers. Since Cal could not see the mini-bus occupants, he dared not shoot at the raiders. Where the hell were Mia and the rest of them? Maybe they were held in one of the raiders' vehicles? He had a rocket launcher, but dare not use it.

Nor could he leave the cover of the SUV to get any closer. What a stupid place to stop!

This was so frustrating. Every last item was being stolen while he looked on, powerless to intervene.

Finally, the raiders were almost finished, so four of them climbed into their vehicles. One remained hiding behind the mini-bus with a rifle aimed in Cal's direction. The raider fired a shot, which struck Cal's SUV, forcing him to crouch lower. Another. Then another. Cal heard the shattering of windows being shot out. Shards of glass fell on his neck. Cal poked his rifle over the car's bonnet and fired a quick burst high in the air, so as not to risk hitting one of his friends. Now, at least the raiders would know he was armed.

It made no difference. The raider continued to shoot into the car. A horrible thought occurred to Cal—what if one of those bullets hit the explosives he was carrying? Grenades, mortar shells, and rockets were stacked to the roof—if the shooter hit one of them, a monumental pyrotechnic display would ensue. Suddenly, hiding behind the SUV seemed a bad idea.

The shooting stopped, and he heard the revving of engines and screaming of tyres. Poking his head up, he watched the two vehicles speed into the distance. He moved around to the other side of his SUV. Two tyres, plus all the windows and headlights, were gone. He was going nowhere.

Then he noticed flames inside the bus, spreading rapidly. He sprinted over to it.

George's body slumped over the steering wheel. They had shot the poor sod through the windscreen with a high-powered rifle. Mia's body sat next to him—also shot through the windscreen. Her precious bread-maker lay smashed on the side of the road. The flames were spreading to the entire vehicle, so Cal held his arm up to protect his face from the heat as he circled the bus. Acrid fumes caught in the back of his throat. James' body lay on the floor, but there was no sign of Sharon. The bastards must have kidnapped her.

Cal stepped back, the heat of the fire becoming intolerable. He could do nothing as the vehicle became an inferno. He gagged when the smell of burning flesh assaulted his nostrils.

The thieves had stripped the bus of everything valuable and left. They had killed anyone in their way. It was the cold-blooded murder of innocent people seeking a new life, including possibly the country's last living dentist. All for a few cans of food.

What now? They had taken Sharon. He had to rescue her!

Cal looked at the sorry state of his SUV. The spare tyres were underneath his stash of armaments. It would take at least an hour to unload and fit them. Full darkness would have fallen before he was ready to leave. The thieves might be in any direction, with a sixty-mile head start. Without headlights or windscreen, he would have to drive at a snail's pace. He had no way to track them—vehicles left no marks on asphalt roads.

It was hopeless. Cal sat on the ground and held his head in his hands.

☣☣☣☣

# Cal's Journal

I've barely eaten tonight. The deaths of poor George, Mia, and James have sickened me. When I'd fixed my SUV, it was dark, so I camped by the side of the road. Not ideal, but I'm so knackered and depressed it was the best I could do.

Some people say the Yellow Death is a new start and a chance to make a better society. Bollocks! Nothing's changed. Most folks are still selfish arseholes. The only difference is there's no law, police, or courthouses to curb the worst excesses of humanity. I shouldn't be surprised, it's exactly what I was expecting. That's why I've been stockpiling weapons. However, this was the first act of wanton brutality I've actually come across, and it was sooner than expected.

Scavenging is still easy, so why did the raiders attack the mini-bus? Were they lazy? Did they think the bus contained something they couldn't scavenge? Perhaps they were hoping to capture the occupants for some unthinkable purpose? Maybe it's their idea of fun. One thing's for sure—I may be paranoid, but I'm not paranoid enough. What happened to the mini-bus might happen to any vehicle travelling along that road, including mine.

I'm writing this as I lie in my sleeping bag, exhausted, but unable to sleep. What's the expression—too tired to sleep? I think it's more a case of too troubled. I can hear a sodding owl nearby, which isn't helping. Every few moments, he lets out a banshee screech, which gives me the creeps. I wonder what an owl tastes like?

At least while I'm awake, I can appreciate the sky. It's fantastic tonight, with a full moon casting a silvery light over the countryside. The air smells clean and fresh. The moonlight is making the clouds glow. They're parading over my head like a moving display of sculptures from a mad artist. George, Mia, and James should be enjoying this sky.

Should I have done more to help them? If I'd given them more weapons this morning, it would have made no difference, since they never stood a chance. If I'd joined their group (which was never going to happen) most likely I'd have been shot with them. And tonight it was bad luck that I arrived too late to help—nothing I could do about that.

So why do I feel so guilty?

This wasn't what I imagined when I reinvented myself after the Yellow Death. I was going to put my pathetic life behind me and become a fearless warrior—defending the weak and beholden to nobody. I even changed my name, for God's sake.

I want to make a difference!!! I'm not cut out to be a farmer, or a cook, or anything to do with children. I don't have the mindset for normal jobs and I hate working in teams. Military knowledge is the only thing I excel at. If I can't use that, then what am I good for? Today was my first proper test of being in danger, and I cowered behind my car. All my fancy weapons proved useless when it came to an actual fight. It sucks.

It's Sharon I feel so guilty about. She'd said she wasn't safe with George. How right she turned out to be. She wanted to join me and—who knows—it might have worked out fine. Sharon knew how to take care of herself. Perhaps she would have taught me a trick or two. It would be safer with both of us travelling together and we would've shared the chores. If the worst came to the worst and we couldn't stand each other, we'd have parted ways again. No harm done.

But I panicked as usual. Simply being close to an attractive woman pressed all my anxiety buttons. The thought of my sodding precious routine being interrupted sent me into a terminal mind-spin. I must have looked like a complete idiot to her—stuttering and blubbering.

I didn't see her body inside the bus, so I assume they took her with them. She's a good talker, so maybe right now she is sitting around a campfire, laughing, joking and getting drunk. Perhaps she's telling those bastards how pathetic George and Mia were and how she's so grateful to be with some real men. Who knows, in a few days, she might be leading the group.

I hope so. I really, really hope so. The alternative is too horrible to imagine, and it would be all my fault.

## chapter six

# JOHN GROWS UP

TIMELINE: 23 YEARS BEFORE THE
YELLOW DEATH

"Saying you 'have' something implies that it's temporary and undesirable. Asperger's isn't like that. You've been Aspergian as long as you can remember, and you'll be that way all your life. It's a way of being, not a disease."
       John Elder Robison (1957– )

Sarah stood in the doorway to their activity room and observed John working with his mathematics tutor. Mr Hussein was the perfect mentor for John—calm, patient and willing to correct John if he fell into what Sarah considered 'Aspergery behaviour'.

'Aspergery behaviour' represented small mannerisms which marked John out as peculiar. Top of her list was his finger rubbing. For the first five years of his life, John had been an obsessive thumb-sucker. This caused callouses on his thumb and threatened to push his teeth out of shape. Sarah tried many remedies to no effect, so was delighted when John grew out of it, almost overnight. Unfortunately, John replaced thumb-sucking with intensive rubbing of his thumb against his index finger whenever he became nervous—which was often.

Other autistic behaviours included avoiding eye contact and ignoring questions. Mr Hussein would pick up on these things and insist on the correct behaviour. "Did you hear me, John?" he would say, "I can't tell if you heard me if you don't answer". John would act surprised. From his point of view, he must have heard Mr Hussein since they sat next to each other. Mr Hussein always waited patiently until John relented. Sarah chose all of John's tutors carefully. They must have outstanding recommendations and excel in their field. They also needed the patience of a saint.

When John was old enough to attend school, Sarah home-tutored him. There was no question of him attending a state school where he would be eaten alive. She investigated several specialist private schools, but none were within travelling distance, and she had no intention of sending him to boarding school.

With John now in his ninth year, she felt her decisions had been justified. John exceeded at every measure of academic excellence and, in most categories, he was outstanding.

Charles suggested John missed out on the social aspects of school. Sarah was convinced that if John attended a state school, he would spend every break standing alone in a corner of the playground, trying to look invisible. John's quiet nature and strange behaviour made him the perfect prey for school bullies. Charles loved his son, yet did not understand him. Perhaps not surprising, considering how little time Charles spent at home.

Sarah profoundly disagreed with her husband about John—and just about everything else. Charles was now

# JOHN GROWS UP

UK-based, but they still lived on opposite sides of the country. She had expected him to put pressure on her to move into his quarters, but he never mentioned it. On the contrary, Charles pointed out how John would suffer from the disruption. Charles joined her when he took leave, but there was little warmth between them.

When they first married, she always became deliriously excited when he was scheduled to return on leave. No more. She dreaded the discussions about John. Sarah resented Charles coming home after hardly speaking to either of them for months, yet feeling he knew exactly what John needed to 'put him back on track'. In his opinion, that meant putting his son into a 'normal' school to experience "a bit of rough and tumble".

Sarah did plan for John to attend a conventional school in the future. But not quite yet. She had two years before he started Secondary School and much work still to be done in preparation.

In the meantime, using a variety of methods, she worked on gradually changing his behaviour patterns and gently teaching him how to relate to others. Perhaps John might never think like a so-called 'normal' person, but she hoped they would train him how to at least act normal.

☣☣☣☣

"Gosh, John. Isn't this wonderful?"

Sarah and John stood in a field watching a re-enactment of The Battle of Naseby—a pivotal encounter during the English Civil War.

In front of them, opposing lines of pikemen pressed against each other, shouting and screaming abuse.

"Hold the line!"

"God save the King!"

"To the colours!"

"Make ready!"

To the right, a company of musketeers raised their weapons and fired a volley, creating a cloud of smoke with a thunderous roar. A dozen cavalry burst from the treeline, their riders brandishing swords and colourful flags.

When John remained silent, Sarah looked down.

John gripped his tablet and frowned.

"John? Isn't this wonderful? Are you enjoying yourself?"

At that moment, six cannons discharged a salvo, creating a booming crescendo, with clouds of white smoke. Each cannon jumped backwards as it fired.

A further line of pikemen advanced from the left, their pace measured by drummers at each end.

The spectators exuded a collective excitement, gasping and cheering.

John turned to Sarah. "This isn't what happened at all. They've got it all wrong."

Sarah attempted to remain calm. "Well, I expect they have to use a bit of artistic licence. I think the aim is to give a rough idea of what a medieval battle was like. Did you expect them to be really killing each other?"

John screwed his face up. Clearly disapproving.

*Oh dear! Why can't he just enjoy it, like everyone else?*

John had developed an obsessive interest in military history during his tenth year. It was the latest in a long line of peculiar narrow interests. Unlike the others, this one had stuck. He had even started talking about a career in the army. Sarah had mixed feelings about it, but used it as an excuse to get John out of the house.

A cloud of acrid smoke from the musket fire reached the crowds and caught the back of Sarah's throat, causing her to cough.

"Are you okay?"

The voice came from a man standing next to them. He was watching the battle scene with his son—about the same age as John. He had a kind face which showed concern for her.

"Yes, I'm fine thanks." Sarah attempted to suppress her coughing.

The simulated combat continued. Reinforcements arrived. The Roundheads and Cavaliers continued their manoeuvrers.

Sarah split her attention between the antics going on in the field and the man to her right. He was about her age and quite attractive. He was a tad overweight, as was his son. In fact, now she thought about it, the boy was a miniature version of his father. They both held burgers and simultaneously took a bite, which made Sarah smile.

The boy was John's age and, like John, he must have been interested in the military. Could this be a potential friend? It would be great if John had a friend. Just one friend.

Sarah leaned in their direction. "Do you come to these re-enactments often?"

He turned and smiled. "Yes. Whenever we can. Simon and I are thinking of joining up this year. I'm saving up for a musket."

"Oh, that sounds lovely. I think it's great that these groups bring history to life. It's so different to watching it on a TV screen."

The man beamed. "That's right. You get to learn about history, get some fresh air and make lots of new friends. Women can take part as well, if you're at all interested?"

Sarah glanced at John, who seemed fixated on his tablet. "What do you think, John?"

"About what?"

"About joining a re-enactment group like…"

"Brian. My name's Brian. And this is my son, Simon."

"Hello, Brian. I'm Sarah, and this is my son, John."

"Lovely to meet you, Sarah. How about it, John? Would you be interested in joining the re-enactment group with Simon and me?"

John looked at Brian. "No, thank you. It all seems a bit...well...silly. Like playing at soldiers. Besides which, you're both far too fat to be medieval peasants."

Sarah's guts twisted. "Oh, God. I'm so sorry."

She grabbed John's arm and pulled him away; her face glowing red with embarrassment.

"For God's sake, John. Why'd you have to say that?"

"What?"

"Why did you say they were a bit—"

"Obese?"

"Yes. No. I mean—"

"But it's true!"

"That doesn't matter! I don't give a fu—I don't care if they were a bit overweight. I don't care if they were the fattest people on the goddam planet! They were nice people, and you insulted them. How do you think they feel now? How do you think *I* feel now?"

John stared intently at his feet, remaining silent.

Sarah took a slow, deep breath. "Oh, John, come here."

She gave him a big hug.

For a few seconds, John stood stiffly, arms by his sides, before relenting and returning the hug.

"I'm sorry, Mum. I didn't mean it."

"I know you didn't. Never mind. How about an ice-cream?"

"Yes, please! With hundreds and thousands?"

Okay. Hundreds and thousands and millions, if you want."

*I know you didn't mean to cause offence. But that's the problem. You don't even realise when you do it.*

☣☣☣☣

# John's Journal: Age 10

# JOHN GROWS UP

This is my first-ever diary entry. Dr Kendall came up with the idea. He says I dislike talking to other people, so I should record my thoughts and feelings in a journal. He says it will be a good outlet for me and stop me from bottling things up inside.

So Mum bought me this fancy leather-bound book which even has a small lock, so I can keep my writing private. That's what she says, but I know Mum secretly kept a key for herself. I've asked her for a padlock with a number combination and she's agreed, but she wasn't happy about it. Sorry, Mum.

Writing with a real pen on paper is weird, but Dr Kendall insisted. He said if I typed my journal into a computer, I might change it over and over, trying to get every word perfect. He wants me to get used to living with mistakes because that's what's normal.

Ha ha! So, I type everything into my laptop first. Then when I'm totally happy with it, I copy it into this journal. Sorry, Dr Kendall, nice try.

I don't understand what I'm supposed to write in this thing. 'Write down your feelings,' he said. Feelings are happening and changing all the time. Which feelings should I write about and why? This makes no sense to me. Perhaps I should keep a log of my emotions in a spreadsheet, so I could create graphs and track them over time. Never mind, I'll give this a go for Mum's sake. She tries so hard to make me normal.

So here are my feelings for today. Most of today I was happy, but right now I'm annoyed. We went to the tank museum. The place was cool, and I bought a model kit of a Sherman tank in the gift shop. They drove an Abbot self-propelled gun over a muddy assault course, which was outstanding. The engine was roaring like a lion and throwing out clouds of black smoke. Mud splattered everywhere and some of the crowd got splashed, which was funny. I wish I'd been in it rather than just watching.

You have to be next to a real tank to appreciate how massive it is. So impressive.

But there was one tank they got wrong. It was a German Panther. It's a fantastic tank. One Panther could take on four Shermans. Pity they were so expensive and kept breaking down. The one in the museum had two of its road wheels made of steel. All the rest were made from cast iron. I know they only made wheels that way in the M.A.N. factory. But I noticed the turret had an infra-red night sight fitted. No tanks from the M.A.N. factory had those night sights.

The museum people got it wrong. How irritating!!!

I tried to explain this all to Mum, but she didn't seem interested. She wouldn't let me tell the man at reception. That was also annoying.

So, tomorrow, I'll email the museum and tell them about their mistake, so they can put it right. These things are important and I'm sure they'll want to know.

## Chapter Seven

# Cal & The Invitation

TIMELINE: 1 YEAR AFTER THE YELLOW DEATH

"Of all the ways of defining man, the worst is the one which makes him out to be a rational animal."

Anatole France (1844–1924)

In the early days following the Yellow Death, Cal encountered a few other survivors. They were clearly still in shock and trauma. Some acted like zombies, whilst others existed on the verge of weeping. Although Cal understood these reactions, they made him uncomfortable. He was ill-equipped to play the part of a counsellor or therapist. Thus, for a time, he kept himself to himself, enjoying the solitude, with the complete freedom and independence it brought.

After several weeks, even Cal felt the need for company, so began approaching other survivors—after checking for hostile intentions and threats.

The first meeting was with a middle-aged couple and a thirteen-year-old girl. They would not have admitted to it, but Cal noticed they had formed into a surrogate family to replace their lost ones. Their stories were unremarkable, but Cal picked up useful information about a few embryonic settlements, which he duly marked on his maps.

The next day, he met a quartet with a sixty-two-year-old—the oldest survivor he'd seen thus far. Initially, they were wary about Cal since having had a terrible experience with a group of young thugs. They spoke of trying to arm themselves after their encounter, but found others had already stripped local police stations of all the weapons. This was what Cal had predicted. He gave them two assault rifles and trained them for an hour before they parted company.

The most surprising group Cal encountered comprised a man in his forties travelling with his son and daughter. The father told Cal how the entire family succumbed to the Death, including his wife and daughter. Yet the disease never became serious in the three survivors. Clearly, a few people carried some level of immunity.

The father praised God for sparing two of his children. Cal wondered why he did not curse God for killing his wife and daughter—and the rest of humanity. Religion made no sense.

So the pattern continued, with Cal meeting other travellers, or newly established settlements. The people he met carried stories of other groups, so he learnt of developments as distant as Cornwall and Wales. His maps became dotted with the locations of fledgling communities.

Other travellers often invited him to join their group, but he always declined—of course. A meal and exchange of news was all he wanted—any further contact created a sense of unease.

The horror of the red mini-bus came as a rude awakening. The stench of burning flesh and diesel was still fresh in his memory. Clearly, some people would murder without a thought.

Cal needed to up the ante. His Lexus SUV was trashed, so he commandeered a black Land Rover Defender—a stunningly beautiful vehicle to Cal's eyes. He had to grit his teeth before butchering it by bolting on ugly steel plates with mesh over the windscreen. He fitted oversized run-flat tyres. A bank of floodlights and smoke grenade launchers on the roof rack completed the 'Mad Max' visage.

Cal also invested two days to develop further insurance in the form of an explosive flak jacket. He replaced the armour plates with plastic explosives linked to a dead-man's trigger. Pressing the trigger armed the device and, if he released it, there would be one hell of a bang. He called it his 'thunder-jacket' and linked it by radio to an even larger bomb in his Land Rover. While he wore his custom thunder-jacket, nobody would dare harm him—at least that was his hope.

Cal was aware of the irony of wearing an explosive vest and driving around in a mobile bomb as a way of keeping safe. The world had gone mad.

Thus prepared, he felt ready to meet and greet fellow travellers.

☣☣☣☣

On a delightful, balmy September day, Cal lay on his front, observing a group of people through binoculars.

Travelling groups were normally small. If a group expanded to double figures, they usually settled in a permanent home. Thus, Cal was surprised to come across an assortment of vehicles lined up outside a service station on the outskirts of Exeter. He spotted them from a distance, parked his Land Rover, then closed in on foot, following his normal habit when meeting strangers.

Clustered around the forecourt and car park were a petrol station, convenience store, tourist information centre, and a diner. After only a year of inattention, the place was in a sorry state. Weeds pushed up through cracks in the concrete and asphalt. Windows were grimy. Signs advertising special offers were faded. A large fabric banner flapped loosely at one end, hanging limply over the store entrance. A BMW estate car with shattered windows was parked at the side. The tyres were flat, with the body peppered with bullet holes—presumably it had been used as target practice by somebody.

The convoy included a spacious luxury motor caravan, three smaller camper vans, three trucks and two SUVs. The grandest of the motor homes had a slide-out central section, doubling its width. Several men carried stores from the shop. Two others operated a pump, sucking fuel from underground tanks. Their exertions under the warm sun caused them to work up a sweat. They wore a mixture of military and civilian clothing.

Directing operations was a tall wiry man with a sloping forehead and classic crew cut hair style. Strangely, he wore a pinstripe business suit, complete with neck tie. He looked as if he was ready to chair a business meeting. This man was obviously in charge. He casually sipped water from a bottle, whilst watching the others working. Two women hung up laundry out to dry on an improvised line. The only weapons visible were three rifles leaning against an SUV.

The leader checked his wristwatch and blew a whistle, which was the signal for his men to take a break. He climbed into the largest motorhome, whilst his men sat and relaxed. Others came out of the store and joined them. A woman brought out a tray of chilled beer bottles for the men. One of them pressed a bottle against his forehead and sighed with pleasure. The scene was easy-going and convivial. Someone started a card game, and another tried to entice a pigeon with breadcrumbs. Cal counted at least ten men and two women.

Fascinating! This group was the grandest and best-organised outfit since the Death. Cal wanted to know more. They had plenty of supplies, so would not need to steal from him. After all, they had parked next to a supermarket and could select whatever took their fancy.

Cal walked back to his vehicle, donned his thunder-jacket and switched on the radio link to the explosives in the back of the Rover.

A short while later, Cal drove slowly up to the service station, using only the electric motors. The Land Rover was virtually silent, except for the crunching of tyres on gravel. They watched him approach, but were unsure how to react, so stood and stared. He reverse-parked by the largest motorhome.

The leader stepped out of the camper and eyed the Land Rover quizzically, paying attention to the bolt-on armour plates. A smile appeared on his face.

"Good day, sir. Those are...interesting modifications you have on your vehicle. Did you add them yourself?"

"Hi there," Cal said. "Yes. It took me the best part of two days, but I feel a lot safer."

"Well, it's not a pretty sight, but I expect they do the job."

"I'm not interrupting anything, am I? Because I can drive on."

"Oh, no, not at all. We're resupplying. Please stay. In fact, I was taking afternoon tea. Perhaps you'd join me?"

Cal resisted smirking. Afternoon tea? Was this guy for real?

"Okay, thanks, I'd love to." He opened the door and stepped out. "My name's Cal."

They shook hands.

"Gibson. Royce Gibson, pleased to meet you...Cal."

Cal kept his left hand in his pocket, gripping the trigger to the thunder-jacket.

They stepped inside the massive motor home. The interior was reminiscent of a boutique hotel with plush furnishings. In a world full of dirt and decay, the spotlessly clean surfaces and polished fittings seemed incongruous. Gentle classical music played in the background.

Gibson led Cal to the dining table to join two other men.

"May I introduce Colonel Richard Fellman, my second-in-command and the man in charge of all security matters."

Cal shook hands, but instinctively disliked Fellman, who sneered rather than smiled, his lips hiding under a black bushy moustache. Even though he was sitting, Cal could tell he was over six feet tall and carried a little excess weight. He was taking more than his fair share of the bench seat, forcing the other man to perch on the end.

"And this is Lieutenant Roberts, the only other officer in our group."

"Please, call me Adam," the lieutenant said. Adam's handshake was as meek as his demeanour.

Cal and Gibson seated themselves. A young woman, who was not introduced, served tea and fruitcake. She did not speak, and the others ignored her. The cake was moist and fruity with a hint of cinnamon. Definitely freshly baked.

Gibson slurped his tea. "So, Cal. What brings you to Exeter?"

"Nothing in particular. I'm surveying most of Devon, mapping the resources and settlements. I'm also looking for a good place to settle down if I can find a suitable community. I was just passing through and saw your convoy, which piqued my curiosity. I've travelled throughout the South-West and you're by far the biggest group of people I've seen on the road."

Gibson smiled. "Why, thank you. Yes, I seem to have collected quite a few followers. But this is only the start. It's about time somebody got things organised. There are too many individuals and groups wandering around randomly, using and wasting precious resources. Present company excepted, of course. Please tell us more about what you're up to."

Cal chewed on his cake and swallowed to give him time to think. "As I say, I've been moving around gathering intelligence about where communities are being set up, what skills they have and what products they're likely to be trading. It's clear to me that small groups cannot be self-sufficient and they'll need to trade. Different places will have unique skills and products. For example, coastal settlements will probably have a surplus of seafood. I'm also studying how we're going to survive in a post-industrial society. I have a large collection of books in my Land Rover."

Cal sipped his tea, savouring the steaming, potent brew. Royce and Fellman exchanged glances. Cal focussed on their expressions and cursed his inability to decipher what they were thinking.

"That's very interesting and commendable," Fellman said. "Few people seem to plan for the future, as you obviously are. I wonder, are you travelling alone?"

Cal tensed. "At the moment, yes." He waited for their response, ready to show his dead man's trigger if he detected the slightest threat.

"I see," Gibson said. "Don't you get lonely being on your own?"

"Generally, I'm self-sufficient, and I meet up with other travellers from time to time. But I'm tired of my own company. That's the reason I pulled in when I saw you. A chance to hear a human voice and pick up some news."

"Indeed, so. Tell me, Cal, I couldn't help noticing you have a selection of modern weapons in your vehicle. Do you have a military background?"

"In fact, I do. I was an army captain. The infantry, to be specific." Cal had repeated the lie so often, it slipped off his tongue.

"Seen any action?" Fellman said.

"Some. Afghanistan, Syria, and a couple of other hot spots."

Fellman's eyebrows raised, "Syria?"

"Unofficially, of course. Training the Kurds."

"Really, that's impressive," Gibson said. "Those skills must come in handy in our current state of affairs. I'd like to hear your views on some security matters. Would you consider staying for the night? I have a guest bedroom in my motorhome. It's extremely comfortable and I can promise you a good meal and a hot shower."

A surge of anxiety crept up Cal's spine, yet he could think of no polite way to refuse. And he relished the idea of a hot shower. What's the worst that could happen?

"Yes, I'd like that, thanks." Once committed, he relaxed slightly and took his hand off the detonator in his pocket.

"Excellent, excellent indeed," Gibson said, smiling. "I'm sure that you and Colonel Fellman will have much to talk about. He served in Afghanistan as well."

Fellman grinned as icy fingers of dread clamped around Cal's neck. Much of Cal's past was a fabrication. He had never set foot in Afghanistan, or Syria, nor had he served in the regular army. Suddenly, he regretted agreeing to stay the night.

## Chapter Eight

# JOHN GOES TO SCHOOL

```
TIMELINE: 20 YEARS BEFORE THE
          YELLOW DEATH
```

> "And now I know it is perfectly natural for me not to look at someone when I talk. Those of us with Asperger's are just not comfortable doing it. In fact, I don't really understand why it's considered normal to stare at someone's eyeballs."
> 
> John Elder Robison (1957– )

Sarah picked up her ringing mobile phone. The display said 'caller unknown'. That would be either a spam call, or Charles. She was not sure which she preferred less.

"Hello."

*"Oh, hello Sarah, it's only me."*

"Charles. What a surprise. Hang on a minute while I put this on speakerphone. How are you?"

*"I'm absolutely fine, thanks, and you and John?"*

"Yes, yes. All good, thanks."

*"Great, great. Yes. Listen, I'm phoning with bad news, I'm afraid. I won't be able to come back next week after all."*

"Oh Charles, we've planned outings and everything. John was looking forward to it."

*"I'm sorry. It can't be helped. I only found out an hour ago and I can't tell you why. It's a matter of national—"*

"Security. Yes, it would be."

*"Sorry. You know how things are."*

"Yes, Charles. I know just how things are. I was hoping you'd spend some time with John and talk to him about school."

*"What do you mean?"*

"Well, he's been at Great Torridge School now for half a term, yet I've no idea how he's settling in."

Charles paused before answering. *"So why don't you just ask him?"*

"Oh thanks. I never thought of that. You think I don't try? Every day I ask how school is, and he mumbles 'fine' or 'okay'. Have you made any friends? 'Not yet'. Are you being bullied? 'No'. How are the teachers? 'Fine'. Do you have a favourite teacher? 'No'. If I get him to string two words together, I'm on a winner. The only subject we can have a proper conversation about is bloody warfare. Ask him how Hannibal moved elephants across the Alps and you can't shut him up."

*"So he's still in his military phase, is he?"*

"Oh, God, yes. Last night I saw him browsing the internet for replica assault rifles, for Christ's sake."

Another period of silence. Such an annoying habit shared by both Charles and John.

*"That's not so bad. When I was about his age, I was collecting knives and hankering after an air rifle. At least he wasn't trying to buy a real one."*

"If that's supposed to reassure me, it doesn't."

*"Isn't this all sort of normal for a boy of his age? It won't be long before he's a teenager."*

"God help us when that happens. I realise I'm looking at this as his mum, but normal for his age would be football and girls, not bloody assault rifles."

*"Well, yes. But I had no interest in football either. It's not compulsory. Are you worried he's being bullied?"*

Sarah realised she was furiously rotating her wedding ring and made a conscious effort to stop. "Yes, of course. It's always been one of my worries sending him to normal school. I don't have any evidence he's being bullied, but how could I tell? Unless he comes home with a black eye and his uniform torn to shreds, I wouldn't know. John's so secretive."

*"I'm sure it's all fine. You've been working hard for years to normalise him, and hopefully, this is a sign you've succeeded. He's not punched anyone, or absconded, or set fire to the school, thank God."*

"Not burning down the school isn't exactly my yardstick for success. As far as I know, he's not got any friends, joined any school clubs, or done anything that normal boys do."

*"So you'd like me to speak to him?"*

"Yes. That would be great, but he hates phone calls. It would need to be in person."

Charles sighed. *"Well, it'll be several weeks before I can get away. This emergency thing is complex. Is John unhappy?"*

"No. At least I don't think so. I've never known somebody to be so content with their own company. He seems so...self-contained. Sometimes I wonder if the world ended tomorrow, leaving him as the only survivor, how long it would be before he even noticed."

Charles laughed. "And is that good or bad?"

"I don't know, but it's not normal."

## John's Journal: Age 13

I hate school. What a ridiculous waste of time and energy. I learn more in an hour alone than in an entire day at school. Time spent travelling to and from school is totally non-productive. There's time wasted walking between lessons, waiting for the teacher to turn up, roll calls and breaks. Every lesson has interruptions by arseholes who think it's funny to taunt the teachers. Also, we're always stopping for questions from people who can't keep up. All wasted time!

Mom says attending school should be much more than gaining knowledge, it's about life skills. Well, I now know the routes which avoid bullies and can stop twats dripping spit down my neck on the bus. So, I guess I've gained useful life skills. Being invisible is the greatest survival skill. Blend in. Stay under the radar. Don't be the first or last at anything.

Sadly, that doesn't work with sports, because I'm utter crap at sports. The worst part of the week is the double sports lesson on Wednesdays. First, there's the torture of the communal changing room and everybody staring at my skinny body and pointing at my prick. I'll never forget the time I wore my sports kit under my school clothes. I thought it was a great idea, but everyone laughed.

After changing, it's outside into the cold and a muddy field, wearing nothing but shorts and a T-shirt. It's insane. If I go outside in winter, Mum tells me to put on a coat and hat and gloves or I will catch a cold. But at school, it's fine to run around a field in the rain half-naked.

# JOHN GOES TO SCHOOL

When they pick the teams for the footie, I'm nearly always picked last. It's me or Fat Pratty. It's a good day when I get chosen before Fat Pratty, who wobbles when he walks and can't run to save his life.

After the team picking, there are 90 minutes while I stand shivering by the goalposts trying to keep warm. Whenever the action comes close to me, the others run around me. Nobody ever passes the ball to me—not since they found out I'm as likely to fall over it as kick it. In most matches, I don't even get to touch the ball.

Everyone gets so excited when they score a goal. Jumping, whooping, shouting, hugging—urgh! Even Pratty joins in. Who cares? Mind you, I hate it when we lose. Then somehow it's my fault because I didn't do something, or I did the wrong thing. They call me a dickhead, or a waster. Mr Clarke does nothing about it.

Mr Clarke hates me. He won't let me wear gloves. "Run around a bit more and you'll warm up," he says. Bastard.

The worst part is the showers. Mr Clarke watches as each of us goes naked through the communal showers. I wonder if he's a perv, or likes to torture boys. The water is either boiling hot or freezing cold. Surely they could get the temperature right if they tried?

I don't get sport. It's an arbitrary set of rules from the past. Everybody tries to prove they can follow the rules a bit better than everybody else. Team sports are the worst. If your team wins or loses, what part did you play in it? Did your team win because of your efforts, or despite them?

It's not that I hate physical activity. When Mum takes me swimming, I love it. Swimming feels natural. And I enjoy recording my times and getting better and better. But I don't care if I can swim a little faster than somebody else. It just doesn't matter.

Today was different. The heavy rain flooded the footie pitches. Hurray, I thought. So, Mr Clarke said we would do a cross-country run instead. Three miles! Booo! I've never run more than a mile, and that nearly killed me.

When we started, I hated it. I was cold and wet and my lungs were burning and I got the stitch. But I carried on running because I wanted it to end as soon as possible. By the time I passed the mile marker, I'd warmed up. My body went into a rhythm. It was a bit like swimming. Natural. Like it was meant to be. I wasn't fast, but I just kept on going. Even up the big hill in the middle, when everyone else started walking.

I started overtaking the boys who got picked before me for the footie team. That was great, so I ran faster. I've found something I'm actually good at.

I finished 8th out of 47 boys. Mr Clarke didn't believe it at first. He was asking around if I'd cheated or taken a shortcut. Afterwards, he asked me if I wanted to join the school cross-country team. No way. Why should I care if Torridge School has—by coincidence—faster runners than another school I've never heard about? Mr Clarke said I was letting the school down. Guess what, Clarkey—I don't care.

I'm going to ask Mum for a pair of proper running shoes, so I can go out running whenever I want. I wonder if I could run a marathon?

## Chapter Nine

# CAL MEETS GIBSON

TIMELINE: 1 YEAR AFTER THE YELLOW DEATH

"We are called to be architects of the future, not its victims."
                Richard Buckmaster Fuller (1895–1983)

When afternoon tea with Gibson had finished, Cal moved his belongings from his Land Rover to the guest bedroom in Royce's motorhome. These included a hidden knife and snub-nosed revolver pistol. He locked his car, but chose not to set the booby traps in case he had to leave in a hurry. Nobody searched him on re-entering the motorhome. Gibson clearly thought he presented no threat. Sloppy security.

They offered him first use of the bathroom to clean up for dinner. He noted the dining table being laid out formally, so removed his thunder-jacket, since it would be unsuitable for such an occasion.

After showering, he sat in the lounge and tried to relax whilst rehearsing how he would answer questions from Gibson and Fellman. Over the past hour, a bank of grey clouds had covered the sky and light rain peppered the windows.

A woman hurried to bring the laundry in off the line. Three other women prepared dinner in the motorhome's tiny kitchen. So far, every woman Cal had seen was young and attractive—surely not a coincidence? They all wore skirts——another oddity. Even Cal detected their mood was subdued. There was no banter or small-talk between them. The atmosphere felt stilted and business-like.

Tendrils of anxiety uncurled inside Cal's guts. Something seemed very wrong with this setup.

A tall, slim woman served him chilled white wine and snacks while he waited, but she made no attempt at conversation and avoided eye contact. She returned later to top up his glass.

"Thanks," he said. "What's your name?"

"My name? Sabine, sir." Her accent was French. She straightened up and brushed long black hair from her face.

"There's no need to call me, 'sir'. My name's Cal."

He smiled and held out his arm to shake hands. Sabine checked behind her, and assured nobody was watching her, tentatively shook his hand quickly. Her obvious nervousness gave Cal the willies.

"I suppose it must be nice, living with all this luxury?" Cal said.

"Yes, sir. It is very good. Is there anything else you would like?"

"Would you like to join me with a glass of wine?"

The surprise on her face was unmistakable—even to Cal. "Oh, no thank you, sir. Is not allowed. Please, I must go to help with the cooking. I have much still to do."

"Sorry, I didn't mean to hold you up."

"Thank you, sir," she said, scurrying to the kitchen.

*What was that all about? She wasn't just wanting to get back to do the cooking. She seemed nervous, maybe even scared. Why can't she have a glass of wine? This doesn't feel right. What the hell have I stepped into?*

☣☣☣☣

Gibson strode in a few moments later, wearing a dinner jacket and bow tie. It struck Cal how much he resembled Joseph Goebbels——one of Hitler's closest henchmen—who Cal had seen in old newsreels. Gibson had the same hawk-like face with a sloping forehead. But the similarity in the way he moved was the most striking——he strutted and remained aloof, confident of his authority.

"Ah, good. I'm glad to see you're being taken care of. Personally, I like to start with something a little stronger. Sabine! Whisky, if you please."

"Yes, sir. Right away."

She appeared a moment later with a glass of whisky with ice.

"Good. I'm glad you remembered the ice this time. And draw all the curtains, will you? Can't you see it's dark outside?" He turned to Cal. "Takes ages to get them trained," Gibson chuckled. "But it's worth the effort."

Gibson meant for Sabine to overhear the comment, and Cal felt embarrassed for her.

Gibson took a sip of his drink. Colonel Fellman entered the motorhome wearing a dress uniform. He shook the rain off his jacket and ordered a gin and tonic, then sat down with Cal and Gibson.

Cal did his best to relax, despite internal agitation. Everything he knew of the conflicts in Afghanistan came from books and documentaries. If Fellman started reminiscing, Cal feared he would be exposed as a fake.

The hosts began by talking business and making plans for the next few days. Sabine served entrees of caviare with French toast. She opened another bottle of wine and poured each of them a glass.

Gibson slurped. "I enjoy a good Sauvignon Blanc. The scent always reminds me of freshly mown grass." Cal noticed Fellman smirking to himself.

Cal was a caviare virgin, and the experience came as a surprise. The fishy, salty beads slid around and under his tongue, and he took a generous gulp of wine to rid himself of them. That was something from the old world he would not miss one bit. He noticed Fellman grinning at him. "How do you find the caviare, Cal?"

"Er...It's not something I'm used to, I must admit."

Gibson crunched toast and chewed fish eggs appreciatively. "It's not the best. But we all have to make sacrifices."

*Since when was caviar and white wine a sacrifice?*

Gibson resumed talk of their forthcoming activities, which provided the perfect opportunity to launch into his vision for the future. This was clearly his pet subject. Fellman must have heard it many times.

"You see, Cal. People need organising. I've always thought so, and the Yellow Death proved it. We've had an entire year since the fall of civilisation and what has been achieved? Absolutely sod all. Groups are still wandering about like lost children and using—in fact, squandering—precious irreplaceable resources left over from a time of plenty."

"You'll get no argument from me on that point," Cal said.

"We've found shops where much of the stock has been ruined, simply because some selfish person left the door open." Gibson was clearly enjoying himself, thinking he had an appreciative audience.

"Now I know everyone needs to eat, so they should take enough to survive. BUT NO MORE! And they have a responsibility to make sure their actions don't cause destruction of what is communal property. Unfortunately, some people have gone feral. They act like every day is Christmas."

A delicious hammy aroma wafted over from the kitchen. Pots, pans, and crockery clanked as preparation came to a head. Cal's stomach growled in anticipation.

Gibson drained his glass. "We'll move on to the red now," he shouted to the kitchen. "And we're ready for the main course." He dabbed his napkin on his lips.

"Do you know what I did before the Yellow Death, Cal? No, how could you? Well, I was the Chief Executive of Devon County Council. I have experience of organising, of managing people and budgets and resources. That's exactly what we need right now—somebody bringing organisation to the chaos, whilst we still have something left to save."

He peered towards the kitchen. "What's taking them so long?" Another large swig of wine. "Now where was I? Oh, yes. There's no central or national government any more. So it's up to the regions to govern themselves. I must be the most senior official who survived in Devon, so it's my *duty* to take charge."

Cal resisted the urge to mention the minor point of democracy and elections, not wanting to annoy Gibson.

Sabine returned and waited while Gibson tasted a sample of the red wine and nodded to show it was good enough to be poured.

"Most of the old laws no longer make any sense—we don't need parking fines or television licences any more, eh?" He chuckled. "So, I've been writing a set of principles which we can all live by. I'm also creating a body of men to enforce the rule of law. We've already started leaving posters at every shop we come to, warning against looting. People can take essentials, but no more. And they must leave property secure. But that's only the start. When I have a complete set of regulations, I'll distribute copies all over Devon."

Gibson's words sounded reasonable, yet Cal still felt tense. Gibson's absolute confidence he had a right to impose his views on everyone else was unnerving. It was the dictator's mindset. Questions popped into Cal's mind. How would settlements survive without stocks of food to carry them over winter? When did building up a reserve of supplies become hoarding? What was the punishment for disobeying? Cal was aware his own activities in creating caches fell foul of Gibson's new regulations.

However, he bit his tongue, feeling that his tentative relationship with Gibson would not last long if he started asking awkward questions.

"It sounds like you've got this well thought out," Cal said. The main course arrived. Gammon and pineapple with mashed potatoes, peas, and green beans.

"This looks fantastic," Cal said. "I haven't eaten so well for ages."

Gibson stared at his plate. "It's not bad. All canned, unfortunately, but that will change. I hope in a few months time, settlements will produce fresh food. Sabine! English mustard, quickly, woman!"

"Yes, Sir. Coming right up."

"She always forgets something," Gibson said.

Cal took a tiny sip of his wine. "I assume you'll trade some of your canned goods for fresh food from the communities?"

Gibson and Fellman smiled.

"Trade? I don't think so," Gibson said. "Obviously, keeping an organisation like mine running will be expensive. This is only the beginning. I have over a dozen men who've committed to the cause, but if we're to establish law and order throughout Devon, we'll need hundreds. We're looking for a place to create a permanent operational base. Somewhere that can be self-sufficient and with good roads."

"And a river," Fellman said.

"Oh, yes, of course. One of my men used to be an engineer. We're planning to have full electricity at the new headquarters. We'll have solar panels and wind turbines, but that's no good on a windless night, eh? Anyway, my engineer chappie says if we're near a fast-flowing river, he'll instal a hydro-electric plant. As much electricity as we need twenty-four-seven. Not bad, eh? I see no reason at all why we have to degenerate into the Stone Age."

"Certainly not. That sounds great," Cal said.

"Anyway," Gibson said, between mouthfuls of food and gulps of wine. "As I was saying, it'll take significant resources to govern the whole of Devon, so naturally, we'll expect the settlements to make a small contribution as taxes."

"What if they don't want to pay the taxes?" Cal said.

"Ha! My dear boy, taxes are never voluntary," Gibson said.

Fellman gave one of his sneer-grins. "That's where I come in."

"Indeed," Gibson said. "My security forces will be available to defend settlements from incursions and threats. Those same security forces will also be essential to maintain order. Every government needs the ability to back up its words. However, I doubt it'll be necessary to use strong-arm tactics. I'm sure most people will see the sense of what we're doing. We shall ask for a modest contribution for bringing order and security to the region. Personally, I expect most settlements will be overjoyed to see organisation being restored."

*Of course. A new Government demanding taxes is just what everyone has been missing.*

"Tell me, Cal," Fellman said. "Where exactly were you stationed in Afghanistan?"

Cal almost choked.

*Here it comes. This is where things might get difficult.*

He took a sip of wine to give a few seconds to collect his thoughts. "Camp Bastion mainly, though we did a few stints in-country. To be quite honest, I doubt if I could remember, or pronounce the names of the compounds we stayed in."

"Camp Bastion," Gibson said. "Well, there's a coincidence. Isn't that where you were stationed, Dick?"

"Yes, indeed," Fellman said. "Although it's not that much of a coincidence. Half the bloody army lived in that shit hole."

Cal's guts twisted further.

*Well, that's just brilliant!*

"I heard conditions were rather harsh?" Gibson asked Cal.

"They were quite basic, of course. We slept on camp beds and the toilets were pretty rank, but we made do. The worst times were when they burnt the waste matter from the latrines. Just poured petrol on it and threw a match to it. The smoke and stench kept the Taliban away better than any guns we had. But any soldier who expects five-star luxury is in the wrong job."

☣☣☣☣

*Thank God that's over. For now at least.*

Cal sat alone at the dining table. With the main course finished, Gibson visited the bathroom and Fellman said he needed to check on the guards. Cal had a few moments to himself in silence, which was bliss.

He rested his face in his hands and closed his eyes. For the past half hour, Gibson and Fellman had questioned him about his combat experiences, drilling down into ever more detail. Several times, Cal was forced to fabricate stories, hoping nothing he said would be called out as a lie. If Fellman noticed anything suspicious, he kept it to himself.

What started as a pleasant meal, became an interrogation. Towards the end, Gibson changed tack and directed questions at Fellman. What was that all about? Maybe Gibson was testing Fellman? After all, Gibson only had Fellman's word about his career in the Army. If Gibson believed Cal was a genuine combat veteran, he could use Cal to find out if Fellman had been lying to him.

God's teeth! This was a nightmare. Cal wished he had not drunk so much. But it was difficult not to without appearing rude and ungrateful. He reflected on Fellman's answers. They were reasonable enough, but vague and lacking detail. Similar to his own answers. Possibly Fellman wasn't all he claimed to be?

Sabine arrived and began clearing the dinner plates. When she moved to pick up Cal's, he gently held her wrist.

"Wait a sec, please. What's going on here? What's the setup? Really?"

Her eyes darted around the room. Checking whether she was being watched. But she remained silent.

"Please. I need to know what the hell I've got myself into."

Sabine leaned closer and whispered.

"Whatever Gibson offers, you accept. Do not say 'no' to him."

"But what—" The bathroom door opened and Gibson shuffled out. Cal released Sabine's hand and she made herself busy.

"Shall I bring dessert, Mr Gibson, sir?"

"Yes, woman. Quick as you can. And more wine."

Fellman also returned to the table, just as Sabine brought three bowls of steaming treacle sponge with custard. Absolute heaven.

As Cal savoured the sweet goodness, he pondered on recent events.

*What is Fellman hiding? He has some military knowledge. More than you can get out of books—such as the nicknames soldiers give their kit. What if he served in the military, but never went to Afghanistan, or any combat zone? Has he been lying to Gibson about his experience? Perhaps Fellman used to be an army administrator, or in the catering corps? Or possibly...*

Cal almost choked as the idea occurred to him.

*What if Fellman had been in the Territorial Army? A weekend warrior exaggerating his career to impress people? Just like me!*

Cal suppressed a smirk. Gibson thought his second-in-command was a hardened combat soldier. Yet, his fledgling army was being led by a solicitor, or a baker. Gibson had questioned both Cal and Fellman in each other's presence. He was probably hoping if one was lying, the other would spot it. But since they were both lying, neither would take the risk of outing the other.

Glasses of cognac came next. Gibson lit up a fat cigar, Fellman took a cigarette. Cal declined. Anxiety and booze is a potent combination. Cal's head was muzzy and he had to concentrate to follow the conversation. He watched his hosts drinking heavily, so hoped they were in an even worse state than him.

"When do the women eat, Royce?" Cal said.

"Oh, they'll have a bite to eat later, I suspect. You don't need to worry about them, they can fend for themselves. That's one bloody thing they can do well—cook, eh?"

Gibson and Fellman laughed.

Gibson took a long drag of his cigar. "In all seriousness, Cal. Our society—before the plague," he belched. "Well, quite frankly, it was corrupt. Rotten to the damn core. Well overdue to collapse. If it hadn't been the Yellow Death, it would have been some other pandemic, or global warming, or nuclear war, or the sodding Muslim terrorists."

Gibson interrupted his diatribe to pluck a sliver of errant tobacco off his tongue.

"Trouble is, we've forgotten the natural order of things. Look at nature, for instance. Males and females are designed for different roles. The males hunt and the females take care of the young. That's how it's been for most of human history and we've prospered and grown because of it. It's only recently we've turned everything on its head. Giving women the vote was one of the worst decisions ever made. Give them a sniff of power and they wanted more. Eventually, we ended up with women working, whilst good men sat at home, idle. Kids brought up by childminders and coming home to empty houses. Who benefits from all that? God did not design women to be leaders. They're not lacking in intelligence, but they let their emotions control them."

He stopped ranting, to puff his cigar vigorously and slurp his brandy. His eyes fixed in the distance, lost in his own drunken, macabre thoughts.

Cal's mind spun, and not only from the booze. This world view was so outrageous, crazy and just plain wrong. He thought of many examples in nature where females were the dominant gender, such as hyenas and spiders. Humanity struggled for millennia to develop a society where human rights and equality became enshrined in law. Gibson proposed to sweep those advancements away on the basis that equality was unnatural! Nevertheless, Cal forced himself to stay quiet. Arguing politics with a rat-arsed bigot would have no good outcome.

Gibson assumed Cal's silence was a sign he agreed with the discussion.

"I'll tell you, Cal, it's no coincidence that after thousands of years of growth, civilisation collapsed less than a hundred years after we started giving women more rights than men. AIDS was the warning. A completely new sickness with no cure, spread by promis... promiscru... promiscuity and homosexuality. AIDS became an illness of the morally corrupt. It wasn't the decent, hard-working white middle classes which were affected. Only the queers and the fucking liberals. They died in their millions. AIDS was a preventable disease. We knew exactly how the virus was transmitted and how to avoid it. Yet it ravaged Africa because the blacks couldn't keep their dicks to themselves. Well, good riddance. AIDS killed no one who was worth a damn." He slammed his fist on the table for emphasis.

Gibson suppressed a belch. "Would you like a coffee, Cal?"

The question took Cal by surprise. Gibson had been in full ranting mode. "Er...yes. Thanks. Black, please."

"What Royce is trying to say," Fellman said, more calmly. "Is that we believe it is necessary to get back to traditional values. Christian family values which served us so well for hundreds of years. The Natural Order. The organisation we're creating is more than an attempt to bring a degree of order. We're not just glorified quartermasters. We intend to introduce a sense of morality to our future society—something which was sadly lacking in our previous so-called civilisation. We've tried multi-culturalism and liberalism and—quite frankly—it didn't work. We had a sick society. Sick! This is our chance to start afresh based on time-honoured principles."

Gibson slapped his palm on the table. "Hear, hear. Well said, Dick."

Sabine brought a tray with a pot of coffee and poured a cup for each of them.

Gibson resumed, his speech now slower and slurred. "Listen, Cal. We have a mighty task ahead of us. Mighty task. We've started on our mission, but have a long road ahead and much to do. I want good men. Lots of 'em. To be perfectly honest, some of my lads are rough around the edges. They lack training and discipline. Dick is doing a grand job bringing them into line, but he can only do so much. We'll need ten times the number of men, so I must have some excellent officers. You've impressed me, Cal. You've got good credentials, you know how to take care of yourself and you're smart. We've both got similar thoughts about what needs to be done."

Another puff of the cigar and sip of brandy, before he continued. "I'd like to offer you a position here, Cal. As an officer, naturally. You used to be a captain, so that's what I'll make you for joining me. You'd be second-in-command to Dick here as regards security matters. That's a very fair offer. I'm sure you'll agree. I can guarantee you wouldn't want for anything. And you can keep your crazy car if you'd like. We'd all get along just fine. So, what do you think?"

Cal scratched his chin, giving him time to respond. Gibson's ideas were as repulsive and despicable as the man himself. He talked about conserving supplies and yet lived like a king. His so-called new society was a throwback to the dark ages. But how would he react if Cal refused his offer? Cal remembered Sabine's warning.

"Wow. I wasn't expecting that. It's a magnificent offer, Royce. I'm impressed by what you've said tonight and honoured you'd think of me so highly. This is a massive decision for me. I've been alone for the last year, so it would be a big lifestyle change. I'd like to consider it for a while. Do you mind if I sleep on it?"

"No, no, not at all. Wise man. Best not to rush into things. I appreciate that. We'll talk about it over breakfast. We do a substantial breakfast here, I can assure you. Nobody goes hungry who works for Royce Gibson."

*Nobody but the women.* Cal thought.

## Chapter Ten

# John's Teenage Years

TIMELINE: 16 YEARS BEFORE THE
YELLOW DEATH

"In adversity remember to keep an even mind."
Horace (65–8 BCE)

Sarah's eyes scanned the sideboard, which held a set of framed photographs of John at different ages. The most recent showed him on his 16th birthday when she took him on a visit to the Bovington Tank Museum. He was sitting in the driving seat of an armoured car and beaming—one of the few photos she had of him smiling. She found it hard to believe he was almost an adult—in some ways, he still acted as a child.

She gripped her mobile phone and willed it to ring. Charles promised to call her at eight p.m. with information about John's latest problem. Charles had many faults, but he was punctual.

When the phone burst into life, the display reported 'Caller Unknown'. That would be Charles.

"Hello, Charles?"

*"Hi Sarah, how are you? Are you alone?"*

Sarah reflexively scanned the room.

"I'm fine. And yes, I'm alone. John's in his room. He's hardly left there since he got back from the Army Assessment. That's two days now. He's devastated. He was pinning his hopes on officer selection. Did you manage to find anything. Was he that bad?"

*"Yes, is the answer to both questions. I spoke to one of his assessors about it. I shouldn't have approached the assessment team, you understand? So what I'm about to say must be in the strictest confidence, or I'll be in hot water."*

"Yes, of course. This is just between you and me."

*"Great. Well, I was told John was excellent in the fitness and aptitude tests. That's about all the good news, I'm afraid. It was downhill from then on. The personality assessment categorised him as...I wrote this down...here we are—INFJ-T."*

"Speak English please, Charles."

*"That simple four-letter code means he's quiet, obsessively logical, and organised. It's the least common personality type. What's more, John is rated as ninety-seven per cent introverted. Ninety-seven per cent, for God's sake! I think we both know that fits John to a tee. Unfortunately, it's pretty much the opposite of what the army wants in someone who might lead troops into battle."*

"Okay, no surprise there. Anything else?"

*"Plenty. There was a group discussion about contemporary affairs."*

"Oh, Lord."

*"Yes, precisely. Apparently, John sat through it, barely saying a word. When he did manage to contribute, he appeared to be several seconds behind the group. The outdoor practical exercise was also a disaster. John was in a team, navigating an obstacle*

*course. I was told that John appeared to be working in isolation. Rather than being part of the team, he was getting in everyone else's way."*

"Oh dear. He must have been completely out of his depth."

*"I've not mentioned the best part yet—the individual interviews. John showed an excellent knowledge of military matters, but that didn't earn him many points—after all, he would get that from the army training. Unfortunately, John's nerves got the better of him. He became reserved and stuttered. The assessor noted long pauses while John considered how to answer. Worse still, they regarded some of his opinions as, shall we say, controversial?"*

"What does that mean?"

Sarah heard Charles turning over sheets of paper.

*"Here we are. Well, for example, John argued that democracy wasn't the best system for choosing a government. He said something to the effect that if you allow a bunch of idiots to decide who should govern, they'll choose another idiot. Then he named the Prime Minister. He was also pretty disparaging about the Monarchy. Just think how bad that sounded, considering he'd have to take an oath of allegiance."*

"I can imagine. Did John propose a better system than democracy?"

*"Unfortunately, yes. He said a benevolent artificial intelligence would make the best government."*

Sarah closed her eyes. "Oh, John, John, John, what were you thinking?"

*"So you can see why they put him in the lowest category. And in my view, they got the assessment bang on. At least they didn't give him any reason to apply again. I've always said the army wouldn't suit him. It's a very close-knit communal life—you can't go and lock yourself away in your room whenever you feel like it. You should have talked him out of applying."*

Sarah sat bolt upright. "Really! Should I? Well, Charles, when have you ever successfully talked John out of anything?

Anyway, he needed to find out for himself, or he'd always be wondering."

Charles paused for an uncomfortably long time before replying. *"Yes, perhaps you're right. He'll get over it soon enough. He must be overdue for moving on to another interest? Hopefully, something harmless, like stamp collecting. Personally, I think we've dodged a bullet, if you'll excuse the pun. God knows what would happen if John ever had to lead soldiers into combat for real."*

☣☣☣☣

# John's Journal: Age 16

Oh my God, what an awful weekend. I just got back home from Westbury after what they call an 'Army Officer Briefing'. It's actually a series of tests to prove whether a person is good enough to join the army as an officer. I thought I was doing OK, maybe not the top candidate, and they caught me out a couple of times, but I thought I'd scrape through.

Yet they told me I'd been dumped in the lowest category and rated totally unsuitable to be an officer. Cat 4 means I'm so useless I couldn't pass even with extra studying. WTF!!!

Was I that bad?

We started with a fitness assessment, which I passed easily—better than most of the candidates. Then there were aptitude tests where I scored highly as well. So far, so good.

The outdoor practical exercise turned into a disaster.

The goal was to traverse an obstacle course without touching the ground. They provided planks (which were too short) and rope (which had knots in it). I guess the idea of the trial was to see if any of us would emerge as a natural leader. God's teeth!

Everyone tried to stand out by shouting orders at everyone else. Chaos reigned!!!!

If only they'd appointed me as leader, I'd have been fine. But all that screeching made me anxious. Totally unrealistic!

So I kept quiet and tried to ignore the shouting. We were falling over each other. I accidentally trod on somebody's hand and she called me a retard. I trust the assessors will mark her down for that. People were getting frustrated and angry. We struggled to build a bridge with the planks and rope, but it all crashed to the ground. Needless to say, the team didn't complete the course in the time allowed. I overheard two candidates mumbling it was my fault! I hope I wasn't marked down because of those twats.

Next came a group discussion, where we all sat in a circle. The assessors suggested topics to talk about. Strangely, not one topic concerned military matters. Everyone tried so hard to impress. They all butted in and blurted opinions without thinking. Every time I opened my mouth to speak, somebody else jumped in. So after a while, I stopped trying and let them waffle on. If they don't want to listen to my views, that's their loss.

The last test was a private interview with a colonel. That was weird. I hoped to show my knowledge of warfare and military history, but he wasn't interested in that. The colonel wanted to know what I'd do if I heard one of my soldiers making a racial slur. He also asked if it was ever right to disobey an order. From his reaction, he was surprised at my answers.

Anyway, something I did or said pissed them off royally, because they made it clear I should not bother to apply again. Shit! I was so sure they would pass me and then everything would be sorted. Now what am I to do?

Mum tried her best to console me. She offered to take me to the Torridge Inn for a Thai meal, but I wasn't in the mood. She keeps saying how good I am with computers and techy stuff and how I would make a brilliant computer programmer.

True, but it's not what I want to do. Absolute bollocks. Sod the stupid army with their stupid current affairs discussions. Surely to God, they need warriors, not debaters?

☣☣☣☣

John's eighteenth birthday passed almost unnoticed. Naturally, he did not want a party. Who would he invite?

A week later, Sarah sat on the living room couch, anxiously twisting her wedding ring around her finger. Outside, a turbulent wind thrashed the windows with rain. She had made a cup of coffee, but it remained untouched. Unconsciously, she kept glancing toward John's bedroom door, willing for it to open.

Today was a big day. Students throughout the UK would receive their 'A' level results. John had studied for two years and his grades would decide which university he would attend—if any.

Most students returned to school to collect their results in person. A chance to meet up with friends. A good excuse to either celebrate or commiserate. To say goodbye to their tutors. One last look at the place which had occupied their lives for seven years.

Not John. John had made special arrangements to receive his results by email.

Two hours ago, he shut himself in his bedroom. There he would remain—alone—until his results arrived. Then what? Would he come out and tell her the news? Or would he stay in his bedroom? Surely, he must realise she was just as desperate to know the results as he was?

Sarah looked at the drinks cabinet and decided it was too early to visit the gin bottle.

*Come on John! Don't keep me waiting.*

The bedroom door opened at last. John stepped out, grinning. No jumping for joy, whooping, or screaming at the top of his voice. Just a grin. Yet seeing it allowed Sarah to give an enormous sigh of relief.

"Four A-stars and one plain A. Autism Man wins the day."

"Oh darling, that's wonderful." She moved to hug him and ignored the slight tensing of his body as she embraced him.

*If this doesn't merit a big hug, I don't know what does.*

After a few seconds, he gave in and hugged in return.

"Goodness, it's been a long road, but you've made it," she said.

"Yeah. Nottingham Uni, Computer Science, here I come!"

She released him and sat down. At last, she took a sip of her coffee and screwed up her nose, finding it was cold and bitter. "I know what—we should go out and celebrate. Where would you like?"

"The *Torridge Inn*, please."

Of course, his choice would be the *Torridge Inn*. Always the *Torridge Inn*, where Karl would find them a dark, cosy corner away from everyone else. After fifteen years of intensive therapy, John still needed routine. Sarah wondered how much difference those interventions had actually made.

Never mind. What counted was her boy had grown up, become independent and was about to go off to Uni. John's rejection for army officer training left him depressed for months. Now he could look to the future. Such a shame Charles would not share this moment, but Charles had never been here when it mattered. When he had finally waltzed off with a young bimbo, Sarah barely noticed any difference. Provided he continued to pay the bills, they were better off without him.

Sarah studied her son. He was on a rare high and getting these passes boosted his confidence. Sarah had been meaning to talk with John about a delicate subject. She would never find a better time...

"John, sit down for a second, would you?"

"Er...Okay. What's the matter?"

"Nothing. Nothing at all. It's just that I was wondering... You've been at school for, what, seven years now? You've never once wanted to bring home a friend, or gone to a friend's house—at least to my knowledge."

John sat motionless.

"Come on, John, don't make this difficult. You've proved you're not thick. Have you ever had a school friend?"

He started rubbing his thumb and finger together.

"Well, not really. There've been people at school I've liked, and they seem to like me. We hang out in the lunch hour and chat a bit. Sometimes we send each other funny videos and stuff. But that's it."

"Has nobody ever invited you to their house, or the cinema, or a meal?"

"A few times. I kept saying no, so they stopped asking."

"But why?"

"I suppose they got fed up with asking."

"No, I didn't mean...Why didn't you accept their offers?"

"I didn't want to. That's not true—I wanted to...but I was nervous. I didn't think I would fit in, because I never do. And I don't get all the social chit-chat and stuff. Besides, most things I enjoy doing are best done alone. Like running. You know I like to run. So does Thomas. He said we should go for a run together. But why? I don't like running with somebody at my side. Either Thomas would need to run at my pace, or I'd need to run at his pace. And we'd have to arrange it all beforehand. I enjoy running when I feel like it, at my own pace. I particularly don't want to hold a conversation when running."

"But don't you want some...companionship? People run with friends because it's nicer than being alone.

John made a long sigh, something Sarah rarely saw.

"I understand. It's true I get a bit lonely at times. When I see others socialising and having fun, I know there's something missing for me. I want to be part of the group. But whenever I'm with other people, I'm anxious—all the time. I just don't fit in. I'm not stupid, but when I'm with several people and everyone's talking, I'm always half-a-second behind. I think about what to say, but before I open my mouth, somebody else is speaking. Usually, I miss my turn to talk. Sometimes, I say the wrong thing, which is even worse. I've learnt it's not worth the hassle."

"Oh, John. That's so sad."

"It's the way I am. Most of the time, I'm okay with it. There's nothing wrong with a square peg until you try to hammer it into a round hole."

"That's really quite profound. Is that what I've been doing? Trying to hammer a square peg into a round hole?"

He smiled. "Perhaps it's more like you've been trying to smooth the corners off the square peg."

"And I've not been very successful, have I?"

"I'm not very normal, if that's what you mean. But you've worked so hard, Mum, and given me the very best education. You've helped me be the best I can be. When I need to, I can pretend to be normal. It's just that it's difficult, so I don't do it unless I have to."

She nodded. "I understand."

*I think I really do understand at last. Perhaps for the first time. We should have had this conversation years ago.*

"But what about girls? You've grown into quite the handsome man. You shouldn't have any trouble finding a girlfriend."

John blushed at the mention of the opposite gender.

"Hells bells, Mom! You know what I'm like trying to talk to a stranger. Multiply that ten times with a pretty girl. I get so nervous, I can't speak. I break out into a sweat."

"Well, that's definitely going to be a problem. What will you do about it?"

"Perhaps there's a dating app for people with autism?"

Sarah laughed. "Perhaps there is. I expect two ASDs would get on together brilliantly. You could bore each other to death, lecturing about your special interests. But can you imagine what your children would be like?"

## Chapter Eleven

# CAL & SABINE ALONE

TIMELINE: 1 YEAR AFTER THE YELLOW DEATH

"When faced with two options, favour the boldest."
                              Chay Blyth CBE BEM (1940 - )

Royce Gibson staggered to bed, almost comatose with alcohol. Cal was hugely relieved the evening ended without the lies about his past being revealed. The hours of warding off Gibson's probing, together with the booze, left him shattered. More than anything, he wanted to lie down and sleep. That luxury would have to wait. First, he had to devise an exit strategy. Instinct and Sabine's warning told him Gibson would take a refusal of his offer badly.

Gibson was someone who thought people were either for or against him. He was charming to his friends, but when Cal refused Gibson's offer to join the convoy, he would instantly become the enemy. That might prove to be fatal.

So, Cal sat on the end of the bed and imagined various escape scenarios. Ideally, he would simply slip out into the darkness and disappear. But he had seen Fellman posting guards who would be watching out for exactly that. Even if Cal got to his car unseen, he would be vulnerable to gunfire driving away. Too risky.

Perhaps he should pretend to join Gibson's group and slip away later? Unfortunately, it would be difficult to keep up the deception and, after only one evening pretending to be a combat veteran, he was a nervous wreck. Any plan involving subterfuge was unappealing, since Cal feared Gibson would see through any story he invented. Somehow, he had to get out soon, without relying on his feeble social skills.

The obvious choice was leaving at first light, taking Gibson as a hostage, allowing him to drive away without being shot at. But the idea of physically restraining Gibson, whilst holding a gun to his head, and somehow getting into his car, was terrifying. If Gibson panicked and started struggling, things might get messy.

These possibilities churned over in his mind until a gentle knocking on the door startled him. The rainstorm had passed over, but water dripped noisily outside, so he wondered if he had imagined the knocking. It happened again, louder this time. Cal opened the door a crack to find Sabine. Her long black hair flowed over her shoulders like an inky waterfall. She wore only a short, sheer negligée, leaving nothing to the imagination.

"Please, may I enter?" she whispered.

Cal was taken aback. "I–I'm not–"

"Please, open the door," she said with pleading in her voice. Cal stepped back to let her in, closing the door behind her. The exotic, spicy waft of fragrance struck him.

"W–what are you doing here?"

"I am here, compliments of Mister Gibson. I am to make you comfortable in whatever way you may wish. Mister Gibson says he saw you looking at me tonight during dinner. He says if you decide to stay, you'll be seeing a lot of me."

"I can see a lot of you already. Sorry—I didn't mean that to sound like...like, oh shit. I don't know what I meant."

Sabine stood next to him, almost naked, her nipples pressing through the thin material of her negligée. The room suddenly seemed stifling and Cal began sweating, so wiped his face with his hands.

*Christ! This can't be happening.*

He took a deep breath to gather his wits.

"Okay, now listen, Sabine. You're very pretty. But I can't...can't be doing this. I can't just–just use you like this. It would be taking advantage of you. It just isn't right. What the hell are they thinking of? Honestly, it's nothing personal. You're very beautiful but, no. Tell Gibson that I appreciate the sentiment, but no thanks."

She frowned. "Please. You do not understand. If you send me away and Mister Gibson thinks I have not pleased you, then I will be punished. It will be bad for me."

"Oh, shit!"

Cal scanned the small room, noting the small bed, small cupboards and tiny desk. Everything was miniature, with only a narrow walkway around the bed. "Oh well, you'd better get into bed then. But just to sleep, mind."

She quickly slipped under the sheets and covered herself. Cal sat on the edge of the bed, vigorously rubbing his finger and thumb together for comfort, wondering where he should go.

Sabine pulled back the sheet on his side of the bed. "Come. There is nowhere else, unless you plan to stand up all night."

Cal was wearing nothing except boxer shorts and turned his back to her so he could pull on combat trousers before sliding into bed. Now he was even hotter.

They lay on their backs in silence, side-by-side whilst avoiding touching, despite the narrow width of the bed. The situation was awkward and embarrassing. Cal felt the need to say something.

"Are you French?"

"Ssssh, the walls are super thin. You must whisper very quiet."

"Okay, sorry."

"Yes. I am French. I come to UK to study marine science at Plymouth University."

"Impressive. Sounds interesting."

"Oui. I mean, yes. Very. Better than washing dishes and laundry."

"Yeah. I don't doubt it. Why Plymouth?"

"It had largest marine science department in Europe and I wanted to improve my English."

"Okay. Your English is actually pretty good."

"Thanks. I've been here for nearly three years. Was about to do my finals when the plague came. I try to get back to family, but the lock down came so quick."

"Yeah. I remember. It caught us all out. So, how did you get to be part of this crazy outfit?"

"Please keep your voice down."

"Sorry. I forgot."

"There is five of us. We are all held against our wishes. I was travelling with a young man named Peter. He was lovely boy. Kind. Always smiling. One day we were loading up our car with supplies from a shop and Gibson's convoy arrived. They accuse us of looting. They say we steal food. Gibson says as punishment, I serve him for six months. He had no right. Peter was angry and he try to punch Gibson. They shoot him like an animal. So, now I work for Gibson. During the day I cook and clean and…and when night comes…"

She did not need to finish the sentence. "If I work hard, do good job, things are...bearable? But, if I make mistake...then is the punishment."

The story confirmed Cal's suspicions.

"How long...How long do you have to, er, serve, Gibson? I mean, when do you get freed again?"

"They no say. Last time I ask, they just laugh."

"Shit. That's terrible. I'm so sorry."

"Is not your fault. At least I am still alive. Better than Peter. He was only twenty years old."

"How old are you, if you don't mind me asking?"

"I was twenty-two yesterday."

"Oh, happy birthday for yesterday."

As the words came out, Cal realised how pathetic he sounded, so he wanted to say something else to move on. "Has anybody tried to escape?"

"No. Is not possible. They remove our shoes and tie us up at night. But, if we tried, they would hunt us down. If they catch us, the punishment would be unbearable. And, if I did escape, it would be so bad for those left behind. Gibson says if one of us runs away, everyone left behind is to be punished real hard. So, nobody tries."

"Oh, I see. So, he's got you hook, line and sinker."

"Pardon?"

"Just an expression. It means...it means you're trapped."

Sabine nodded slowly.

Cal paused before breaking the silence. "The sex thing. How often..."

Sabine cleared her throat. "There are five women and fourteen men. The men are allowed a woman each week if they have followed their orders. You can do the maths. Gibson never touches us. Fellman is the worst. He enjoys to give the punishments. Fellman is a...a..."

"A sadist?"

"Yes, that's it. You cannot imagine what it is like here for us. Tonight I forget to put out the English mustard. It is such a small thing. But tomorrow I may be punished, or they may forget about it. I do not know. They want me to worry about it over the night. Perhaps I will go hungry tomorrow. Perhaps it will be something worse. Fellman is a bastard. He likes to be inventive with punishments. Who eats English mustard with tinned ham? How was I to know? Pigs. Maybe I will be lucky and they forget about the mustard."

Another long, uncomfortable silence followed before Sabine spoke again. "Will you accept Gibson's offer? Will you stay here?"

Cal considered whether to tell her the truth. His pause was enough for Sabine. "Ha! You do not trust me. You think I may be a spy for Gibson?"

"Well, I—"

"Is okay. I understand. This place is like poison. It makes everyone suspicious. But you give yourself away by your silence. If you were planning to join Gibson, you would have said so straight away."

Cal felt foolish. Sometimes, it seemed just about everyone could read his mind. It confirmed he should not try to lie his way out of here.

"You are safe," she said. "I am no spy."

"You would say that, wouldn't you?."

"If I were a spy, you have already given yourself away."

"Good point."

"I am no spy. I swear."

She made the sign of the cross over her chest.

Cal made a move to hold her hand, but lost his nerve. "I believe you."

He turned and noticed her silhouette in the dark. The rise and fall of her breasts under the thin blanket.

"You're absolutely right. I'm not staying. Gibson's a nutter and Fellman makes my skin crawl. Their ideas are repulsive.

What he's planning is a protection racket, creaming off the excess from the settlements. They need him like a hole in the head. I plan to leave tomorrow."

Sabine turned to face him. "You must be careful. Gibson will not let you leave. There was another like yourself. He tried to go away and Fellman had him killed."

"I suspected that might be the case. Don't worry, I've an exit plan. Well, the start of one anyway."

"Can you take me?"

*Oh shit. I didn't see that coming.*

"Sabine. I can't. It'll be difficult enough to get away on my own. I'm sorry."

She sighed. "I understand."

"Listen, if I get a chance—"

"I say I understand."

They lay in silence again for several minutes. Cal heard her breathing. He could smell her scent and sense the minutest movement she made through the mattress.

He desperately tried to focus on the details of his escape tomorrow and to go over every possible eventuality. Was there any way to bring Sabine along with him? He found it impossible to think straight. An almost naked woman lay next to him. An ogre wearing hobnail boots stomped inside his head. He was so drunk. The air felt intolerably hot and stuffy. He struggled to breathe. Bedclothes stuck to him with sweat.

Cal rolled to his side and stood up. He was desperate for cool fresh air and fumbled with the window catches, but they would not open more than an inch.

"Sod it!"

He stood with his back to Sabine, panting.

"Cal?"

He turned to face her. "What?"

"Tomorrow, when you go. Please take me with you."

"But...I–I already told you—"

With one movement of her arm, she swept the sheets away, exposing her body. Her meaning was obvious.

"You mean...you mean, if I help you escape, you'll let me..."

"Yes. Anything to get out of here. Anything!"

Cal rubbed his face. "But I can't. It's not possible. Gibson won't let me just walk out of here and it'll be twice as hard if I try to take you."

"Then try twice as hard. Are you not a soldier? You have guns."

He gritted his teeth in frustration. "Dammit, it's not that easy."

Of course, she would have overheard the conversation at dinner and his fabrications of being an experienced combat soldier. She must think he could shoot his way out, like a wild-west gunslinger. Sabine did not know the closest he had come to real battles were video games. She was pinning her hopes on a fraud.

But she was desperate. She would literally have done anything to escape, and who could blame her?

"If I took you with me. If somehow it were possible—and I'm not saying it is—but if I could, what about those left behind?"

"If I ran away, Fellman would punish those left behind. But, if you ordered me to go with you, I would have no choice. So he would not punish the others."

Cal wondered if that was true. Fellman sounded the sort who would punish the remaining prisoners to vent his anger—or simply for fun. However, Sabine needed to believe Fellman would not harm her friends, and perhaps she was right. He considered the escape again. Maybe, just maybe, he might actually bring her along. There was extra risk, certainly, but if he had a gun to Gibson's head and wore his thunder-jacket, they would have to do whatever he demanded—wouldn't they?

He exhaled deeply. "God's teeth. Okay."

"You'll do it? You'll take me with you?"

"Yes, yes. I'll take you with me."

"You promise?"

"Yes. Yes, of course. Tomorrow, you go free. I promise."

She stared into his eyes in the dim light, searching for the truth in his words.

"Good, good, thank you so much. Perhaps...if you get the chance...you help the others too?"

Cal sensed hysteria rising in him. "Oh yes, of course. Why not? And perhaps I'll ask for a box of Gibson's finest cigars and some of his fucking caviar too, while I'm at it."

Sabine had a confused expression, but she remained silent.

Cal consciously took several deep breaths of the muggy air.

"Yes, yes, yes. If I get the chance, I'll try to rescue your friends as well. Promise. Cross my heart and hope to die. Jesus H Christ, how did I get myself into this mess?"

She nodded. "Okay. Thank you. You can come to bed now." She patted the mattress next to her.

"No, no. You don't have to—y'know...that's not why I'm doing this."

Sabine paused for a few seconds, clearly finding it hard to believe he would not take his prize. "Really? So you're not going to..."

"No."

"Do you not find me attractive? Are you...gay?"

"Yes. No. I mean I'm not gay. And I do find you attractive. I'd have thought that was pretty bloody obvious. But unlike just about everybody else who survived the Death, I like to think I still have some shred of morality."

Sabine nodded to herself. "You are a rare thing in these times. A man with conscience and self-control. It's a pity I didn't meet you first instead of Gibson. Thank you."

Besides the headache, Cal realised he was now quite nauseous and craved solitude. "How much longer do you need to stay here—to prove you've done your duty, I mean?"

"I can go now. If you wish. It has been long enough. If anyone asks, you had good time. Yes?"

"Yeah. Sure. I've had the time of my life. Now if you wouldn't mind leaving? It's nothing personal, but I've got a pounding headache and really need to get some sleep. That's not going to happen with you lying next to me."

Sabine climbed out of bed, kissed him on the forehead, and left.

Cal flopped down on the bed and sighed with relief. That had been intense. Barely a minute passed before he realised what a terrible mistake he just made by sending Sabine away. They were supposed to be escaping together tomorrow and should have made plans. Shit! He was so knackered; he was not thinking straight. Too late now. He was committed.

☣☣☣☣

Cal set his alarm for five-thirty a.m. and was wide awake after the first note of 'Mad World' had played. The thought of his audacious escape plan filled him with dread. Adrenaline pumped into his bloodstream, which only seemed to make his pounding headache worse.

He swilled back paracetamol tablets with his water bottle. Outside the window, the sky showed the first inklings of light. Overnight rain had soaked the ground.

He used the bathroom, then dressed and prepared himself, including putting on his thunder-jacket. He waited, mentally preparing for what he was about to do.

At last, Cal heard Gibson leaving his room and tramping to the toilet. He listened for the toilet flush and sounds of Gibson returning to his bedroom, before slipping out into the corridor. Gibson shambled back towards his bedroom, his silk pyjamas hanging limply from his frame.

Gibson turned as he heard footsteps behind him, to find Cal's stubby revolver inches from his nose.

Cal gripped the detonator trigger of his thunder-jacket in his spare hand.

"Good morning, Royce. I've thought about your offer and decided to decline, so I'll be leaving now."

"Fine, fine," Gibson croaked. "Just go, please go."

"I intend to, but I need to make sure I'll not get a bullet in the back, so I'm taking you with me. Just for a little while. You're my insurance policy, understand?"

Gibson gave a slight nod.

"Good. First, we're going outside to my car. Nice and slow, with no sudden movements. Okay?"

"Yes, yes. Please don't shoot. There's no need for violence."

Cal moved with Gibson to the door, keeping his revolver pointed at Gibson's head. Gibson pushed down the door handle, and they walked out and shuffled around the outside of the motorhome towards Cal's Land Rover. The morning air was chilly and made Gibson shiver. He gingerly stepped in his bedroom slippers, which soon became soaked. They moved to the rear of the motorhome, before a guard spotted them and raised his weapon.

"No, no," Gibson said. "Lower your guns, no shooting, no shooting."

The soldier lowered his rifle a little, yet remained wary. Cal's heart thumped, and he took several deep breaths to steady his nerves. Three other soldiers arrived and formed a half-circle around them. Cal continued to step towards his car with Gibson, until he reached the driver's door.

"Okay, Gibson," he said. "I'm going to take the women with me. All of them. I want you to order them out here."

"Alright, alright, anything you say. Take them."

"Stop right there!" It was Fellman. Cal swivelled to see Fellman gripping Sabine by the neck with a gun to her head. Behind Fellman, two more soldiers held other women the same way.

"Let me tell you what's about to happen now," Fellman shouted to Cal. "You're going to lower your weapon and release Mister Gibson. I'll start counting and, if you've not surrendered when I reach five, I'll shoot this young lady's nose off. Then I'll count again, but next time it'll be a bullet to what little brain this bitch has. After that, I'll move on to another one. I'm sure you get the picture."

Cal detected an undertone of smugness to Fellman's voice. Fellman was enjoying this. Cal realised Fellman had nothing to lose since he probably cared little for whether Gibson lived or died in this game of dare. Maybe Fellman wanted Gibson to die, leaving him to take over the leadership. Cal realised his hostage was not as valuable as he first thought.

Cal glanced at Sabine, her face contorted in pain from Fellman's grip.

A gust of frigid wind blew through the camp.

"If I release Gibson," Cal said. "You'll kill me."

"Of course we will. We can kill you any time. One word from me and you'll have half-a-dozen bullets in your head, but I'd prefer to get Mister Gibson out of the firing line. You're about to die. The only question is, whether you're going to watch these five bitches die before you have your turn."

Cal swallowed hard.

*Bloody hell. This has gone very bad, very quick.*

Cal remembered his thunder jacket. Although he gripped the trigger, it had momentarily slipped his mind.

"If you kill me, then Gibson, and you, and everyone else in this camp, will die as well. Look here, I'm holding a dead-man's trigger. If I release the button, five kilos of C4 in my flak jacket will detonate. That should be enough to kill everyone within ten metres. For good measure, my car has another ten kilos that'll go up as well."

The soldiers reflexively took a step backwards.

"Bollocks, you're bluffing," Fellman said, with a sneer.

Gibson whimpered.

"Okay. Tell one of your goons to open the tailgate of my car."

Fellman nodded to one soldier, who approached the Land Rover and carefully opened the rear door to peer inside. "Oh shit, Sir. There's a stack of green blocks with wires coming out and a red flashing light on top. There's some writing. 'Block Demolition Charge Four' it says."

Fellman stared towards Cal. "You might still be bluffing. How do I know that's actually explosives?"

"One way to find out."

Fellman gave one of his sneer-smiles, "Cute. Very clever. I underestimated you. So what do you propose?"

"I get in the car with the five prisoners and Gibson, then drive away. I'll let him go after I've travelled, say, five hundred metres down the road. We part our ways, no hard feelings."

"Not acceptable. There's nothing to stop you killing Gibson when you're out of here. We keep the women as hostages for Gibson's safe return."

Cal's mind scrambled for a solution to the dilemma. "How about this——I only take Sabine?"

Fellman frowned and looked down at the woman in his grip. "Why Sabine?" Then he smiled. "Oh...last night. Your little fuck buddy. I see you've developed a fondness for her."

Cal cursed as he realised his mistake. By singling out Sabine, he gave Fellman extra leverage.

Fellman slowly put his pistol in his holster and, having freed up his arm, grabbed Sabine's hand. He took hold of her middle finger and bent it backwards until she screamed in pain.

"Stop!" Cal said.

Fellman smirked, knowing he had the initiative again.

"Got a soft spot for this one, have you? Y'know what, I don't think you'll shoot Mister Gibson and I don't think you'd deliberately set off those explosives either. That would kill you and your precious girlfriend here. The only thing keeping you alive now is that sodding dead-man's trigger. So, I suggest you get in your car and fuck off while you still can. And if Mister

Gibson is not back here safe in five minutes, I'll kill the women and you can be sure this one here will be slow and painful. Is that absolutely fucking clear to you?"

Cal did not like it one bit, but saw no alternative. Several trigger happy thugs still pointed rifles at him, any of them might accidentally pull the trigger. A sharp pain in his chest reminded him to breathe. Dammit! He needed to end this now.

"Agreed," he said after a few seconds. "But I want your word you'll not harm any of the women. They had no hand in this. They knew nothing about it."

"You're hardly in a position to bargain, but it's a small thing. You have my word, I'll not touch them. Now sod off before I change my mind."

Cal let Gibson get into the driver's seat. He kept his pistol aimed at Gibson's head and held up his other arm to show everyone he had his thumb on the dead-man's trigger. Carefully, he walked around to the passenger side and climbed in.

"Drive off, nice and slow," he said to Gibson.

As the Land Rover left the site, Cal's eyes locked with Sabine's for a second and his stomach churned with guilt.

☣☣☣☣

"Stop here."

Cal had allowed Gibson to drive until they were well out of sight of the convoy. The car came to a halt.

Gibson switched off the engine, before turning to Cal. "You know, it's not too—"

"Shut up!"

Gibson frowned, not used to such treatment, but he stayed silent.

Cal wound down the window and listened for sounds of pursuit, whilst keeping his eyes on the rear-view mirror. Nobody was following them. But if he didn't release Gibson soon, that might change.

"Get out of the car and kneel down"

"Kneel down? What? On the road? You've—"

Cal raised his pistol to Gibson's forehead.

"Go on. Refuse. See what happens."

A few moments later, Gibson knelt on the road facing Cal.

*What the Hell do I do now? I should shoot him in the head. He's scum and the world would be a better place without him. I don't need an enemy like Gibson running around Devon. Who knows when our paths would cross again and he's the sort of person who'd hold a grudge. Better to end it here. Do everyone a favour. End it now.*

Cal raised his pistol and pointed it at Gibson's forehead.

Seconds passed.

A dense murder of crows flew overhead, their caw-caw-cawing seeming to mock him.

"You'll not shoot," Gibson said with a sneer. "I would, but that's the difference between us, isn't it? I've got the guts to do what's necessary, while you—"

"Just shut the fuck up!"

This time, Gibson would not shut up. "Before the Yellow Death, I was running the whole of Devon and, in another year, I'll be running it again. I was born to lead, Cal, you must see that. Why don't you accept the inevitable and join me? It's not too late, you know. What I said about needing good men is true and you've impressed me—even though you've lied through your teeth about your past."

Cal could not prevent the surprise showing on his face.

"Yes, Cal, I know you were lying about being an officer in the army. Just as Fellman has lied to me. I suspected Fellman was exaggerating about his past and last night convinced me. The fact that neither of you exposed the other showed you were both lying. You're not the only one who can pretend to be drunk. My guess is you were in the Territorials—am I right?"

Cal remained silent. This was too much to take in. Gibson had seen right through him, yet had not mentioned it. But why hadn't Gibson confronted Fellman before now?

Gibson appeared to read his mind. "Y'know what Cal? I don't care. It doesn't matter if Fellman wasn't an army officer, because the important thing is he can do his job. Dick controls the men and follows my orders. And he knows enough to create an army from nothing. Same goes for you, Cal. You're intelligent and you can handle yourself well, so I don't give a rat's arse whether you were a bank manager or a bank robber. Join me and help me build a new society."

*What would happen if I killed him now? Nothing. Fellman wouldn't kill the women. They're assets to him. There's nothing to be gained by killing them. Fellman would probably be glad to be rid of Gibson.*

Cal tightened his grip on his pistol and pressed it against Gibson's forehead. He inhaled deeply.

Gibson closed his eyes and made a tiny whimpering sound.

*Gibson's a monster who presides over murder and rape. He plans to bully countless peaceful settlements. Gibson deserves to die. But shooting a defenceless man in the head—what would that make me?*

For an age, Cal stood motionless with his finger pressing on the trigger. Inner turmoil froze him. At last, he lowered his gun and gasped for air, realising he had not been breathing.

In silence, he climbed into his car, slammed the door, and drove away. As the wheels spun, he heard Gibson shout after him.

"We'll meet again, Cal. Bloody well count on it."

☣ ☣ ☣ ☣

Cal drove at speed, turning randomly at junctions. His heart pounded, and he gripped the steering wheel tightly. He needed to put distance and time between himself and the convoy. Gibson would probably not chase him, but he was in no mood to take chances.

When panic and anxiety reduced to the merely uncomfortable, Cal pulled off the road and skidded to a halt in an overgrown picnic area, shielded by trees. Ancient oaks and elms surrounded him. The sun shone in an almost cloudless sky, and the clearing was a patchwork of deep shadows and bright sunshine. A year ago, this sheltered glade would teem with families enjoying the warmth of the sun and the peace of nature. These trees witnessed the rise and fall of a civilisation. They looked down on Cal in judgement.

He slammed his fists against the steering wheel several times. "Fuck! Fuck! Fuck! Fuck!"

What an almighty balls-up. Instead of liberating the women, he barely escaped with his life. Some hero he turned out to be. Fellman grabbing the prisoners and using them as a counter-hostage was predictable. So why did he not predict it? With hindsight, Fellman's move was obvious. Cal had been incredibly naïve. No, that was too kind—he'd been stupid; and drunk; and tired; and stressed to the point where he couldn't think straight. He had been so riddled with anxiety that the first setback with his plan sent him into a full-blown panic attack.

But what was the alternative? What should he have done instead?

Cal rested his forehead on the steering wheel and tried to steady himself by taking several long, deep breaths. Now he was alone again, a myriad of possibilities queued in his mind. Perhaps he should have called their bluff and shot Gibson in the head in front of them. What could they do with his finger pressed on the detonator to his thunder-jacket? What if he pointed his pistol at Fellman and shot him? Although Fellman held Sabine closely, he was only a few yards away and a head shot would have been easy. They dare not shoot back.

If only he'd shared his plans with Sabine and got her to help, instead of acting on his own as usual.

By wearing his thunder-jacket and with a gun to Gibson's head, he should have taken charge and been giving the orders. All he needed to have done was keep a cool head and show a modicum of courage. Fellman called his bluff and found him wanting. He'd panicked and blew his chances—and the chances of those poor women. This was all his fault.

Cal remembered when he'd been interrogated on a T.A. training exercise, ten years ago. On that occasion, he panicked and folded with embarrassing speed.

This was just the same. His aspirations and reality proved to be a universe apart. When presented with danger, he imagined acting cool-headed and courageous—yet in truth, agitation and blundering ruled his actions. He was fine making plans in theory, but when actually put at risk, or when he had to think fast, he fell to pieces. He always had. Even meeting strangers at social events sent him into a spin of anxiety.

Was this the sort of person he wanted to be? Was he content to lie in bed at night imagining himself as a hero when, in reality, he fumbled and disintegrated into hysteria at the first hint of danger?

He was ashamed but, much more than that, he was angry with himself. Really furious. A white-hot fury.

Kicking the car door open, he stamped over to a picnic table, bringing his right fist down on it with all his might. To his surprise, the timber shattered. He held his throbbing hand against his stomach and cradled it with his other hand. "Fucking hell! That really hurts." Several minutes later—when the pain dulled and became tolerable—he examined the table. The damage was impressive.

Although the table was old, the timber was sound. When he pressed the plank next to the one he just split, it felt quite firm. A pity he did not summon such courage a couple of hours ago when it mattered. Punching the hell out of a picnic table did nobody any good.

He walked back to his car, rubbing his fist, which throbbed painfully. His knuckles were bloodied.

What to do? What to do? Why was he such a wuss? What was the difference between a hero and a coward, ultimately? Perhaps only a decision. Turn and fight, or turn and run.

Back inside his Land Rover, Cal closed his eyes, continuing to rub his sore hand. A childhood memory came unbidden to him. A man giving a speech as he opened a new building in Plymouth harbour. Sir Charles Blythe was a national celebrity and hero. His notoriety stemmed from rowing across the Atlantic, then sailing around the world single-handed. Remarkably, Sir Charles had two prosthetic legs. Charles Blythe had raised millions for charity.

Cal's mother dragged him along to the event, hoping to inspire her reclusive son with a real-life hero. She carried a copy of Sir Charles's autobiography and, much to Cal's embarrassment, she approached the great man to sign it. Sarah and Sir Charles chatted for some time before Charles signed Cal's copy of the book and added a dedication.

Later, when Cal was back in the safety of his mother's car, he read the inscription:

*To John. When faced with two options, favour the boldest. Sir Charles Blythe.*

Fourteen-year-old Cal had thought the advice was stupid. *Favour the boldest option!* What a recipe for disaster! However, he never forgot that phrase and now it made sense. The phrase was poor advice if his goal was to live a long, boring life. But was that what Cal wanted?

He reviewed his life, both before and after the Yellow Death. At every age, when faced with a tough choice, his default mode was to avoid the boldest option—to take the safe, comfortable path. Cal's nature was to avoid risks, and his mother had unwittingly encouraged him. She had always protected him from the big, bad world. This is where it led him, and he didn't like the destination.

He thought back to the red mini-bus and Sharon's parting words: "You live a nice, long, boring, lonely life." He was doing precisely that.

Surges of mixed emotions flooded Cal to the point where he became dizzy. He clamped his eyes shut and breathed deeply. For years, he had been fooling himself. Imagining himself as one person, but acting like another. God's teeth, what an idiot!

This was an epiphany. Today's incident forced him to see himself as others must do. A clash between the inner and outer perspectives.

*When faced with two options, favour the boldest.*
*When faced with two options, favour the boldest.*

That simple phrase changed everything. Is that what separates a hero from a coward? From this point onwards, he vowed to use that phrase to guide him. If it resulted in a bullet to the head, so be it. Better that than living as the snivelling wimp he'd become.

Somehow, just making the commitment made him feel better about himself. The past was unchangeable, but lessons could be learnt from it to forge a different future.

Yet the guilt from deserting Sabine and the others still felt like a rock in his belly. At least they were no worse off than before he arrived.

Or were they? He gave Sabine hope and then ripped it from her. How must she feel now, after being promised freedom, then having it snatched away? The devastation was written on her face when he drove off and left her. She said he was a good man. Was he?

*When faced with two options, favour the boldest.*

If he was going to live by that phrase, he should start now. Right now! Was it too late to free Gibson's prisoners? It would be crazy to go back now, wouldn't it? Sabine said there were fourteen of Gibson's goons. Those are long odds. But maybe he should follow their convoy at a distance, then wait until dark? Possibly plant explosives under the vehicles where the soldiers slept? Perhaps pick them off from a distance with his sniper rifle? What if he destroyed Gibson's motorhome at night with a rocket launcher? Possibilities stacked up in his mind.

He didn't have a plan, but ideas bounced around his head. He could still make this right—but only if he found the convoy again.

*When faced with two options, favour the boldest.*

Cal started the car engine and began to drive back to Exeter, thinking of the many ways he might free the captives. He felt a new sense of purpose. When he neared the service station, he parked his car and closed in on foot.

The convoy had gone.

He consulted his map. They might have gone North on the A377 into Exeter City and be anywhere in Exeter. Alternatively, they might have gone South, where they would hit the A30, at which point the choice was North or South? If they chose the latter, they would meet the M5 motorway and be halfway to bloody London or Plymouth, depending on which direction they chose.

He racked his brains, trying to remember if Gibson or Fellman had said anything about their future destinations, but his mind came up blank. They might be anywhere. If this was a movie, he would search the service station and find a vital clue to help catch them. But this was reality, and he had absolutely sod all.

In frustration, he kicked an empty petrol can which clattered across the forecourt, prompting a rat to scurry for cover.

He was desperate to put right his failure, so, on impulse, ran to his Land Rover. The convoy would travel slowly. Cal still had a chance! He uncoupled the trailer and started the engine, then pressed hard on the accelerator. Both the petrol and electric motors kicked in and the acceleration pushed him back into his seat. He thundered down the A377, touching ninety miles per hour.

At the junction with the A30, he chose left at random. It mattered not which direction he took—only speed was important. After a further two miles, he filtered left on to the M5. Three empty lanes spread out before him.

He pushed harder on the accelerator and felt the Land Rover surge forward. The speedometer nudged past a hundred and an ominous clunk sounded from above. Cal thought about the overloaded roof rack and the consequences of hitting a pothole at this speed.

*When faced with two options, favour the boldest. Sod it!*

He pressed the accelerator to the floor, and the engine screamed in response.

After half-an-hour, the Land Rover passed the outer limits of Bristol.

*That must be a world record.*

Cal's reserves of adrenaline were running low. He realised that if he had picked the same direction as the convoy, he should have caught them by now. He took his foot off the pedal and let the Rover gradually slow to a halt. Quite possibly, he had spent the last hour travelling in the opposite direction to Gibson and might be further away than when he started. Alternatively, the convoy might have pulled off somewhere, and he passed them without realising.

"Dammit to Hell!" This was hopeless. Maybe he might bump into Gibson's convoy in the future or hear about it from travellers on the road. He could do nothing for now, but this was unfinished business.

At least he had tried. Next time would be different. He vowed to himself that next time would be very different indeed. Sabine was the last victim he would abandon. Gibson had been the last bully he would run from. Whatever the consequences.

## Chapter Twelve

# JOHN GETS HIS GUN

TIMELINE: 9 YEARS BEFORE THE YELLOW DEATH

> "Much learning does not teach understanding."
>
> Heraclitus (540–480 BCE)

"Got a problem, John?" Gordon asked from the next desk. John was scowling at his computer screen. For two months, he had worked in a small office with a dozen other staff for 'WebExpert SW', a website creation business. The office was pleasant enough, with windows looking out over the town centre. A scattering of large pot plants and comfy chairs amongst the workstations led to a relaxed atmosphere.

John was a website coder and developer, known in their firm as a 'dev'. Gordon was a designer. John made things work, whilst Gordon made them eye-catching.

"It's Primasolve, they've seen our latest mock-up and want it changed, yet again! Guess what, they prefer the shopping cart to work like it did in version one."

"You're kidding?" Gordon said. "What version are you on now?"

"Six. We've got to start charging for all these modifications to the spec. We're going round in circles."

Gordon smiled. "You'll get used to it."

"Will I? Building a custom website should be straightforward. We have a detailed spec agreed with the clients."

"Yeah, but you know the sales team. They promise potential clients a bucket load of bespoke features just to get the contract signed. But most websites have a similar format so people can easily navigate them. Once you start faffing with the basics and end up with something that's distinct or unique you find customers can't work out how to place a friggin' order."

"By which time I'll have spent days writing thousands of lines of code, only to learn the customer hates it and wants something more familiar."

"Like I say, it's the way the world works. Don't sweat it."

"I know I shouldn't, but I'm good at this." He lowered his voice so only Gordon could hear. "I can write code twice as fast as some senior programmers, but what's the point if I have to do everything twice?"

Gordon continued to stare at his screen, typing as he spoke. "You get your paycheck at the end of the month, don't you? That's what really matters."

"I suppose so."

*Is it? Is that what really matters? Wasting my time creating code which never gets used? Creating a website to sell stuff which nobody needs, just so I get paid, so I can buy food, so I can continue to write more useless code.*

Gordon pressed the 'Enter' key on his keyboard with gusto. "And send! Another fantastic world-beating website design winging its way to an undeserving customer." He glanced over at John. "So, if you find this job so moronic, why'd you spend three years at uni studying it?"

"I enjoyed *learning* about coding. I love learning. It's actually doing it all day, every day, that's so bloody monotonous. If only I could work on a project that's innovative or worthwhile—something which would benefit humanity, then it wouldn't feel so bad."

Gordon laughed. "Benefit humanity! Jeez, did you pick the wrong job?"

"I didn't exactly pick this job. It was the first offer I got after uni. I was so pleased to get a regular job with a regular paycheck. I'm not expecting to change the world, but it would be nice to do something worthwhile. For God's sake, just take a look at this next project."

John angled his monitor so Gordan could see the screen. "It's going to be a website for a company which makes bespoke clothes for rabbits and guinea pigs. The Bunny Boutique!"

Gordon leaned back to see an image of a guinea pig wearing a bowler hat and waistcoat. "Aw, he's so cute. Almost makes me wish I had a little piggy."

John returned to his keyboard, but his mind was stuck in the past. At the end of his degree course, he had once again applied for the Army. An engineer battalion this time. He imagined constructing bridges in far-flung parts of the world. The rejection letter hit him like a brick. It mentioned his previous performance at officer selection and wished him luck finding a suitable career elsewhere. The army was desperate for new recruits, but apparently not him. Was he that seriously flawed?

So here he was—creating websites for followers of bunny fashion. The idea of doing this until retirement made him want to jump off a cliff. There had to be something better.

☣☣☣☣

The staff at 'WebExpert SW' benefited from a small dreary kitchen. It had space for two tables plus a work surface with a basin, toaster, and microwave. Its redeeming feature was a view of the local park, providing entertainment such as teenagers pulling branches off trees, or stray dogs shitting on the footpaths.

Gordon entered the staff room, out of breath. He had dashed into town during his lunch hour to buy groceries and now had only a few minutes to eat his sandwiches.

"Hi John," he said, panting as he grabbed his lunch box from the fridge. "Any tea in the pot?"

John was preoccupied with his Kindle, so seconds of silence followed before he responded. "What? Oh, sure. I made it about five minutes ago, should still be just about okay." He didn't bother to look up from his Kindle.

Gordon sat at the same table as John and began rapidly stuffing his face.

John looked up. "What's that smell?"

Gordon smiled. "Egg sarnies with sandwich spread, my favourite."

"Ugh!" John resumed reading.

Gordon swallowed. "You ought to get out more in your lunch hour. Take a walk around the park, maybe? The weather's lovely today."

John glanced out of the window at the park. "Hmm. I prefer to read."

Gordon peered at the screen of John's Kindle. "What are you reading now?"

More silence, until John noticed Gordon waited for an answer.

"Sorry, I was miles away. What were you saying? Oh, the book. Yes, it's called 'Apache'. The memoirs of a helicopter gunship pilot in Afghanistan."

"Uh-huh. I've noticed you reading military books before. Are you interested in that sort of stuff?" Gordon's mouth bulged with sandwich, making his speech barely comprehensible.

"Yeah, I guess I am. I've been following military history for years."

"Ever thought of taking it a step forward? Doing it for real?"

Gordon's cheeks bulged like a hamster.

"What? You mean join the army?" John said.

"Yes. No...well, sort of... I'm talking about the T.A. The Territorials. You know I'm in the T.A. don't you?"

John chuckled. "Yeah. I've seen you at your desk on Monday mornings, looking half dead." Gordon leaned closer. "Yeah, well, I may be knackered. But that's 'cos of all the great stuff I've been doing all weekend. You should try it."

"What? Me become a weekend warrior? I don't think it would suit me."

"Why not?" Gordon said, forcing the last of a sandwich into his mouth. "You like to keep fit. You might take to it. Where else are you going to get paid to blow-up stuff?"

*Where else indeed?*

John had never considered joining the T.A. Surely, that was playing at soldiers rather than a serious business——one step up from paint balling? Still, beggars can't be choosers and he would get to handle actual weapons.

Gordon took a huge swallow to clear his mouth. "Do you know what we were doing last weekend?"

"How could I?" John said.

"Firing anti-tank rockets on Salisbury Plain. I got to fire a live NLAW missile. They cost twenty grand apiece and make a hell of a bang! Tell you what. We're recruiting at the moment. Why not come along to tomorrow's training night and check it out? No commitment. Just have a look."

"Hmm. I'm not sure." John's guts churned at the prospect.

"Come on, what harm can it do? Something unmissable on telly is there?"

"You seem keen to get me involved. Do you get a bonus for getting recruits?"

"No. Of course not. More's the pity. I just think you might find it fun."

John rubbed his chin but said nothing.

"Well, it's up to you. But if you want to actually do something instead of just reading about it," he pointed to John's Kindle, "then come along at eight p.m. tomorrow night at the T.A. centre in Barracks Road." He glanced at the wall clock. "Jeez, I need to go."

He gulped the last of his tea and left, leaving a pile of crumbs on the table, which brought a disapproving frown from John.

That evening, John sat at his laptop and Googled the T.A. He found the T.A. and regular army had identical equipment and training standards. T.A. soldiers had served in Iraq and Afghanistan, and were doing U.N. peacekeeping duties. They received normal army pay, with a training bounty on top. The money would be useful, but the idea of actually getting to use assault rifles and rocket launchers really excited him—and that didn't happen often.

☣☣☣☣

The following evening found John parking his car at the Wyvern Barracks & Training Centre. His guts churned with an uncomfortable conflict of nerves and anticipation. Sitting in the safety of his vehicle, he glanced around the various imposing buildings. Tall metal-spiked fences surrounded the barracks. In the car park, mean-looking military vehicles sat alongside civilian cars. A large sign proclaimed 'Parking For Authorised Persons Only'. Was he an authorised person?

This was too much. A terrible mistake. He was about to leave, when another car pulled up next to him. Two men dressed in combat fatigues stepped out and began putting on berets.

"You here for the T.A. induction training, mate?" One of them shouted with a smile.

"Er...yes. I suppose so. I think."

"Follow us then, mate. We'll sort you out."

They took him to a room where several officers sat at desks doing paperwork. A lieutenant made him welcome and asked a few questions. When he found out John was a friend of Gordon's, he escorted John to a large hall to meet Gordon's section leader—Corporal 'Smartie' Smart. Several dozen soldiers—mostly men— chatted convivially in small groups. John barely had time to say hello to Smartie before an officer shouted for the soldiers to assemble for roll call.

Smartie leaned towards John. "Take a seat while we do the admin bullshit. After roll call, stick with me. We've got a treat in store tonight." He scooted off to line up with the others.

After the roll and a pep talk by the C.O. the company broke up into sections for individual training.

Smartie's section went into a separate room with John tagging along.

Seven men from the section were present, including Gordon. The Corporal started out by reviewing last week's training, before moving on to that evening's subject—observation and fire control.

They watched a video of an infantry platoon crossing open ground. The viewpoint was a soldier's eye view of the terrain. Smartie pointed out landmarks and gave them labels. Without warning, the platoon came under heavy fire and the picture paused.

Each trainee scribbled down the gunfire they had seen. John had been given a writing pad and pencil to join in.

After a few seconds, Smartie picked a soldier to read out his observations to the group:

"Right of trees, fifty metres, small arms. Left of trees, thirty, M.G. Left of house, fifty, mortar. Left of gate, ten, small arms."

It took a moment for John to understand the code being used.

"Very good," Smartie said. "Anything to add to that, Gibbons?"

"I got all of that, plus, right of gate, twenty, troops moving."

"Excellent. Remember lads, don't only focus on gunfire and smoke. We need to know all enemy positions—even if they're not shooting. Sometimes, gunfire is a distraction from a more important target. The movement Gibbons spotted might be a mortar or anti-tank team setting up. Good spot, Gibbons. Davies, you got anything else?"

John realised he had missed several enemy locations.

*Oh, God. Please don't ask me to report to the group.*

They repeated the exercise several times with different scenarios. John improved at spotting the enemy, but relief washed over him when the session finished without having to speak aloud to the section.

It was time for a quick ciggie break. John found himself at a loose end since he did not smoke or vape. Not knowing what else to do, he hung around with the others outside in the dismal smoking shed, keeping his distance from the foul fumes.

Gordon was with them using an e-cigarette, which surprised John as he never smoked at work. By this time, darkness had fallen and a persistent drizzle tickled John's face and neck. The soldiers talked about girlfriends and football—subjects for which John had no wish to contribute. This reminded him of the dreaded school playground, standing alone—the outsider looking in.

Perhaps coming here tonight was a huge mistake?

When Smartie called them into the main hall for the 'special event', John considered walking to his car and driving off, until Gordon encouraged him. "Stick with us, John, this'll be great."

☣☣☣☣

For the last hour of training, the entire company assembled in the main hall. They had laid out rows of chairs for a talk. At the front, a tall, burly sergeant, who pulled his beret so low it covered his eyebrows, stood behind a row of tables displaying a variety of small arms.

"Okay, lads and lassies. Settle down. I'm Sergeant Bailey from the Regimental Armoury. That means I get to play with all the good stuff. Now then, I'm sure you're all kick-ass warriors and can handle Brit kit with your eyes closed. Otherwise, we're fucked if we go to war."

Pause for laughter.

"Colonel Braithwaite has arranged for a demo of weapons from other countries less fortunate than ourselves. Being able to use these weird foreign buggers might just save your life one day."

He picked up a mean-looking machine gun with a long barrel and bipod. John instantly identified it as a Russian PKM.

"Who can tell me what this beast is?" the Sergeant asked.

John scanned the audience and saw only bemused faces. Was he the only one who recognised it? Apparently so. He wanted to show off his knowledge, but nerves got the better of him, so he clasped his hands tightly together and remained silent.

"Nobody, huh?"

"Looks Russian," somebody shouted out.

"Well done, that man. If you ever come up against the Russkies or their allies, this is what'll be hurling bullets in your direction."

Sergeant Bailey continued showing several assault rifles and light machine guns used by various armies around the world. John recognised them all from books and videos—but it was exciting to see them for real. He sat up straight, his attention focused on every word and movement the sergeant made. The atmosphere was relaxed, with the audience asking plenty of questions. For John, this was a real 'kid in a candy shop' moment.

As the American M4 assault rifle was being shown, one soldier asked, "Is it true they've got a reputation for jamming?"

The sergeant laughed, "All guns will jam if you don't clean them," implying he thought US troops were less fastidious in cleaning their guns than Brits. "Of course, the Russian AK47 over there never jams, 'cos all the parts are so fucking loose."

The audience laughed and John surprised himself by joining in. A poke at both the Yanks and Russkies—top marks.

After the talk, the soldiers inspected the firearms, huddling around the tables. John mingled with the rest and they ignored the fact he was wearing civvies. He was simply one of the lads—a novel experience for him.

A British SA80 assault rifle sat among the other weapons for comparison, but the soldiers ignored it. John picked it up reverently. It fitted snugly in the crook of his arm, as if the weapon was part of him. He inserted the empty magazine and cocked the rifle, appreciating the satisfying click. In his arms, he held a machine he'd seen many times on TV, but this was the first genuine encounter.

John had often wondered how he would react to holding a real modern assault rifle. Would it feel like what it was—a mass produced tool made from pressed steel and plastic? Not in the slightest—this was something special. The weapon was lighter than expected. The grips felt warm and smooth—as if they were moulded specially for his hands. This object represented the culmination of hundreds of years of development. Light, reliable, accurate, deadly and comfortable. John held the rifle with reverence, as if he cradled a religious icon. This must be what Beethoven experienced when he discovered the piano.

John picked up the AK47—the assault rifle used by Russia and a favourite with terrorists. This was a battered Chinese copy with a folding bayonet attached under the barrel. It felt heavy, clumsy, awkwardly balanced, with a crude wooden fore-stock and butt. It even rattled when he shook it.

What a revelation! He could have quoted all the statistics about these weapons, but you could not truly understand the difference between them without holding them. It occurred to him he'd gained a greater understanding of these guns in the past hour than after years of study and research. Imagine being able to actually shoot them!

Gordon came up behind him. "What do you think, John?"

John was smiling. "Fantastic. Bloody fantastic."

"So, you'll seriously think about joining?"

"Oh, yes!"

"That's great. It's not like the old days when you had to sign your life away. Try it out and if you don't take to it you just stop coming. Before you leave, go back to the office and they'll give you a welcome pack."

"Cool. By the way, I never knew you vaped."

Gordon laughed. "I only do it here. Even the wife doesn't know. It's part of fitting in. Speaking of which, if you're joining, you should give yourself a nickname."

"What do you mean?"

"Well, I reckon we have at least four Johns in this company, so you'll not be called that. Everyone has a nickname, even the officers, although they might not know about it. In our collection of John's we have Jonny, Tall John, Jack, and Bricey. I'm Gordo around here. Sergeant Smart is just Smartie. If you don't come up with a nickname yourself, somebody else will. What do your friends call you?"

John didn't have any friends.

"Just John, I suppose."

"Well, that's no good, is it?"

John rubbed his chin. "Why is somebody with the name of John called Bricey?"

"It's his surname—John Bryce. What about you? Can you make something from that monster surname of yours?"

John considered it. He hated being forced to decide on the spot, and his chest tightened. "Er...Well. Callaghan-Bryant. Bry? Calla? Cally? I know, what about just Cal?"

"Hmm. That works. We don't have a Cal. It's short and sounds cool to me. Think about it before next week. Get in first. Whenever somebody asks you your name, you tell them it's John, but your friends call you Cal. Don't give anyone else a chance to make up a nickname for you, or fuck knows what you'll end up with."

"Okay, right. Thanks for the advice. I will."

For the entire drive home, John grinned inanely. Sitting next to him on the passenger seat was an information pack with the forms to enrol.

Next week, a doctor would perform medical screenings. Provided John passed, he would take the oath of allegiance to The King and become a real soldier.

He even had a new name to go with it. He had never liked his name. It was too common. If a teacher shouted 'John' in the playground, half-a-dozen boys would turn their heads. And as for Callaghan-Bryant—ugh!—so embarrassing. He always had to repeat it two or three times. His surname was a mash-up of his parents' surnames and he hated it. But, he liked 'Cal'. It was short and sounded good. It would be a great name for a movie hero.

Joining the T.A. was like taking on a new personality. Outstanding.

## Chapter Thirteen

## CAL MEETS JULIET

TIMELINE: 14 MONTHS AFTER THE
YELLOW DEATH

"No one would choose a friendless existence on condition of having all the other things in the world."

Aristotle (385–322 BCE)

Cal's Land Rover crawled at a walking pace through the pretty village of Holsworthy. After the Yellow Death, Cal tried to avoid towns and villages. They were littered with corpses which attracted wild animals and feral dogs. Empty towns were creepy—who knew what might be round the next corner? However, it had been fourteen months since the Yellow Death and scavenging was becoming difficult. Population centres were the best places to find anything worthwhile. He drove in 'creep' mode, using only the electric motors. The car windows were lowered, and he listened for the sounds of other people.

Holsworthy had been a typical small Devon market town, with thatched cottages from the Middle Ages nestled next to modern bungalows. They all had one thing in common—their neatly manicured gardens had become so overgrown it became difficult to tell where one finished and another started. Mother Nature had begun to inexorably reclaim her territory from the upstart humans.

Coming up ahead was a major road junction dominated by a convenience store and petrol station complex. Cal braked to get a proper view.

'Davy's Supastore' was a large multi-purpose affair which used to be the hub of the town. Dirty, faded signs advertised offers on groceries and booze. Inside the store was a post office, pharmacy, and bakery. The adjacent café claimed to sell the best cream teas in Devon, served with scones baked on the premises. Cal's mouth watered at the thought of them. Devonshire cream tea—that's something he was unlikely to enjoy again anytime soon. Four petrol pumps stood under a covered area, one of which showed damage from someone trying to get at the precious contents.

Several vehicles were parked around the store. However, one stuck out as deserving of his attention. The yellow Nissan Pathfinder SUV was a recent addition and stood out. Although caked in mud and dirt like all the rest, it had clearly been driven recently. Vehicles, which had not moved for several months, had a distinct pattern of accumulated filth and grime—often accompanied with flat tyres. Somebody must be in the shop.

He reversed his Rover into a minor side street, then watched the store through the windscreen, ready to drive off at the first sign of a threat. Despite being mid-November, the sun shone in an almost cloudless sky and the slight breeze was pleasantly warm. Since the Yellow Death, the weather systems were crazy.

The summer had been miserable, and now they were experiencing a winter heat wave.

Cal imagined how this place used to be. Buzzing with life. A focal point for the locals and tourist traffic tempted by the aromas of coffee and warm pastries. Families would be crowded around the picnic tables, their dogs patiently waiting for scraps of food.

The store was already showing signs of decay. The windows were filthy. Signs displaying special offers were peeling and fading. Weeds poked out of cracks in the tarmac. Various planters on the forecourt displayed dead and decaying vegetation. The overflow from a blocked gutter badly stained one wall. A hanging sign warning that CCTV was in operation swung and squeaked with each gust of wind.

Ten minutes passed with no sound or movement from the shop. Cal was tempted to drive on. That would be the safest choice.

"When faced with two options, favour the boldest," he mumbled to himself. "Okay, let's say hello. It might actually be somebody pleasant."

He donned his thunder-jacket and shouldered his combat shotgun. His advance towards the store was slow and deliberate, stopping several times to look and listen. Still no sound or sign of movement. The shop appeared desolate and cleared out, so he wondered what anybody could be doing inside all this time.

A quick scan of the Nissan Pathfinder was revealing. He saw no weapons, but the SUV was loaded with supplies. A stack of boxes covered the passenger seat which meant the driver was a loner—ideal. Many of the boxes were medical products, which was odd. He noticed a hairbrush and tube of moisturiser on the dashboard. Probably a woman.

The main door to the store had been forced wide open, making his entry easy and quiet. Once inside, he heard movement from the back—and humming. Sounded like a woman.

A loud crash broke the silence, followed by the splintering of glass as something fell on the floor. "Dammit!"

Definitely a woman's voice.

The store had a strangely unpleasant smell—musty, like wet cardboard, with a hint of decay. Before the Yellow Death, the narrow corridors and high shelving would have made it seem cramped. However, with the shelves now empty, it appeared barren and sad. A few crumpled boxes littered the floor, along with rodent droppings. If Cal needed paper towels, pickled gherkins, or cake cases, this was the place to be. Otherwise, the shop was a disappointment. He passed the news-stand with the headline on a yellowed copy of 'The Times' declaring, 'New Hope for Plague Cure'.

*Yeah, that turned out well.*

As he moved towards the back of the store, the light became dim and he waited for his eyes to adjust.

The woman was behind the counter of the in-store pharmacy. He watched her going along the shelves, throwing items on to a growing pile of drugs in a shopping cart. This was not random looting—she was picking items with care. He noted from the back view she had a trim figure with long, fair hair in a ponytail sticking out through a red baseball cap. She wore a white sleeveless T-shirt and faded jeans. Her bare arms and clothes were covered in grimy stains from working in the dusty shop. On the countertop behind her was an automatic pistol.

She disappeared around the corner and he picked up her gun, swiftly removed the bullets and put the empty pistol back on the work surface. Cal stepped into the middle of the store, where he was easily visible.

She came back around the corner, dropping the armfull of boxes, then grabbed her pistol from the countertop. She gripped it with two hands, pointing directly at Cal. "Don't move!"

"I wasn't moving."

"Who are you?"

"I'm Cal."

She tightened the grip on her pistol. "That's not what I mean. What are you doing here?"

"I wondered what was going on in an empty derelict store, that's all." Cal nodded towards the shopping cart full of medical supplies. "You must have quite a headache?"

She frowned, glanced at her gun, then shook it up and down. "This is too light. You've taken the bullets out, haven't you?"

He nodded. "Well done. Not many people would have noticed that."

She lowered the gun. "Damn."

"Relax. I don't mean you any harm. I just didn't want to get shot by accident. Of course, I'd rather not be shot at all, if that's okay?"

Cal put the handful of bullets on the countertop.

She gave a small smile. "I don't normally shoot people before we've been formally introduced. Jesus, you scared the shit out of me, creeping up like that. Couldn't you have shouted 'hello' when you came into the shop?"

"I didn't know if you'd be friendly. You might have shot me on sight, either deliberately or accidentally."

"Fair enough. What did you say your name was?"

"Cal."

"Cal?"

"Yes. Just Cal."

"Okay, just Cal. I'm Juliet. Juliet Davenport."

"Are you stocking up with medical supplies?"

Juliet tensed as if being accused of a crime. "Is that a problem?"

"No. Not at all. Just curious, that's all."

She nodded. "Okay. Listen. I'm thirsty and filthy and this place stinks. So how about we get some fresh air and have a cup of tea?"

"Sounds good to me."

☣ ☣ ☣ ☣

The cup of tea. The British national drink since 1750. It could be said that tea was one of the building blocks of the British Empire. When a visitor enters the home of a Brit, they will inevitably be offered a cup of tea. Tea is bound into the DNA of every true Brit and provides the common ground between strangers.

Cal sipped his tea. "Ah, that's wonderful, but I miss fresh milk."

"Oh, please don't start that," Juliet said.

"Start what?"

"For the last two weeks, I was travelling with a couple who constantly moaned about what they missed since the Yellow Death. It was like some bizarre game to them. Their names were Winnie and George, but I called them Whiney and Grouch—not to their faces, of course." Juliet switched to a high pitched whinging voice. "Oh, I do miss watching Eastenders. Oh, I'd kill for a cream cake. Oh, wouldn't it be nice to eat a banana again?" She switched back to her normal voice. "I split up with them yesterday. I didn't tell them the real reason, of course."

"It'll get a lot worse," Cal said.

"What will?"

"Stuff we'll have to do without. We're still living off the excesses of a previous civilisation. 'Dead Man's Legacy'." He held up his mug. "This tea probably came from India. Coffee comes from God knows where, hot chocolate—"

"Enough! You're depressing me. Look, when proper tea runs out, we'll make nettle tea, or rose-hip tea, or something like that. When coffee runs out, we'll grind up roasted acorns. People are inventive and adaptable."

"Have you ever tasted rose-hip tea?"

Juliet shrugged. "Once. It was horrid."

They were on a patch of long grass behind Davy's Supastore, enjoying the sunshine of the clear late-autumn afternoon. Juliet sat cross-legged. Cal was crouching, which was the best he could do, given the fact his back was stiff from awkwardly lifting a crate the previous day. Every few minutes, he had to change position to relieve the pressure on his lower spine, but he tried hard to appear casual.

Juliet was in her early thirties, with an intelligent face and lively blue eyes. Cal was immediately attracted to her.

"Where's your car? I didn't see it out the front." Juliet said.

"Oh, it's parked about fifty yards up the street. Standard procedure. I like to creep up on people."

"Yeah, I noticed."

"Sorry about that. There's some nasty people about. I've found it's best to, well, be safe than sorry. Perhaps you should think about being more careful yourself, travelling alone. You are on your own, aren't you?"

"For the moment, yes."

"See, that's what I mean. You shouldn't tell strangers you're alone. You should have said you were with a group of ex-SAS soldiers who'd return in a few minutes carrying machine guns."

Juliet laughed. "And if I'd made up such a ridiculous story, would you have believed me?"

"It's the principle I'm talking about. You need to look out for yourself. Nobody else will."

"You're travelling alone. I suppose that's allowed because you're a man?"

"No—well, I am a man, obviously. But I'm a trained soldier with a shitload of weapons and I'm very careful. I wouldn't park my vehicle outside the shop. I wouldn't drive around in a car that looked like a large banana, and I wouldn't leave my only weapon on the counter."

"Maybe that gun wasn't my only weapon?"

"No?"

"I've got my winning smile and charming personality."

Cal shook his head. "Oh, Lord. Just how have you survived this long?"

Juliet went silent and stared into her empty mug. Cal feared he had soured the mood and wished he'd kept his mouth shut. "Listen, I'm sorry—"

"No, don't say anything. You're right. I should be more careful and I used to be. But it's difficult to keep it up—always looking over your shoulder. Avoiding strangers when the thing you want to do most of all is to have a friendly chat with another human being. I've seen some bloody appalling things since the plague—it's sickening what people do to each other. Each time I come across an atrocity, I get extra careful. But it doesn't come naturally to me. After a while, I start to let things slip. Like today. I know putting my gun on the counter was stupid, but it's so inconvenient to carry it all the time. Maybe I'm too trusting. Too hopeful that every stranger won't be a potential rapist."

Cal sympathised, but his compulsive personality meant he never cut corners where security was concerned. He would feel naked without a gun somewhere on his body. He decided discretion was the best policy and did not offer any further criticism.

"Is there any more tea?" he said, changing the subject.

"Sure, here you go," Juliet said, handing him the pot. "I'm quite aware it's risky being on my own, but being with others doesn't guarantee safety. Take Whiney and Grouch, for example. They were so noisy, you could hear them a mile away and they'd be hopeless in a fight. I didn't feel any safer with them. They were more of a liability. About a month ago, I found a coach that seemed to have come from London. It'd been attacked. Ten bodies on board. Two were only teenagers." Her face screwed up at the memory of it. "Being in a group didn't help them. At least when I'm on my own, I don't attract too much attention."

"Except for your banana-mobile. That was how I found you, by the way. More tea?"

Juliet held out her mug for Cal to fill it. "I'd rather be travelling with somebody else," she said. "But I've decided until I find someone I can trust, I'm better off on my own."

"Here, have a spoonful of horrible powdered milk."

"Thanks."

Cal stared into his mug, watching the milk powder dissolve, turning his drink from black to orange. "Travelling in a group has advantages, but I agree you must find the right people."

Juliet sipped her tea. "So, you've not met anyone in all the time you've been travelling?"

"Not really. I'm a bit of a loner and I'm extremely security conscious, as you'll have already gathered. Anyone I hooked up with would have to go along with my procedures. There was a young woman a few months ago… She asked if she could travel with me, but I said no. Perhaps travelling alone had become such a habit, I didn't consider it properly. Maybe it wouldn't have worked out, but I should've given it a trial for a few days. It was a missed opportunity. Other than that, I've not found anyone I'd like to pair up with."

"Wow. So you've been completely alone for, what… fourteen months?"

"Yeah. Just as well, I like my own company."

A cool breeze wafted through the trees and Juliet shivered. "I'm getting a bit chilly. If you don't mind, I need to get a fleece from my car. Back in a minute."

☣☣☣☣

While Juliet was busy at her car, Cal's mind was free to cogitate.

Juliet appeared to be a capable, young, fit, intelligent woman who was travelling alone! Unbelievable. So she travelled in a stupid bright yellow SUV—that's not the crime of the century.

Juliet said she wanted someone to travel with, but it had to be the right person. Could he be the right person? Has Christmas come early this year? He told himself not to get carried away. This was crazy thinking. Why should she want to join up with him? Surely she would prefer another woman or a mixed group? Juliet knew nothing about him and would have learnt to be wary of lone males. Besides, how would she take to all his security procedures?

Juliet returned, wearing a blue fleece and striped bobble hat. She sat down cross-legged and poured another mug of tea, adding a spoonful of milk substitute. "I think I'm actually starting to like this powdered milk."

Cal's eyebrows raised. "Seriously?"

Juliet grinned. "No. I'm joking. It tastes horrible."

"Agreed. For a moment, I was worried you'd gone insane. I might try taking my tea black."

"Perhaps you need to make friends with somebody who owns a cow?"

"Good idea. I'll put it on my 'To Do' list."

"So, what did you do before the Yellow Death?" Juliet said, in between sips of tea.

"I was a soldier."

"Oh right. That must be useful given our present situation?"

"It comes in handy. What about you, what did you do before everything went pear-shaped?"

"I'm a doctor."

"Really? You're really a doctor?"

"Yes," Juliet said and smiled. "Why'd you find that so surprising?"

Cal paused for a moment. "So far, I've not met a survivor whose previous job is going to be one iota of use in this new world. I met a dentist once, but he was killed. So you're a doctor—that's brilliant. We're going to need doctors. You're worth your weight in gold."

"I'm glad you think so."

"We are talking medical doctor, aren't we? Not a doctor of mathematics, or something like that?"

"No, no. I'm a genuine medical doctor. Before the plague, I was a paediatrician at the Royal Devon and Exeter."

"Was that why you were collecting all those drugs—because you're a doctor?"

"Yep, the tools of my trade. Obviously, there are other things I could use, like x-rays and MRI scanners, but we can kiss them goodbye. At least I can do some good with the right drugs and some basic pieces of equipment."

The Sun's heat was fading fast and neither of them wanted more tea. Their break was coming to a natural conclusion, but Cal was surprised to be feeling quite comfortable chatting with Juliet. Instead of looking for excuses to end the conversation as normal, he would have happily talked with her for hours.

Another chilly breeze rustled the nearby hedge. Juliet put her cup down. "Sorry, but the temperature's really dropping now. I need to move on and find somewhere to camp." She rose to her feet.

Cal wanted to shout, 'no, stay longer', but of course he remained silent and stood up with her. Juliet walked off to her car while he packed his portable stove and other utensils into his rucksack. When he walked over to Juliet's SUV, she was struggling to fit her latest medical supplies into the back of it.

Cal noticed she had donned a red padded anorak. "Feeling warmer now?"

"Yes, much better, thanks. This time of year it goes cold quickly in the afternoon."

"Yeah, but it's November. In any normal year, I guess we'd all be wearing overcoats by now."

Juliet was shoving a heavy box into the gap between the car window and a large stack of supplies. "Get... in... there! I really must tidy out this damn car."

"What are you planning to do with the medical stuff you've collected? Obviously, you'll not fit anything else in your car."

After forcing the boot of her SUV to close, she turned and faced him. "Well, I expect that'll be tomorrow's task—finding somewhere safe and secure. I've got a map with all my hiding places marked on it." She paused. "I guess I shouldn't have told you that. I've just given you an incentive to hit me on the head and steal the map."

Cal laughed. "It crossed my mind. Not to steal from you, of course. But maybe you should have kept that information to yourself until we got to know each other better?"

"You just said 'got to know each other better'. Do have something in mind?"

Cal swallowed and blushed.

"Seriously, what do we do now?"

"What do you mean?"

Juliet leaned back on her SUV. "Okay, we've established we don't want to shoot each other yet. We've had a nice cup of tea and a pleasant chat. I think we seem to get on fine. We both agree it's best travelling in a group—if you can find good companions. So where do we go from here? Do we both climb into our jeeps and go our separate ways, or what?"

Today had been the four hundred and sixty-fifth day that Cal had checked his mobile phone to find no reception. Throughout all that time, he had been alone and even he was missing human company, especially now winter was drawing in. The evenings were long and lonely.

Juliet had hinted they camp together tonight, and his guts churned with anxiety at the idea. What would she make of all his booby traps and security measures? Would she think he was a paranoid nut case? Would he be able to follow his comfortable routines and habits? It would be safer to give an excuse and part company.

Then he remembered Sharon. He had panicked when she'd asked to join with him and, later on, he'd bitterly regretted turning her down. Now he was doing precisely the same thing again. Could he not learn and adapt?

## CAL MEETS JULIET

*When faced with two options, favour the boldest.*

Cal realised he'd been standing in silence for several seconds and Juliet still waited for a reply.

*What the hell? What's the worst that can happen?*

"It'll be pitch dark in a couple of hours," he said. "Usually, around this time, I'd look for somewhere to camp for the night. Off-road where I can hide my truck, preferably near a stream. I prefer to set up camp and recon the area before nightfall. You're welcome to join me, if you want—no pressure."

Juliet smiled. "Thanks Cal, I'd like that very much."

"I passed over a bridge about a mile north of here. Looked like a clean stream, good place to camp. Unless you have any other ideas?"

"No, that sounds fine. I'll follow you. There's one more thing I want to get from the store."

She walked back to the shop and returned a moment later, carrying a case of wine. "The shelves are cleared of booze, but look what I found under a desk in the office. Have you got room for it in your Land Rover?"

"If I haven't, then I'll damn well make some."

A few moments later, Cal waited in his Land Rover as Juliet drove up the street to meet him.

When Juliet noticed Cal's SUV jutting out of the side road. She smiled. Her eyes were drawn to the bolted-on armour plates and massive roof rack with spot lights and smoke grenade launchers. She lowered her window and shouted, "You've seen too many Mad Max films."

Cal smiled. "You're just jealous. Follow me. And don't get too close. I don't want to be associated with that slab of butter on wheels."

# Chapter Fourteen

# JOHN & THE INTERROGATION

TIMELINE: 8 YEARS BEFORE THE YELLOW DEATH

> "Education is an admirable thing, but it is well to remember from time to time that nothing that is worth knowing can be taught."
> Oscar Wilde (1854–1900)

John returned home on Friday after a tiresome day. He spent most of the last week building a bespoke website, and today's testing highlighted several problems. On a different day, he might work late and fix them—tonight he had other commitments.

After a brief shower, he donned his uniform. Everything needed for the weekend had been neatly packed before leaving for work that morning. Nevertheless, he worried something vital might have been missed, so he unpacked and re-packed every item. John's pulse raced, and he had to make a conscious effort to stop his hands from shaking as he ticked off his meticulous checklist again.

When his parents split up, the divorce settlement provided his mother with a lovely, traditional two-bedroom cottage with gardens in the Devon countryside. They lived on the edge of Little Barton, a picture postcard village with a traditional duck pond and thatched pub. If you removed the cars and satellite dishes, it would look like a relic from the middle ages. One attraction of the house for Sarah was the self-contained chalet at the far end of the garden. She wasted no time offering it to him and it was too convenient to turn down—even though he knew she planned it to watch over him.

As John left his chalet, he walked across the lawn and into the house.

"Anything you need before I shoot off, Mum?"

"No, I'm fine. You go off, dear. Have a lovely time with your army buddies. And do be careful. Don't go shooting yourself in the foot like your Dad did."

Since John completed his basic training, he had been a regular attendee on T.A. weekends. The training normally followed a repeating annual schedule, but this coming weekend promised to be special and exciting.

Because of the latest flare-up in the middle east, elements of the Parachute Regiment were being sent for a six-month tour as U.N. Peacekeepers. They had been enjoying an extended holiday in the UK and, before they left, their C.O. was honing their skills with week-long war games. John's platoon would act as a live enemy for the final two days of the exercise.

When John arrived at the barracks in Exeter, the usual pre-weekend bustle was already in full swing. Soldiers signed out weapons; collected ration packs; loaded equipment; checked vehicles and radios. Roll-call followed, with a briefing about what they should expect. Their platoon commander—Lieutenant Greene—read out the guidelines for the upcoming exercise. Most of the advice was fairly standard and obvious, including guidance on dealing with civilians they might meet by accident.

They boarded coaches for the journey to the Dartmoor training area. John was already exhausted. After a busy week, he would usually think about winding down and going to bed. He dozed fitfully on the coach.

At around eleven p.m. they finally arrived at what appeared to be the official middle-of-nowhere. Torrential rain greeted them. The moment they stepped off the coaches, they became fully tactical—no lights, no sounds, their faces smeared with camo paint. With the moon skulking behind thick clouds, the inky blackness covered them like a cloying blanket.

A five-mile tramp in full kit brought them to a wood where they snatched a couple of hours of sleep, spreading out their ponchos as improvised tents.

John was shaken back to consciousness at three a.m. for his stint at guard duty. He had made a rookie mistake of sleeping on a slope, so had slid out from underneath his poncho. His sleeping bag was soaked and cold. Sodden trousers clung to his legs.

Two hours later, he was on a reconnaissance patrol and wading waist-deep through an icy stream. Through night-vision scopes, they monitored activity at a farmhouse for an hour, before being recalled.

As daylight filtered through the grey scudding clouds, John lay face down on soggy grass amongst the trees. His section had arrived at this abandoned cottage two hours ago and set up an ambush for an enemy patrol. John shivered, wondering what the hell he was doing here, when he could be tucked up in a cosy bed at home. Despite being uncomfortable, he struggled to stay conscious.

Something caught his attention. Through the morning mist, he watched dark moving shapes silhouetted against the dawn light. The adrenaline started pumping. Had anyone else seen them? He heard nothing from his own patrol, spread out on either side of him. Had they all fallen asleep? The Paras were perilously close now—they needed to open fire—NOW!

Blinding flash! One hostile set off a trip-flare. Everyone in John's section began rapidly firing. Staccato gunshots hammered the air. The enemy responded. Thunder-flashes arced above and exploded. Flares soared in the sky. Banshee screams and shouting from all sides. Crimson acrid smoke caught the back of his throat. A maelstrom of light and sound and smoke engulfed the area. The Paras turned and disappeared into the trees.

It lasted under twenty seconds.

John's section withdrew to a staging area and heated a meal from their ration packs. John sat hunched over a pouch of baked beans with sausages, revelling in the tomato sweetness. Simply holding the warm pouch was a luxury beyond compare. As John shivered in his damp clothing, a Land Rover pulled into the staging area. The muck-smeared passenger window wound down to reveal Lieutenant Greene.

The lieutenant scanned the huddled group and smiled. "Great work today, guys. Baxter, Tommie—I'm hearing good things about you. Keep it up. Cal, you're looking bedraggled. Get some hot grub into you. Jolly good. Listen everyone, the big show's on tomorrow morning. Let's give the Paras something to remember us by. Yes?" He turned to his driver without waiting for an answer. "Back to HQ, please."

The torment continued throughout Saturday. They dug foxholes and filled them in. They trudged from one nondescript muddy patch to another. Rain repeatedly started and stopped, never giving them time to dry out. Towards evening, they attacked a farmhouse occupied by the Paras. It might have been the same building John had watched the previous night, but he was too tired and disorientated to notice.

In the early hours of Sunday morning, the entire platoon assembled in a large tent. Each soldier grasped a steaming mug of tea or coffee as if their lives depended on it. Lieutenant

Greene addressed the group. He looked as if he had just stepped out of a hot shower—which might well have been the case. His uniform was spotless.

"Drink up, guys. We're about to go into the big event."

He pointed to a drawing on the whiteboard.

"The paras have bedded down here. We are to split into six groups and strike with a coordinated attack at daybreak. Let's give the fuckers a rude awakening, eh?"

John wondered what exactly the good lieutenant would do during this attack, but knew it was best to keep his mouth shut.

"The Colonel will follow progress from HQ, so let's put up a good show, eh? When this is over, I've arranged a good feed before we all head off home."

The lieutenant seemed disappointed by the muted response.

☣☣☣☣

By five a.m. after a long trek in the dark, John was in position, lying on his belly again. The others in his section lay in a line to his left. Thick fog clung to the undergrowth. The air was as still as death. It was not quite cold enough for frost, but plenty cold enough to make John feel utterly miserable in his sodden clothes. The first light of dawn crept over the horizon, bringing no warmth.

It began with a tremendous flash in the sky from a para-illuminating flare.

Somebody shouted, "Fire," so John slipped off the safety catch and let rip towards the enemy camp. He had 120 rounds of ammo and intended to use every one.

The platoon unleashed Hell on the paras.

Bangs, flashes, gunfire, detonations, shouts, and screams broke out from all directions. Billowing clouds of red and green smoke drifted across the landscape. The sky erupted with flares like demons bursting forth from another dimension. The pungent stench of white phosphorous and nitrocellulose jolted John's senses. For a brief time, all discomfort was forgotten as adrenalin-fuelled excitement took over. John fired over and over, loaded and fired again—his heart beating as fast as the flashes from his gun barrel.

John was so intent on shooting, he never noticed two soldiers creeping up behind him. By chance, a Para patrol was returning to camp as the assault began and they turned tables on their attackers.

Being captured during a training exercise is the ultimate embarrassment. John had little time to reflect on this as two burly soldiers grabbed him from behind, then dragged him into their camp. Two of John's colleagues suffered a similar fate. The sounds of battle were dying out. No doubt most of his mates would withdraw to enjoy a hot breakfast and swap exaggerated tales of brave exploits.

John's immediate prospect was to give the soldiers of the Parachute Regiment practice in prisoner interrogation.

☣☣☣☣

"Stand absolutely still and keep your eyes on the ground, you little shit!"

As the sounds of battle faltered, the paras pulled a hood over John's head and tightened the draw-cord around his neck until it pinched his skin.

The hood obscured all light, restricted the air, and stank of vomit. After a few breaths, Cal was gasping whilst beads of sweat formed on his brow. They ordered him to strip and left him standing naked in the open, holding his arms high. Whilst his head boiled in its bag, the chill November air stole the heat from his bare skin. He shuddered. Worse than the cold was the sense of being exposed and vulnerable. By the time his boots, trousers, and jacket were returned——minus laces and belt——his feet were wooden.

After dressing, they forced him to lie spread-eagled, face down in the icy mud. Still hooded, he lay for an eternity, straining to hear what was happening around him. Besides the breeze stirring the trees and twittering of birds, the area was deathly quiet. Had they left him? Was he lying alone in the middle of nowhere as part of some cruel joke? He shivered, a combination of fear and cold.

*What's happened to my rifle? God, I hope they picked it up. I could be court-martialled if I've lost it. They must've picked it up. They wouldn't leave an assault rifle in the woods, would they? What if they forgot it?*

Of course, he dare not ask.

They had forced John to lie with the palms of his hands pointing upwards. His twisted arms ached. Time seemed to have stopped. John's mind drifted and gradually his arms untwisted into their natural state. Without warning, he felt pressure on his right hand. Somebody stood on it, forcing it back into position, crushing it into the gravel. John cried out, but was too afraid to move.

*This isn't right. It's a sodding training exercise, for God's sake! Why isn't Lieutenant Greene stopping this? Does he know what's going on?*

Time passed. Excruciatingly slowly. Impossible to tell how long. At first, John's hand throbbed until both hands became so cold he lost feeling in them. He heard the crunching of boots coming closer, and tensed. His arms were wrenched behind his back and tightly restrained with a cable tie. Rough hands dragged him across the ground before throwing him into the rear of a truck. Two other bodies pressed against him. Perhaps they were his mates, but he remained silent.

The truck made a journey over rugged terrain. He was thrown about and banged his head several times.

At journey's end, they dragged John out, freed his hands and made him lean against a wall with his arms and legs outstretched——the classic stress position for interrogation. A wave of dread passed through him. This wasn't good.

*Oh, God! How long can this last? It feels like they're just getting started. Can't see anything. Can't breathe. Christ! Everything hurts so much. Can't feel my fingers or toes. Is that shouting and screaming? Can't hear anything above the noise of that damn car engine revving. Must get a grip. This is a standard sensory deprivation technique. I've read about this. It doesn't help to know that. How long has it been now? Seems like hours. Arms, legs, burning. Feel sick. How long now? Oh...my arms...hurt so much. Can't take much more of this. Perhaps, if I can bend my arms and knees a little. Just a bit. Take the pressure off for a moment——*

Something smacked him hard on the back of his legs and he collapsed.

"Stand straight, you fucking piece of shit!" shouted a harsh voice a few inches from his ear. He struggled to assume the stress position again, with adrenaline holding him rigid.

"Name?" screamed the Voice. It was so loud and close, it hurt his ear.

"Er, Cal–J–J–John–Callaghan–Callaghan-Bryant, Sir."

"What was that you said? Don't you even know your name, you little tosspot?" bellowed the Voice.

"I–I–I–It's—"

"Shut Up! Shut the fuck up! You sorry piece of shit. Stand straighter. Straighter! What's wrong with you? Can't you even stand up? Fuck me, what a sorry sight you are. Is this the best the army can do?"

"I–I—"

"What part of 'Shut up' didn't you understand?"

The shouting went on and on. The Voice insulted in ways he could not have imagined. The Voice asked about his sex life. The Voice accused him of being impotent and having a tiny dick. In between the insults and threats, the Voice bombarded him with questions. Questions came so fast he could hardly think. John was nauseous, numb, scared, cold, confused, suffocating, hot, agonised, disorientated, and he answered every question as best he was able.

He told them his name, serial number and rank. Eventually. For a time, his army number—which would usually run effortlessly off his tongue—was lost from memory. That brought another torrent of abuse from the Voice as John blurted out random numbers. He would have told the Voice anything. It confused him. He braced himself for the next bout of abuse, but the only noise was the sound of the engine revving. The Voice had gone.

But for how long? Seconds, minutes, hours. Time lost all meaning. There was only now. Only agony. In the complete and utter darkness of the hood, lights formed and swirled in front of John's eyes. He knew they were in his imagination, but couldn't stop his eyes following them like a cat chasing a spotlight on a wall.

He gasped for air inside the hood as if he were running a marathon. The draw chord cut painfully into his neck. He needed more air! The Voice was back again. Shouting and demanding. Accusing and insulting. Questioning and more shouting. John's hands and feet were numb, yet his head roasted, with stinging sweat running into his eyes. He told the Voice everything. Anything to stop the shouting, to make it end. What did he have to do to make it stop? Nausea spread from his guts to his throat in a slow, inexorable wave.

*Oh, Christ! I can't throw up inside this goddamn hood.*

Again, he noticed the stink of vomit from a previous incumbent of the hood.

The Voice continued to scream at him, but somehow sounded more distant—otherworldly. He found he could ignore the Voice. His mouth tasted of metal—as if he had licked an iron bar. Weird! He was dimly aware of shaking uncontrollably—or was he? His body felt disconnected. Coloured lights spun around his head. He floated within infinite space. Nothing mattered any more.

For the first time in his life, John fainted.

☣☣☣☣

When John awoke, he found himself in the cab of a Land Rover with his hands tied to the steering wheel. The car was a short distance from a derelict house where, in the early morning light, he saw one of his mates standing in the stress position against a wall. At last the fog had lifted, revealing a clear blue sky. The low sun cast long shadows. A handful of soldiers casually stood around, some smoking. John found it difficult to believe this was the hell hole where he had been abused to the point of collapsing.

A wave of overwhelming relief passed over John. Thank God.

His fingers and toes tingled as the feeling returned to them. He looked at his reflection in the rear-view mirror, expecting to see a bloody welt where the draw cord had cut into his neck. Only a thin pink line was visible.

Then came shame. He had told them everything. Absolutely everything. Fellow British soldiers questioned him for a few hours. They barely touched him, yet he had been so terrified and confused, he said anything to make it stop. His two mates were still out there. They had not fainted. They didn't blabber like babies. John bet they remembered their army numbers.

What a twat. Why did he give in so easily? This was only a sodding training exercise, for God's sake. He only had to keep his mouth shut for a couple of hours. Perhaps this was something to do with autism—some instinctive panic reaction? John was never in any real danger. Why did his brain go into a complete meltdown? What a plonker.

A new sound cut through the air—a screaming Land Rover engine. No—two or more, coming closer, fast. Around the bend in the road came four Land Rovers at high speed, spraying water and mud in their wake. What the hell was going on? Soldiers jumped out, and he recognised them! His mates were here. This was a rescue. A real rescue, not something pre-planned.

"Here! Here! I'm over here!"

John struggled to free his hands. A moment later, the door flew open.

"Cal. You okay?" Gordon said.

"Gordo, my hands!"

A massive knife appeared, and in seconds, John was free. He saw a tussle going on at the house. Nothing serious, a bit of jostling and wrestling. Soldiers on both sides grasping and pulling each other to the ground, or pinning them to walls. The sheer numbers of the rescue team overwhelming the few paras.

The other two prisoners were freed and led to the rescue Land Rovers. They acted dazed and confused.

"C'mon Cal," Gordon shouted and slapped him on the shoulder. The two soldiers ran together towards the house and jumped into the nearest Rover.

Engines revved. Wheels spun and gravel was thrown backwards as the Rovers accelerated. The soldiers of The Rifles began shouting with glee. Seconds later, they were speeding away. John's comrades cheered, laughed, and slapped each other on the back. One man had a bloody nose, yet he seemed not to notice.

John sat silent and numb, gasping for air.

☣☣☣☣

Late on Sunday afternoon, Sarah was pruning the roses in her front garden, wondering whether to stop for a cup of tea and a scone. Most of the garden had been tidied for the winter, but the roses and fuchsias proudly displayed their red and purple blooms, which glowed in the fading sunlight.

The sound of a car coming up the lane drowned out the orchestra of bird song. She smiled as John pulled into the driveway next to her. John got out, dragging his webbing and bergen rucksack after him. Goodness! How dishevelled—filthy, crumpled clothing hung from his slumped shoulders. Traces of camouflage paint framed his face and red eyes. Most unlike John!

"Hello dear. Gosh, you are a sight. Oh, dear me, you pong a bit as well. Did you have a nice time?"

John gave an unconvincing half-smile. "Yes, Mum. I had a great time, but I'm knackered now."

"Never mind. You're filthy. I trust you're going to have a shower before anything else?"

"Yes, Mum."

"I'll put the kettle on and make us a cup of tea. Mind you take those boots off before going into the house."

"Sure, Mum—although I don't think my bare feet will be much cleaner."

Sarah watched him trudge towards the front door.

*Boys will be boys. I hope he enjoyed his war games.*

☣☣☣☣

John sat at his workstation, staring unseeing at his computer screen. His hands rested by his keyboard. The rain front which had tormented him on Dartmoor now flung heavy droplets against the windows, creating a low rumbling, interrupted by occasional thunder and lightning. The weather provided the perfect accompaniment to his mood.

The events of last weekend churned over in his mind. Trying to find something positive about his humiliating performance. He looked at the graze on the back of his hand. At the time, it hurt as if his hand was being crushed. In reality, he suffered only a few surface scratches, not even worthy of a sticking plaster.

Last evening, he had gone to bed at seven p.m. The earliest for as long as he could remember, yet he had lain awake for hours. Today he felt exhausted, and ached in a dozen places.

Building websites never seemed so trivial and pointless.

A cup of coffee appeared next to his hand. He glance upwards and saw Gordon, who wore a broad smile. "Thought you looked like you needed it. Pretty intense weekend, eh?"

"Thanks. Yes, that's one word for it. How come you're so...lively? I feel like death warmed up."

Gordon sipped his own drink. "Don't worry. I'm feeling knackered as well. But I'm used to it. That was your first real hard weekend. When you've been doing it a while, you learn survival tricks—like how to sleep curled up in a muddy trench and not falling asleep on a slope. Besides, I didn't have to go through the inquisition. Whilst you were spending three hours standing against a wall, I scoffed bacon and eggs." He took another slurp of coffee and wheeled his chair over to sit next to John. "How was that session, by the way? It looked harsh."

"Horrible. I've experienced nothing like it. I didn't think they could rough people up like that in training."

Gordon shook his head. "Me neither. I've never seen anyone go so far. That's why we came and rescued you. We watched from a distance and decided you'd suffered enough. Lieutenant Greene's put in a formal complaint. If that's what they do in training, can you imagine what the fuck they do to real prisoners?"

John was silent for a moment. Normally, he was secretive about his feelings and would never tell his mother about the interrogation. But when you've shat in the same hole as somebody, you form a bond. Army buddies hold no secrets.

"You know I fainted? I actually goddamn fainted like a little girl."

Gordon could not suppress a small grin. "Yes. I heard. Don't sweat it. It happened at the end of a tough weekend. You were exhausted, disorientated. Remember, those were professional interrogators, and they deliberately tried to break you."

"They succeeded. And nobody else fainted."

"I spoke to Gerry and Bricey on the coach home. They both came pretty close to it."

John's boss stepped out of his office and walked past them towards the kitchen.

Gordon changed the subject quickly. "I think we should make these fonts bigger and move the banner further down the page. It'll look more prominent and get the message over better." They waited until the coast was clear.

John spoke first. "There's no getting round it, I panicked. I lost control. I was fucking useless."

Gordon lowered his voice to a whisper. "That's why we have training. Next time, you'll know what to expect. You'll do better. Drink your coffee and stop overthinking it."

Gordon wheeled his chair back to his desk.

John nodded and dutifully took a sip of his drink without tasting it. Was he overthinking it? He was relieved Gordon brushed off his miserable performance under interrogation, but John could not dismiss it so easily.

The interrogation had been a disquieting experience. John had read true stories of immense bravery, where people resisted unimaginable torture for months. John hoped it would be the same for him. After all, he was cool and logical—wasn't he? Before last weekend, he imagined gritting his teeth and telling the interrogator to go to hell.

But that was not how it happened. Not at all. In reality, he folded under the slightest pressure. He panicked and acted like a complete wimp. If a movie hero had caved in so quickly, John would have been scathing about them.

Gordon reassured him he would do better next time. Would he? Or would he panic again? Was this a lack of experience, or a basic flaw in his personality? Making quick decisions had never been his strong point. Anxiety was never far away—lurking in the shadows, ready to grab him by the balls, turning him into a stuttering idiot.

John made a point of planning everything to the nth degree. Every Plan A had a Plan B, C, and D. Nothing was left to chance. That was how he survived life. That way, he avoided unpleasant surprises and the need to react quickly. Whatever happened, John always had a plan to follow.

Except last weekend he didn't. He never expected to be captured, nor could he have predicted the interrogation. John had been caught unprepared. He had been complacent. But he could learn from it.

Gordon was right. John would act better next time, but not for the reason Gordon believed. John would relive the interrogation in his mind and rehearse exactly what he should have done. He would do it again and again. Each time with a different scenario. Whatever the interrogators did, John would have an answer to it. If there was a next time, it would be different.

Of course, the biggest mistake was getting captured. That was stupid. So, he would also replay that incident and plan how he should act.

This should be a solvable problem if he put his mind to it.

## Chapter Fifteen

# CAL MAKES A DECISION

TIMELINE: 14 MONTHS AFTER THE
YELLOW DEATH

> "Accept the things to which fate binds you, and love the people with whom fate brings you together, but do so with all your heart."
> Marcus Aurelius (121–180)

*So far, so good. I haven't ballsed it up yet,* Cal thought.

A few miles from Davy's Supastore, Cal found a track off the main road, running parallel to a small bubbling stream. Juliet and Cal reversed their SUVs into the bushes next to each other. Cal brought out a saw, then began removing tree branches. A few minutes later, he had hidden both vehicles under foliage.

They both collected wood, then Cal shot a rabbit in an adjoining field.

"Shall I light a fire?" Juliet said.

Cal looked around. "Do you mind if we wait another fifteen minutes? It's still quite light and I don't want smoke leading anybody else here."

Juliet shrugged. "Fine, but don't blame me if dinner's late."

"I'm going for a walk. Be back in about twenty minutes." Cal shouldered his rifle and walked off for his evening reconnaissance of the area. As usual, he left an emergency pack near the campsite. As he circled their vehicles, checking for escape routes and hazards, he reflected on the experience so far with Juliet. Being alone with a woman would usually reduce him to a stuttering fool. Yet, he found himself surprisingly relaxed in Juliet's presence.

Perhaps this was partly because of Juliet's personality. Her job involved putting people at ease and she was good at it.

What also helped bolster Cal's mood was the environment. He never fitted into what passed for normal society, with the many conventions, rules, and fashions. In this alternative world, Cal felt in control. Nobody gave him orders. The new lifestyle suited him well—he was healthier than ever and wanted for nothing. Living alone, relying on his own wits and guile, had created a sense of confidence, which all the years of schooling and therapy had failed to do.

In fact, he felt as if he was in his element.

When he walked back into camp, there was a spring in his step. He was looking forward to spending the evening with Juliet.

He began the daily routine of setting trip wires around their campsite.

"What are you doing?" Juliet shouted as she gutted the rabbit.

"Booby traps. Trip flares and tear gas, to be precise. I don't like surprise visitors."

Juliet frowned. "I don't want to seem ungrateful, but what if I want to wee in the night? I've lived this long without experiencing tear gas and I'd like to continue that way."

"Don't worry. I'm setting the gas grenades in a horseshoe shape around the front of the trucks. Best not to go wandering this way. Around the back, I'll set the trip flares and show you where they are in a minute. They'll wake us up if anyone approaches during the night, but there's no real harm done if you set one off by accident."

"So, do you think they'll work? I mean, if anything creeps up on us."

"Well, I've not woken up with a badger in my tent yet."

They stewed the rabbit with canned vegetables and potatoes. While the meal bubbled over the open fire, they sat in the dark, drank tea, and chatted. The river gently gurgled in the distance. Occasionally, an owl hooted. The night was cold and cloudy, so they both covered their legs with sleeping bags.

"The stew smells gorgeous. God, I'm hungry," Juliet said.

"If you want, I've got some snack bars in the car."

"No thanks. I'd rather wait. This is going to be wonderful. I've not had fresh meat for weeks. The smell is delicious." She poked at the stew with a spoon. "It's taking ages. Maybe we should have roasted the rabbit?"

"Hmm. Nice, but all the fats drop off into the flames. Wasted calories. This way we get all the goodness."

"But it would have been so tasty. Are you always so damned practical?"

"Not always. For instance, why don't we open one of those bottles of wine?"

"Now that's a fantastic idea."

"Better still, how do you fancy mulled wine?"

An hour later, they both sat with their sleeping bags pulled up to their chests, eating large bowls of rabbit stew and drinking steaming red wine. The crescent moon hid behind the clouds, so the only light was their campfire and head torches.

They had swapped stories about incidents they had seen since the Yellow Death. Cal had told Juliet about the red mini-bus, but had avoided any mention of his caches.

"God, I needed this," Juliet said.

"What? The booze or the food?"

"Both. And the chance to sit down and relax... and talk. You're a superb cook, this stew is delicious."

"Me? I'm a crap cook. I thought it was mainly you that did the stew."

"It was. I'm being polite. Isn't it odd that before the Death we cooked with all sorts of spices and flavourings. Now we simply stick a few bits of meat into a pot with some veggies and bit of salt. Boil for an hour and it tastes like heaven. I really appreciate the flavour of every chunk of veg and morsel of meat."

"I guess our tastes adjust. You're right about this being delicious. It's great to have hot food in your belly to warm you up, if nothing else. However, I'd still say you have to go a long way to beat a good curry."

Juliet laughed. "A very long way indeed. India, to be precise. It's going to be some time before you enjoy another vindaloo."

"True." He spooned a particularly large chunk of rabbit into his mouth. Despite the myth, it was not like chicken at all. More chewy and dry, which he liked, but it also had a more intense flavour—gamey and earthy. Of course, he had only ever eaten chicken raised on intensive farms with processed feed and growth hormones. A wild chicken might taste entirely different—if wild chickens even existed.

He looked through the campfire at Juliet. She returned his gaze and smiled. With the light from the flames dancing on her face, she was beautiful. This was... nice, cosy, companionable... perfect. There was nowhere else he wanted to be. The conversation was relaxed and natural. In moments of silence, there was no awkwardness between them. Cal could not remember being so comfortable with another person. "You were telling me about your time as a doctor."

"Oh yes. Well, after med school, I worked as a junior hospital doctor at the John Radcliffe in Oxford. I wanted to work with children, so moved to Exeter three years ago when an opening came up in paediatrics. I loved it most of the time. Fixing up kids was so satisfying. It wasn't only healing the kids, it was the reaction of the parents as well. Of course, sometimes it was hard. You can't help getting emotionally involved more than is good for you."

She sipped her drink. "On my first day at the Royal Devon, another doctor approached me. Kevin was quite handsome. I tried to put him off. New job, new apartment, my hands were full without starting a new relationship. But he was patient and persistent. Eventually, I agreed to go out with him. We became steady and often slept over at each other's places, although we both still kept our own homes. I had a cat called Napoleon." Juliet was silent for a few seconds. "Kev and I were talking about setting up home together. Then the plague arrived and everything went to hell. Kev was one of the first to go down with it and...

She paused to wipe her eyes before continuing. "Sorry. One of his friends told me he was planning to propose. Apparently, he'd been carrying a ring around for days, waiting for the right moment."

Juliet's voice petered out, and she became quiet, lost in her own thoughts as painful memories welled up. Cal wanted to help, but was nervous about saying something sounding crass or insincere. Experience had taught him it was better to remain quiet than say the wrong thing. If they had been sitting closer, he would have put his arm around her. But in the end—as usual—he did nothing.

A few moments later, she came out of her reverie.

"Sorry about that. I didn't plan to burden you with my troubles. You're a good listener."

"I'm a better listener than a talker, that's for sure."

Juliet put her mug down and blew her nose. "When I returned to my flat for the first time afterwards, Napoleon had gone. I stayed there for three days, hoping he'd turn up. That scrawny cat was my only living link to the pre-Yellow Death world, but he'd disappeared. I hate not knowing what happened to him."

"I expect he wandered off to find food when his normal source had dried up. There was no way he could know you'd come back."

"Yes. That makes sense—but I'd love to be able to give him a cuddle. Sorry, I'm being morbid again." She threw more wood on the fire, which crackled gratefully and spewed a shower of sparks upwards. "Would it be very bad to open another bottle?"

"Very, very bad. I'll get the corkscrew. Do you want it warmed up?"

"I don't mind, you choose."

Cal topped up her mug straight from the bottle.

"So you didn't go through the fever at your home then?"

"No, no. I was at the hospital. Most of us stayed and worked right through it. When I got sick, I just lay down on a bed, ready to die. I was exhausted, and I'd seen so many die that I never even considered the possibility I might live through it. By then, I didn't much care one way or another. Kev had already gone. So had my parents. When I eventually woke up—days later—there was an empty IV drip in my arm. Somebody must have tended to me for part of the time. I'd been told we'd run out of meds, but I'm guessing they put some to one side for the medical staff. Maybe that's what saved me."

Juliet sipped from her cup, and Cal waited for her to continue.

"When I had enough strength to get out of bed, I wandered through the corridors. It was spooky. Not only the corpses—I'd got used to those. It was the structure itself. A hospital should always be bursting with noise and life, but it was totally silent.

## CAL MAKES A DECISION

The hospital was dead. I realised straight away we were back to the Stone Age—medically, that is. The place was packed with technology; scanners costing millions of pounds, operating theatres, dialysis machines, all of them nothing more than s crap.

"All my training and experience seemed to be useless. How could I set a broken leg without x-rays? How could I cure an infection without antibiotics? We're back to doing amputations with the patient having to be tied down. People are going to die from the most trivial injuries."

She brushed her hair out of her face. "When I think about it, that's what hit me the hardest after the Death. When the initial shock was over, I was left feeling useless. A doctor isn't a nine-to-five job, it's a life. I spent nearly all my time around the hospital. All my friends were other medical staff. The Yellow Death took away my reason for being."

Cal offered her the bottle, but she shook her head. "All of your training must count for something?"

"I didn't think so right away. We'd got so used to all our high-tech tools. But I came round to thinking that those few of us who survived, especially those with skills, have a duty to preserve whatever we can. We can't let everything we've learnt over centuries be lost. So I resolved to do two things. Firstly, to create medical supply dumps. So I looked for buildings which were secure and dry, and began storing important drugs and equipment for the long-term. I took out any batteries, wrapped equipment in cling film and that sort of thing."

"That's what you were doing this afternoon?"

"Yes, I'm still at it. Protecting irreplaceable medical supplies. But we must do more than hold on to the past. Eventually, drugs will run out, or simply get too old to use. So, I've been learning about how medicine used to be practised. Just how do you amputate an arm if there's no painkillers or anaesthetic and only thirty seconds before the patient bleeds to death? A few weeks back...Perhaps I shouldn't tell you this?"

"Go on. I doubt you'll manage to surprise me."

Juliet cleared her throat. "Well, a few weeks ago, I noticed an injured sheep in a field. It was in a terrible state. Lower jaw missing and face half gone. I expect it must have been attacked by a fox or a feral dog or something. Nothing I could do for it so I put it out of it's misery."

She paused. "Then it occurred to me how I could treat it as an opportunity. I got out my surgical instruments and practised amputating limbs as if it was a live human. Just as well that I did because I made a right mess of the first one. I've no training as a surgeon and it's not easy—especially when you're trying to do it in under a minute."

"Holy crap. I was wrong. You have managed to surprise me. That's amazing."

Juliet smiled. "I've also been studying the use of herbs and natural remedies. You'd be surprised how many modern drugs are based on wild plants. There's a stack of books in my jeep I've read through. It's like med school all over again."

"That's great. It's exactly what I've been thinking since day one. Preserve what we have and prepare for when we no longer have Dead Man's Legacy. If only more people thought the way you do. Nobody else seems to think long term."

Juliet poked the fire with a stick. "After I woke up, I was numb for a while, like everybody else. But I knew there must be survivors. Since I was working in the hospital when the first cases arrived, I saw how a handful of patients somehow hung on. Even before I went down with the fever, I realised this was the end of civilisation, but there would be a few survivors. That gave me a head start over most people, and being a doctor gives me a reason to carry on."

Cal sipped his wine. "Have you been working all on your own?"

"Unfortunately, yes. I've travelled with a few groups for short periods, but couldn't raise much interest. Everyone wished me luck, but they all had something better to do.

Most folk are acting like they're in some sort of delayed shock. Post-traumatic stress, I expect. I met one woman six months after the Yellow Death who had watched her husband, eight children and four grandchildren pass on in front of her. That poor woman dug graves for all of them. How the hell do you get over that? She felt so guilty for surviving—it was as if a weight was pressing her down. I reckon the only reason she carried on was because she was Catholic and suicide is a mortal sin. In her heart, she wanted to lie down and die."

Juliet stared into the fire, lost in her thoughts. "Anyway, that's what I've been doing. Saving what I can and preparing for the future. We can't carry on scavenging forever. What about you? What have you been up to for the past year?"

Juliet's question startled Cal. He had been intent on listening to Juliet's story and ideas. Now he had to justify what he had been doing since surviving the Yellow Death, and the prospect sent his mind into turmoil. The evening had been going so well.

*How much should I tell her? She's trusted me. I have to do the same—right? But what will Juliet think when I say I've spent my time storing guns, bombs, and rocket launchers—machines of death? She'll wonder if I'm crazy. She might start telling others about the nutter who has made massive weapons caches all over Devon. Anybody with that knowledge would recognise it was me, and then I'd become a target. Everyone would want to steal my stashes. Or am I being paranoid? Why would she do that? I don't plan to go around telling everyone about her medical caches.*

*When faced with two options, favour the boldest.*

"You've gone silent," Juliet said. "Don't you approve of what I'm doing?"

Cal realised he had been silently staring into the fire for several moments.

"Oh, Good Lord, no. Please don't think that. Actually, I'm in awe of what you've done. It's exactly what needs to be done.

Everybody should be doing something similar. I've been sort of doing the same thing—but different."

"Now you've got me intrigued. So, what have you been up to?"

"After the Yellow Death, I had a similar epiphany to yours. To be honest, for a time it was like being king of the world. Nobody told me what to do. I could go into any shop and pick whatever took my fancy. For a while, that gave me a real buzz."

Juliet laughed. "I remember going into a department store and trying on loads of super expensive boots. It was a strange time. I was in terrible grief and shock. But I had to put that in the back of my mind somehow to survive from day to day. When it came to the surface, I would just burst into tears. I cried every day for a long time. Going through a shop and trying on jewellery, clothes, and ridiculously expensive perfume was a distraction...But it felt hollow, or shallow. Papering over the cracks. That sort of thing should be done with friends. It just reminded me I was alone."

Cal put another log on the fire, sending a shower of sparks into the night. "I get that. When I drove out of the showroom with my brand new top-of-the-range SUV, I was chuffed. But after driving down an empty road for a few minutes, it somehow took the shine off it. Like you said, it was shallow. But something else occurred to me. Something... darker. Something which scared me."

Juliet glanced up at him and frowned. "Go on."

"I realised I could do whatever I wanted." He paused, letting his statement to sink in.

"So?"

"That idea scared me. I'm not the sort to take advantage of others. But there's plenty who are. I've studied warfare all my life and if there's one thing I've learnt for sure, it's that the veneer of civilisation is very thin. Most folk need little excuse to turn into animals."

"That's a pretty pessimistic view of humanity. There've always been plenty of good people...Martin Luther King, Nelson Mandela—"

"Yeah, but for every good person you can list, I bet I can give you ten evil dictators. Before the Death, everyone believed we were cultured, civilised and respected each other's civil rights and so on. Yet there were terrible atrocities happening all over the world. And there always has been. For instance, when the Soviet Army reached Berlin in 1945, they systematically raped over a hundred thousand women. In the Vietnam war, an entire company of US soldiers rampaged and slaughtered over five hundred defenceless villagers. You only had to watch the news to hear of civil wars, school shootings, mass rapes, terrorist attacks—"

Juliet held up her hands. "Okay, okay, I get the point. There's a lot of bad people around. I don't need convincing—I saw my fair share on a Saturday night in the Emergency Department."

"Sorry. I get carried away." Cal picked up his cup, then decided he'd drunk too much already. "Anyway, I felt with no police, army, courts, or any mechanisms of law, some people would go wild. And I'm being proved right. For instance, the red mini-bus and the coach you found with the ten bodies. Initially, everybody grabbed whatever they wanted, so there was no need to steal. Now it's getting difficult. Some folk will establish settlements and start growing their own food. But that'll be hard work. There'll be those who'll want to take an easier path."

Cal poked the fire with a stick. "I saw this coming from day one. I asked myself, what do people need to defend themselves against aggressors? Answer: Weapons! So I created weapons caches. I've made dozens of secret ammo dumps across Devon. Also, like you, I realised this would be a stop-gap. We'll soon run out of ammo, or it'll become unreliable. Then we're back to bows and arrows. So I've also been doing my homework. Medieval warfare—manufacturing gunpowder and so on. Like you, my truck has a stack of books. The only difference is mine are mostly about how to kill."

He inhaled deeply. "So. Now you know my dirty little secret."

Juliet tilted her head back and started laughing. "Jesus, Cal. What a pair we are. The Angel of Mercy and the Angel of Death."

Cal noticed the light of the fire flickering on her face. Juliet was lovely, and he felt, well, dirty next to her. Florence Nightingale sharing a glass of wine with Attila the Hun.

"Listen, if what I've said disturbs you, if you don't feel safe camped here, I quite understand. I must come across as some sort of gun-toting nut case. If you like, I'll take off and camp somewhere else."

She looked up at him, and in the firelight, he could see she was smiling. "Don't be silly. I'm perfectly safe with you. Well, safer than I would be without you, anyway. One advantage of working shifts in the Emergency Department is you learn to judge people pretty fast. There's nothing wrong with arming yourself—you already know I carry a gun. A gun is just a tool, no different to a scalpel. What matters is what you do with it."

"I'm relieved you think that way."

"It's still early days and we hardly know each other yet. There's still plenty of time for me to form a poor opinion of you. One thing puzzles me, though. I can see why you'd want to store sufficient weapons for yourself and your friends, but why do you need so much?"

"There's two reasons. The first is that weapons will become a useful currency. Remember that money is worthless, probably the same with gold and jewels. Let's say in a couple of years I need something from a settlement—food, shelter, medical help, whatever. How do I buy it? I suspect the offer of a good rifle, with ammo and training, will be very welcome. Weapons are my nest egg."

"Yeah, I guess that makes sense in a weird sort of way."

"But that's not the major reason. Have you noticed how it's always the bad guys who have the guns? People tend to believe others are like themselves—that's a fundamental part of human psychology. Good people expect other people to be good. So they won't think to arm themselves until something bad wakes them up. By then it'll be too late. You can bet one of the first thoughts for most of the surviving shitheads will be to get their hands on some guns. I want to help the good guys. To even the score."

"And how will you decide who are the good guys?"

"The good guys are usually the ones being beaten up by the bad guys."

"I've drunk a teeny bit too much wine. That almost makes some sense. I'm going to put up my tent and get ready for bed."

They both erected their small tents side-by-side behind their SUVs and prepared for bed. Half-an-hour later, both laid in their sleeping bags in their respective tents. Cal felt strange knowing somebody was lying only a few feet away, and he quite liked the idea. He had lived a solitary life long enough.

"What time do you get up in the morning?" Juliet shouted.

"Six. You don't need to shout. I'm right next to you."

"Sorry. Did you say six? Won't it still be dark then?"

"Yeah, but I always get up at that time. Is that a problem?"

"Well, I guess not, but I've drunk a little too much. Don't expect me to be ready to jump out of bed that early."

"No, problem. Take your time. I'll try not to wake you up."

"Goodnight, Cal."

"Goodnight, Juliet."

"And Cal?"

"Yes."

"Thanks."

"Okay, no problem."

*Thanks for what? For being nice? For sharing food? For being a half-decent human being and not raping you? Sometimes people say the strangest things.*

*Yet, in a way, I also feel gratitude towards Juliet. But for what? It's the first night since the Death I've not camped alone. I've not talked—or laughed—so much for as long as I can remember. And it was so...natural. So relaxed. I've drunk too much and that must be part of it. But I've got drunk on my own before and just become miserable. Juliet made me...happy. I'd almost forgotten how that felt.*

He lay in his sleeping bag, warm and cosy. This had been the best night since the Yellow Death, and he should have fallen asleep in an instant. Yet he could not. Something niggled at the back of his mind. Something he should sort out.

Both he and Juliet had drunk a lot of wine and he suspected neither of them was used to alcohol recently. Juliet had giggled towards the end and slurred her words. Cal thought of the booby traps and tear gas grenades dotted around the camp. What if Juliet got up in the night for a pee and stumbled about in the dark? The air outside was frigid and pitch black. Although he wore only shorts and a T-shirt, he was quite cosy inside his sleeping bag. The last thing he wanted was to go outside again.

Cal rolled over and tried to get to sleep, to put the thought of those gas grenades out of his mind. It would not work. "Damn, damn, damn!." He climbed out of his soft cocoon, left his tent and crept around the camp, disconnecting the tripwires to the tear gas.

When he finally returned to his tent, he immediately fell into a deep, contented sleep.

☣☣☣☣

The next morning, Cal's phone alarm sounded at six a.m. as usual and the sounds of Mad World drifted across the campsite. From inside her tent, Juliet half-sang, half-croaked along with some of the words.

"Morning, Cal."

"Morning, Juliet." Cal unzipped the flap of his tent. "Looks like it's going to be a lovely day. Blue skies and fantastic sunrise."

"I'll take your word for it. That's a lovely song, by the way. Do you understand the lyrics?"

"Something about depression and loneliness."

"And you picked it to wake you up every morning?"

"What can I say? I like the tune."

Cal spent a few moments in his sleeping bag, stretching his back and working the muscles around his lower spine. The exercises continued outside the tent as he inhaled the crisp morning air. A light frost had powdered the landscape with white. The orange sun hovered above the horizon.

"I'm going for a run."

The zipper on Juliet's tent came down and her head poked out of the flap.

"What?"

"I'm going running. Be back in about an hour."

"Are you absolutely insane?"

"Most definitely. The booby traps are disconnected, so it's safe to move around. The sun's up. Do you want to come?"

"Christ, I've been sleeping next to a madman. And my head hurts."

"Sure you won't come?"

"Fuck off and don't disturb me again unless you have a mug of coffee." Juliet pulled her head back into the tent.

☣☣☣☣

On the run back to the campsite, Cal noticed a strange odour. It took a second to recognise—frying bacon. He was still a couple of hundred yards away from their camp and, as he approached, the smell became stronger.

*Who'd have thought cooking smells carried so far? Must be more careful about that.*

Juliet was sitting by the campfire preparing breakfast. The frying pan sizzled over the open fire.

"Wow, that smells good," Cal said.

"Really! Would you like some too?"

Cal flushed. He assumed Juliet would have done enough for both of them. "I-I-I'm sorry, I thought—"

"What? That I was cooking for both of us? Of course I am. Relax, Cal, you're far too easy to tease. It'll be cooked in about ten minutes if you'll be ready?"

"You bet."

Breakfast was delicious. Cal savoured every mouthful. Juliet had sliced and fried some tinned ham, which they ate with baked beans and scrambled eggs. It was a taste explosion—meaty, salty, smoky, fatty, chewy, eggy goodness. Porridge would seem very bland after this feast. The pièce de résistance was real fresh coffee. Cal cradled the steaming hot mug in both hands as if it was a religious icon. Juliet was apologetic about the ham being charred at the edges, but Cal was amazed how well she had managed on an open fire.

"I don't normally eat like this," she said. "Usually I have porridge, but thought this was a special occasion."

Cal laughed. "This'll be the first time for a year I've not started the day with porridge."

As he scraped the plate clean, he reflected on how content he felt. He lived by routines and, if they were disturbed, he became agitated. Because of Juliet, his normal ways had been tossed aside. He had slept without booby traps, missed out exercises and eaten ham and eggs for breakfast. His normal routine had been shot to pieces. Yet he was completely at ease.

Afterwards, they cleared away the dishes and started packing the vehicles. Both moved unhurriedly, giving each other uneasy glances and half-smiles. What would happen next? Juliet finally closed the boot of her car and leaned against the back of it as Cal packed the last few items into the Land Rover.

"Okay Cal," Juliet said, echoing their conversation from yesterday afternoon. "What now?"

"Now?"

"Yes now! Good God, you don't make things easy, do you? What are we going to do now? Shall we say goodbye and drive away on our separate ways? Maybe never seeing each other again. Is that what you want?"

"No. No. Not at all. What would you like to do?"

Juliet sighed.

"Okay. I'll put my cards on the table and hope I'm not making a fool of myself. Sit, please." She pointed to the ground, and they both sat down. Juliet pushed the hair away from her face. "I enjoyed last night, Cal. I enjoyed talking to you and I enjoyed the meal. I've not laughed so much since...well, for a long time. It was fun and I've not had much fun recently. Also, I slept really well last night. And it wasn't only the booze, either. I felt safe for the first time in ages."

"I'm glad to hear that. Last night was good for me too."

"Good. The thing is, I think we have similar ideas. You're one of the few people I've met who's focussed on planning for the future. I don't know how you feel, but I'd like to try travelling together for a while. Just for a trial period. I've tried travelling with several groups and it hasn't worked out. But I'm willing to give it another go with you. That's if you're interested? We can help each other with our caches?"

Cal nodded. "Yes. That sounds brilliant. I'd like that a lot. And, if you wish, I can train you on using weapons and defending yourself.

"Great, even better. But there's just one problem. You're hiding something from me. I'm a doctor and I've taken hundreds of case histories, so I can tell when somebody is holding something back. Last night, whenever we talked about the past, you were, vague, evasive, and changed the subject. That makes me nervous, Cal. What have you done that's so bad you're keeping it from me?"

"Nothing, honest."

"This reminds me of trying to coax the symptoms from a child. Since the Yellow Death, we've all done things which would have been unthinkable before. Have you killed somebody? Are you being chased by somebody?"

"No, no, nothing like that, really."

"Then what? Speak to me, Cal. You've been lying to me about something. You can't expect me to trust you when you're holding back from me."

Cal knew she was right. If he didn't reassure her, she would drive off and he would be alone again. But what to say? So much about his past was fabrication. He'd repeated the lies so many times he almost believed them himself. If only he hadn't mentioned all the bullshit about combat in Afghanistan and Syria yesterday—he couldn't go back on that now.

He realised many seconds had passed between them in silence. Juliet waited, but soon it would be too late to do anything. He had to give her something.

"Okay. You're right. The truth is I'm autistic. Asperger's Syndrome to be exact, although I know we're not supposed to call it that any longer."

"Oh," Juliet said and nodded slowly to herself.

"Do you know what that is?"

"I'm a doctor, Cal."

"Oh, yes, silly. Of course you do."

Juliet smiled. "I see. Your shyness. The long pauses. The routines and need for security. I'm surprised I didn't pick up on it myself. You hide it very well."

"Oh, thanks. Apparently I'm a mild case and trust me, I've had a shitload of therapy."

"So, you're not a mass murderer?"

"No, well, not yet anyway."

"Good. Let's hope it stays that way. In that case, I suppose we'd better decide where we're going today?"

## Chapter Sixteen

# JOHN & AARIKA

TIMELINE: 5 YEARS BEFORE YELLOW DEATH

> "I remember the first time I had sex—I kept the receipt."
>
> Groucho Marx (1890–1977)

In a dark corner of a bar which blasted pop music loud enough to hurt John's ears, he sat at a table with three T.A. buddies.

"Well, bugger me with a bargepole," Danny said, slapping his hand on the table and spilling their beers. "Cal's still a fuckin' virgin."

The others laughed.

"It's not a crime," John said, staring into his beer.

"It fuckin' should be. How d'you get to be twenty-seven years old and still be a virgin?"

"I-I guess I'm not good with women," John said, suppressing a belch.

"Even so—twenty-seven! That must be some sort of record."

John wished he could curl up and die. This was not how he wanted to spend the only day of leave they had been granted during the two-week annual training camp. When the soldiers of the fourth battalion of The Rifles were briefed about coaches taking them into Cologne, the cheering must have been heard back in the UK.

John initially hoped this was his chance to explore the culture of the German city. Perhaps a trip to Cologne Cathedral or the Roman-Germanic Museum. His buddies had other ideas, so a massive pub-crawl became the objective of the day. Not wanting to spend a day alone in a strange foreign city, John went along reluctantly. He regretted his decision. This was their tenth bar and thus, the tenth tankard of strong German beer. John struggled to focus his eyes and the urge to vomit hovered just below the surface. Yet he felt compelled to keep drinking with his mates.

With John were three buddies from his infantry section. Danny, Martin and Stuart had completed basic training with John and were the closest he had to real friends.

Each year, TA soldiers were expected to attend a fortnight long training camp. This year was a special event. The entire battalion had been transported to Germany to take part in joint Anglo-German-American manoeuvres.

Exercise 'Stand Together' was planned for the second week of the annual camp. The first week comprised practising relevant military skills. The highlight for John was his first experience with fast assaults from helicopters. Jumping from a moving chopper was an exhilarating moment he would never forget, and never wanted to repeat. Unprepared for the effect his heavy equipment would have on his legs, John collapsed in a heap, face down in mud.

As is often the case when men get drunk together, the conversation centred around sport, women and sex. The lads had taken turns to relate stories of macho sexual conquests—no doubt exaggerated. When John remained silent, the probing questions began. In his drunken state, he let slip about his complete inexperience of sexual encounters.

Martin put his hand on John's shoulder "Jesus Christ, Cal. No wonder you're always so bloody quiet and wound up. You've got to be ready to explode?"

"No, no, really. It's not—"

Danny grinned widely. "Now we know why he takes so long in the bog, eh, lads? Bet he must wank himself silly." The three others burst into raucous laughter. "I'll tell you what though, we're in the perfect place to fix Cal's embarrassment. Drink up lads, we've got some urgent business to sort out."

☣☣☣☣

Danny bent to speak to the cab driver through the open car window. The other three hovered behind him in a shop doorway, trying to stay out of the rain. "Are you able to take us to the Eros centre?"

The driver looked at the four men and smiled. "The Pascha? Sure. Any cab driver in Cologne could take you there with their eyes shut. Get in."

Boris, the driver, spoke almost perfect English and talked profusely about their destination——he appeared quite proud of it. "Many cities have an eros centre of one sort or another, but ours is the finest. The Pascha is the biggest brothel in the whole of Europe. Over a hundred and twenty rooms spread over twelve stories and each one dedicated to giving young men like yourselves the best time of your lives."

"Are you sure it's legal?" John whispered towards Danny.

"Yes, of course. Trust me. This is all totally fucking legit and above board. Sex on demand with German efficiency. All the women are registered and have regular medical checks. Each room is professionally cleaned every day. The building even has a beauty parlour and restaurant."

"I heard some women practically live in the place," Stuart said. He was the oldest member of the quartet and the only one married.

"I'm still not sure this is a good idea," John mumbled.

"You're right," Danny said. "It's not a good idea, it's a fucking brilliant idea."

After paying the modest entry fee, the quartet entered the ground floor of the Pascha, which was given over to a nightclub.

They pushed through the crowds and found their way to one of the quieter tables. It might have been any nightclub anywhere. Strobe lights punctuated the darkness, accompanied by more throbbing music assaulting John's ears. The men ordered beers from a waitress whose clothing was not designed for modesty. It was a miracle of engineering that her breasts stayed inside her bra when she leaned over the table. Her sweet, spicy fragrance hit John like a slap in the face.

He glanced around, frantically rubbing his thumb against his finger under the table. No amount of alcohol could prepare him for this onslaught on his senses. The place was heaving with drunken men and scantily clad women. The air felt clammy and stank of unwashed bodies and beer.

"Why are there no women customers in here?" John shouted, trying to penetrate the noise.

"Are you serious? They're not welcome," Danny said. "This is not exactly the best place for wives and girlfriends, is it?"

"I guess not."

"Jesus, will you take a look at that!" Stuart said, pointing to the stage where six women wearing nothing except white wigs and matching silver micro-skirts were now gyrating erotically and spraying each other with foam.

John's guts churned, and beads of sweat ran down his forehead. This was horrible. His idea of complete hell. Crowds, noise, flashing lights. Everything strange and unusual.

*Please let this end.*

"Are we really going to do this?" Martin said.

"Sure, why not?" Danny said.

"I think I'm going to be sick," John said.

"Oh no. You ain't getting out of it that way, my man. If you need to puke, then go puke first." Danny said. "The toilets are over there."

John considered visiting the toilets, if only to escape the cacophony, when their drinks arrived.

The same waitress deposited each of their beers on the table with a complementary bowl of nibbles. All eyes transfixed on her bosom.

"Danke, fraulein," Danny said, handing her a five Euro note as a tip, which she took without comment.

"Bit ungrateful," Danny said.

"Probably because you just insulted her by calling her a fraulein," Stuart said. "Best not try speaking German, eh? She was actually wearing a name badge, if you'd taken your eyes off her tits."

"Okay. Fair enough. But I'd still like to bury my face in those babies."

Stuart pulled John's beer away from him. "I think you've drunk enough for one night lad, we don't want you disappointing the ladies, do we?"

John's head spun. "I really don't—"

"You really don't what, Cal?" Danny said. "You really don't want to wait much longer? Understood. We'll move on in a minute. First, let's get these beers down us, yes?"

"I can't believe this place," Martin said. "Is it true they've got a money-back guarantee?"

"Satisfaction guaranteed. You can't say fairer than that," Danny said.

Martin grinned. "Holy shit." He looked at Danny. "What about you——are you planning to sample the goods?"

"Well, I might take my pecker out for a bit of exercise, since we're here. When in Rome, as they say. Let's see what's on offer first, eh?"

☣☣☣☣

The quartet left the nightclub area and entered the main hotel. Seven of the twelve floors were set aside for the professional women. The men strolled from floor to floor, walking through the plushly decorated corridors. Most hotels are furnished in bland neutral colours, but the Pascha was quite different. The walls were dusky pink, the doors and frames with their elaborate carvings and recessed lighting were a deep burgundy with gold motifs. Slow, repetitive music pervaded every corridor, and the air was heavy with spicy exotic scents.

Outside each room, a woman sat on a high stool ,displaying a welcoming smile. Their apparel varied from scanty lingerie to sleek evening dresses—depending on their target audience. All clothing had been chosen to ensure ample flesh was on display.

Danny whispered, "C'mon John. This is the third floor we've been on. You must've seen someone you fancy by now. What's taking so long? Just give me a nod."

"Yes. No. Okay. It's not that easy. I'm quite particular. I usually only fancy blondes. And they need to be slim."

"Yeah, so? Take a look around. Ninety per cent of these beauties are blonde and slim. You're not here to marry her you know."

"Yeah. I know. Sorry. It's just that—"

Then he saw her at the end of the corridor and, in a fraction of a second, he decided. He jabbed Danny in the ribs hard enough to make him cough—but Danny got the message.

She was petite with straight shoulder-length blonde hair, huge blue eyes, thin lips and a chiselled nose. John thought she was gorgeous and felt himself blushing. Her standard welcome smile extended further as they stopped next to her.

"Hello, *jungen*."

"Hello there yourself," Danny said. He was a telemarketer, so was quite comfortable negotiating, unlike John, who stood rigid with nerves. "And what do they call you, sweetheart?"

"Ahh. You English, yes?"

"That's right. England's finest. Except old Stuart here who's half Scottish, but we don't hold that against him."

"Good, I like English boys a lot. My name is Aarika. It means a rose."

"A rose between several thorns," Stuart said under his breath.

"You boys are *soldaten*...soldiers, yes?"

"That's right, Aarika. Fourth Battalion, The Rifles," Danny said.

"Ahh, so you are here for the war-games?"

"Absolutely."

"We have many soldiers come here today. English, Deutsch, Amerikana. Many boys missing their girlfriends, yes?"

Stuart and Martin shifted uncomfortably, being reminded of partners back in Devon.

"Tell me, Aarika," Danny said. "Who makes the best lovers, the English or the Americans?"

"Oh, English, of course," she said, with a smile. "But the Yankees they..." she rubbed her fingers together as the universal sign to show Americans have a lot of cash.

"Look, Aarika. You can help us out with a little problem here. You see our friend, John," he pulled John out from behind him. "Well, he needs female company and, let's just say he's got no experience. No experience at all. He might need some guidance." He winked at her.

"Guidance? Oh, I understand." She appraised John quivering in front of her. "He is *männliche jungfrau*—a virgin, yes?"

"Sorry, yes. I'm afraid he is. But we're hoping that's about to change."

"You didn't have to tell her that," John whispered into Danny's ear.

Aarika smiled knowingly. "Is no problem. Aarika has made many boys into men. I am excellent teacher. But it takes a little more time than usual. You pay more, yes?"

"How much?" Danny said.

"What service is it you are wanting?"

"Well, just the normal."

Aarika put her head back and laughed out loud. Other women nearby were listening and joined in. "Around here, there is no normal."

Stuart was getting increasingly uncomfortable. "Just straightforward sex, one man, one woman, face to face. Nothing kinky. No trimmings."

"Okay. You are nice boys," Aarika said. "I do special deal, one-fifty. Cash."

"What!" said John, then quieter behind Danny's back, he continued, "I don't have that much cash left."

Danny was unperturbed. "Oh come on now, Aarika. That's a bit steep on a soldier's pay. How about one hundred?"

There was some negotiating between Danny and Aarika, whilst John did his best to appear invisible. They set the final price and John counted the last notes from his wallet. The others chipped in to make up the difference. The deal had been struck.

☣☣☣☣

Aarika closed the door behind John. There was a finality which instantly wiped out the effects of the alcohol and everything focussed into astonishing clarity. John took a deep breath.

The room was small and dominated by an immense bed. Mirrors on the walls and ceiling created multiple images of himself and Aarika. The walls, carpet and luxurious bedding were shades of blue. Sets of twinkling fairy lights hung around the perimeter. The air was warm and clammy, with a musky scent. A dull repetitive thudding from the night club music resonated through the walls. It was a Santa's grotto for perverts.

"Relax John. This will be fun. Have you had much to drink?"

"Just a little. I'm not sure I—"

Aarika unbuttoned his jacket and began to slip his clothing off.

"If you need to vomit, there is washroom next door," she pointed to a door. "If you are sick in here, I have to charge extra, for the cleaning and lost time, you understand?"

"I-I'm not going to be sick." He thought he might be sick.

Aarika expertly stripped off his clothes leaving him naked before her. 'John Junior' was fast asleep. John felt his face flush with embarrassment.

Aarika stood in front of him. She wore an ankle-length red dress which clung to her body. A slit at the side revealed her smooth thighs. In one easy, practised manoeuvre, she slid the straps over her shoulders. The dress dropped to the floor, leaving her naked, save for a red jewelled thong and stockings. John's eyes gaped open, and he swallowed hard. Despite fear and anxiety, he felt a stirring between his legs.

"Now, John," she whispered into his ear. "You are going to have to do better than that."

She walked behind him and smoothly slid her hands up and down his body, frequently visiting his member. Aarika was a professional, an expert in the art of arousal.

She whispered in his ear, "Let me tell you secret, John. I have never had to give refund for lack of satisfaction."

Wherever her fingers roamed, his skin tingled in response, until he involuntarily let out a whimper. Occasionally, she allowed her long fingernails to gently scrape John's skin. John's cock now stood at attention. Aarika produced a condom out of nowhere, like a magician, then expertly unrolled it over 'John Junior'.

Aarika stood before him and pulled him close. Her breasts rubbed against his chest. "Now, listen. This is important. Put your hands wherever you want, yes?" She grabbed his wrists and placed his hands on her buttocks. "But not your lips. No kissing. You understand, yes? You are not my boyfriend. If you try kiss me, I call security." She pointed to the big red button beside the bed.

John nodded and gulped. Aarika walked backwards, pulling him with her onto the bed. He felt her smooth, warm skin start to gyrate rhythmically against him, igniting primitive passions.

*Oh...My...God!*

☣☣☣☣

Twenty minutes later, John appeared from Aarika's room, grinning like a squirrel in a nut factory. His shirt buttons were undone to the waist. Only Stuart waited for him.

"How'd it go, mate?"

"Bloody marvellous. I can't believe it. I want to do it again."

John was in love. Aarika was a goddess. He had asked for her email address and telephone number.

"Don't be silly," she had replied. "Go back to England and find yourself a nice English girl. And never, never, tell her about this night."

The four friends began the walk across the city to rendezvous with their coach. John staggered for a hundred metres before vomiting his last few pints of beer down his legs and onto the pavement.

So it was that John Callaghan-Bryant lost his virginity aged twenty-seven, thanks to a massive intervention by his army buddies. However, next day he could remember little about it, except for Aarika's face which was impressed on his memory forever.

# Chapter Seventeen

# Cal & Juliet

TIMELINE: 15 MONTHS AFTER THE
YELLOW DEATH

"Can there be a love which does not make demands on its object?"
                          Confucious (551–479 BCE)

For the first few days after Cal and Juliet joined forces, they remained as separate units.

At the start of each day, they packed their respective possessions into their own SUVs. They slept in their own tents and travelled in their own vehicles. During the day, they both worked on a mutually agreed project.

The evenings were spent planning the following day, cooking and eating together. This was when they chatted and learned from each other. Cal showed Juliet how to use firearms, as well as the habits he followed to survive in an unforgiving world. In return, Juliet related her ideas for medical care in the future—including surgery using only basic equipment, with hypnosis for anaesthetic.

As the days passed, both relaxed and developed a joint routine, although it would be more correct to say that Juliet learnt how to fit into Cal's routine.

After one particularly long and tiring day, they sat by the campfire in the dark. In order to finish and seal a cache of medical supplies, they had worked later than usual. Heavy cloud cover obscured the moon and stars but, in addition to the cheerful fire, six wind-up battery lanterns illuminated their camp site.

Juliet sat on a cushion with a blanket over her shoulders. She watched as Cal laid out a small plastic sheet to clean his rifle. "This is cosy."

Cal scanned his surroundings as if he had been completely unaware of them. "Yes. I hadn't thought about it, but you're right."

"Are you sure you're okay with the extra lights?"

Cal gave her a reassuring smile. "Sure. It's a small thing. Morale is important."

Juliet remembered their second night together. She had set out several lanterns around the camp, hoping to make it cheerful. Cal pointed out the waste of resources, mentioning how even rechargeable batteries had a limited lifetime. Juliet had been crestfallen. Was this what life was going to be like? Sitting in the dark to eek out the life of rechargeable batteries?

The next day, Cal had apologised. The following evening, he had set out a dozen lights. Juliet recognised how he strived to make her feel comfortable, even at the sacrifice of his precious routines.

A pot of water bubbled over the fire. Juliet dropped two pouches of army 'Meal Ready to Eat,' ration packs into it. "Two delicious madras curries coming up in exactly eight minutes." She pressed the timer button on her wristwatch. "What would you like to do tomorrow? We've been storing medical supplies since we met. Now it must be your turn?"

Cal knelt on the plastic sheet, with parts of his SA-80 laid out in front of him. He rubbed a long metal rod with an oily rag.

Juliet waited for Cal to answer her question. She was aware Cal spent a lot of time in his own world. When focused on a task, he became oblivious to his surroundings. Juliet had seen this many times in autistic children. She had learnt to attract their attention before speaking. If she intended to stay with Cal long term, she would need to get into the habit of doing it again. It was quirky, but she could think of worse faults to have. "Cal, did you hear me?"

Cal looked up. "Sorry, what?"

She smiled. "I asked what you wanted to do for the next few days. Isn't it about time we collected some more of your weapons?"

"Oh, I see. Right. Well, for a start, I don't regard them as my weapons. I've always treated them as a sort of communal resource to which I'm the custodian. You know, making sure they don't get into the wrong hands."

"Sorry, I stand corrected, Mr Pedantic. But my question still stands."

"To be honest, I think I'm done with collecting weapons. I've got enough to equip a small army and they're getting hard to find locally. Devon was not exactly the military hotspot of the UK and I prefer not to travel long distances anymore. There's no point storing more ammo than will get used in the next, say, twenty years. After then it'll become unreliable. The worst sound in the world is pulling the trigger in combat and hearing nothing but a click."

He returned to cleaning his rifle.

Juliet nodded. "Fair enough." She noted when he was speaking, he stopped cleaning his rifle, seemingly unable to do two things at the same time—another feature she often saw with autism. "So, shall we concentrate on medical stuff for a couple of weeks?"

A few seconds elapsed before he looked at her with a surprised expression. "Weeks?"

"What?"

"You said, 'weeks'."

"Yes, I did, didn't I? Has that scared you? The fact I'm talking about us being together for weeks?"

Cal's hands had stopped moving again, and he appeared to be deep in thought.

"No. Not at all. It's just…Well, I'm surprised. I didn't know how you were feeling about us…I mean, about the arrangement. I was concerned one night you'd tell me you were ready for us to go our separate ways?"

"Really? You were worried that might happen?"

He dropped the metal rod and rag, then sat back. This was obviously something which demanded his full attention.

"Well, yes. I didn't know what you thought of me. About all my security procedures and habits and stuff. I've tried to fit in with your needs, but I wasn't sure if it was enough. I know I'm pretty weird."

"Oh, Cal, what it must be like to be inside your head. Haven't you noticed I've been having a wonderful time? Yes, you're a little…unusual. You wouldn't win any prizes for conversation, but I think we're getting along fine and travelling with you is far more pleasant than being alone. I feel safe with you and you're the first person I've met who I can say that about."

His eyebrows shot up. "Oh. You think so? That's fantastic. I'd no idea. So you want to carry on travelling together, like, sort of permanent?"

Juliet grinned widely. "Don't get carried away. I'm not ready for wedding vows yet, but I would say our trial period has been a success and we need to start making some long-term plans. If that's okay with you?"

"Yes, please!"

Juliet's wrist watch beeped. "Great. Dinner is served."

She fished the pouches out of the water with her fingers. "Ow, ow, hot, hot, hot."

"No kidding, Sherlock. Shall I call a doctor?"

They cut open the pouches and ate the curry out of them with spoons. Cal used the boiling water in the saucepan to make mugs of tea.

"This stuff is actually quite tasty," Juliet said. "It's nicely spiced. How do these meals rate from a nutritional point of view?"

"Not too bad. MREs were never intended to replace normal food long-term, but tests on soldiers living off these meals for weeks have showed no adverse effects."

Juliet sipped her tea. "How long do they last before they go off?"

"Most of them have a three-year use by date, but that's conservative. If they're stored properly—the cooler the better—they should last over ten years. That's one reason I'm hiding them away in cool dark places. A handy tip is you can tell if they've gone bad because the pouch becomes bloated."

"Well, that's something I'll definitely look out for. I don't want to live through the greatest pandemic in the planet's history, only to be killed by a dodgy curry."

☣☣☣☣

Cal placed a pile of boxes into the trailer of his Land Rover. It was parked outside the main entrance to the North Devon District Hospital in Barnstaple. The roundabout in front of the entrance—which had previously been neat lawn— was now a miniature jungle. The hospital used to be the primary medical hub of north and Devon, although compared to city hospitals, it was small. The modern buildings were only three storeys high and laid out over a wide area with lawns and trees.

Cal took several long breaths of the cool, clear air to flush his lungs of the foul musty smell which hung inside the buildings. Juliet came out moments later and did the same. The day was cold, cloudy, and dry. An east wind brought a further chill to the air, and they both wore thick coats and gloves.

They were now sharing the Land Rover. It had been a difficult decision for Juliet to give up her SUV and combining all their kit into one vehicle had been a struggle. Nevertheless, fuel was becoming hard to find and running two vehicles was an extravagance. The Rover was the obvious choice due to Cal's security modifications.

Juliet jumped up and down, swinging her arms to warm up. "Fucking hell, I hate this."

"Maybe the hospital wasn't such a good idea?"

"It was a good idea, but I must admit I'm struggling with the practicalities of it."

In the war against the Yellow Death, hospitals had been the battlegrounds. It had been a short and very one-sided war. Hospitals became no more than morgues piled high with bodies. Towards the end, people died wherever they happened to be lying with no one to move them. Thus, most survivors of the pandemic avoided hospitals—they were gruesome, containing little of value.

Nevertheless, last evening, Juliet suggested the nearest hospital might be worth investigating for medical supplies. Cal had been surprised.

"You're kidding right?" he'd said. "Didn't the hospitals use all their medications fighting the plague?"

"Not necessarily. Stuff like I.V. drips will have been used up, but many meds were useless against the plague, so there should be plenty left. I'm hoping we might even find antibiotics."

"No way."

"Yes way. Listen, where I worked, we gave the first patients antibiotics as suggested, but they had no effect. Most people died so fast, the drugs never had a chance to work. Then we had a memo come round telling us to stop prescribing them because they needed to be saved."

Cal frowned. "Saved for what, for God's sake?"

"I don't know. Then we had another directive saying all pharmaceuticals should only be given to medical staff. It was total chaos. Patients and relatives were getting angry. The staff were dropping like flies. Those left standing spent more time doing crowd control than anything else. Even if we wanted to prescribe antibiotics, there were no staff to do it. We ran out of beds, then trolleys, then chairs. After that, we laid people on the floor in the corridors. It got so bad, we couldn't even get to some patients. There's no way you would understand how desperate we were. It was bedlam... confusion... mayhem. Nothing we did seemed to help."

Juliet became quiet, her face downcast. She blinked as though trying to hold back tears.

"And you want to go back into one of those hell holes?"

"I don't want to, but I think it's worth a look. They may be a goldmine."

Juliet had been correct. They found the pharmacy well stocked. They also discovered a delivery van from a drugs company parked outside the hospital. The pharmacy was situated near the main entrance, so they did not have to venture far inside the building. Nevertheless, the stench was dire. In the reception area, dessicated bodies lay on scattered gurneys, others sat slumped, mummy-like in chairs, their faces wearing a rictus grin. All waiting for medical help which never came. A large whiteboard stood inside the doorway with the message 'GO HOME' printed in huge capital letters. Underneath, somebody had scribbled 'Sinners repent'.

"Have you seen the 'Use By' dates on these boxes?" Cal said. "Some are only a year ahead."

Juliet nodded. "I know. Don't worry, that's okay. It's like the expiry dates on your ration packs—they're ultra cautious. Those dates are when the manufacturer guarantees the drugs will still be one hundred per cent effective. But most drugs will still be effective ten or more years past the 'Use By' date if they're stored correctly. Otherwise, what I've been doing for the last year would be a complete waste of time."

A chill breeze blew over them, and Cal pulled the zipper on his coat higher round his neck. "There's one other thing that's been bothering me."

"What's that?"

"Imagine if you had an accident or caught an illness and died. All the medical supplies you've stored would never be found by anyone. They'd be lost to humanity."

Juliet sat on the edge of the trailer and wrapped her arms around her body. "That does concern me. I always leave some supplies behind—I never clear a place out totally. Anyone looking for drugs where I've been will still find something. In fact, if I find drugs stored well, then I leave them where they are and just mark the location on the map."

"So anybody could come along and steal them?"

"It wouldn't be stealing them. I don't own them. They'd have as much right to them as anyone. I assume that if somebody goes to the effort of taking medical stores, they must need them. Most times, though, I take the supplies and hide them somewhere secure, like we're doing today. You must understand that prescription drugs can do more harm than good in untrained hands. If you take the wrong drug, or the wrong amount of the right drug, you might kill someone. Honestly, it might be better if all these drugs were lost to humanity, rather than having untrained people trying to use them."

Cal held up an energy bar and Juliet took it gratefully. "Surely, if you have an infection, any antibiotic is better than nothing?"

"Not necessarily. Some are broad spectrum and others work best on specific infections. If you took a random antibiotic, it might help, but at best it wouldn't be the most effective treatment. And some have powerful side effects. If you gave Vancomycin to someone with a history of kidney problems, you'd probably kill them."

"Shit. I had no idea."

"I wouldn't expect you to. There's a reason why it takes seven years to become a doctor. Even then, we get called junior doctors. I used to hate that term."

"I can imagine."

Juliet bit from her energy bar and chewed whilst talking. "Any how, I'm with you now. If I fell off a cliff, you can make sure all the meds I've stored get put to good use."

"That's if I can understand the codes on your maps. It all looks Chinese to me."

"Good point. I'll teach you all the codes tonight. I think I can just about trust you now." She smiled. "My dream is to find a settlement somewhere in mid-Devon, not far from good roads. I'll set up a medical centre so people from all over Devon can come for treatment. With luck, we might attract a few other surviving medical staff. Either way, I plan to start training others and we all need to begin learning traditional medicine for when supplies of the modern stuff runs out."

"That would be brilliant if you could pull it off."

"It doesn't make sense for somebody with my training to be ploughing fields and milking cows. But if I'm to get this off the ground, I'll need supplies of pharmaceuticals and equipment. Lots of it."

"Which brings us nicely back to the reason we're freezing our tits off outside this giant morgue on the coldest frigging day of the year."

Juliet nodded and put the last chunk of energy bar into her mouth. "It'll be worth it. I reckon we need two more trips to the pharmacy, and we'll be done here. Are you ready?"

"I can hardly wait," Cal said, pulling his buff over his mouth and nose.

"Okay then, let's take a deep breath and run."

## Chapter Eighteen

# JOHN & BRITNEY

TIMELINE: 4 YEARS BEFORE THE YELLOW DEATH

> "Almost all of our relationships begin and most of them continue as forms of mutual exploitation, a mental or physical barter, to be terminated when one or both parties run out of goods."
> W. H. Auden (1907–1973)

John was with Sarah in her Devon cottage, preparing his breakfast porridge. He added small dollops of milk and stirred the bowl until the mixture was just the right consistency. It went into the microwave for exactly thirty seconds to bring it to the optimal temperature. After the microwave pinged, John topped his bowl with two spoonfuls of chopped nuts, one of seeds, and two of plain yoghurt.

Sarah watched him go through the ritual and sighed. Would it kill him to change the routine for once? Even the nuts must be the correct type—almonds, walnuts and brazils, definitely not cashews. Sometimes, Sarah was tempted to rebel by doing something outrageous, such as sneaking cashews into the mix.

They sat in her kitchen, looking through the French doors into the garden. The early morning sun cast long shadows. The borders were a festival of colour. In the middle of the lawn, sparrows, blackbirds, thrushes, and other birds fought over the bounty set out on the ornate bird table.

Breakfast together was part of their morning routine since John quit his job with WebExpert to become a freelance web developer. It had been a smart move—he was earning twice the money and chose his own hours. A bonus was avoiding the tedium of office politics. But, without a job to force John into town on weekdays, he became more reclusive and 'Aspergersy', as Sarah would say.

"Have you got much work at the moment?" She said.

"As much as I want."

"And what exactly does that mean?"

John sighed. Here we go again. The frequent questioning of his life was becoming tiresome. John appreciated all his mother had done for him, but it was time for her to let go and start enjoying her retirement instead of worrying about him.

"It means I can earn two hundred quid an hour, so could survive by working ten hours a week. Of course I work a lot more than that, but I'll not flog myself to death, to make money I don't need." He gulped a spoonful of porridge.

"How many hours do you put in?"

"Around twenty-five hours a week. Of course, it varies a lot. I've got a deadline to meet in a few days, so I'll be at it all day today."

"But John, those are part-time hours."

"Part-time hours, full-time pay. Not bad, eh? Remember, the work is incredibly intense. If I tried to work eight hours straight, my head would explode."

Sarah frowned and put down her coffee cup. "What if you're ill, or work dried up? You need some security behind you."

"Mum, I'm a web developer. As long as I can move my fingers, I can work. My commissions come from global notice boards. Work won't dry up unless people stop using the internet. I've got plenty of savings and putting more away each month."

"Oh, I suppose you're right."

"Listen Mom. I really appreciate all you've done for me. All the education and therapy and setting me up in the cabin and stuff. But I'm a big boy now. I can look after myself. Your work is done."

Sarah returned to her toast and marmalade for a while. The silence was ominous. John rarely started a conversation.

"I sometimes wonder what on earth you do out there, stuck alone in your cabin all day. It's not healthy."

"Mum, I'm not in my chalet all day. I go running, I mow the lawns, I go to the T.A. And we walk to the village together several times a week. As for what I do when I'm in the chalet—apart from paid work, of course—well, I'm developing a highly realistic war game simulator. There's been nothing like it before. It'll allow people to re-enact real historical battles with accuracy down to individual soldiers. When it's complete, I might make a fortune from it. Historians will love it."

Sarah smiled. "That's brilliant dear. You're very talented, you know. I'm sorry, I'll shut up now. I don't want to spoil your breakfast with my concerns. I just wish you had a few friends, or even a nice girlfriend."

Sarah could see John flush at the mention of a girlfriend.

"It's not that easy, Mum. Little Barton is like a retirement village. I'm not likely to bump into Miss World on the daily walk to the bakery am I?"

☣☣☣☣

John stared at the list of women displayed on his computer screen. None of them appealed to him.

He had tried online dating agencies. They sounded good in principle, but were not working out well. His limited interests and hobbies generated few matches, and he was finding it impossible to locate a strikingly gorgeous female who was fascinated with military strategy and tactics. It didn't help that he lived in the arse end of nowhere.

On the occasions when he went on a date, the real-life women failed to live up to their profiles. They turned out to be less attractive, less interesting and wholly incompatible. The feeling was mutual, with none showing the slightest interest in a second date.

John was aware he was the problem—introverted and socially awkward, with nerdy hobbies and a mundane lifestyle. He would struggle to find a partner if he were the last man on earth.

Internet dating seemed a dead end, but what else was there? John rarely ventured further than the village, where most of the residents were retired. Even though he was twenty-eight years old, most folk called him 'Young John' or 'Sarah's John' as if he were still a school boy.

John closed the lid of his laptop, depressed as usual. The wall clock displayed three p.m. He had logged six billable hours of work on a lucrative contract which earned him more money than most people made in a week. However, the coding was intense and left him mentally exhausted. He needed to escape from the computer screen. For once, the outside world invited him, with warm sunshine and a light breeze. Perfect for a tour of the lanes and local woods on his mountain bike.

An hour later, John pedalled hard uphill. He passed a silver Audi parked on the roadside. An elderly couple sat in the back seat. A third person knelt on the grass verge by the nearside front wheel.

John pulled over and saw a young woman struggling with a wrench.

"Hi there, need any help?"

She stood up, wiping her forehead with the back of her hand, leaving a black oil stain. John noticed she was petite with long blonde hair in a ponytail. Her blue eyes were perfectly framed with matching eye shadow. This was someone who took great care with their appearance.

The woman smiled at him, showing her perfect white teeth. "Oh, thanks. That'd be great. I've got a flat. I know how to change a wheel, but the sodding nuts are too tight for this silly little wrench they give you."

"Let me have a go." John held out his hand for the wrench and peeked into the car.

"Hi," John said to the couple in the back.

"Oh, hello there, it's Sarah's John, isn't it? From Willow Cottage?" The man said.

"Yes, that's right."

The elderly man poked his head out of the window. "Britney, this is John from the village. He's the son of Sarah, a good friend of ours. He lives in her garden."

"What, like a gnome?" Britney said.

John flushed. "No, not quite. My mother has a chalet which I live in—until I get my own place, of course. It's quite spacious."

"I'm sure it is. Hello John, I'm Britney, everyone except my parents call me Brit." She held her hand out, but stopped when she noticed her oil-stained palm.

"Pleased to meet you...Brit." John said. "Now let's sort out this tyre."

John wore padded cycling gloves and had no intention of being shown up as a wimp. The bolts were stiff, but the first three succumbed to brute force. The last one refused to budge.

"What if we try together?" Brit said.

John was dubious. The tyre iron was tiny, with barely enough room for four hands. "Well, we could give it a go."

Brit knelt down next to him and they lined up their hands before pulling with all their strength. No movement.

"Damn," Brit said. "Guess I'm going to have to call out the AA after all. Mum's going to be late for her hospital appointment."

"The problem is leverage," John said, gasping. "Let's both try holding the wrench at the end. Put your hands over mine."

"Are you sure? I don't want to hurt you."

"It's okay, I've got padded gloves."

Brit came closer to him and did as he suggested. Their proximity made him conscious of his sweaty clothing. Her perfume was a mix of flowers and spices, so he wondered what foul stench he must emit.

"After three," John said. "One...two...three!"

The nut abruptly surrendered, and they both fell backwards. John's hands burned with pain, but he ignored it. Replacing the tyre after that was child's play. Brit climbed back into the driver's seat.

"Drive carefully until you can check the pressure," John said.

"I will. Listen, I feel terrible rushing off after you've been so much help," Brit said. "But I'm taking Mum to a clinic appointment in Barnstaple and we're running late now."

"No, that's fine. You go on. I was glad to be of service."

"I'm staying with my parents until tomorrow night. If you're free tonight, maybe I could buy you a drink in the White Hart to say thanks properly?"

The elderly lady piped up. "Oh, yes, that's a good idea. I'm sure you two would get on well."

*What? This is too good to be true. This sort of thing doesn't happen to me.*

"Er, yes, sure, I'd love to. What time?"

"About eightish?" she said, shutting the car door and starting the engine.

☣☣☣☣

"Er, Mum. I won't be joining you for dinner tonight. I hope that's not going to be a problem?"

Sarah was hoeing one of her flower borders. She stopped and turned to look at him.

"Is everything all right? You're not feeling ill are you?"

John smiled. "No, Mum. I'm fine. I'm going to the pub."

"What? The pub? The White Hart? But you never go to the pub. You never go anywhere."

John sighed. "Thanks for the vote of confidence. Anyway, tonight I am going somewhere."

Sarah stood silently, resting on her hoe, waiting for more.

"Okay. If you must know. I'm having a drink…with a girl—I mean a woman—a young woman."

Sarah frowned, then beamed. "A real woman? You mean you're having a date?"

"Yes. No. Not really. It's not a date. It's just a drink. It's no big thing."

"My son is meeting a real woman at a pub for a drink. When did that ever happen before? Don't tell me it's no big thing. Who is she? How did you meet? Is it Jane from Brownhill Farm? No, I bet it's Katy from the bakery, isn't it? I know you had your eyes on her for a while. C'mon inside. Let's have a cup of tea and you can tell me all about it."

*Oh bugger!*

☣☣☣☣

John stood outside the 'White Hart' pub, checking his appearance reflecting from a window. His hands felt empty. Towards the end of his interrogation by Sarah, she had asked what he was taking as a gift for Britney.

The thought had never occurred to him until that moment, but having been put into his mind, it swirled about like a tornado causing destruction. This was NOT a date. Or was it? Surely, it was only a courtesy 'thank you' drink? Or was it? Was Britney just being polite? Could she have fancied him when he was hot and sweaty? Perhaps he should take a gift, just to be on the safe side.

But if he took a gift, and it was just a courtesy thank-you, he would look like an idiot. What gift should he take, anyway? Chocolates were the obvious choice, but what if she was dieting, or was dairy intolerant, or allergic to nuts? If she was vegan, chocolates might offend her. Not chocolates then. So it had to be flowers. But what if she had hay fever? Wouldn't flowers be sexist? And where would he buy a bouquet at short notice?

*Why did everything have to be so bloody complicated?*

He should have declined the invitation. Should have said he was busy tonight. Now he was standing outside the pub wishing he had a box of chocolates in his hands, not knowing whether he was about to have a date or a quick drink.

*Let's get this over with.*

He pushed open the door and stepped inside. The 'White Hart' was a traditional pub with a low roof made lower by massive oak beams. A variety of horse related equipment and ancient muskets adorned the walls and a musty-beery aroma hung in the air. If not for the giant wall-mounted television, he might have been stepping through a time portal into the 16th century.

Brit sat at the bar, chatting and laughing with the bartender and two customers. Other than Brit's group, the pub was empty. John clenched his jaw. She was here to meet him, not the village idiots. How could he make the others disappear? He paused by the entrance, unsure what to do.

Brit noticed John and gave him a brief smile before turning to her other suitors. "Sorry guys, my date's here now. I've gotta go. It's been lovely catching up with you. Good luck with the competition on Saturday, Jim."

She hopped off her barstool and wobbled for a second on her heels before walking over to John. She was stunning. Her blonde hair was loose with jazzy jewellery things weaved into it. She wore a sparkly red mini-dress which clung to her as if she had sprayed it on. John wanted to eat her up.

*She had said her 'date' was here! I'm her date! I should have brought flowers, or chocolates, or something.*

Supremely confident, she embraced him. "So glad you came. I hate being stood up."

"I–I, surely nobody would stand you up? You look fantastic, by the way."

"Why, thanks. Believe me, it's happened. Some men are real dicks."

"I should have brought you some flowers, I—"

"Don't be silly. Where would you have got flowers? Besides, this is my treat to thank you for this afternoon. Come on, let's get a drink and sit where the bar creepers can't overhear us. I'm buying."

Brit ordered a rum and coke. John picked a local ale called the Dartmoor Destiny. The bartender poured the deep amber liquid with pride, ensuring it had a thick frothy head. Cal sipped and nodded appreciatively—the hoppy citrus flavour was smooth and more-ish.

Brit and John sat in a secluded corner. John was mindful of his mother's advice, shortly before he left home:

"Now John, remember the rules of a pleasant conversation which Dr Kendall taught you?" Sarah had said.

"Yes, Mum, of course."

"And rule number one is?"

"Brevity is best. Don't get carried away and give Britney one of my world famous tedious lectures on a subject nobody is interested in."

"Good. Particularly resist talking about your plans to develop a war game simulator. That's a definite turn-off. And rule number two?"

"A question for a question."

"Which means?"

"When I've answered a question, remember to ask something personal back."

"Great. Something personal. Don't ask her views on the Vietnam war, or nuclear weapons."

"Of course not. I'm not stupid."

"Well, that's debatable. But, if you can keep to just those two rules, I'm sure you'll get on fine. You're quite presentable, you know. If I were thirty years younger..."

"Oh God, Mum. That's gross."

So, John avoided speaking of his war game simulator, or the finer points of website coding, or the reasons for the collapse of the Roman Empire. He asked Brit about her interests and hobbies. That took some time, since they included running; swimming; surfing; tennis; football; horse-riding; painting and photography. Furthermore, she was learning to play the guitar and volunteered for the local Young Enterprise Scheme. Her life was a maelstrom of activities, and John felt pedestrian in comparison.

"To be honest, it's too much, and I should cut some stuff out. I get totally knackered, which is one reason I come here every fortnight. It's lovely to see Mum and Dad, but it's also my chill-out time. Sometimes I spend most of the weekend asleep, which is embarrassing."

John supped his beer. "How did you get involved in so many things?"

"I'm too accommodating, I just can't say 'no'."

John cleared his throat. "Lucky me."

Brit smiled at him and sipped her drink.

John's face flushed. "It, um, is very peaceful around here."

"Yeah. I'd die of boredom if I lived here all the time, but it's what I need every couple of weeks." She paused. "Sorry, I just realised what I said. You do live here all the time."

"That's okay. You're right. This place is pretty dull. The highlight of the month is the pub quiz. Fortunately, Barnstaple's only thirty minutes drive away and I train with the TA a couple of weekends each month, which can be intense."

"Oh, yes. Tell me about that. It sounds exciting."

As the evening wore on, more punters entered the pub. Almost without exception, new customers would greet Britney like she was an old friend. Brit was far more familiar with the villagers than John, and she was insanely popular.

A young farmer came over and stood by their table. Jack had a mass of curly ginger hair and his shirt sleeves were rolled back to reveal substantial tattooed biceps. John sat patiently as Brit and Jack nattered to each other. John noticed Jack glancing down Britney's cleavage. He gritted his teeth and began rubbing his thumb and forefinger together. Jack continued to casually drink his pint and seemed in no mood to move on.

One of Jack's friends shouted from the bar. "Hey, Jack. The darts is starting. You're up next."

Even John could read the irritation on Jack's face as he weighed up his options.

"Okay, mate. Just coming. Get another round in will ya."

Britney smiled at John. Such perfect teeth. "So, alone at last. What have you got against Jack?" Brit asked.

"What makes you think I've got something against him?"

"Well, there's your silence for the last ten minutes, you're gripping your glass so hard that your knuckles are white, and your face looks like a pig in a bacon factory."

"Oh. Is it that obvious? It's not that I dislike Jack. In fact, I barely know him. It's just that, that—"

"John, you're not jealous, are you?"

John blushed again.

Brit took his hand and leaned forward. "Don't worry. He's not my type... But you are."

*Wow! Unbelievable! Say something back—quick.*

"Me too...I mean, I-I—"

"I know what you mean, John. Relax, will you? I don't bite. Well...not in public, anyway."

They talked until closing time. John discovered Brit was single, claiming to be too busy for all that romantic crap. They walked back to her parent's house under a beautifully clear, starry night and stood together next to her parents' front door. John remained immobile whilst his mind fumbled for what to do now. This was unexplored territory. Brit bent forwards and gently kissed him on the lips.

"That's all you're getting for now. My parents are still awake upstairs and I don't want them opening their window to see me being groped. You'd give my dad a heart attack—I'm still his little girl."

"I wasn't going to—"

"Sssh! Listen, I'll be back here in two weeks. Maybe we could meet up again? If the weather's good, you should take me to the beach. How about some surfing?"

*Take her to the beach. Where she'll be wearing a bikini. Hell, yes!*

☣☣☣☣

John saw Brit regularly. Every two weeks, to be precise. On their second date, they visited Woolacombe beach on the North Devon coast. To John's dismay, the sun was not warm enough to encourage Brit into a bikini. Nonetheless, their picnic on a blanket developed into steamy petting, brought to an untimely end by a wet golden retriever looking for a missing ball.

On their fourth date, following a good meal and a few glasses of wine, Brit suggested it was time for John to show her his chalet. Fortunately, he had prepared for this eventuality by spending hours cleaning and hiding all clues to his geeky nature. Barely had the door closed before she pressed him against the wall and passionately kissed him.

She stared directly into his eyes and smiled. "Fuck me. Now!"

Despite the alcohol in his veins, John panicked. But Brit was experienced and masterful in this area. She played him like a musical instrument—guiding and encouraging every move until they both lay sated and exhausted. John's second experience with a woman felt a universe apart from the twenty minutes in the *Pascha* with Aarika.

From then on, John lived for her visits. He had a real girlfriend, and she was as hot as hell. At the next TA weekend, he delighted in boasting, showing off her photograph to anyone who could not get away fast enough.

Britney's visits often clashed with TA training. It was a choice of sex or mud—no competition. So the army saw a lot less of John.

On two occasions, John stayed the weekend with Britney in Bristol, but they were uncomfortable mishaps. Britney had a vast social circle and being with her meant being with her friends. John was ill at ease with group mingling and fitted into Britney's social life like a turd in a swimming pool.

So they fell into a comfortable routine of meeting every fortnight, always in Little Barton. Some weekends, they spent all of Saturday on the beach, or exploring the countryside. Sometimes, it would just be the evening. Usually, they had sex.

The arrangement was perfect for John. Their short time together made it exciting and special. For most of the time, John was free to follow his nerdy interests and routines. Britney's brief visits filled all his social needs. He wanted it to stay this way forever.

But nothing stays the same forever.

# John's Journal: Age 30

It's over. Brit's dumped me. We were having the usual Saturday night meal at The White Hart. Everything seemed fine at first. With hindsight, Brit was acting a bit strange. She drank more than usual and tried to get me drunk as well. I was hoping she had a special game planned for afterwards. Something exotic in the bedroom, perhaps?

How badly did I read her? The bombshell dropped after dessert. "John, this has been lovely as usual, but there's something I need to tell you."

Apparently, she's got a boyfriend in Bristol. Been going out with the bastard for ages, but sounds like they're getting serious. In a few weeks, they're moving in together. Brit banged on about what a wonderful person I was and we should keep in contact as 'friends.' Blah, blah, blah. I'm sure we won't. If we ever speak again, I'll be surprised—unless she needs a car tyre changed.

I thought we had something special going on, but I've been an idiot. Clearly, I was her bit on the side, a convenient distraction when she visited her parents. Brit was the highlight of my week, a few hours of bliss in an otherwise pointless existence. But she had a whole other life, an exciting career and a massive social circle. She's attractive, intelligent, sociable and wealthy. Of course, she'd find a proper boyfriend who was compatible and they're going to settle down and have gazillions of kids. Who'd want to be stuck with me for life? Absolute bollocks.

So what now? It took 28 years to find my first girlfriend, so I can look forward to another when I'm about 56. If I'm lucky!

☣☣☣☣

"Would you like another coffee, love?"

John sat and stared into his empty coffee cup.

"John?"

"What? Sorry Mum, I was miles away. Yes, thanks, another coffee would be great."

Breakfast in the Callaghan household had become a sombre affair since John's break up with Britney. Today, even the weather contributed to the mood, with the sky packed full of thick dirty clouds threatening to piss down at any moment.

"Do you have any plans for today?" Sarah said.

"Just the usual. I've got some coding to do. Are we going into the village?"

"Yes, that would be nice. I need to get a birthday card for Elsie."

Sarah filled his coffee cup. John remained silent.

"You haven't mentioned your war games simulator thingy for a while."

"I've given that up as a bad job."

"Oh dear, you spent a lot of time working on it, didn't you?"

"Yeah. Tell me about it. There's a reason nobody's ever done it before. It was far more difficult than I expected. No matter what I did, when I repeatedly simulated an actual battle, the results would be different. Not only different to the original conflict, but different each time I ran it."

"Hmm. Isn't that sort of like real life? You've told me the course of a battle could alter because of the weather, or a single soldier picking up a flag and starting a charge."

"Yeah, you're right. So, in reality, you can't predict combat with any certainty—there's always a big randomness factor. And, logically, that means what I was trying to create is pointless. A realistic simulator will produce random results. That's the conclusion I reached, which is why I've abandoned it. Pity I didn't realise that six months ago."

"How disappointing." Sarah began rotating her wedding ring. "You haven't eaten much. How about another slice of toast and marmalade?"

"No, ta." John sipped his coffee, staring blankly at the work surface.

Sarah looked at her son. "Will you be training with the TA this weekend?"

"No. Not this weekend."

"Okay. You don't seem to do that much recently?"

More uncomfortable silence. Sarah waited patiently for the cogs in John's brain to gear into motion.

"No. I suppose not. To be honest, I don't feel like it much anymore. There's a repeating yearly training cycle, so basically I've done everything seven times already. And I'm fed up with being wet and cold and muddy and it's hard work for me to pretend to be one of the lads. Most of them regard getting pissed on the Saturday night as the highlight of the weekend, but I hate doing that, so usually volunteer for guard duty. I still do enough weekends to qualify for the annual training bounty, but I'm not sure why. It's not like I need the money."

Sarah nibbled a piece of toast ineffectually. "John. I wonder...was I right to put you through all that therapy?"

"What do you mean?"

"Well, when I look at you now, it seems you're not exactly thrilled with your life."

He huffed. "Really. What gave it away?"

"I'm being serious. You don't have the personality to socialise with other people, but you're not happy on your own. When you were younger, your interests would change regularly, and you were totally engrossed with every new hobby. You sometimes spent days on your own and you'd be quite content. But your interests haven't changed for years and you've become bored with them—and nothing new has come along to replace them. You seem stuck in a rut."

Sarah reached over and held his hand.

"I worry that my meddling has turned you into a half-way house. You still can't fit into society, but you're no longer comfortable to be on your own. Perhaps if I'd let you blossom into your own natural autistic self, you would've been satisfied leading a solitary life. I've tried to normalise you and ended up with a hybrid. Goodness, that sounds awful, doesn't it? I didn't mean to say it like that."

John laughed.

"Oh, Mum. Maybe you're right. But, in truth, I doubt the therapy had much effect on me. And you were doing what you thought best. It was Kendall who was advising you. Doctor Meddle. And he was only following the latest trends in psychology, which I expect have completely changed since then. Don't blame yourself. Maybe I was destined to become a depressed lonely git."

## Chapter Nineteen

# CAL'S PERFECT LIFE

TIMELINE: 18 MONTHS AFTER THE
YELLOW DEATH

"We're all a little weird. And life is a little weird. And when we find someone whose weirdness is compatible with ours, we join up with them and fall into mutually satisfying weirdness — and call it love."
Robert Fulghum (1937– )

*Almost December and still warm enough to be wearing a T-shirt. The weather's gone insane.*

Cal stirred the breakfast porridge, bubbling gently over an open fire. His morning run, exercises, and wash were complete. He added another dash of water and a spoonful of powdered milk to the simmering goo, then gave it a stir.

The breeze changed direction and blew wood smoke into his face, making his eyes sting. He stood up and walked backwards to get clean air, rubbing his eyes as he did so.

Apart from a few thin cirrus clouds, the sky was an uninterrupted blue canvas. The sun hovered low above the distant hills, and the warmth felt good on his skin.

When he recovered, he noticed Juliet walking towards the camp after her morning ablutions in the nearby stream. She wore only leggings and a tee-shirt which displayed her figure wonderfully. Her hair hung loose and damp. She carried a towel and bag of toiletries.

Cal sat back down, but continued to watch her progress. As she came into the campsite, Cal noticed she was not wearing a bra, since her nipples stood proudly underneath the thin material.

Cal stared, his manhood responding instantly, causing him to shift position to disguise the effect Juliet was having on him. Their eyes met for an instant, and Cal flushed with embarrassment as he directed his gaze intently on the porridge.

Juliet lifted her towel over her chest. "Sorry, I wasn't thinking. That was a bit blatant. Sometimes I forget I'm not living alone now."

"No, no, no. Sorry, I shouldn't have been...I mean, I didn't intend to stare, but-but—"

"But you couldn't help gawping at my breasts?"

"No! I mean, yes. Damn! Sorry."

"Relax, Cal. It'd be pretty strange if you didn't look. It's not like you've been creeping down to the stream to spy on me...Or have you?"

"NO! Of course not. I wouldn't dream of it. Well, I might dream of it, but I'd never do it."

Cal's face flushed again. He remembered that one time. They had camped right next to a stream. With Juliet so close, it would have been difficult to avoid seeing something. He'd only had a quick peek.

*Bloody hell. I am human. What am I supposed to do with a hot girl walking around naked?*

Juliet donned a thick fleece before sitting down next to Cal. She began rubbing her hair with the towel. "How's the porridge?"

"Almost ready. Another couple of minutes should do it."

"Tell me something, Cal. Are you gay?"

Cal's eyebrows shot up. "What? No. Why would you ask that?"

Juliet shrugged. "Just wondering. You've never spoken about a wife or girlfriend and, until a few moments ago, I haven't seen you show any interest in me."

Cal lifted the porridge off the fire and began spooning it into two bowls, attempting to avoid eye contact. "I find it uncomfortable talking about private stuff, that's all. Here you go." He passed a bowl to Juliet.

"Thanks. Pass the sugar, will you? I fancy something sweet this morning." She added a teaspoon of sugar to her bowl and stirred it in before tasting it. "That's better. You know, Cal, if we're travelling together permanently, you're going to have to be more open. To be honest, keeping your past such a secret is getting a bit creepy. It's not normal."

Cal laughed. "I've never claimed to be normal."

They ate in silence for a moment until Cal relented. "Sorry. You're absolutely right. I'll try to be less secretive. I just don't want to scare you off."

She smiled. "I don't scare that easily. So, let's start with relationships. What is your relationship history? Are you…Were you single? When was your last relationship? Come on, spill the beans."

Cal felt his guts tighten. What should he say so he came across as reasonably normal?

*When faced with two options, favour the boldest. Just speak the truth.*

"I've had one girlfriend. Sort of."

"What does that mean?"

Cal told her about the weekend relationship with Britney.

Juliet listened in silence and nodded from time to time as she ate her porridge. "And you've never contacted Brit since you broke up?"

"No."

"You didn't feel the urge to find out how she was getting on? She was your first real grown-up relationship after all."

"I thought about her, but never plucked up enough courage to contact her. I didn't want to bother her. I assumed I'd be ancient history, and she'd get in touch with me if she wanted to. Besides, after we broke up, I was in a terrible state for a while. Things weren't going well for me."

"I see. And she was your only relationship?"

He nodded and moved his spoon around his bowl for a few seconds without eating. "Well, there was one other time."

*Why am I telling her this?*

"Oh, yes. Go on."

"Once…years ago. I was in Germany with the army. I got very drunk. More drunk than I'd ever been. I kind of went with a prostitute. Only the once. It's never happened again and it never would. My mates sort of…coerced me. God, that sounds pathetic."

Cal didn't dare look at Juliet to see her reaction, so fixed his eyes on his porridge bowl. He waited for a reaction. And waited. When Cal could bear the silence no more, he finally looked up at her. Juliet was smiling broadly, and they both burst out laughing.

"Oh, Cal, what are we going to do with you? For God's sake, eat your porridge before it's stone cold."

Cal began spooning the mush into his mouth.

Juliet hung a kettle of water over the fire. "So, you're definitely not gay?"

"No, definitely not."

"Just a little inexperienced."

"I guess you could say that."

"That's okay. I can work with that."

*What the hell does that mean?*

Juliet put a second spoonful of sugar in her porridge and smiled. "Now, tell me all about this night with a prostitute. That's something I've got to hear about."

*Oh, God.*

☣☣☣☣

Juliet drove along the A377, towards Exeter, with Cal sitting next to her, cradling a rifle in his lap. Every few seconds, the wiper blades swept across the windscreen to clear the persistent drizzle. Today's aim was to find an organic wholesaler somewhere north of Exeter. They hoped to find a warehouse brimming with canned and dried food, which was undiscovered by other survivors.

Cal dozed, but woke up when the Land Rover detoured down a minor side road. "What's going on?"

Juliet grinned to herself. "Wait. Be patient. You'll see."

She turned into a small lane preceded by a faded sign, leaning at an odd angle, which declared; 'Paradise Valley - Leave Your Cares At The Entrance'. The lane opened to reveal rows of dirty caravans standing amongst tall grass and weeds. One had caught fire at some stage, leaving only a blackened chassis. The grey scudding clouds added to the gloomy scene. The site contained a huge outdoor equipment shop. Juliet ignored the front car park and drove around the back, where they would be hidden from the public road.

Cal noted with satisfaction how Juliet had begun following his security habits.

Juliet turned off the engine. "I want to grab a few things. Won't be long. You coming in?" She got out and briskly walked to the shop without waiting for an answer.

Cal shrugged, scanned the area, slung his rifle over his shoulder, then followed her inside.

Before the Yellow Death, the place had been an outdoor living superstore, selling everything needed for the adventurous holiday maker. Since then, it had been plundered, with the main doors smashed in and much of the stock taken. The store was as cold inside as the car park, and Cal shuddered, hoping Juliet's detour would be over soon. Discarded items littered the floor with debris blown from outside, completing the picture of decay.

Cal scrunched up his nose at the stink of mould and damp cardboard. Prominent signs advertised the shop's biggest sale ever—how true that turned out to be.

Juliet walked to the camping and trekking section, where there was still a reasonable selection of sleeping bags, mattresses, and similar equipment. Cal was side-tracked by portable stoves and he mooched around for spare gas cannisters.

"Cal, come over here, will you? I need your opinion on something," Juliet shouted from across the store.

A rat scuttled outside at the noise. Cal walked over to Juliet, who stood in front of a line of brightly coloured sleeping bags hanging on a rail. She slid them along one by one until stopping at a double with red and yellow stripes. She stepped back to admire it.

"Well, what do you think?" Juliet said.

"About what?"

"The sleeping bag, silly. Do you like it?"

Cal frowned. "It's okay, I suppose. A bit colourful for my taste."

She grabbed the sleeping bag and rubbed it between her fingers. "Hmm. Lovely and soft. Do you think it would be comfy?"

"Well, yes. I expect it would."

"Excellent. Shall we take it then?"

He looked at her quizzically. "Why? What do you want a double sleep... Oh."

She nodded, smiling.

"What? You don't mean...For us? You and me? For us to sleep in...together?"

"Well, you can sleep. I was planning on doing something far more exciting."

"Oh...Oh, yes. Good God. Well yes, of course, definitely...Fantastic, thanks."

He realised he was babbling, so took a deep breath. "Sorry. You took me by surprise. I didn't realise you were thinking of me in that way."

"I know. That's part of what makes you so appealing. Okay then, if we're sharing a sleeping bag, we're going to need a bigger tent."

They returned to their vehicle carrying their latest acquisitions. Cal beamed like a dog in a sausage shop.

"Cal, please take that inane smile off your face, it's not attractive."

"Sorry."

"About our new sleeping arrangements."

"Yes?"

"Do we need to pay a visit to a pharmacy?"

"What for?"

"Come on Cal. Put two and two together, will you?"

"Oh, I see. Yes. I mean no. No, we don't need to visit a chemist. I've got some...things in my car."

"Of course you have. I should have known. You're a man. Civilisation may have ended, but you wouldn't be caught without a condom, just in case."

"As a matter of fact, they make excellent emergency water carriers."

"Yeah, and I'm sure that's why you carry them."

☣ ☣ ☣ ☣

Cal silenced his phone alarm a second after it sounded. He had been awake for some time, simply lying back and experiencing bliss. Outside, the first light of dawn appeared. Wind rattled the canvas of the tent. Cal couldn't care less. Inside the sleeping bag, he felt warm and dry. Better still, he lay with a naked, beautiful woman pressed against him.

*Hell's bells. Life doesn't get any better than this.*

The evening after they visited the outdoor store at Paradise Valley and acquired the new sleeping bag, Juliet surprised Cal by deciding to sleep separately as usual. Their double sleeping bag remained in its plastic wrapping.

Juliet had explained her position over breakfast. "I wanted to have the new tent and sleeping bag ready. Just in case."

"Just in case of what?"

"In case you decide to take our relationship further than simply being travelling companions."

"Well, I do. Definitely."

"Excellent."

"So, that's settled."

"Not so fast, Romeo. I'm not some German prostitute."

Cal blushed at the mention of Aarika. "Sorry. I didn't mean to imply—"

"Woo me."

"What?"

"You heard. I'm a woman, not a vending machine. Woo me. Romance me. Entice me."

Cal had nodded thoughtfully. "I-I don't have much experience at wooing."

"Well, you'd better get learning fast then, hadn't you?"

Romance did not come naturally to Cal. What to do? What to do? Before the Death, he might have sent a bouquet of flowers, or a box of chocolates. He could have texted sweet nothings to her, or arranged an expensive meal at a posh restaurant. But all the mechanisms of civilised romantic foreplay had vanished. Now it was two people travelling alone in a post-apocalyptic landscape. How do you introduce romance to that? Yet somehow he had to rise to the challenge. The stakes were high. He needed to think about it logically.

So, he began complimenting Juliet on her looks. That proved to be relatively easy, since he only had to remember to say out loud what he was thinking. He began to anticipate her needs and perform minor acts of kindness, such as laying out a cushion and blanket for when she returned from her morning ablutions. Once, he collected a bunch of red flowers from a garden and presented them as a bouquet. If there was any heavy lifting to be done, Cal made an extra special effort to do the lion's share—diverting Juliet to a less manual task.

The evenings saw the biggest change. Cal made a supreme effort to talk and have real grown-up conversations on subjects other than warfare. He asked Juliet about her life—favourite movies, books, and foods. They discussed politics, religion, and a dozen other subjects. In turn, he revealed more about himself.

One night, when they were both sozzled, Cal told the truth about his military career—or lack of it. He had feared Juliet would think less of him, but she laughed hysterically and complimented him on his deception. With that secret exposed, Cal was able to relax and talk about anything and everything with her. Juliet was the first person in his life he felt totally at ease with.

These developments had culminated the previous evening. When the evening meal was finished, they enjoyed a glass of red wine. Cal noticed Juliet rotating her shoulder. They sat on opposite sides of the campfire as usual, with several battery lanterns glowing nearby.

"Got a problem?" Cal asked.

"My shoulder's sore. I think I slept awkwardly last night, because I woke up with a stiff shoulder and all the lifting today has aggravated it."

"Why didn't you say before now. I'd have carried those boxes for you."

"I don't like to make a fuss. And I don't want to be the helpless female either."

"I'd never think that about you. Everyone has an off day. We're a team and help each other out."

"I guess so. It's really not so bad. Probably be okay in the morning. And don't you dare tell me I need to see a doctor."

Cal poked the fire with a stick. "How about I give it a rub? See if I can't loosen it up a bit?"

They gazed at each other over the flames. Although the pair had become closer over the past couple of weeks, physical contact remained a rarity.

"Okay, that would actually be lovely," Juliet said. "Tell me you've been hiding the fact that you're a trained masseur."

"Sorry, no. But how hard can it be?"

Cal stood up, went around the fire, and knelt behind Juliet. She wore a thick fleece over her pyjama top. He placed his palms on her bare neck and began rubbing gently and rhythmically.

"Oh, that's heaven. Are you sure you've not had training?"

"I must be naturally talented. It's about time I found something I'm instinctively good at." He pressed his thumbs into her spine and moved them up and down her neck.

"How's that?"

"Soooo good. But it's not helping my shoulder."

Cal sat down crossed legged behind her. He transferred his hands to her shoulders, still on top of her fleece.

"Hold on a sec," Juliet said, taking off her fleece. The air was chilly, but they were close enough to the fire to feel the heat on their faces.

"If it makes it easier, you can go underneath my top."

Cal hesitated, and his breath quickened. He slid his arms underneath the bottom of Juliet's pyjama top and started caressing her shoulders again. The sensation of his fingers sliding over her soft skin was exquisite. He sensed her relaxing and responding to his movements. It felt good. It felt sensational.

# CAL'S PERFECT LIFE

Juliet moaned with pleasure. "I used to love having a back rub. I can't remember when I last had one. God, that's lovely." She tilted forwards, lowering her head, inviting Cal to go lower.

Cal ran his thumbs up and down Juliet's spine and again she moaned.

Cal felt himself become erect and resisted the urge to gyrate his thighs. The suggestion of a shoulder rub was made in good faith, but now his body coursed with desire and he regretted the offer. When this was over, he would have to sneak off for some private time.

Cal's fingers squeezed and rubbed, moving away from Juliet's spine and outwards to her shoulders, then progressing down her back. He fought the craving to reach around and cup her breast. This couldn't carry on much more. Juliet became increasingly relaxed, but Cal was about to explode with frustration. His hands now rotated in the small of her back, just above her buttocks.

After a couple more minutes, she sat up straight. "That was fantastic. You, sir, have a gift." She rotated her shoulder again. "That's much better. Thanks."

Juliet turned to face him and smiled. "Now it's your turn."

*Oh! I wasn't expecting that. Should I present my back to her?*

Juliet leaned forward and gently planted a kiss on his lips. Then sat back and smiled.

Cal was stunned. Was that what she meant by his *turn*? And was that the end of it?

Juliet continued to sit and face him, looking into his eyes.

*When faced with two options, favour the boldest.*

Cal leaned forwards and kissed her. Slowly.

Juliet stood up and, for a second, Cal feared he had done something wrong.

"C'mon, get up," she said.

He did so, wondering what was happening now. The pair faced each other in the flickering firelight. Inches apart. Juliet put her arms around him and drew him close. They kissed again—for a long time. Cal wanted it to go on forever. This was not like Britney—that had only been animal passion. This was also animal passion, but with something else, a yearning, a wish, an urge to get closer to Juliet than was physically possible. He wanted to get inside her skin, to be one with her—it could only be love.

Their lips parted.

"At last," she said. "I was wondering if you'd ever pluck up courage to do something."

Cal didn't know what to say, so kissed her again.

"Listen," she said. "I know it's late and dark, but how about putting up that two-person tent we've been lugging around?"

Cal erected the new tent in a blisteringly fast time, whilst Juliet unpacked the double sleeping bag.

☣ ☣ ☣ ☣

The melody and lyrics of Mad World entered Cal's consciousness. He lay in absolute darkness and had to fumble about to silence his phone alarm.

Juliet's arms wrapped around him from behind.

"Are you awake?" he said.

"I've been awake for ages. I'm so cold I can't sleep. This has been the worst night ever."

"What? Even dressed like the Michelin man?"

Over the last month, the nights had become progressively colder. Most mornings they had been greeted with a frost. The previous evening, Juliet had climbed into their sleeping bag wearing several layers, including her thickest fleece, gloves, and thermal socks.

"Yes. Even dressed like the Michelin man, I was freezing fucking cold. And don't you dare say I was wearing too much clothing."

"It was the last thing on my mind."

"Good. What about you? You must have felt the cold?"

"Hmm. Maybe a little." Cal had been chilled for most of the night, but was reluctant to admit it. He switched on his head torch, which lay next to the sleeping bag. The walls and roof of the tent were bulging inwards.

"Just a sec." He pulled himself out of their sleeping bag.

"Oh, Cal. For God's sake. Can't we just stay in bed until it gets light, at least?"

"I said, just a sec. I'm checking on something." Cal zipped open the bottom of the outer tent flap. A clump of snow fell inwards.

"Holy crap!"

"What is it?"

"It's snowed. I mean really snowed."

Juliet crawled to join him at the entrance.

"Oh, my word. It's beautiful."

Although the sky was a deep ultramarine, the snow reflected enough light to view the landscape clearly. The vista was ghostly. An almost perfect uninterrupted white. The snow was thick enough to cover most objects, with only trees standing proud. Even they struggled under the weight of snow, which burdened their branches.

"Well, I think we can say the winter heatwave is truly over," Cal said.

"What are we going to do?"

Cal slid back into the sleeping bag. "We could build a snowman."

"Seriously, you dick, we can't travel in this weather. Even if we could, living in a tent is ridiculous."

"Hmm. I agree. Come back to bed."

Juliet did so, and they hugged each other.

"It's time for Plan B," Cal said.

"Plan B? I didn't even know we had a Plan A."

"That's why you're not in charge."

She punched him in the arm.

"Ouch!"

"Serves you right. Chauvinist pig."

"So, do you want to hear about Plan B or not?"

"What I want most of all is a wee, but I'm not sure if I can be bothered to go outside."

"It's going to get very wet and steamy in here if you don't."

"Okay. I'm going for a wee. You dig out the gas stove and put the kettle on."

A short time later, they sat cross-legged inside the tent, cradling mugs of steaming tea in their hands. The eastern sky had turned mid-blue, signalling the sun was struggling to make an appearance. The only light in the tent was their head torches.

"So, genius. Tell me about this Plan B."

Cal slurped his tea. "Okay. Well, although the weather has been unusually warm since the Death, I suspected it might not last. The planet is warming up, but one effect of that is the weather's becoming extreme and unpredictable."

"Yes, I know all that. I used to watch the news as well. So what is Plan B?"

"Before we met, I was scouting out potential sites for settling down—both temporarily and permanently. I needed to know there were bolt holes I could go to in an emergency. For example, if I was injured and needed to lay up somewhere to heal. So, I've prepared half a dozen places which are suitable for temporary winter retreats."

"Oh wow. That's great. Where are they?"

"The nearest is less than fifteen miles away. It'll be a struggle to get there in this snow, but trust me, the effort will be worth it. It's called Rockbeare House. Used to be a farmhouse. I think some rich family must have bought it a few years ago and went to town modernising the house and grounds. It's got log fires and a range cooker. Best of all—wait for this—it has solar panels, a wind turbine, and a ground source heat pump. There's a well for water and a septic tank, so it's pretty much off-grid."

"Wow. That's fantastic. But what about food?"

"I've left supplies in a barn nearby. We can supplement those with hunting and perhaps fishing from their lake. Of course, I also removed the... bodies... Mom, Dad and three kids. I found them all huddled together in the same bed."

Cal became silent. Sometimes the horror of the Yellow Death crept up unexpectedly.

Juliet reached over and held his arm. "You okay?"

Cal looked up. "Yeah. Sorry about that. Anyway, the place is ideal for sitting out the worst of the weather. We could sit out the cold spell watching some movies whilst relaxing in front of a log fire. I might even arrange a hot shower. Sound good?"

"Oh, God. It sounds perfect. There's just one tiny weeny thing."

"What's that?"

"You've just told me we could have spent the last two months living in luxury rather than freezing our tits off. I've spent every morning trying to wash in an ice-cold stream and now you tell me about hot showers and log fires. Why the hell didn't you say something earlier?"

Cal paused, feeling slightly deflated.

"Erm, I...Well, I wanted it to be a surprise."

"It is. It's a lovely surprise. But it would have been a lovely surprise two weeks ago."

"I guess I was waiting until we really needed it. Once we hunker down for the winter, we'll be using our supplies rather than building them up. The farmhouse is pretty remote. Apart from a few neighbours, there'll be no more scavenging until we hit the road again."

Juliet sipped her tea. "Oh. Okay. I suppose that makes some sense. But in future, it would be nice to be kept in the loop. I'm not a child who needs looking after."

"No. No. Of course not. Sorry. It won't happen again."

"Good. So tell me. Is there a Plan C you've been keeping to yourself?"

Cal laughed. "Maybe. But that's on a need-to-know basis."

☣☣☣☣

The campfire burned brightly, creating an aura of light and warmth holding back the darkness. Mutton stew bubbled enthusiastically and gave off meaty aromas. Cal and Juliet both stared into the fire in silence, gripping mugs of tea. They had only recently begun travelling again after spending three months at Rockbeare House during the worst of the Winter.

The first six weeks at Rockbeare had been bliss for Cal. Living in luxury, alone with the woman of his dreams. They watched movies, cooked, shared hot baths, played games and made love. They proved to be evenly matched at playing chess and their daily game became increasingly competitive, with prizes and forfeits adding to the interest.

As the days became longer, Cal developed itchy feet. They were wasting time. Juliet was comfortable and reluctant to leave. However, she had to agree they had scavenged everything within the local area and it was not tenable to stay there long term. Cal argued if they were going to settle in a permanent location, they needed to find a larger group.

Juliet pulled the hood on her coat over her head. "God it's cold. I bet there'll be another frost tonight."

Cal suspected Juliet's comment was a jab at him for making them leave Rockbeare House in March, when Spring was still battling for dominance over Winter. He chose not to respond and stirred the stew, staring closely at it. "How the hell can you tell when this is done?"

Juliet took the spoon off him, removed a chunk of potato from the pot, blew on it, and then carefully nibbled it.

"Give it another fifteen minutes."

"How d'you do that? How can you simply poke the food, or nibble it and know how much more it needs cooking?"

"How come you can't? It's a basic life skill any normal ten-year-old can do."

Cal sat back down and switched off his head torch.

"Are you angry with me?"

"A bit pissed, yes."

"Is it because I wouldn't stay at Berryfields tonight?"

"Exactly. That was a wonderful settlement. The people were friendly. They were doing exciting things with solar panels and the water turbine. It was fascinating to learn what they were up to, and they were keen to hear our news. They were so grateful we told them about the blacksmith in the next valley. And we did a good trade."

Juliet pointed to the mutton and vegetables boiling in the pot. "But you barely exchanged words with them and were itching to get away. It would've been lovely spending one night in a proper bed and having human company."

"I'm human."

"Barely."

Cal had no reply, so stirred the stew to appear busy. The silence dragged on for several minutes before he relented. "Okay. I'm sorry. I know what you mean. And I saw you were unhappy when we left. In fact, I almost turned back."

"So, what was the problem?"

Cal sighed. "I don't really know. I could pretend I didn't want to put us in their debt, but that's bullshit. The truth is, I was okay in their company for a short time, but it soon became...uncomfortable. That's the best way to describe it. All those questions about where we'd been and what we'd done."

"So what's wrong with that? They were only curious about us. It's completely natural. Most folk would be glad to talk about their adventures. I would. It's called conversation."

"I know. Sorry."

Juliet was glaring at him. "You talk of settling down somewhere, but in reality, you can't spend more than an hour with strangers without getting anxious. Strangers are only strangers until you get to know them. We'll never find a permanent home if you run away after an hour."

"Sorry."

"Don't just keep saying 'sorry' and stop talking. That doesn't help, you irritating man. Tell me what's happening in that excuse for a brain you've got."

Cal sat back and pondered how to respond, but before he formulated a reply, Juliet continued. "Part of the problem is this macho persona you've created for yourself, isn't it?"

Cal frowned. "What do you mean?"

"You've invented this false past in which you're a combat veteran and military superhero. I understand why you did it. But it's doing more harm than good—if it ever did any good. Are you aware that individuals with autism are notoriously terrible liars?"

"Yes, I was told about that. It's true that I hate deception—both giving and receiving."

"And yet you've set yourself up so you have to lie about your past to everyone you meet. Doesn't that seem a little bit bonkers?"

"Well, if you put it that way."

"Cal, there's nothing wrong with your past. You were a web developer, and I'd put money on the fact that you were a damn good one."

"Yeah, well—"

"It's a skilled job. Not everyone could do it. There's nothing to be ashamed of. I understand you want to be seen as a military expert, but you served in the TA infantry for seven years and you studied warfare for decades. So you are a military expert. Why invent a load of bollocks about fighting in Syria when you've never set foot in the country?"

"That's a fair point. It seemed like a good idea at the time. I didn't anticipate the consequences. It probably was a mistake."

Juliet sipped her tea. "Well, it's decent of you to admit that. Thank you. And stop poking the stew."

"Sorry."

"And stop saying sorry."

"Sorr—" He drank from his mug. "There's something else."

Juliet sat up. "Well, go on."

"Remember, I've said I'd received therapy for my autism."

"Yeah. You've never wanted to talk about that, but I've wondered about it."

"Well, I had an awful lot of therapy—the 'full monty'. No expense spared. Personal tutors, child psychologists, mental games, coordination exercises. I had more therapists than relatives. All from the age of three, for Christ's sake."

"When did it stop?"

"The therapy? I don't think it ever did."

Cal read the confused look on Juliet's face. "What I mean is Mum was always trying to push me and encourage me to socialise and leave my 'comfort zone' as she called it."

"Oh, I see. Mothers do that sort of thing. In her eyes, you'd always be her little boy."

"Yeah. Well, I suppose I can't blame her. The psychologist sold this package to my mum as some sort of fix. Dr Kendall told her the human brain is extremely pliable in young children. What did he call it? Neuro—"

"Neuroplasticity."

"That's it. He told my mum it could be moulded. He said they would rewire my brain."

Juliet frowned. "Well, I'm not sure I agree with that. If it were possible, there'd be no adults with autism. They taught me autism is a fundamental part of the personality. You simply can't train somebody out of it, only help them cope with it better."

"That's my point. What if all the therapy didn't rewire my brain? What if the results of all those therapies was I learnt some new tricks, habits, and behaviours which help me fit into what passed for normal society? A couple of years back, Mum wondered whether she'd been right to try to normalise me.

She was afraid she'd created... what did she call it? A hybrid. Somebody who was no longer happy alone, but unable to mix socially. The worst of both worlds. I'm starting to think all I got was a bunch of coping techniques which need to be practised, or I lose them again."

Juliet moved closer and put her arm around him.

"I think I understand. You're worried you've been on your own for so long now you're losing your ability to mix with others? Perhaps regressing back into full-on autistic behaviour?"

"Yeah. Something like that. Thinking back, the first months following the Death were great for me. I could do whatever I wanted, and there was plenty of everything. That must sound awful when most survivors were in terrible shock and grief. But for me, months passed before I felt any sort of loneliness. Even then, all I needed was an occasional meal with other travellers. Just before I met you, I was in a dilemma. I realised travelling alone on the road was becoming untenable, and I was genuinely missing human company. Yet the idea of joining with another group terrified me. I'd have to be sociable and fit in with others and lose all my freedom."

"And then you met me?"

"That's right, and it was perfect. We just clicked, and you fulfilled all my needs for companionship. If only the two of us could keep travelling forever, I'd be a happy bunny. I realise that's not normal, or even healthy. And I understand most folks, including you, need a social circle of friends and colleagues—but I don't."

"Cal, that sounds so sad. And you know, living like we do is becoming impossible. Scavenging, or whatever else you want to call it, is getting more and more difficult. Being on the road is getting more and more dangerous. We have to settle down somewhere and you've said yourself we can't be self-sufficient on our own."

Cal nodded. "Very true. It's driving me crazy. I can't live with people and I can't live without them."

"Listen to me. You've been to uni and held a regular job. So you can live with other people. We must find a settlement which is right for us. Perhaps one where we get our own house or living quarters. I'm a doctor and you're a military guru, so any settlement will be glad to have us. I reckon you just need more practice being with people. The more time you spend mixing with others, the better you'll get at it. If you make an effort to socialise, to meet others, to talk—and I mean properly talk—eventually those techniques may become ingrained. Talking becomes a habit, so you don't have to make such an effort any more. And it would help if you weren't making up stories about being a war hero."

"I guess you're right. I'll tell you what, the next time we meet people, I'll try my best to be more sociable. Promise."

"And less of an arsehole?"

"Yes, much less of an arsehole."

"And will you seriously think about dropping this military hero bullshit?"

"Okay. I'll think about it."

"Good. Thanks, Cal. That's all I can ask for." Juliet squeezed his hand. "That stew must be ready, if you haven't poked it to death. I'm starving."

*Shit. What have I let myself in for?*

## Chapter Twenty

# John's Exploding Disc

TIMELINE: 2 YEARS BEFORE THE YELLOW DEATH

> "Panic is a sudden desertion of us, and a going over to the enemy of our imagination."
> Christian Nevell Bovee (1820–1904)

John was attending a battle-shoot weekend. They were highly popular and one of John's favourites in the TA training schedule. This was a chance to have a go at live firing every infantry weapon in the British Army's inventory. They would also be using interactive firing ranges and laser tagging gear to simulate real combat. This was just the type of thing John had joined the TA to do.

Unfortunately, the preparation was hard and tedious. Transporting mountains of ammunition from the armoury to the firing ranges was tough. Everyone helped out, creating a long queue of soldiers outside the armoury. In turns, they walked through the small armoured door and returned a few seconds later, straining under the weight of a metal box or canister.

John waited in line with the other troops. The soldier in front of John was a behemoth—over six feet tall and built like a yeti on steroids. Four ammo boxes remained in the current stack and yeti-man bent to pick up two of them. Most soldiers carried only one box at a time.

John was proud of his physical fitness, so followed the example of yeti-man. He bent over to grab the two crates on the floor. They were an awkward shape, with sharp edges. He bent lower and lifted with all his strength. Nothing. The crates refused to budge. He was aware of the others watching him from outside the door. It would be humiliating to have tried and failed, so he braced and prepared for another supreme effort.

"Aaaargh!"

Instant white-hot searing agony exploded in his spine. He felt as if molten lava was being poured on his bare skin—but worse, because this was inside him. It was the most excruciating pain imaginable. It did not lessen as the seconds passed. John's torso was in spasm, forcing him into rigidity. Embarrassing as it was, he couldn't straighten up, nor lower himself to the ground. He had become a statue.

"You okay, mate?" the man behind him said. John could only whimper in response. It took four of them to carry him out of the bunker and lay him on the grass, curled into a ball and moaning.

He spent several pain-filled hours in the local Accident and Emergency Department until a doctor gave him the bad news.

"The X-rays show that you have a prolapsed disc."

"A what?"

"Your spine consists of bones——vertebrae——which are separated and cushioned by shock-absorbing flexible discs. These intervertebral pads have a soft inner core. You put too much pressure on a disc when you tried to lift that weight.

Essentially, it bursts and is now pressing on the nerves of your spinal cord. Most people call this problem a slipped disc, but it hasn't physically slipped or moved, more like exploded."

"Oh, Christ. That sounds bad."

"Well, it's not good. The disc will heal by itself, but it'll take some time. Unfortunately, there'll always be a weakness and a predisposition to aggravate the problem. Also, the damaged disc will be misshapen and flattened, so it won't do such a good job of absorbing shock. There'll be a tendency for the disc to press and squeeze nerves in your spinal column, causing pain. If it becomes persistent, we can refer you to a specialist pain clinic and, as a last resort, there's the option of surgery. But we're a long way from thinking along those lines. With any luck, in time you'll make a full recovery."

The doctor gave John a professional, patronising smile, which John found unconvincing.

An ambulance transported John home, flat on his back. He felt as if a white-hot knife had been inserted between his vertebra. Every bump in the road brought a fresh wave of agony.

☣☣☣☣

"Hello, John. How are you feeling today?"

Dr. Chandra stood next to Sarah at the foot of John's bed. The doctor held a well-practised smile.

John lay flat on his back and adjusted his position, only to be rewarded with a stab of pain.

"Ow! To be honest, I feel bloody awful. Same as yesterday and the day before that. I don't seem to get any better. And I'm in agony. Every movement is agony. But if I stay still for too long, my back seizes up, which hurts even more. I can't tell you the pain I have to go through just to take a piss."

The doctor nodded sympathetically. "And it's been four weeks now?"

"Four very long weeks. The Valium and Ibuprofen don't seem to do very much. Can't you give me some more of that morphine based stuff?"

"I'm sorry. That wouldn't be a very good idea in the long-term. And sadly, your recovery is likely to be a long-term process. Are you managing to sleep?"

"Not much. Sometimes I fall asleep due to complete and utter exhaustion. But when I turn or move in my sleep, the pain wakes me up again."

"I'll prescribe some sleeping tablets. You should be getting your first visit from the physiotherapist tomorrow. The exercises they'll get you doing will be somewhat...difficult. Especially in the early stages. But it's important we get you moving and prevent your muscles from wasting away if you're going to get better."

"Am I...Am I actually going to get better? I've really fucked up my back. This much pain must mean there's some permanent damage?"

The doctor took a deep breath. "John. I'm confident you will get better than you are now. Much better. But it will take time. And whether you'll make a one-hundred per cent recovery is uncertain. First, we need to let nature take it's course. The body has remarkable healing abilities when we give it a chance. Later on—if necessary—we can talk about other treatments. Tell me, are you able to work? I understand you're some sort of whizz at computer programming."

John shook his head. "No way. I'd have to balance my laptop on my chest. It's not practical. Besides, my head is so woozy from the drugs."

"Pity. It might help to take your mind off your discomfort. Well, I'm sure you know best."

The doctor let himself out, leaving John alone with Sarah.

"Do you mind if I open a window a little? It's starting to smell in here."

"Sorry. Go ahead."

Sarah sat next to John's bed.

"The woozy head thing. That's not just the drugs is it?"

"What do you mean?"

"John, I'm not stupid. I see what goes out in your recycling bins. I can smell the alcohol on you."

John let out a sigh. He had been dreading this conversation. "It's the only thing that dulls the pain. It helps me sleep."

"You're not supposed to mix booze and those—"

"I know! I'm not an idiot. But you don't have to live with this pain all the time. I want to cut my fuc—my head off."

Sarah nodded and put her hand over John's.

"I know it's hard. We'll get through this together, you'll see."

"I hope so. I expect you're feeling pretty smug about the work thing?"

"What d'you mean?"

John gave a rare smile. "Remember when I was boasting how financially secure I was. How I said as long as I could move my fingers, I could work? That sounds pretty hollow now doesn't it?"

"I wasn't going to mention that, but it did occur to me. Never mind. We all live and learn."

☣☣☣☣

Weeks turned to months, with the passage of time marked by weekly visits from a physiotherapist to record his so-called progress and adjust his therapeutic exercise regime. Even the physiotherapist struggled to stay positive. John watched Winter turn to Spring, then Summer, through the windows of his chalet which had become a prison.

He worked his way through a variety of pain relief machines and devices bought off the internet, but only alcohol brought any meaningful comfort.

Life was miserable and tedious. Hours felt like years. The chilling prospect of spinal surgery began to sound more and more tempting.

☣☣☣☣

# John's Journal: Age 32

Received a letter today from the Army. I've been medically discharged, in other words, scrapped. I'm not surprised. It's been 18 months since I injured my back and it doesn't seem to get much better. None of my so-called TA buddies have contacted me for months, but I've not contacted them either. I genuinely thought I had real friends, but it appears not.

I do those exercises the physio gave me religiously—despite the pain. Occasionally, there's an improvement, but if I make a sudden movement, or twist without thinking, it's back to square one.

Mornings are the worst. I always wake with my back in a spasm. Just getting out of bed is agony. It loosens up after a while, but I've got to move carefully to avoid aggravating it.

I get about in slow motion like a snail. Painkillers don't do much. A few shots of vodka help—but the pain is always present under the surface. Mum refuses to buy me more than a bottle a week, so I've been ordering booze online. Eventually Mum will guess and I'm not sure what she'll do then—probably start vetting the mail.

Mum paid a surprise visit to my cabin today and said what an awful mess it was, with an overpowering stink of sweat, curry, and farts.

She really lost her rag and I don't blame her. When I looked in the mirror, it wasn't a pretty sight. Red sunken eyes and yellow teeth. Not had a haircut or shaved for God knows how long. A hippie would look good in comparison. Anyway, Mum ran back to her cottage in tears. Well done John. Must make an effort to shave and cut my hair tomorrow, for her sake at least. It's not as if I even like having a beard.

What I'd do for a decent night of sleep. The moment I fall asleep, the back pain starts to increase. At most, I'll get a two-hour stretch before waking. I wriggle a bit, change position, and then I'm good for another hour or two.

I checked on Brit's Facebook page today. She's married with one kid and a second on the way. I considered emailing her, but don't want her to know how low I've sunk.

I'm living off my savings now. It hurts to sit at a desk and I can't be bothered to do any website coding. Besides, I'm not getting any more commissions. I made a few careless mistakes on the last couple of sites I coded. Not sure whether it was the booze or lack of sleep. Whatever. I got a few complaints and bad reviews from clients, so new enquiries have dried up.

Going running is impossible, of course. But I take a short walk up and down the lane each day. Otherwise, I'd never leave the cabin. Beginning to hate these four walls.

Next week I've got an appointment with a spinal consultant. About bloody time. I'm not getting my hopes up, but I'm desperate to try something different. Surgery is risky and not always successful, but I'm willing to give it a go. Anything is better than this.

☣☣☣☣

"John, what are you doing here?"

"Morning Mum. How's things? I thought I might have breakfast with you. Is that okay?"

"Why yes, that'd be lovely, dear. What a nice surprise. We haven't done that for months." She closed the cover on her iPad and put it to one side.

John hobbled to the breakfast bar and sat down. The early morning sun through the French doors painted bright rectangles on the floor.

Next door's rooster gave a raucous 'cock-a-doodle-doo'.

John smiled. "Blimey. He's a bit late today. The sun's been up for hours."

Sarah began filling the kettle. "Maybe he had a late night. What about you? How are you? Is there still a lot of pain?"

"It's worst in the mornings. I'm in my loosening stage at the moment." He wriggled in his chair. "But, overall, I'm much better. I think I'm seeing some benefit from those cortisone injections. Look at me—I'm actually sitting in a chair like a normal person."

"That's wonderful. How long since you had the last injection?"

"About two weeks, so if they're going to do anything, now's about the time when I should see some improvements."

"Fingers crossed. I haven't soaked any porridge. Would you like toast and marmalade? Coffee?"

"Yes and yes, thanks. Since this is a special occasion, I'll skip porridge for once."

"This is lovely. It's so, well, normal."

"Yes. And it's going to be normal again. I've wasted enough time moping in my cabin. My back feels stronger than it has for months. If it doesn't keep improving, I'll press for surgery. I've spent too long lying down."

She put a mug of steaming coffee in front of him and slid four slices of bread into the toaster. "I'm so glad to hear you say that. Shall I put the news on?"

He sipped his coffee. Hot, strong and smooth, just how he liked it. "Yes, please. Sounds like it's gone crazy in America. Did you see the reports last night?"

She frowned. "Yes, I did. It's happened so fast, I can't keep up with it. They said hospitals in New York were overwhelmed and not taking new admissions. That's terrible."

"Yeah. It's worrying. It's as if COVID-19 has a faster, meaner older brother. That quarantine's not turning out well."

"No. Those scenes of their National Guard soldiers firing on those poor people running through the roadblocks. It was horrible."

The aroma of toasting bread wafted across the room. "That has to be one of the best smells in the world," John said.

Sarah grinned as she pointed the remote control at the TV in the corner of the kitchen.

*"...cases reported in six other cities in the U.S. The President has made an executive order prohibiting non-essential travel between states and all flights into and out of the country have been cancelled..."*

"Oh my Lord, how awful. Have they no idea what it is?" Sarah said.

"I've not seen anything confirmed, but plague keeps being mentioned. Something about lumps in the neck, and armpits."

"Plague? Goodness, isn't that ancient history? Here's your toast, dear."

"Thanks. I Googled it last night. The plague's never gone away. There are still cases every year in parts of the world."

*"...anyone with signs of fever, or aches and pains, should stay at home and self-isolate. Report any symptoms to your physician but do not go to the ER..."*

Sarah turned away from the screen. "I was going into the village today to post a parcel. It looks like it's promising to be a lovely day for a stroll. I don't suppose..."

"Sure, I'll walk with you. Just give me time to do my physio stuff and tidy my cabin a bit. I'll not be walking very fast though."

"That doesn't matter. I'm in no hurry. By the way, you look much nicer without that horrible beard."

He rubbed his bare chin. "Thanks. It feels better too."

*"...some victims develop a yellow pallor which has led to the Mayor of New York calling the outbreak the Yellow Death..."*

Sarah picked up the remote control again. "Do you mind if I turn this thing off? It's giving me the creeps."

"No problem."

*"...W.H.O. has confirmed this is not a Coronavirus related disease, but a completely new—"*

The screen went blank.

"That's better," Sarah said. "As if there aren't enough bad things happening without talk of a new disease. Plague indeed!"

John ate his toast in silence.

# Chapter Twenty-One

# Kim & The Outbreak

TIMELINE: At the time of the Yellow Death

> "There are no great humans, only great challenges that ordinary humans are forced by circumstances to meet."
> William F Halsey (1882–1959)

Like John and Sarah, millions of UK citizens learnt of the new 'Yellow Death' disease the same morning over breakfast as they watched in horror at the events in America. In South London, one of those people was Kim Sullivan. She rushed to get herself and her three-year-old daughter ready to leave the house—whilst keeping an eye on the television.

"...*unconfirmed reports of the National Guard firing live ammunition on civilians trying to break out of the cordon in Bedminster...*"

Katy sat at the kitchen table, stirring her Coco Pops with a spoon. "Mama, where's Daddy?"

"Daddy's not here Katy. Remember, I told you he had to go to Bristol to visit Grampy 'cos he's a bit poorly? Now eat up your cereal quickly, there's a good girl. Mummy needs to get to work."

*"...claimed that photographs posted on Facebook showing long queues outside hospitals are fakes and were actually taken during the last Covid-19 pandemic..."*

Kim glanced at her wristwatch and cursed under her breath. Leaving for work in the morning was always a rush. Without Nigel here to help, she had fallen behind schedule. She checked herself in the mirror whilst waiting for Katy to empty her bowl. An independent observer would have described Kim as an attractive thirty-two-year-old, with her jet black shoulder length hair framing an oval face with striking ebony eyes. Yet Kim saw only limp hair, smudged lipstick, and puffy eyes.

"Katy, pleeeese hurry up, we have to go."

Twenty minutes later, Kim pulled into her mother's driveway. She grabbed Katy from her safety seat and rushed to the front door, pressing the bell several times.

Kim glanced at her wristwatch again. "Come on, come on."

"Mummy, will Daddy be home tonight?"

"Not tonight, darling. He'll be staying with Grampy for a few days yet, but maybe we can Facetime him, okay?"

Kim surveyed the oppressive grey clouds, which were about to piss down on them. Where the hell was her mother?

The door opened. Rachel was an older version of Kim, but with shorter hair. Rachel considered ageing to be an enemy to be resisted, so did not tolerate a single grey hair. "Ah, Katy, how are you today? I see you've brought Panda with you, lovely. Do come in, I've got the telly on ready for you to watch Peppa Pig."

"Yay!" Katy rushed past Rachel into the living room.

Kim handed Katy's bag to Rachel. "I can't talk, I'm late. See you about six?"

"Fine, whenever you're ready. I'll give Katy some tea before you arrive. Oh, by the way, did you see those terrible news reports about the plague—"

"Sorry Mum, I really have to go. I'm late and the traffic's awful this morning. Speak tonight, yes?"

During the drive to the Library where she worked, Kim would normally tune her radio to Capital, where upbeat music and banal showbiz gossip would cheer her up. Today she switched to BBC Radio 4 where the *Today* programme was covering the situation in New York. Hard facts were vanishingly rare, with only a mish-mash of conflicting stories. A virologist claimed this outbreak to be a hoax, since no virus could spread as fast as the reports suggested.

When Kim pulled into the Library car park—five minutes late—she knew little more than when she left home. She hoped the situation was exaggerated. After all, they had become used to new diseases appearing regularly: bird flu; swine flu; Mad Cow disease; bat blight; Coronavirus, and so forth. The first reports were always worrisome. The media inevitably jumped on the story and predicted the end of the world. When it became clear the new disease was manageable, the media would speculate about mutations into something worse. Kim wanted reassurance this was a false alarm.

She entered the Library through the main doors and relaxed before mouthing the word "Sorry" to her colleague who was supervising the information desk. The Library oozed an atmosphere of studious calm, which was the main reason she loved her job. That and the books—the Library was one of the few places with more books than her house.

Most days in the Library passed in a flash. Not today. Kim looked at the wall clock every few minutes. She noticed few customers, with only the internet terminals being used. Sometimes the Library felt more of a technology hub than a book repository. She hated it last year when the council had replaced bookshelves with yet another bank of computer workstations.

Her colleagues talked incessantly about the outbreak, or followed the news on their phones—usually both at the same time.

When Kim finally left work, she was weary of idle speculation, so played music in the car. She almost forgot about the situation until a car pulled up next to her with both occupants wearing face masks.

*Christ Almighty! It didn't take long for panic to start.*

After a day of listening to doom-mongering, Kim wanted a bottle of wine. They usually only drank at weekends but, with Nigel absent and all this crazy talk, she would make an exception. Kim made a minor diversion to the nearby Tesco Express.

The store was crowded—way more than normal. Customers packed shopping trolleys with essentials. Most people went about their business in silence with a sense of urgency. No casual browsing of the special offer shelves today. Grab and go was the order of the day. The atmosphere was contagious, so Kim felt the urge to join in. She loaded milk, bread, and cheese into her basket—not sure if she needed any, but best to be on the safe side.

In the drinks aisle, the shelves of bottled water were almost empty. She reached for the last five-litre bottle, but another woman grabbed it first. Their eyes met, and they both smiled politely.

"It's okay, you have it," Kim said. "I've probably got plenty at home, anyway." She lied, but wanted to avoid a confrontation.

"Thanks, it's all gone crazy, hasn't it?"

"I'm sure it's nothing." Kim noticed the woman's trolley had enough toilet rolls to supply an army.

The woman saw Kim's eyes focus on her hoard and hurried off, looking guilty.

*Toilet rolls. Toilet rolls. Remember Covid. Whenever there's a crisis, everyone runs out of toilet paper.*

She strode to the toiletries aisle to be greeted with more empty shelves.

"For God's sake, what's wrong with everyone?"

Kim's chest felt tight and her breathing became rapid and shallow. She needed to collect Katy, then get back home fast. To close the front door and feel safe.

Neither of the self-service tills was working. The queue for the only supervised till stretched along an entire aisle. Even so, most folks left a gap between themselves and the person in front. A woman pulled her scarf up over her face.

"Shit! I don't have time for this." Kim set her basket down on a stack of Coke cans and left the shop empty-handed.

That evening, alone with Katy, she missed Nigel terribly. After Kim had put Katy to bed, she sat on the sofa wishing she had bought that bottle of wine after all. She sat through the news reports and the special documentary on Channel 4 about the crisis. They covered the quarantine around New York and showed horrific pictures of panicked citizens fleeing the city. Thousands of video clips showing chaos and panic were uploaded onto YouTube and social media every hour.

If Nigel had been with her, they would have talked about it at length and made plans together. Being alone at this time sucked. Before he left, they had agreed he would call her when he could. Kim's eyes kept wandering to the phone, willing it to ring. She dozed off, hugging a cushion. When the telephone rang, it took a few seconds for her to remember where she was.

"Hello?"

*"Kim, it's me. How are you?"*

"Oh, Nigel, thank God. I was hoping you'd phone."

*"Is something wrong?"*

"Only the entire world going mad."

*"Oh right, the Yellow Death thing. That's partly why I'm phoning. How's Katy managing without her favourite parent?"*

"She's fine. I don't think she's realised you've gone yet."

*"Ha, ha."*

"How's your Dad?"

*"Not too bad. He's in hospital and having a battery of tests. They still don't know why he collapsed. It might have been a mini-stroke. He'll probably be coming home tomorrow, but they'll be doing further tests over the next few weeks."*

"That's a relief. Thank God it's nothing too serious. Do you know when you're coming back? I miss you—there's a backlog of laundry and dishes building up."

*"I'm sure there is. I must show you how to use the washing machine, one of these days. Seriously though, about me coming back—I was actually going to suggest the opposite. How about you and Katy coming down here to stay with us for a few days?"*

"Oh, I see. Er... Won't that be difficult with your dad coming home? He'll need looking after."

*"Clearly, it's not ideal, but I'm worried about this Yellow Death thing."*

Kim was taken aback. Surely the idea of fleeing London for the countryside must be an overreaction?

*"Kim? Are you still there?"*

"Sorry, yes. I was just surprised. There've only been cases in New York, hasn't there?"

*"So they say—if you believe them—which I don't. But if they're telling the truth, how long will it stay confined? I trust nothing coming from the Government. I certainly don't trust them to tell us if cases turn up in London. Their priority would be to prevent panic. Look at what's happened in New York."*

"Yes, but tomorrow? I'd have to pack for me and Katy. I've got work, I can't just not turn up. Katy has kindergarten tomorrow—they're doing some sort of baking and she's so looking forward to it. And what about my mum? I can't run off and abandon her."

*"Bring your Mother if you want to. She can sleep in my parent's caravan in the garden."*

"Ha! Good luck getting Mum to sleep in a caravan."

"Well, we'll sort something else out then. The important thing is that we're all together."

"Nige, this is very good of your parents, but it's all too quick. Let me try to get time off work and I'll speak to Mum. There's no need to panic—one day won't make any difference."

*"Well, okay, I suppose. We'll see how it develops. But keep your eyes on the news. If things get worse, I want you ready to jump in the car at a moment's notice."*

"Oh, Nigel, you're so masterful."

"I'm serious."

"Sorry, okay. We'll talk about it tomorrow. But you check with your dad when he gets home. I suspect the last thing he wants when he's convalescing is a bunch of refugees landing on his doorstep."

"Nonsense, he always loves to see Katy…and you, of course."

"Of course. Listen, I'm bushed, it's bloody hard work without you here and I need to get to bed. Give my love to your Mum."

*"Will do, love you."*

☣☣☣☣

The situation deteriorated the next day. On the breakfast news, there were reports of outbreaks in other US cities plus rumours of thousands dying in New York. A White House Press Release warned against fake news. Kim watched a video on YouTube purporting to show long rows of bodies outside a New York hospital. The scene was chilling—but was it real, or some idiot's idea of a joke? No doubt some people would take bizarre pleasure from using AI to generate deep fake videos. You could not trust anything these days. Even the BBC made mistakes sometimes.

In London, life continued almost like normal. This was still a 'foreign' problem. Kim went to work as usual and Katy attended kindergarten. However, an undertone of menace and suspicion haunted the streets. Everyone waited for the inevitable announcement about the disease reaching the UK. The Government provided bland reassurances which reassured nobody.

That evening, when Katy was asleep in bed, Kim sat in front of the television eating a bland macaroni-cheese ready-meal. Her phone rang and she smiled when Nigel's name popped up on the screen.

"Hi Nige."

*"Hi Kim, how's things? How's Katy?"*

"Just a sec while I switch off the TV. That's it. We're all good. Not died of the plague yet."

*"Ha, ha. Very funny."*

"Sorry. Katy made a gingerbread man at kindergarten today."

*"Excellent. Did it taste good?"*

"How dare you! Mr Ginger is now Katy's new best friend. She's taken him to bed with her and I don't think he's going to be eaten anytime soon."

*"Oh dear. And what happens when Mr Ginger starts to become Mr Mouldy?"*

"I'm hoping by then we'll all be back together and you can deal with her temper tantrum."

*"I can hardly wait. Have you decided about coming down here?"*

"Sure. I have to go to work tomorrow, but I've booked a weeks' holiday starting the next day. In a week, we'll have a much better idea whether this is serious. There's no way Mum's coming, though. She said she'd lived in that house for forty years and she was planning to die in it."

*"Well, let's hope that's not soon. Are you sure you have to work tomorrow?"*

"Yes. If I want a job to go back to. Which I do by the way. This isn't the end of the world, y'know."

*"Okay, fine. Fingers crossed that things don't get any worse. I read the Government has plans to cut off London if there's an outbreak."*

"Rubbish. Where did you read that—Scaremonger.com?"

*"Actually, I think it was The Guardian."*

"Well, even so, they couldn't possibly know for sure. The media are speculating like everyone else. Anyway, there hasn't been a single case in the UK. All flights from the US are cancelled. With luck we may escape it."

*"Yeah, we'll see. Stable doors and all that."*

"Listen, Mr Pessimist. The day after tomorrow, you and me sipping Prosecco as we admire the view over the Bristol channel. Yes?"

*"It's a date. Have we still got those boxes of face masks somewhere?"*

"I don't know. If we have, they must be in the garage."

*"See if you can hunt them out and bring them with you, will you? I tried to order some online today and everywhere's sold out."*

"You're kidding. What's got into everyone?"

*"I expect most people are being cautious, like me. Nobody wants to get caught out. Mom's gone and ordered a massive grocery delivery with lots of long-life milk and stuff, just in case."*

"Why am I not surprised? By the way, how's your dad?"

*"He's back home with us. Very chipper. It's as if it never happened. This afternoon we had to stop him from going out to mow the lawn. He hates enforced resting and being treated as an invalid."*

"Fantastic news. I'm glad to hear something's going well today. Give your parents my love."

*"I will. Mum's already started baking cakes and biscuits for you and Katy. If you don't get here soon, they'll overwhelm us."*

"Please remind her I'm supposed to be on a diet."

*"Sorry. Mum doesn't recognise that word. When she gets stressed, she starts baking. You'll have to sneak a few biscuits under the table for the dog."*

"I can't do that. Benji already needs to be dieting more than me. He's the fattest labrador in Bristol."

*"Fair enough. We'll just have to put the excess biscuits into stock for the apocalypse."*

"That's not funny anymore. I'm officially banning all jokes about the end of the world."

☣☣☣☣

The following day, Kim overheard a conversation about people presenting at London hospitals with symptoms of the plague. The Government strongly asserted that all was well and preparations were in place in the 'unlikely' event the disease crossed the Atlantic. The Transport Minister announced an immediate forty-eight hours ban on flights in and out of the UK. The Scottish Assembly unilaterally closed the border between England and Scotland, which brought vitriolic outrage from Westminster. This rather negated the Government's assurances that the situation was under control.

Kim saw the effect of the crisis everywhere. Three library staff phoned in sick, although nobody believed they were ill. It didn't matter, since the library remained deserted. Long queues formed outside local stores and petrol stations. Shops limited the number of items which could be purchased. It became commonplace to see people wearing masks. If anybody dared sneeze, they would find themselves in a very lonely place.

More than anything that day, the atmosphere of distrust and alarm lurking just below the surface unsettled Kim. Strangers would stare at you in the street, looking for any sign of illness. It seemed every individual had developed a magnetic field which repelled everyone else. People went about their business with heads down, faces covered. Citizens were scared.

And still the Government denied any cases in the UK.

"Hello Mum."

*"Oh, hello, Kim. How are you?"*

"I'm all packed and ready to go first thing tomorrow. Are you sure you won't come with us? Even if this plague thingy doesn't hit us, everything's gone crazy. It'll be nice to get out into the countryside."

*"It's very kind of Nigel's parents to invite me, but you know we don't really get on with each other. I've got plenty of food, so I'm happy to hunker down until this madness passes."*

"I don't like leaving you here alone. What if this doesn't just pass?"

The silence stretched out.

"Mum?"

*"Sorry. I was just—it doesn't matter. Listen, Kim. You need to be with your husband. Hopefully, this will turn out to be an unexpected holiday for you and you'll have a great time. If not...well, then your family still needs to be together. Either way, you're better off in Bristol with Nigel. But my home is here, no matter what."*

After putting the phone down, Kim felt bereft. She hated the idea of leaving her mother behind. But the desperate urge to get away from London was irresistible. She looked at her watch. Eleven-thirty. Perhaps she should leave now? Drive through the night? No, she was too exhausted. It would be crazy to fall asleep at the wheel and crash the car. Tomorrow would be fine. First thing tomorrow they would get out of London.

☣ ☣ ☣ ☣

Sleep eluded Kim. She lay in bed, completely washed-out, yet her mind raced. Had she packed everything she needed? She must remember to shut off the heating and water before she left tomorrow. She must remember to clear out the fridge before they left. Oh, and she had to phone Katy's pre-school and tell them she was away for a few days. So much to remember.

Kim climbed out of bed. She looked in on Katy, then grabbed a notepad, before returning to bed.

*Okay, let's write down everything I need to do tomorrow. Get it off my mind, so I won't forget anything.*

Her list grew. As she wrote the various tasks, her mind felt lighter. Eventually, Kim found herself dropping off to sleep with pen in hand. She jolted awake.

*Damn! Did I set my phone alarm to wake me up tomorrow?*

Kim picked up her phone and checked the alarm settings. She could not resist tapping on the BBC News app and at once regretted it. Every item on the Top Story's page was plague related.

A deep sense of unease permeated every bone in her body. Once again, she left her bed and went to Katy's room. Katy slept peacefully.

*Get a grip on yourself, Kim. You're losing it. You have to keep strong for Katy.*

Kim made a hot water bottle, which normally soothed her. She soon overheated and tossed it on the floor. The time was two a.m. She felt so alone and so wanted to speak to Nigel again. But if his phone went off at this time, it might wake up his parents and she couldn't risk that. Damn!

Finally, Kim picked up her Kindle and switched off her bedside lamp. She was part-way through reading *'Flowers In The Attic'* about a family who kept their children hidden in the loft of their home. It was a poor choice, given the circumstances. Kim's eyes mechanically scanned the words on her Kindle, although their meaning skimmed over her consciousness, like pebbles across the water.

Before long, her troubled mind could no longer resist the need for sleep and her eyelids closed...

Kim gazed at the many birthday cards on her bedroom window and bookshelves. She had turned thirteen the previous week, and her party had been a lavish affair with many gifts. Children and adults she did not even recognise turned up. She had revelled in being the centre of attention. After all, she was a teenager now—almost a woman.

The sound of laughing in the street drew her to the window. Her bedroom was on the second floor, providing an excellent view of the comings and goings below. At the weekends, she would see people leaving their houses, dressed up to enjoy London's nightlife, and she would imagine joining them. In a few years, a handsome man would escort her to the ballet in his posh limousine. Life was good and the future exciting.

Kim surveyed her bedroom. On the opposite wall was a poster of the Russian ballet and, to her left and right, bookshelves strained under the weight of her personal library. Kim was an avid book reader and collector. She loved old books, especially if they carried inscriptions and notes from previous owners. An antique book was a piece of history. Sometimes, she would open one of her vintage volumes and sniff the pages, imagining all the people who held it before her.

Kim loved her bedroom. Her sanctuary. Mother allowed her to help choose the furnishings, and it contained all her prized possessions.

At that moment, she was completing her homework. Mom was out as usual. On Thursdays, it was the bridge club. In the past, Dad used to go with her, but nowadays he was always too busy—due to his important government job. So Dad stayed at home to look after Kim and Toby, which meant shutting himself away in his office.

Father expected his children to stay in their bedrooms and not disturb him doing his secret government business. That suited Kim fine. Except tonight would be different.

A curt rapping on her the door startled her. Dad walked in and closed it behind him. Kim swivelled her chair to face him. He was a tall man with a receding hairline, which he tried to conceal with careful combing. Kim rarely saw him out of a business suit and he wore one now, although it was creased.

"Hello Kimi," Dad said. "What are you doing?"

"Just some stupid French homework. Why do we have to learn French, anyway? Can't they all speak English?"

Normally, that might have sparked an interesting discussion, but tonight, he seemed distant.

"It's the law. We have to pander to the bureaucrats," he said.

He meandered around her room, examining it as if he had never seen it before. He scanned her books on the shelves, her ornaments, and jewellery box. Then he began touching them, almost like a blind man feeling his way. His fingers traced the outline of Orlando Bloom's face on her 'Lord of the Rings' poster. During this examination, he said nothing. It started to creep Kim out. This was her stuff, her personal stuff, and he was invading her privacy. Kim stiffened as his hand passed over her journal, and sighed with relief when he left it alone.

He snapped out of his reverie, locked the door, and put the key in his jacket pocket. Kim and Toby both had locks on their doors, but no key. The keys were for locking them in their rooms when they needed to be punished. Kim could not remember a time when Dad had locked himself in the bedroom with her and could think of no good reason for doing so. Kim's chest tightened and her breathing became fast and shallow. Instinct told her to run. To get away. Something terrible was about to happen. But she was trapped.

"I need you to do something for me, Kimi," Father said with a stern voice.

"Okay." Kim's voice came out as little more than a squeak.

Her stomach churned, and the room suddenly felt hot and stuffy. She had never seen Dad act this way. This was all so wrong. She must get away.

"Come over here, please."

Kim rose up on shaky legs and stood in front of her father. Had she done something wrong? Had she broken one of the many rules she and Toby needed to follow? At least he wasn't carrying the feared hosepipe.

"Get down on your knees."

"What?"

"Do not question me. Get down on your knees. I will not ask you again."

Kim did as she was told, her breath coming in shallow gasps. Her head was level with his crotch, so she stared at the floor. Without ceremony, he unzipped his trousers and released his penis, which jutted out at attention.

Kim gasped. Never had she seen an erect penis in real life and now her Dad's hovered inches from her head. A stench of of stale urine and cheese struck her, so she screwed up her face. She tried to stand up, but he pressed down on her shoulder.

"Stay," he commanded, as if speaking to a dog. She stayed and trembled, eyes closed tightly.

"Now Kim," he said, "I want you to lick it...lick it, slowly."

Kim opened her eyes and looked up in disbelief.

"What? I don't understand."

He took out a short piece of hosepipe from the inside of his jacket. Kim recognised it as the instrument used for giving stern lessons. Her spine turned to ice.

"I said lick it. NOW!"

Kim woke with a start, gasping for air. The room was dark, and she lay in bed.

"Fuck, fuck, fuck!"

She had not endured that particular nightmare for years. Not since she finished with all the psychotherapy shit her mother put her through. She hoped that was all behind her—that awful part of her life was locked behind firm mental doors—wasn't it? Why now?

Kim walked to the bathroom and drank cold water from the tap. Her pyjamas stuck to her back, so she pulled off her top and threw it into the laundry basket.

It was obvious 'why now' when she thought about it. After years of therapy for depression and anorexia, she built herself a fortress to protect her from the past. This comprised a nice job, a loving husband, a pleasant home, and now a wonderful daughter. Those may not be exciting and not what she dreamed of when she was a little girl. Yet her life was safe, comfortable, secure, and predictable. Considering her history, this comforting security was all she wanted.

After graduating from university, a friend talked Kim into taking up karate against her better nature. The formality of the dojo brought comfort. Everyone dressed the same and gender was left at the entrance. With time, Kim's strength and agility magnified, but more importantly, she regained confidence in herself. She had passed three grades and wore an orange belt when one of her fellow students asked her out on a date.

Nigel was an incongruity. A black belt who could split a plank of wood with his fist, yet was gentle, caring, shy—and handsome. He treated her like a princess. Nigel helped Kim move on with her life and put the horrors of her teenage years behind her.

But overnight, the world had gone to shit, and the future was a black hole. Nigel—her rock—was not here to hold her hand and reassure her. Perhaps she was more fragile than she thought. Recent events must have stirred up memories and resurrected insecurities. It seemed her past had not been buried deep enough.

Kim opened the door to Katy's bedroom to reassure herself. Katy slept safely. Katy was perfect. Katy was pure. Katy had a lovingly devoted mother and father who would make sure she received the best of everything. No man was ever going to force his dick into Katy's mouth. No man was ever going to thrash her with a piece of hosepipe.

Kim returned to bed, but sleep eluded her. A door in her mind had been kicked open, and she did not know how to shut it. She feared falling asleep and putting herself at the mercy of her inner mind again.

Unfinished business. That was what the psychologist mentioned at their umpteenth session together. Kim never had an inkling why her father broke the sacred trust with his daughter.

He never apologised, never explained, made no attempt to contact her. Years passed, then he died of a stroke. Any chance of resolution, or understanding had passed. Unfinished business.

The situation was different with her mother—to an extent. Kim saw Rachel most days, and she was the devoted grandparent. On the surface, they had a close relationship. On the surface. Yet Kim knew she held a deep resentment of her mother. After three years of abuse, Kim finally escaped by videoing a session with her father and showing it to Rachel. The consequences were unexpected.

Rachel sent Kim to live with her aunt and uncle. The story given to friends was Kim needed to be closer to school. Nobody believed it, but nobody questioned it. In London's polite society, one did not delve too deeply. Rachel protected Kim from her father and made sure she wanted for nothing. At the weekends, Rachel, Kim, and Toby went on outings together. Life appeared to be very polite and civilised.

Yet they banished Kim from the family home whilst he still lived there, unpunished.

He got off scot-free!

Worse still, that thing could never be mentioned. The past became a closely guarded family secret. Kim never found out whether Aunty Helen knew the real reason she moved in with her. Everyone acted as if nothing had ever happened. The injustice was eating up Kim from the inside.

Months later, Kim collapsed at school and was rushed to hospital to be diagnosed with anorexia. That became the start of a long course of psychotherapy, which only ended when Kim moved out to university.

After dozens of counselling sessions, evaluations, interventions, hypnotherapy, and drugs, the mental health service discharged Kim. But she still remembered the words from the counsellor in her last session. Unfinished business. She felt deep bitterness towards her parents. Yet her father lay in his grave and her mother resolutely refused to discuss the subject. Kim would have to learn to live with it. A wound that had never healed, and this pandemic had picked off the scab.

☣☣☣☣

Making an early start with a small child is easier said than done. The situation was made worse by Kim's lack of sleep and the feeling her head was stuffed with cotton wool. Thus, it was mid-morning before a hot and bothered Kim pulled away from their house with Katy strapped in the rear seat. The car had been crammed with luggage. Dark grey clouds hung low in the sky, which only added to her feeling of apprehension.

The morning news was all bad. Official sources at last admitted suspected plague victims had presented at several London hospitals. Unconfirmed reports claimed some had already died. Each time a journalist mentioned the 'plague' word, Kim's anxiety raised a notch.

The Government advised the public to stay at home unless their journey was essential. Schools and non-essential shops closed, as did most Government and Local Authority offices—including libraries. The UK was close to a full lockdown.

Yet the Prime Minister advised everyone not to panic. These actions were an "abundance of caution". He gave a stuttering speech in the rain and tried to evoke the 'Dunkirk' spirit. "Britain shall prevail".

Kim feared travelling in case the police stopped her for breaking the lockdown. Yet the thought of staying in the city was unthinkable, so she continued with her plans.

Kim's fingers itched to switch on the car radio for the latest news—even if it was little more than speculation. But with Katy listening in the back, she chose a 'Postman Pat' CD. They both sang along to the music as if this was a normal day.

The journey began well but, after half-an-hour, traffic congestion built up. Many cars were stuffed with baggage, so Kim realised she was not alone in breaking the lockdown. Faith in the Government seemed thin on the ground.

When they reached the M4, a cloud of drizzle enveloped the traffic snake. Kim frequently used the windscreen washers to clear the muck thrown up from the road. She tried to remember when she last filled the washer bottle under the bonnet. Vehicles packed closer and became slower until, shortly before junction five, progress came to a halt. The opposite carriageway back to London was empty.

Kim sat for twenty minutes, becoming increasingly frustrated. The queue moved a few yards twice. The log jam disappeared into the mist.

"Mummy, I'm thirsty."

"I know, darling. I'm sorry, but silly Mummy forgot to pack the juice boxes. We'll pull into a shop as soon as we can, okay?"

Another hour passed with no movement. Everyone had turned off their engines, and many now stood on the road. Kim followed suit to stretch her legs. Shouted conversations took place along the line of stranded drivers:

"This is worse than a bloody bank holiday."

"They just said on Capital radio they've blocked off roads out of London."

"So are we in or out of the road block?"

"I dunno, they didn't say."

"Look at those idiots driving down the hard shoulder. What if there's an emergency?"

"I've been trying to get through to the AA for the past half-hour, but it just keeps ringing. Not even a recorded message."

"The BBC just said the PM's in a COBRA meeting and he'll be making a special announcement within the hour."

"Oh, great. I feel so much better already."

"About bloody time they took control of this mess."

Kim paced back and forth, nibbling her fingernails. Her mouth had become dry, and she cursed not bringing a bottle of water. A sense of complete helplessness gnawed at her belly. She picked up her phone to call Nigel and her mother, to let them know the situation, but the screen displayed 'no network'. How could there be no network? Other people complained their phones had stopped working—some received a message reporting a temporary outage because of essential maintenance.

Men relieved themselves at the side of the motorway. Kim envied them, regretting her last cup of coffee before leaving.

A police helicopter buzzed overhead like an angry wasp.

An awareness of foreboding and intense wrongness settled upon Kim. She stood on one of the country's major highways, which had become a giant car park. How long could this go on for? What if people left their vehicles and started walking? A few abandoned cars would permanently block the road. Where were the authorities? Why wasn't somebody sorting this out?

The opposite carriageway remained clear. The thought of taking down the central barrier occurred to her. A group of men began talking about it. She needed to do something—this waiting and not knowing was excruciating. But she had to stay strong for Katy.

"Mommy, I want pee-pee."

*Oh, God, no. That's all I need.*

"Okay darling. Just a minute. You'll have to go on the grass verge."

*So will I, if things don't get moving soon.*

A few cars away, somebody shouted. "Wait, listen everyone."

The talking stopped and, in the distance, the roaring of engines starting could be heard—hundreds of them—a veritable tsunami of noise rushing towards her. The crowd cheered and Kim could not help smiling as she started her own car engine.

At last, they began moving. Initially, their motion was start-stop-start-stop, but after a few hundred yards, they picked up speed and a few drivers tooted their horns. Vehicles sped from the other direction, going into London. The blockage must have been cleared.

"We're on our way again, Katy. We'll stop at the next service station. Everything's going to be okay now."

The euphoria did not last long. After a mile, they came to a massive roadblock of commercial trucks, military vehicles, and police cars. Both the soldiers and police were armed and appeared cautious. A long section of central barrier was missing. Traffic was being directed to move onto the opposite carriageway and go back towards London.

"No, no, no, no. This can't be!"

Kim was desperate to pull over and reason with them. She had to get to Bristol. But cars, trucks, and vans were packed tightly together, so she was carried along with the tide of humanity. Those few drivers who stopped to protest were waved on—no exceptions. The guards stood unresponsive at the shouted pleas.

An hour later, Kim and Katy arrived home. Kim went to phone Nigel, but her mobile had no network. She sent a text, hoping it would work through the system. Bristol seemed very far away.

## Chapter Twenty-Two

# JOHN & THE OUTBREAK

TIMELINE: AT THE TIME OF THE YELLOW DEATH

"Courage is resistance to fear, mastery of fear - not absence of fear."

                          Mark Twain (1835–1910)

John returned to his chalet after breakfast with his mother, then switched on the TV. The BBC News channel gave the outbreak in America exclusive coverage.

John listened as he went through his physio exercises. For each gram of hard fact, there was a mountain of speculation. The same reports and videos repeated every few minutes with the words 'unsubstantiated' and 'unconfirmed' being used liberally.

A distinguished professor of contagious diseases gave a reassuring assessment. He claimed this was only mass panic, fuelled by media conjecture. The Coronavirus pandemic had sensitised the public, and consequently, we were seeing a massive overreaction to the latest new story. The only thing viral is the spread on social media. Infectious diseases could not travel as fast as news reports showed. Thus, the vast majority of cases will prove to be everyday ailments such as the common cold. Blah, blah, blah.

It all sounded reasonable—if this was a genuine expert sharing his honest views. But John suspected the speaker was a government stooge reading a script prepared years ago for the express purpose of avoiding panic.

John switched off the television, feeling none the wiser and with a sense of unease. Everyone had underestimated COVID-19. Would this be the same?

☣☣☣☣

For the next two days, the crisis in America dominated the news and continued to worsen. The US President confirmed rumours this was a variant of the 'Black Death' plague and said the disease responded well to antibiotics. He assured the nation the situation was under control and there was no need to panic.

Meanwhile, medical services in several US cities became overwhelmed. Many towns took matters into their own hands by putting up blockades and declaring quarantines.

On the third day, social media became rampant with reports of cases turning up in London hospitals, displaying similar symptoms to the so-called Yellow Death. At a press conference, the Prime Minister called for calm. The UK was prepared for any eventuality. He assured the nation the situation was under control and there was no need to panic.

The Secretary General of the World Health Organisation pitched in. She announced the WHO was monitoring developments closely, with specialist teams dispatched to assist and provide first-hand reports. The public should know that since the Coronavirus pandemic, a number of robust measures had been introduced to monitor and manage new infectious diseases. She assured all citizens that the situation was under control and there was no need to panic.

So many reassurances. So why was nobody reassured?

John soaked up as much information as he could, whilst his mother strove to avoid it. Hence, the disease became a subject he never raised in her company. Normally a loner, he itched to talk about this with somebody else—but he had no one.

His back pain reduced daily, so he continued to take breakfast with his mother in her house. She always had a reason to walk to the local shops, and he gladly agreed to escort her for company. Today, the mission was to stock up on baking products.

The day was overcast and cool as John and Sarah strolled towards the village boundary, where hedgerow gave way to picturesque cottages.

Sarah took a deep breath. "Oh, just smell that."

John sniffed the air. "Smell what?"

"The air. It's so clean and fresh. The flowers, the grass. Nature's fragrance. We're so lucky to live in this part of the world."

John sniffed again. He could discern the sweet aroma of some flower or other, and the air did indeed feel fresh. He usually took it for granted—it was just air.

"What on earth's going on down there?" Sarah said, pointing further down the road.

John had been scrolling on his mobile phone, but looked up towards the village. "Has there been an accident?"

They heard shouting.

"No, John, I don't think it's an accident. It looks like a tractor was trying to turn around and got stuck. What a silly place to turn, with the road being so narrow there."

The tractor was ancient, with most of its blue paint replaced with rust. It pulled an even more decrepit trailer, and they were completely blocking the lane, preventing a silver BMW from getting through. The BMW's horn sounded several times.

"Somebody's impatient," Sarah said.

The BMW driver and his female companion were standing by their car with the doors open.

"You've got no bloody right!" the driver shouted.

John recognised the farmer in the tractor as a local man called Eddie. John knew he was in his forties, but his weather-beaten face made him look much older. Curly ginger hair poked out from under a flat cap.

The tractor's engine was not running and Eddie brandished a double-barrelled shotgun. "This gives me the right," he shouted back at the driver.

"Better stay here, Mum," John said.

"Nonsense, this is the most exciting thing to happen in years."

She quickened her pace.

"Listen here. My name's Travis Stiles and I own a bloody house next to the church. I've got every right to come through your blockade."

"I'm sorry, mate," Eddie said. "I've got my orders. Nobody gets past. Nobody."

"Whose orders?" Sarah shouted as she approached.

"Oh, hello Sarah," Eddie said. "It's the Parish Council. Had an emergency meetin' this morning. Most of the villagers turned up. Sorry, you didn't get an invite. It was all a bit of a rush, like. Anyway, they voted to quarantine us for the time being as a precaution. 'Till we know more about what's happening. Nobody comes in and, anyone who leaves don't come back."

"Oh my God!" Sarah said. "That'll be Michael Moore, the officious little toad. It's ridiculous."

"That's what I've been saying," Travis said.

"Ridiculous or not. That's how it is," Eddie said, brandishing his shotgun.

"And what are you going to do—shoot me?" Travis challenged.

"Well, maybe I will and maybe I won't," Eddie said. "But I'll start by shooting that pretty set of wheels of yours." He lowered his shotgun and pointed it at the car windscreen.

"You wouldn't bloody dare," Travis shouted, pulling his mobile phone out of his jacket. "This is fucking insane. It's illegal. I'm calling the police."

Eddie appeared to be uncomfortable. They waited while Travis listened to his phone whilst tapping his fingers on the car roof. "Whole bloody country's gone to pot. They're not even answering a 999 call."

"Let me try, Travis," said his passenger, pulling out her phone, encased in a pink jewel-encrusted case.

Sarah also took her phone from her handbag. "I've got the direct number of the local police station," she whispered to John.

Travis threw his phone on the car seat in disgust. "Look here, man, I've driven six hours solid from London to get here. You wouldn't believe what the roads are like."

"Well then," Eddie said. "You'd best get started back soon, 'cause you've got a long way to go."

Travis reached into his jacket and pulled out his wallet. "If it's a question of money, I've got...let me see—"

"Put that away, city boy. Now you're really pissin' me off."

A young man appeared from behind the tractor's trailer and jumped on the tow bar. He was dressed in scruffy clothing and had a mass of curly ginger hair, making him look a younger version of Eddie. John recognised Jack—the guy in the pub who had tried to flirt with Britney on their first date together.

"What's going on, Dad? Oh, hello there, Mrs C."

"Nothin' to worry about, son," Eddie said. "This here gentleman is just deciding he doesn't want to visit our village after all."

"Oh, hello Jack," said Sarah. "How's your Mother doing?"

"Mum's much better now, thanks, Mrs C. The doctor gave her a tonic yesterday."

Travis's companion piped up. "Travis, I can't get through to the police either. They're just not answering. It's disgraceful."

"Let's get out of here," Travis said to his companion. "This is turning into some sort of fucking village meeting. We'll drive to the Police Station and demand some service. I don't know what we pay our sodding council tax for."

The car doors slammed, and the engine revved as it reversed. Travis shouted through the window. "You haven't heard the last of this."

Jack shouted back. "Mind you don't scratch your shiny paintwork on the hedgerow, now."

Eddie chuckled, "Sodding blow-ins."

Sarah whispered into John's ear. "I've tried phoning the station direct and they're not answering either. It's very strange."

She glanced up at Eddie. "Now we've got them out of the way, how do we get past?"

"Sorry, Sarah, nobody comes past. Nobody. Not even you, I'm afraid."

"Goodness me, Eddie. You can't mean that?"

"Mr Moore was most insistent. Anybody who's out of the cordon stays out."

"And what would you do if I simply walked past your little road block? Are you intending to shoot me?"

"Oh come on now, Sarah. You know I won't do that. But you'll get me in terrible trouble with Mr Moore. A quarantine's no good if folks just keep ignoring it."

"He's right, Mum," John said. "It makes sense."

"Well, it makes no sense to me. We're both perfectly healthy and we've been nowhere near anywhere which could have the disease."

"So you've not been near Exeter, or Barnstaple, or Ilfracombe, in the last fortnight, eh?" Eddie said.

"Barnstaple? Surely they've not gone down with it in Barnstaple?"

"T'was on Radio Devon this morning. They say they're lookin' at a dozen cases in Barnstaple. And Exeter, Ilfracombe, South Molton—it's poppin' up everywhere."

"Oh my God, John, I was in Barnstaple last week and Exeter the week before."

"Calm down, Mum," John said. "Those are big places and they might be false alarms."

Sarah thought about it. "Yes, I suppose you're right. I'm getting carried away."

"I reckon we're all getting a bit jumpy right now," Eddie said. "Let's hope this'll be like that Russian flu last year. Turned out to be nothing."

Sarah nodded and dabbed her handkerchief on her forehead. "Oh dear, well, this is rather inconvenient. I was hoping to buy some bread and flour from Diane's Pantry."

Jack piped up. "Tell you what, Mrs C. If you give me your shopping list, I'll run to the shops and get your stuff for you."

"Oh, would you dear? You're such a good boy. Here we are then. I just need to explain a few things to you."

While Jack raced off to the village centre, John and Sarah sat down on the trailer.

Sarah looked at Eddie. "Well then, you'd better tell us about this meeting."

"Okay, it started with Mr Moore walking around the centre first thing this morning with his bull-horn, calling everyone to the village green for a special meeting. He'd heard about the cases in London and a friend phoned him to say it was in Exeter."

Eddie propped up his shotgun inside the tractor cab. "So him and the rest of the parish council gathered next to the war memorial and most of the villagers joined them. He said once the news of the spread was out, people would flock from the towns and cities looking for safe havens. There might be millions on the move and it would only take one infected person to come here and the entire village would be wiped out."

John laughed. "He doesn't pull his punches, does he?"

Eddie continued. "Anyway, he said we couldn't count on the authorities to act fast enough, so we had to take matters into our own hands. He called for a quarantine, and there was an enormous cheer. I reckon most people were glad to be doing something."

"Pity nobody thought to tell us," John said.

Eddie sat down. "Sorry, John, it all happened so fast. Mr Moore organised a convoy to get as much food as they could from Barnstaple. Everyone in the convoy was to wear a face mask the whole time they were out, or we'd not let them back through the cordon."

"Well, it sounds completely over the top to me," Sarah said.

"Better safe than sorry," Eddie said. "If you two stay in your cottage, you should be safe enough. And if you run short of food, I'm sure we can arrange to leave some here for you. We won't abandon you."

John believed Michael Moore to be an arrogant, officious, pompous twit. But, on this occasion, he had judged the situation well and behaved absolutely correctly. John only wished they were not outside the cordon looking in.

☣☣☣☣

The village had turned John and Sarah into outcasts. All non-essential travel had been prohibited. They returned home to watch events unfold on the TV.

John sat it out with his mother in the cottage rather than return to his chalet. Naturally, Sarah was anxious and needed company. He was the only available choice and, unusually, being alone did not appeal to him either.

John filled every water carrier and bucket he found, then filled the bath with water.

He checked on their food supplies. Food in the freezer would feed them for a fortnight—if the electricity continued to flow. Sarah had a large larder, and canned goods were lined up on every shelf. Sarah loved baking, so they had good supplies of basic stores such as flour, eggs and dried fruit. At least they would not run short of home-made cake!

Being late summer, Sarah's small vegetable patch was in full production, so they harvested salad and fruit daily. They could pick apples and blackberries if they wanted. The cottage had an open fire, and the cooker used bottled gas.

All in all, not a bad situation. They could stay here in comfort for quite a while.

John worried about unwelcome visitors. Anyone travelling to the village would pass their cottage before being stopped at the roadblock and sent back. Those people would be angry and frustrated. Probably tired and hungry after a long, fruitless journey. What if they noticed Sarah's cottage and called in? Before his back injury, John used to practise archery in the garden. He brought his bow and arrows into the hallway, along with the axe from the shed. Sarah frowned at the sight of them, but said nothing. This was a worrying time.

Sarah spent a couple of hours making phone calls to friends and relatives. A surprising number did not answer. Those that did were afraid. Everyone was afraid. Sarah's sister experienced several short power cuts. Sarah's best friend saw youths throwing stones at an ambulance. The world had gone bonkers overnight.

Nothing seemed certain. The Government churned out reassuring statements (which were disbelieved) and instructions (that were ignored). Conflicting and unsubstantiated tales of horror abounded. Rumours were rife. Cabinet ministers contradicted each other. Lacking reliable facts, people filled in the gaps with stories and speculation.

On the television, a string of BBC foreign correspondents took it in turns to confirm cases appearing in countries around the globe. There was no pattern or perception of the disease progressing from one place to another. Mass illness sprang up everywhere simultaneously.

In the UK, queues formed outside beleaguered hospitals. A Channel 4 reporter claimed that folk with mild symptoms hoped to be first in line for antibiotics, or antiviral drugs.

This baffled John. Antibiotics and antivirals? Were they dealing with a bacterium or virus? Most reports indicated the Yellow Death was a variety of plague—a bacterial disease. If so, antivirals were worse than useless, yet people clamoured for them. Nothing made sense any more.

The Health Minister announced the Territorial Army and other reserve units were being mobilised to help with roadblocks and crowd management at hospitals. John wondered if he would get a telephone call. Although no longer on the active list, these were desperate times. Fortunately, the call never came. John was relieved, because he would not leave his mother alone at this time. If his father had been here, it might be different. But his father was never here when it mattered. It had always been just John and Sarah. He would not abandon her now.

Sarah took a deep breath. "I don't think all this is doing me any good. It's a perfectly nice day. The sun's out, the birds are singing, I'm going out to do some weeding. The lawns need mowing too, if you're up to it?"

"I'm watching the news. This is important."

"Well okay, but it might rain later, so best do it while the weather is good."

*The world's falling apart and she's bothered about the lawns. I suppose there's comfort from familiarity.*

"Okay, Mum, I'll be out in a few minutes, just finishing my coffee."

"Is there anything in particular you'd like for dinner, love?"

"No, not especially. But maybe we'd better use something from the freezer—how about a curry?"

"The freezer? Why is that, dear? Oh...I see. Yes. If you think that's best."

Sarah did not stay outside weeding for long. She developed one of her nasty headaches, probably because of the sun, she told John, so she went inside to cool down. When John came back inside after mowing the grass, Sarah was sitting hunched in the armchair. Her face had a sheen of sweat and she clutched her armpits.

She looked up pitifully. "Oh, John."

## Chapter Twenty-Three

# CAL MEETS KEN & SUE

TIMELINE: 18 MONTHS AFTER THE
YELLOW DEATH

"Everything that irritates us about others can lead us to an understanding of ourselves."
Carl Jung (1875–1961)

The day after Cal promised Juliet he would be more sociable, they were driving North-West along the A361 towards South Molton. The town had a good health centre which Juliet thought was worth checking out for supplies. The day was proving to be unusually warm, and the sun shone in an almost cloudless sky.

Juliet drove as usual, since Cal was best suited to shoot back if they came under attack. Despite Juliet looking ahead, she spotted a column of smoke a couple of hundred yards off to the right and reduced speed.

"Look Cal, over there."

Cal saw the smoke trail and his heart sank, but he steeled himself. "I suppose you'd like to have a look?"

"Yes, please."

Using only the electric motor, they crept along a narrow, overgrown lane towards the smoke, stopping while they were still too far to be heard. Cal started checking his weapons. "I don't expect there's any hope of you waiting for me in the car?"

"Sod off."

"I thought not. Okay, bring your weapon, stay a few yards behind me and keep quiet."

Juliet made a mock salute. "Yes, sir!"

Ten minutes later, they were getting close.

"Can you smell cooking? Fish?" Juliet whispered.

"Yes," Cal whispered back. "They're not making any attempt to hide themselves. Either they're not afraid of anything, or they're stupid."

"It smells good, I just realised I'm hungry."

"Want to go back and have some dinner?"

"You're not getting out of it that easily."

"Okay. We're really close now. No more talking."

They came to a hedge overlooking a wide slow-moving stream and, on the bank, was a campfire. Two people lay on towels, apparently dozing in the sun. The man was bare-chested and in his thirties. His skin was black as charcoal and his hair trimmed so short, he almost appeared bald.

Lying by his side was a woman of the same age, wearing a small red bikini. She was slim with long caramel coloured hair and massive sunglasses covering much of her face. Her skin appeared bleached compared to her companion. The pair could have been transplanted from a beach at a Mediterranean holiday resort.

The woman rolled on to her front. "Ken, can you do my back?" She handed him a bottle.

"Sure, hon," he replied, and began rubbing sunscreen over the woman's shoulders. Cal and Juliet frowned at each other. Were these folk for real?

"Are those fish nearly done yet? I'm starved," said the woman. Over the open fire, three fish sizzled on a metal plate.

"Oooh, hot, hot, hot," Ken said, after touching them with a finger. "Yeah, I think they're ready and so am I."

Cal nudged Juliet and pointed to a shotgun lying next to Ken. Juliet nodded, then put down her rifle, stood up and walked through the thin hedge, holding her hands in the air.

"No. Wait!" John mouthed, but Juliet had gone. By choice, he would have watched and waited for longer before approaching them.

"Hi there," Juliet said in a friendly voice.

Cal fixed the sights of his rifle firmly on Ken.

Ken grabbed his shotgun and pointed it at Juliet. "Stop right there," he shouted.

"Okay, okay, I don't mean any harm. I just want to talk. I can turn around and walk away if you'd rather."

The woman raised her sunglasses on to her head and appraised Juliet. "Put the fuckin' gun down Ken."

"Shut up, Susan. You'll get us killed one day."

"Yeah, yeah," Susan said, lying back on her towel. "Why are all men such pricks?"

"I think it's genetic," Juliet said.

"Are you armed?" Ken said.

"Don't be ridiculous. You can see I'm not. And now you should ask me if I'm alone."

Ken paused for a second. "Okay. Are you alone?"

"No, there's someone hidden nearby with a rifle aimed directly at your head. If we meant you any harm, you'd already be dead."

"You're bluffing."

"Well, if I'm bluffing, then I'm harmless, and you can lower your gun. And if I'm not, you're fucked and you should still lower your gun. Either way, you should lower your gun, Ken."

"Told you," Susan said.

Ken's face displayed indecision for a few seconds before he shrugged and lowered the shotgun.

"I think your fish is burning," Juliet said.

"Shit!"

"Men!" Susan said.

Cal shouldered his rifle and walked out into view.

"My name's Juliet Davenport and this is Cal. We saw your smoke from the road as we were passing."

Ken stood up and offered his hand to Juliet. "Hi, sorry about that. My name's Ken, Ken Black and please don't make any jokes. I've heard them all. This is Susan Anderson."

"Hi Juliet. Hi Cal," Susan said, continuing to lie on her front. "We were just about to eat some...slightly burned fish," she said as she watched Ken trying to loosen the fish from the hot plate. "Come and join us."

"Oh, we couldn't," Juliet said. "There's only enough for the two of you."

"Well, we're not going to eat with you looking on drooling. So you can either join us, or clear off," Susan said.

Juliet smiled. "Oh, well, since you put it like that, some fresh fish would be lovely, thanks."

The fish was moist, tender and tasty. Cal sucked the bones to get every last shred of meat. Ken told them he had caught it in the stream only an hour previously. Fishing had been his hobby before the Yellow Death and, since then, it had become a way of supplementing their diet. Ken and Susan usually camped near a river or lake, so he could provide their supper.

"Actually, you're doing me a favour by turning up," Susan said. "To be quite honest, I'm having nightmares about eating fish. I don't want to appear ungrateful, because we never go hungry, but fish every day?"

"Maybe Ken could show us how to fish?" Juliet said.

"Sure, that'd be great," Ken said. "But it's not something you can pick up overnight. I've been at it for years and still learning. I began when I was ten. My Dad taught me. Now, he was a genuine expert."

"Oh, no," Susan said. "Now you've started him off."

Cal and Juliet decided to camp there for the night, so Cal brought the Land Rover closer.

"Jesus man," said Ken. "That's one cool set of wheels."

Ken and Susan lived in an ancient sky-blue Land Rover which had been converted into a motorhome by building a habitation unit on the rear. It was clearly an amateur conversion, being top heavy and ungainly.

Cal frowned at it. "After the Death, you could've picked any one of a thousand motor homes in Devon. Why this?" He gestured towards the vehicle.

Ken laughed. "Why Betty? Man, I've been with Betty long before the Death. Me and her had many adventures before the world went to shit. I wasn't going to abandon her for a younger model. That just wouldn't be right, would it Sue?"

Sue smiled. "Betty was the love of his life long before me. I'd hate to have to make him choose between the two of us."

They clearly loved their contraption, but to Cal it seemed a liability, sticking out like a sore thumb and impossible to conceal at night.

The evening was highly sociable. They sat around and talked, ate and shared stories, as travellers always do. Ken caught two more fish for Cal and Juliet, which were paid for by exchanging tinned ham. Both sides of the party were glad about the change of diet. Susan opened a bottle of brandy.

"We met shortly after the Yellow Death," Susan said. "We hit it off together right away and travelled about for a few weeks. Then we joined a group with a dozen other survivors. We were searching for a place to start out again. Trouble was, we were sort of on the fringe of the group."

"Most of the others were real serious dudes," Ken said. "They acted like we had to follow all the rules from before. One day, I caught one of them putting rubbish in a litter bin. I told him the Council wouldn't be emptying the bins anytime soon, but he just glared at me."

"Perhaps they were finding comfort in following familiar habits," Juliet said.

"I guess so, but that was part of the problem. They were so rigid and stuck up. There were a couple of kids with us and they used them as an excuse to keep us in line. We weren't supposed to get drunk in front of the kids."

"Or swear," Susan said.

"Or fuck," Ken said, laughing.

"Especially not that," Susan said. "They made us pitch our tent away from the main camp in case we made any sounds at night which might let on we actually had some fun."

Ken imitated a wolf howling at the moon.

Cal sat stiffly, attempting to keep his face neutral when he really wanted to frown. This couple acted like big kids. Yet Juliet kept laughing and seemed to be enjoying their antics. He hoped she was only being polite, as was he. This was a horrible mistake. Juliet held out her cup as Ken poured another shot of brandy. Cal declined.

Susan continued the story. "The friction between us came to a head one day when we were scavenging a large mansion for supplies. We found a massive greenhouse the previous owners had used mostly for veggies. Most of it was rotting, but I came across sacks of spuds and something else…"

They exchanged glances and smiled, sharing the memory. "I'd never seen them before, but Ken recognised them straight away."

"Cannabis plants," Ken said. "Hundreds of the bloody things. They were past their best, but I managed to salvage and dry enough to fill three carrier bags."

"Why would they be growing cannabis?" Cal said.

"Why not, man? I'm guessing you've not tried it?"

"They may have grown it for medicinal purposes," Juliet said. "Cannabis has traditionally been used as pain relief for long-term illnesses."

"Whatever," Ken said. "We couldn't believe our luck."

"Until we lit up the first time," Susan said. "Then all hell broke loose. You'd think we'd strangled a baby or something."

"The others told us to burn the entire stash," Ken said.

"So we split. We'd had more than enough of their stupid rules and regulations."

"Yeah. There was too much of that shit before the Death. We've been travelling alone since then. Taking life as it comes and living it to the full."

Cal screwed up his face. This couple was stupid, reckless and inconsiderate. And they shouldn't be smoking cannabis in front of children.

This couple would soon need to join a settlement and rely on those folk who had been grafting to get it set up, while they'd been on an extended holiday. They have nothing to offer the settlers except Ken's world renowned fishing skills. Wasters!

But if Juliet was feeling the same as him, she was not showing it. She laughed hysterically at the stories of their ludicrous antics.

"Shame it's got to end," Susan said.

"Yeah. Finding stuff is getting difficult and we can't live only on fish." Ken said.

"So we're looking for a farm or settlement with a friendly community to make a home."

"One that's near a lake, or river, so I can fish. I reckon my skill is invaluable. Fish is highly nutritious and it'll be my contribution to the settlement."

*So that's it. While most people graft in the fields, that loafer thinks he can stand on a riverbank doing his hobby. They wouldn't be invited to join any settlement I was leading.*

Throughout the evening, Cal stayed quiet. He had no wish to talk of his past, and no interest in how Susan and Ken had spent their time. For Cal, this evening was like dutifully listening to a neighbour describing their holiday photographs.

However, Juliet gave the impression of having a wonderful time. She drank a lot of brandy and did a lot of laughing.

Towards the end of the evening, when everyone but Cal was thoroughly drunk, thoughts turned to the future.

"I've got an idea," Susan said. "How about we all try travelling together? Just for a few days. See how we get on? We'd be safer in a group and could share all the chores."

Cal mentally screamed 'No!' but Juliet, relaxed and with brandy flowing through her veins, turned to him and said, "That sounds like a fantastic idea. What do you think, Cal?"

Cal felt trapped by his promise to be sociable, so shrugged his shoulders. "Fine, just for a trial period, though."

"Wonderful, that's settled then," Susan said. "Let's celebrate." She poured another round of brandy.

☣☣☣☣

Ken and Susan eventually retired to their campervan and, even with the doors and windows closed, Cal could still hear their raucous laughing and joking.

Cal prepared for bed in silence, then climbed into their sleeping bag with his back to Juliet.

Juliet sighed. "Okay, what's the matter?"

"Nothing."

"Oh, don't be so childish. Just tell me what the problem is."

Juliet waited patiently until he spoke.

"How could you agree to join up with that pair?"

"Come on, Cal, they're good fun. Ken and Susan are just the sort of people you need to mix with and there's only two of them. You'll not find a smaller group to travel with. You agreed you needed to mix more."

"Yeah. But not with them. Those two will get us killed."

"Will they? I wonder. They seem to have survived just fine so far, without booby traps and paranoid delusions."

The comment stung Cal. They lay in silence, back to back. After a few moments, Juliet relented.

"I'm sorry, Cal, that wasn't fair of me. I appreciate your caution, but when you meet people like Ken and Sue, you've got to wonder if we don't go a bit too far with the security thing? Maybe we're missing out on life a little?"

Cal said nothing. All he wanted to do at that moment was go to sleep and pretend the world didn't exist.

Juliet turned over to face his back. "Are you worried because you haven't been able to set your trip wires tonight?"

Cal also turned, so they were face to face. "A little, but we're well off-road. I doubt we're in any real danger for one night."

"Then what is it that's really bothering you? Is it because I agreed to travel with them without checking with you first?"

"A bit."

"I'm sorry. I shouldn't have done that. I was in a good mood and got carried away in the moment... and the booze didn't help. Listen, this is only a trial. Just give it a couple of days and see how we get on. Ken and Susan are looking to join a settlement soon anyway and who knows, they may not like travelling with us."

"I suppose so."

Cal had a sinking feeling his perfect life had gone forever.

## Chapter Twenty-Four

# Kim Makes A Choice

TIMELINE: At the time of the Yellow Death

"Plague has hung over human history. The biggest human extinction was after 1492 in North and South America when the mortality rate was 95 per cent, which is enormous. But again, I'm actually giving you grounds for optimism: There were enough to continue."
Margaret Atwood (1939–)

Kim spent the rest of the day at home with Katy. The streets of London had become unfamiliar and terrifying. Everybody acted edgy and treated strangers as threats. Those few venturing out wore masks, or covered their faces. Sirens sounded in the distance, accompanied by the occasional bang or crash of breaking glass. During the afternoon, a persistent drizzle bathed everything in a sheen of wetness.

Kim thought about going to her mother's house. She ached to have some company and worried about how her mum was coping. Normally, the drive would take about twenty minutes, but today? Who knew if she could even get there, with roadblocks, abandoned vehicles and looting gangs. The television was full of pictures of terrible things happening everywhere. Had Kim been alone, she would have taken the risk, but she had Katy to think about.

So she locked the doors and windows, then closed the curtains. The world had turned evil, so she wanted to shut it out. She played a few games with Katy, read her some books, and let her watch a DVD. When Katy napped, Kim watched the news. The lights flickered several times. The phone lines and mobile reception remained dead.

Kim felt the urge to keep peeking through the curtains, checking for danger. Every sound outside made her jump. In the late afternoon, Katy spilled a drink and Kim screamed at her out of frustration, regretting it as the words left her mouth. Katy started crying and asked where Daddy was for the hundredth time.

By the time Kim put Katy to bed that evening, her head was throbbing. She took aspirin, but it made no difference. The doorbell rang, and she flinched. Grabbing a carving knife, Kim raced to the living room window, peering around the curtain to view the doorway.

Her mother waited nervously at the door. Kim breathed a sigh of relief and rushed to open it. Rachel's eyes widened when she noticed the knife in Kim's hand. "Not exactly the welcome I was hoping for."

Kim smiled and put down the knife. "Sorry."

They embraced like never before.

☣☣☣☣

The pair sat at the kitchen table, drinking tea. Rachel reached across to hold Kim's hand as she spoke about her journey.

"I sat around the house all day thinking of you. I spoke to Nigel before the phones died and he said you were on the way to Bristol, so there was no point in me coming round here. But then I saw the traffic being turned around on the TV, so thought perhaps you'd be here after all. By then, the phones were down, so I had no way of knowing. I sat for hours plucking up courage to make the journey. In the end I thought 'sod it,' nothing's worse than sitting here stewing, so I jumped in the car and came over. Quickest journey here I've ever made, there's hardly anything moving on the roads now. Everyone's gone to ground."

"I'm glad you're here. I worried about you too."

"Well, everybody's worried about everybody and everything at the moment. I can't believe this has happened so fast."

Kim looked down and shook her head. "It's crazy. I don't understand what's happening. The Government claims there's no confirmed cases. At the same time, they're blocking off London. This must be more serious than they're letting on."

"I'm afraid it is. That's one reason I had to come and see you. I know the truth. Well, as much as anyone does at this stage."

"How? What?"

"Have you got a drink, something stronger than this, I mean?" She indicated her cup of tea. "You're going to need it."

"We've got a bottle of port left over from Christmas we never opened."

"That'll do for a start."

Kim took two wine glasses from a wall cupboard and poured them both a glass of the dark red liquid. Rachel sniffed her drink before downing half of it in one swallow. "Oh. That's a bit rough."

"Nigel's boss gave it to him at Christmas. He's a renowned skinflint."

"Never mind. It'll do the trick. Top me up again. I'm not going to be driving anywhere."

Kim did so.

Rachel took a deep breath. "Right, where do I start? You're aware your dad worked for the Government, but you never knew what he did. Well, to tell you the truth, neither did I, especially in his last few years—after our 'falling out'. I do know it was connected with national security, counter-terrorist intelligence, and stuff like that. He was pretty high up in the food chain. Over the years, I met many of his colleagues at official functions. There was one man in particular who I got to know quite well." She gulped her port. "In fact, I got to know him very well indeed. We became...familiar."

Kim frowned. "What do you mean...Oh Mum, you don't mean..."

"After that time...I mean, after you'd moved out to live with Auntie Helen—"

"You mean when you *moved* me out."

"Yes, okay, if you wish. After we'd arranged for you to live with your aunt, your dad and I lived separate lives. We never slept in the same room again—how could I after what he'd done to you? We barely spoke. But we still had to attend official functions together—to keep up the appearance of a happy married couple."

"Because it wouldn't do for anyone to think Dad wasn't perfect in any way, would it?" Kim gulped from her glass, gripping it tightly.

Rachel put her hand over her mouth and stared at the tabletop. After a long silence, she breathed deeply and cleared her throat. "Anyway, on one of those tiresome formal dinners, I met one of your Dad's colleagues. A scientist named—"

"Please don't tell me his name."

"As you wish. But you should understand he was kind to me at a tough time."

"Was Dad aware of this?"

Rachel chuckled. "Do you know what? I don't think he did but, to be quite frank, I don't give a fuck whether or not he knew about it."

"Mum! I've never heard you use that word before." They looked at each other and burst out laughing. Rachel pushed her empty glass over to Kim to refill it.

"Steady on Mum. I've never seen you drink like this before either."

"Yes, well. There's never been a time like this before. Nor will there be again."

"What do you mean?"

"If you'll stop interrupting me, you'll find out."

Kim motioned zipping up her lips.

"Good. As I was saying. Me and…the scientist fellow became close friends. Our liaison stopped a long time ago—long before your dad passed away—but we always kept in contact. This morning, to my utter astonishment, I found him knocking at my door. He stayed for about half-an-hour and told me everything. These guys live and breathe secrecy, but he said there was no point in secrecy any more. He wanted to say goodbye to me."

Rachel sipped her drink and stared into the glass.

"And what did he tell you?" Kim prompted.

Rachel sighed. "We're all going to die."

Kim frowned. Was her Mother playing some sick joke?

Rachel stared into Kim's eyes. "I'm so sorry, Kim. This so-called Yellow Death is a variant of the plague. But it's far more transmissible and deadly. Most people are asymptomatic for days after they become infected, but all the time they're spreading it around. And it kills almost everyone."

"But…that's not…possible. That's crazy."

"Less than one percent survive. Perhaps much less than that. Some of the first people to catch it are still hanging on to life in a coma—but their prospects aren't good. The very few who've recovered needed massive medical intervention, and that's gone out the window. Now that the NHS has effectively disintegrated, perhaps everyone will die."

Kim sat back, trying to process the enormity of what her mother had said. "Everyone?"

Rachel nodded.

"But...Katy?"

"Everyone."

"Noooooooooo!" Kim covered her face with her hands and silently screamed inside. This was unbelievable, yet there was not a shred of doubt in her mind about it being true. Everything suddenly made sense. "How...long?"

Rachel shrugged. "Days, maybe. I'm so sorry, Kim. When I found out I had to let you know."

"Why? Why did you have to let me know? What difference does it make? Couldn't you have let me have a few more hours of blissful ignorance? God, this fucking headache is driving me insane. My God! That's it, isn't it? I've got it. I'm already going down with it."

"Perhaps. It's impossible to say. For some people, it starts with a headache. But you might just have an ordinary headache. You've been under a lot of stress. But then, you do work in a library, mixing with all those people. It might as well be a germ factory."

"God, I can't afford to be ill now. I've got Katy to look after."

"That's another reason I came over here. I thought you might need help if you went down with it before Katy."

Kim nodded. "Yes. You're right. Thanks. Sorry. That was a shitty thing for me to say to you."

"It's okay. You've just been told the world's about to end. You have a right to an emotional outburst. I threw a vase at the television. Let's go sit in the living room. We might as well make ourselves comfortable. And bring that bottle with you."

☣☣☣☣

## KIM MAKES A CHOICE

Kim and Rachel walked to the living room and sat side-by-side on the sofa, their glasses fully charged. Kim's head spun with questions, and somebody with a mallet was pounding on the inside of her skull. She swigged back two paracetamol with port.

"You're not supposed to mix those pills with alcohol," Rachel said.

"It's the end of the fucking world, Mum."

"I know, but I was thinking of Katy. She might need you in one piece."

"Shit. Yes, you're right. God's teeth, this sucks."

"Yes. As far as suckiness goes, this is indeed the top of the suckiness pile."

Kim took a deep breath. "What are the other reasons?"

"Sorry?"

"You said one reason you came over here was to help out with Katy. So what are the other reasons?"

"Oh, yes. Well. There are two other reasons." Rachel paused and swallowed. "Firstly, I needed to make peace with you...Over the past...While I still can."

Kim knew exactly what she meant, but this was the last thing she wanted to talk about. Kim remained silent.

Rachel continued. "The thing that happened to you. The reason we sent you to live with Auntie Helen. It was unforgivable."

Kim breathed deeply. "You still don't get it, do you? You talk about the thing that happened to me as though it was some sort of accident. As if I'd got an illness. Why can't you say it like it was? Why can't you say 'what he did'?

"Sorry. You're absolutely right. What your father did to you was unforgivable."

"But you let him get away with it!"

"Well, not really."

"Yes! Really! You sent me away to live with Auntie 'hear no evil' and he stayed living in our house."

"We did what was best for the family. The entire family. We had to consider Toby. And I made sure you were protected. He could never do that thing to you again—"

"That thing? That thing? You can't even say it, can you?"

Rachel sipped her port. Her hands shook so much she held the glass with both hands. "Fellatio. There, I've said it, all right? For three years, my husband forced my daughter to perform fellatio under my roof and I never had a damn clue."

A long silence stretched out between them as they swam in an ocean of painful memories.

Rachel cleared her throat. "We weren't husband and wife after that. I barely spoke to him. But if it had ever got out what he'd been doing—for all those years... There would have been a massive scandal. The story would've been on TV and in the papers. We'd have had a scrum of media rats hanging around our home for months. Dad would've lost his job and there wouldn't have been another at his age. Our house and the villa in Italy were both mortgaged. The cars were on lease. And there was your father's pension to consider. Everything would have gone. No more private school, no more horse riding for you, or music lessons for Toby."

"So you're saying you turned a blind eye to serial sexual assault, so I could have what—fucking riding lessons?"

"It wasn't like that. The family would've been destitute. Living in some bloody council house on benefits. I'm sorry, Kim, but it wasn't a straightforward decision. And if it was only me, I'd have gone to the police station right away. But I had to act for the best interests of both of my children in the long-term. Do you think I wanted to share a house with the man who'd abused my daughter? I felt like smashing his head in with a frying pan. But I had to be sensible, pragmatic, for the sake of you and Toby."

"Did you even consider asking me what I thought?"

"Yes. I agonised over it. But you were only sixteen and, if I'm honest, you were quite...naïve for your age."

"Apart from the sexual assault?"

"What I mean is I didn't think you were in a...a mental state to make sensible decisions affecting the rest of yours and Toby's life. And to be honest, what happened later made me realise I was right."

Kim frowned. "What do you mean? No! You're not talking about the anorexia?"

"Well, that showed what a fragile mental state you were in—starving yourself to death."

"You make it sound like I woke up one morning and decided to stop eating. It was never like that. I couldn't stand the feeling of...of certain things in my mouth. And we both know why that was. It got worse and worse over time. Food was the only thing in my life I could control."

"Oh dear, this isn't going how I wanted it to. What I meant to say was...was, I was a terrible mother. Neglectful. It shouldn't have happened on my watch. For three years, he deceived me. Then you...stopped eating, and I never noticed that either until you collapsed at school. I was so wrapped up with charity events and the bridge club and tennis committee and being the dutiful wife. I forgot about my most important job—which was being a mother. And that's what was unforgivable."

Tears flowed down Rachel's cheeks. "And what was just as bad was standing aside for years before then and letting that man have his own way about so many things."

"The hosepipe?"

"Yes. That damn hosepipe! Sometimes when he used it on Toby, I put on headphones and blasted music so loud it made my ears hurt. Just so I couldn't hear Toby's screams. But it wasn't only the hosepipe. It was all the silly rules and regulations. The etiquette and manners at the dinner table. As if we were royalty. I was weak. I let him bully me for years."

Rachel took out a tissue and blew her nose. "So I wanted to apologise while I still can. I'd been failing you for years and let you down when it mattered most. I was...pathetic and made the wrong decisions. I'm sorry. If I was in that situation again, I'd fight to send him to prison and sod the pension and the villa."

The two women sat in silence for several minutes. Kim had waited years for an apology. For some heartfelt and genuine recognition of the horror she had lived through. Yet Rachel's apology felt like a damp squib—nothing changed, nothing felt different. Perhaps because the real traitor in her family had escaped justice and never made any attempt to atone before he died.

Nevertheless, they might all be dead in a few days. There was no point holding grudges. Kim took her mother's hand. "Thanks, Mum. That means a lot. Pity it took an apocalypse to drag it out, but I appreciate it. And I realise it can't have been easy."

Tears flowed freely down Rachel's face. "Nothing ever is."

"I've had enough of this awful port—tastes like paint thinners. I'm going to put the kettle on."

Kim returned a few moments later with two cups of coffee.

Rachel was looking in the mirror. "Oh dear, with all that crying, my mascara looks terrible."

"Civilisation is crumbling around us, Mum. Who cares?"

"I care. I'm not planning to meet my maker with smudged make-up."

Kim sat on the sofa and rubbed her temples.

"Is your headache not getting better?" Rachel asked.

"Worse. Much worse. I'm going to have to lie down a bit."

Rachel placed her palm on Kim's forehead. "You're burning up. Are your armpits sore?"

"Yes. I've got it, haven't I?"

Rachel nodded. "It looks like you have. The swelling under the arms is the lymph nodes starting to...Oh, what the hell, I don't suppose you need a description."

Kim put down her cup and covered her eyes. "What am I going to do? I can't afford to be ill. I've got to look after Katy."

Chill realisation hit her like a brick in the face. "Katy! Oh shit. I've been with Katy all day. If I've got it—"

Kim froze at that thought and Rachel had no crumb of comfort to offer. They were past the point where well-meaning platitudes might help.

Rachel began rummaging through her handbag. "Which brings me to the last reason I had to come over here." She pulled out a small brown container and placed it on the coffee table.

"What's that?" Kim said.

"Antibiotics. The strong stuff. Brand new, experimental. Knock out an elephant."

"Mum, where the hell did you get these?"

"Same place I got the information—my scientist friend."

Kim stared at the pot suspiciously. "Will they work?"

"Who knows? There's not been time for trials. They're new and powerful and as rare as hen's teeth. That much I'm sure about. Obviously, these pills were never intended for this Yellow Death thing, but the scientists believe they might be effective. I was told selected members of the Government are getting them. These were given to my friend, but he said I'd make better use of them. He hasn't got any children. If you've got this disease, then, from what little we understand, there's nothing to lose by trying them. Take one every six hours."

Kim picked up the pill pot and tipped out the precious contents on the table. "Mum, there's only twelve pills, that's only three days' supply."

"That was all I could get, darling. Let's hope three days is enough."

"Yes, but it's three days for just one person. We all need them."

"No. I'm sorry, but they're no good for Katy. That much is clear. They'd do Katy more harm than good. My friend told me they're only suitable for children over twelve and adults, because of the side effects. They'd mess up Katy's liver."

"Are you sure?"

"Yes. Quite sure. Take them."

"But if I take them, what about you?"

"Kim. Darling. They were never destined for me. I'm getting on a bit now. Even if I took the pills, it would probably do no good. To be honest, I'm not sure I care all that much. Listen, my scientist friend said there's a pattern emerging to this thing. The plague kills almost everyone, but the few who are hanging on, are healthy adults aged under fifty. So there's no chance for a wrinkly like me."

"No, that can't be true. You're not even ill yet."

"No, not yet. But I will be. I've probably been in contact with dozens of infected people—and now you. There's no escape from this. You must be realistic. The only thing that's kept me going these past few years is seeing that you, Toby and Katy are okay. I can't help Toby since he's in South America. But I can help you, and you have Katy to look after. When this is all over, God knows what mess we'll be left with. But, if by some miracle Katy gets through this, she'll need you. Katy can't survive on her own—she won't even be able to get out of the house. You're a wonderful mother, Kim. A damn sight better than I was."

"Don't say that, Mum."

"Hush now, Kim. We both know it's true. I lost sight of what was important and didn't see what was happening in my own house. These pills are something practical I can do for you. It's not much and doesn't make up for everything. But it's something."

"Yes, Mum. It's something. Thanks."

Kim took a pill.

## Chapter Twenty-Five

# Cal & The Ultimatum

TIMELINE: 18 MONTHS AFTER THE
YELLOW DEATH

"You will never truly know yourself or the strength of your relationships until both have been tested by adversity."

J. K. Rowling (1965— )

The two couples had travelled as a group for seven days.

Cal's face had developed an almost permanent frown. *Cal and Juliet and Ken and Susan. It sounds like a title for a road movie. A terrible, hideous road movie.*

The last week proved to be every bit as bad as Cal feared. He despised both of them. The pair were almost exact opposites to him. He worked hard; they were lazy. He planned ahead; they took what life threw at them. He acted with caution; they were rash. Most important of all, Cal was a loner, and they were sociable. Where Juliet was concerned, that gave Ken and Sue the trump card. It also resulted in a constant low level of friction within the quartet.

Juliet enjoyed their company, and had quickly become best friends with Susan. They laughed so much together it began to irritate Cal, although he chided himself for being uncharitable. He wanted Juliet to be happy, but it came at the cost of his own wellbeing.

A thousand-and-one irritations accompanied the Ken and Sue roadshow. The most troublesome was Cal's feeling of vulnerability. Their sky-blue motorhome stood out like a vicar in a brothel and made more noise than a Challenger tank. Cal could not set trip wires around camp and they refused to make any concessions to stay out of harm's way. When Cal pointed out they should not park directly in front of a shop, they chorused, "Come on Cal, don't be so anal" and burst into laughter. He heard that phrase too often.

Last evening, Juliet suggested she and Sue share a vehicle. That left Cal and Ken to travel together. Cal suspected the group hoped he would bond with Ken.

Cal hated the idea and would rather share his car with a hungry alligator, but nobody showed interest in what he thought anymore. Cal also noted with resentment how Juliet did not consult him first. It felt as if the clock had been turned back twenty years, with Cal the friendless outsider in the school playground again.

So, today Cal had spent hours trapped in his Land Rover with Ken. Long silences had been punctuated by Ken's tedious fishing stories. Towards evening, as the sun touched the peaks of distant hills, Cal was near to breaking point. He drove slowly, so they could look for a place to camp. Sue and Juliet followed closely behind in the Rover motorhome.

"Listen, Cal," Ken said, "I know you and I are very different, and we haven't hit it off all that great. But we both see how well

Jules and Sue are gelling, so we need to find a way to get along. Savvy?"

Cal hated Ken referring to Juliet as 'Jules'. Why did he have to debase everything?

"Yes, that would be nice," Cal said, keeping his voice as monotone as possible.

"Y'know we've got more in common than you think. We're both survivors and hunters. We both like beautiful women. I mean, look at Sue and Jules. Both are highly shaggable. You and me... we're lucky men, Cal."

Cal did not regard dipping a hook into a river as hunting. As for Ken being a survivor—that was pure luck, but he let the comment pass. It was true they both appreciated beautiful women, but so what? They both enjoyed shitting. That did not make the basis for a friendship. Cal bristled at the notion of Juliet being shaggable. Where was this nonsense leading?

"Yes, we're so fortunate," he mumbled.

"Y'know, Sue and I were chatting last night. About what a coincidence it was for us to all meet up. Two couples of the same age, bumping into each other. It feels like destiny."

Cal huffed. "The reason we discovered you was because of your smoke trail which could be seen for miles."

"Yeah, whatever. It was lucky we lit that fire then, or we'd have never met."

"Lucky indeed. Particularly lucky it was us that saw the smoke and not a gang of murderers." Cal realised he gripped the steering wheel tightly.

Ken shrugged. "Anyway, like I was saying, we were talking about things and...well...did y'know she quite fancies you?"

"Who, Susan?"

"Yeah, man, Susan. Who'd you think I mean? She said you've got a fit bod, and she gets turned on when you come back from a run, all sweaty, with the heaving chest and all that shit."

Cal looked at Ken with a furrowed brow. "This is one of your jokes, isn't it?"

"No, man, I swear. You must have seen her looking at you?"

Cal thought about it. Perhaps their eyes had locked once or twice. "Okay. Let's say I have. What of it?"

"Listen. Thing is, that Jules is super hot, and she seems to like me. So, Sue suggested…maybe if you and Jules wanted to, well, spice things up a bit…y'know, in the bedroom department. Well, we wondered what you thought about swapsies?"

"What?"

"Oh come on man, don't tell me you haven't eyed up Sue a little—in that tiny red bikini she's so keen on? I can tell you she's not a disappointment in the sack and super obliging, if you know what I mean?" He stuck his tongue out and wiggled it.

Cal slammed his foot on the brakes, causing the Land Rover to skid to a halt. Crates and boxes crashed in the back.

"Whoah, man!" Ken said.

Cal turned to face him, chin rigid and face flushed. "Now you listen. Listen very carefully. If you touch Juliet—and it's Juliet, not Jules—If you touch her, if your eyes pause for a second when you look at her, then I will wring your scrawny, useless neck. Is that absolutely clear?"

Ken held up his hands, palms facing Cal. "Yes, man, yes. Calm down, calm down, it's only an idea. I told Sue you were too—that you'd never go for it. Sorry, man, no offence meant."

"Don't ask if you can fuck my girlfriend and then say no offence meant. And while we're discussing being offensive, if you call me anal one more time, you're going to get very anal with my rifle barrel. Do I make myself clear?"

"Crystal. Jeez, man. Cool it."

Cal looked in the rear-view mirror and saw the women staring back with puzzled expressions.

He started off again. Cal and Ken remained silent for the rest of the journey.

☣☣☣☣

That evening, the usual jollity around the campsite was absent, replaced with uncomfortable silences. Cool damp air promised rain during the night.

When Cal and Juliet fetched their belongings from the Land Rover, they had a moment alone.

"What's going on? What's happened between you and Ken?" Juliet said.

"Why don't you ask him?"

"Because I'm asking you. Because you're supposed to be my partner."

"We argued."

"No shit. What about?"

"I can't tell you now. It's complicated...delicate. Let's talk about it later."

"Fucking hell. Why can't men just get on with each other?"

Cal went to bed straight after the meal and Juliet followed shortly afterwards. The couple lay back-to-back in their sleeping bag without speaking for several minutes. The tent canvas rustled in the wind.

"Juliet?"

"Yes?"

"Are you still awake?"

"I just answered you, didn't I?"

"Sorry. This afternoon. When I was alone in the car with Ken. You'll never believe this, but he asked if we'd try swapping partners—for sex, that is."

Juliet laughed. "Oh, Lord. Was that when you braked and almost drove into a ditch?"

"Yes. And I didn't almost drive into a ditch. I was in complete control."

"Whatever. So, what was your answer?"

"Well, I said 'no', of course. What did you expect?"

"I reckon you probably said a lot more than 'no', judging by his reaction tonight. I wondered what was going on. Poor Ken.

He had no idea what he was getting himself into. I bet Susan put him up to it."

"Yes, she did."

Juliet laughed again. "Typical."

"You seem to be taking this rather lightly."

"And you seem to be taking it rather seriously."

"It is serious. Ken wanted to shag you!"

"And why are you surprised? Am I that unattractive?"

Cal turned over to face Juliet, and she did likewise. The couple lay face-to-face in the dark. "No, of course not. You're not unattractive. What I mean is you are attractive... pretty... beautiful. You know what I mean. That's not the point. Ken had no right asking that."

"Because?"

"Well, because you're mine, of course. Oh bollocks, I don't mean that. I mean, we're together——a couple. You're my girlfriend, partner, whatever you want to call it. Come on, you know what I'm getting at."

In the dim light from the moon filtering through the tent walls, Cal saw Juliet smiling. "Yes, Cal. I do know exactly what you mean, and I feel the same. But Ken and Sue aren't like that. They're much more... flexible. If you talked to them a little more, instead of just glaring across the campfire, you'd realise."

She held Cal's hand inside the sleeping bag. "Remember, they left their last group because of smoking pot. They're just a tiny bit more liberal and laid back than you are, Cal. At least Ken had the decency to ask. It's not like he's trying to go behind your back. Considering how attractive Sue is, I'm quite flattered. Do you find Sue attractive, Cal? That is a super tiny bikini she wears."

"Why does everyone have to keep banging on about that fucking bikini? Okay, I admit Sue is quite attractive. What's that got to do with anything?"

"Well, I just wondered if the prospect of sex with Sue would change your mind?"

"What! You can't be serious...You're winding me up, aren't you? Christ, you had me worried there for a second."

"Cal, I'd no more have sex with Ken than I'd boil my head—even if I fancied him—which I don't. And his breath stinks of fish."

Cal chuckled. "Good!"

"And also, by the way, it's nice to hear you say I'm beautiful. You've not said that before, so if Ken's suggestion has wrung that out of you, it's achieved something."

"Have I not said that before?"

"No."

"Shit. Sorry. I'm not good at this relationship stuff."

"You're doing all right. But sometimes you really put the 'ass' in Asperger's."

Cal lay in silence, wondering how to broach the next subject. He could think of no easy way.

"Juliet?"

"Yes."

"I've been thinking a lot and decided I'm leaving."

"What?"

"I was considering leaving even before today. This business of sharing partners has made up my mind. Ken and Sue are too different. It's like living with Martians. I've tried, honestly, but I can't stand it anymore. Can't stand *them* any more. It would be really, really, great if you'd come with me. I don't want to be alone again. But with or without you, I'm going, tomorrow morning."

"Christ, that came as a shock. You're serious, aren't you?"

"Sorry, yes. I can't understand why you like them so much. Think back to the first morning we were together. You'd slept well and felt safe for the first time in ages. That was because of my booby traps and precautions."

"Yes, I remember."

"Well, there's been no booby traps since we met those two. No hiding the vehicles. No covering our tracks. We travel around like a bloody circus. Doesn't that worry you?"

Juliet considered for a moment. "Well, yes. It does, to be honest. But not so much. I know it makes no sense, but I feel safer in our group. Somehow Ken and Sue make me more optimistic. When I'm alone with you, I expect a bogeyman around every corner. Your paranoia is infectious. Somehow, the world seems a brighter, less dangerous place with them around. Perhaps the world isn't as bad as you imagine? Ken and Sue have survived until now without letting security dominate their lives. Everyone we've met lately has been nice. People are settling down, making new homes, beginning to trade. Things are becoming civilised again."

"Is that right? Remember the red mini-bus? Remember the coach full of dead bodies? What happened to those raiders? Have they all emigrated, or turned into farmers? Trust me, they're still out there. Ken and Sue have been lucky, that's all. I won't rely on luck. Eventually, luck runs out."

Juliet sighed. "So we have to go around constantly checking nobody is creeping up on us. We have to treat everyone we meet as a potential murderer. What sort of life is that?"

"It's not forever. There'll be some sort of civilisation again, perhaps in a few years. But not now. Perhaps the time is right to seriously search for a permanent home. Join a settlement. Travelling is becoming too hard and dangerous."

Juliet smiled. "Ken and Sue are looking for a settlement. Perhaps we can look together?"

"They are not looking for a settlement. I know they say they are, but they're not actively doing anything about it. They just travel from one fishing spot to another, hoping to stumble on the perfect settlement. As usual, there's no plan, only a belief something will turn up. Even if by chance they were to discover Nirvana, would they be accepted? Can you honestly see that pair grafting hard from dawn to dusk? Do you expect the settlers will allow Ken to fish all day and Sue to spend the afternoon sunbathing? In my opinion, Ken and Sue don't genuinely want to join a settlement—they're too lazy."

"That's being harsh, I'm sure they can adapt."

"Huh! If we're serious about settling down, I can find somewhere in a couple of weeks. With our skills, we'd have people begging us to join, but not with Ken and Sue in tow. No, I'm definitely leaving tomorrow. If you come with me, then we can hunt for our forever home together. Otherwise... well, if I'm on my own, it doesn't matter to you what I do, does it?"

"Oh, Lord. So you're going to make me choose. Leave with you, or stay with Ken and Sue?"

"I guess so, sorry. That's what it comes down to."

"Shit. I enjoy being with you, Cal, but I need more. Sue's such fun and we're so great together."

"Look," Cal said. "I know I'm not the world's best conversationalist. But when we've settled, there'll be loads of other people. You'll make new friends."

"That's true, but Sue's special. We get on so well together. If we'd met before the Yellow Death, we'd have been best friends. Shit, shit, shit."

Juliet remained still, her breathing heavy in the silence. "This isn't fair. You break this news out of the blue. Did you expect me to just agree to leave with you tomorrow morning?"

"Well I, I guess, I, yes. I suppose I did. I thought—"

"No. You didn't think. Because if you'd given two seconds thought about how I'd react, you'd realise there's no way I can make that decision on the spot."

She sighed. "Give me a day to decide, Cal. I need to sleep on it and think about it. And I need to decide what this ultimatum says about you and our future together—if there is a future. And, if I do decide to leave with you, I need time to break the news to Sue."

Cal sighed. "Okay, I'll put up with this pantomime for a bit longer."

Cal rolled back onto his side and closed his eyes, but sleep remained elusive. He lay for what seemed an eternity with his mind churning over. Juliet's breathing slowed and, when he was sure she was asleep, he rolled on his back.

The glow of the moon illuminated the tent canvas. Would he genuinely leave Juliet behind if she decided to stay? He meant what he said at the time, but the idea of actually driving off without Juliet filled him with dread. Juliet had changed everything. He did not want to live without her. Bollocks—relationships were so complicated. Why did they have to bump into Ken and Sue rather than a nice, conventional couple?

Cal realised the ultimatum to Juliet was stupid, and he would never leave her. He felt guilty for putting her in that situation. Should he wake her up and tell her of his change of mind? No—too late for that—it can wait until morning. First thing tomorrow, he would apologise to Juliet and clear things up.

Then he needed to show some grit and stand up to Ken and Sue. He could adapt. At least he could try.

A breeze rustled the tent and reminded Cal of how exposed they were without booby traps or trip wires. An elephant might walk into the campsite and they would never know. That had to stop. He felt responsible for Juliet's safety. Security was one of the few things he excelled at. Tomorrow night he would set booby traps and, if the others made jokes, so be it. And he would hide the vehicles properly—even if he did the work alone.

This was the last night they would sleep without proper defences.

## Chapter Twenty-Six

# JOHN & THE YELLOW DEATH

TIMELINE: AT THE TIME OF THE YELLOW DEATH

"Pale Death with impartial tread beats at the poor man's cottage door and at the palaces of kings."

Horace (65–8 BCE)

"This is ridiculous." John tossed his phone onto the living room chair and began pacing. Rachel lay on the couch, simultaneously shivering and sweating. She seemed to have aged twenty years. "The NHS helpline just has a recorded message telling me to go to local medical services. But the GP surgery has a message saying to call the NHS helpline. I've tried dialling 999 several times, but it just keeps ringing. Nobody bloody answers."

"Oh John, I'm sorry."

"Don't be silly, Mum. You've nothing to be sorry about." He sighed. "Listen, I'm going to take you straight to the Royal Devon and Exeter Hospital. They'll be able to sort you out. No point in trying the local surgery for this sort of thing."

"I don't think I can manage the journey."

"Sure you can. I'll help you to the car, so you only have to lie back."

"But what about.... what about packing my things?"

"We'll worry about that later. I can come back and get anything you need. Just give me two minutes. I'm going to change into my old army uniform and grab my bow and arrows.

Moments later, John returned. He scanned the room.

*OK. Calm down. Have I got everything? Postcode for the hospital. Phone. Water. Car keys. I'm sure I've forgotten something.*

Sarah groaned.

"OK, Mum. Let's get going."

Sarah screamed when John helped lift her up. Her clothes were hot and damp. John helped Sarah into the back seat, where she might lie down if she wished. He handed her a bottle of water, which she dropped into the footwell. A steady drizzle in the air The local Heart radio station held a public discussion where attendees shared their difficult stories and offered suggestions for how the authorities should handle the problem.added to the sense of miasma.

The roads were deserted, so he drove fast and made good time. None of the radio stations were playing music. They all talked about the plague. Endless gossip and few facts. Government advice was to stay at home in a full lockdown. Cal listened to a discussion on the radio. A string of scared people related harrowing stories and explained how the authorities could do better. This was truly the blind leading the blind and ignorant.

As they reached the outskirts of Exeter, traffic built up and slowed to a crawl going into the city, although it flowed freely coming back.

"There's a lot of traffic coming out of the city. Not sure what's going on. I wonder if they're evacuating the city?"

Sarah groaned in response.

"Not long now, Mum. We're at Exeter." In the rear-view mirror, her face was grey and twisted with pain.

"John. I'm sorry," she croaked. He didn't understand what she kept apologising for.

A few minutes later, they reached a major roundabout and discovered the source of the holdup. Army land rovers and trucks completely blocked every exit. Armed troops were in charge, a few of them wore full-face gas masks giving them an ominous alien look. The guards directed vehicles to go around the roundabout and return the way they had come. Most drivers complied. Occasionally, someone shouted at the soldiers, pleading to be let through for some urgent reason. They remained resolute—no exceptions.

Cal tried to recognise the soldiers. All were strangers except one: 'Smartie' from his T.A. unit. This was his chance!

John swerved out of the line of traffic to the annoyance of other drivers, who blared their horns. He drove up to Smartie, whilst lowering the car window.

"Hey, Smartie!"

Smartie squinted suspiciously, then smiled in recognition. He pulled his surgical mask down below his chin.

"Hey, Cal. Good to see you. It's Sergeant Smart to you, you goddamn civvy." Smartie pointed to the sergeant's stripes on his sleeve. "What's up?"

"It's my mother, she's ill. I need to get her to the hospital."

Smartie screwed up his face. "Sorry mate, nobody's going through the roadblock. There's a complete ring around Exeter."

"But she's in terrible condition. She needs medical help and I've tried everywhere else."

Smartie glanced into the car at Sarah's pale, sweaty face and shook his head.

"Listen, John. I've seen dozens of people in your mother's condition this morning. The best thing you can do for her is to go home. I know that sounds fucked up, but I was on duty at the hospital earlier, and it's worse than hell there. Half the doctors and nurses have gone down with it and they've run out of everything—even beds. People are lined up on the floor in the corridors. We were clearing the bodies. We carried one after another and made piles out back. When one pile got so big we couldn't reach the top, we just started another pile. Ignore the crap on the TV. It's out of control."

"Jesus. It's worse than I thought."

"And getting worse by the hour. Most of the lads didn't turn up for duty. These guys here are from different units all over Devon. God knows how much longer we'll stay. We don't even have any bullets, for fuck's sake. Go back, John, while you still can. The word is the RAF may start bombing the major roads to stop travel, so you might get stuck in the middle of nowhere. Things are turning nasty—well, even more nasty. People are getting desperate and violent. I see you've got a bow and arrow in there. Keep it handy. Believe me, you're best off in the country. Get back to your house and lock yourself in until this insanity blows over."

"They mentioned new drugs on the TV."

"Bollocks. I told you, ignore anything on the TV or radio. There are no drugs at all. No new drugs and no old drugs. There's nothing. If you've got any aspirin, you've got more drugs than the fucking hospital. Everybody is catching it and everybody dies."

"Everybody? Some people must get better?"

"Honest to God, I don't know, but I've not seen any. Just go home."

John felt frustrated and defeated. His mother was sick, in pain, possibly dying. She had devoted her life to him and now, when she suffered, he was powerless to help. John's mind raced for another choice, but there was none.

"Okay Sarge, I'll go back. Shit!" He banged his fist on the steering wheel, then put the car into gear.

"Thanks, Sarge. Listen, for what it's worth, I was proud to serve in your platoon. I hope things turn out all right for you."

"You too, Cal." They went to shake hands, but stopped short, thinking better of it. The sergeant patted the roof of John's car instead. "Good luck, Cal. You were a good soldier, even if you were weird. Fuckin' bad luck about your back."

As John drove away, he saw the soldiers in his rear-view mirror. They were his comrades and were doing their duty to the last. A feeling of guilt gnawed at him—somebody else he had failed.

☣☣☣☣

When John and Sarah returned home from the abortive trip to Exeter, he helped her to bed and gave her paracetamol. The trip had been a sobering experience. Sarah had always cared for him. Now she was helpless and John was at a loss what to do. For the next twenty-four hours, he split his time between sitting at her bedside and watching civilisation collapse.

Sarah was barely conscious. Even with painkillers, she remained in agony. He tried to get her to drink hot toddies laced with liberal amounts of brandy, but nothing brought any comfort. At times, Sarah burned with fever. An hour later, chills and shivering wracked her body. She would not eat and only drank in tiny sips, finding swallowing too difficult and complaining everything tasted 'funny'. Painful swellings appeared on her neck and armpits which gave off an unpleasant odour of decay. They were too tender to clean, so John could only wipe her face and hands, then drip perfume on her pillow.

John found it difficult to look at her, as she appeared to have aged decades overnight. Sarah took pride in her appearance. She was meticulous in her make-up, even when working in the garden. Now she lay in bed, curled up and bare to the world. He brushed her hair and wiped the dried saliva from her cheeks.

Once, in a rare moment of lucidity, she looked up at him and reached to stroke his cheek. She mouthed something silently before returning to unconsciousness.

On another occasion, she stared directly at him and said "I'm sorry." Why did she keep saying that? What did she have to be sorry about?

The mobile phone reception disappeared quite early. One by one, live television broadcasts were cancelled in favour of recorded shows. Later these were replaced by announcements apologising for the temporary interruption to programmes which, of course, would resume as soon as possible. BBC1 was the last channel to die.

The electricity cut out several times, then resumed. John imagined a few dedicated staff at the National Grid, desperately trying to route a diminishing level of power around the country. Eventually, the lights went out and stayed out.

John still had his laptop and Sarah's iPad, which gave him about twenty hours of surfing for what it was worth. The internet survived a surprisingly long time. It slowed, with pages arriving in fits and starts. Certain sites became unavailable. News websites were not being updated.

Only social media remained active, where desperate people all over the globe sought reassurance from others. Folk derived a little comfort from knowing they were not alone in their fear and suffering.

Conspiracy theories flourished. This was a plot by the Russians; Chinese; Iranians; Taliban, communists, Muslims; white supremacists, etc. Prepare for the foreign invasion! John saw a photograph purporting to be an alien spacecraft seeding the Yellow Death spores across America. Prepare for the alien invasion!

Of course, there were postings with various suggestions for curing or avoiding the disease with herbs, witchcraft, injecting disinfectant, or repenting sins. The nutters had emerged in force.

In the end, it was not the laptop batteries, nor the World Wide Web which stopped John from surfing. His internet connection simply died at the same time as the landline phone.

Evening had arrived and soon he would have to light candles.

John considered making a final journal entry, but if this was the end of civilisation, what was the point? He shut down his laptop and closed the lid, feeling he was saying goodbye to an old friend.

The absence of sound was unnerving. No television or radio, no background hum from the fridge or freezer. He walked outside. The sun was already below the horizon, but the clouds still glowed in a myriad shades of red and orange. Normally, John would be aware of some noises, although most of the time he would be oblivious to them—lawnmowers, hedge clippers and strimmers, cars in the distance, the occasional aeroplane. Now he heard nothing. Strangely, not even the birds sang tonight.

It seemed the world had gone to sleep. The silence was broken by his mother moaning through the upstairs bedroom window. John walked back into the cottage.

"Just coming, Mum."

☣☣☣☣

No television, no radio, no internet. John resorted to his Kindle reader. He had not been reading much recently. A pity, he thought, because he enjoyed reading, but it was so easy to be seduced by all the modern technological alternatives.

John sat by his mother's bedside under the light of a candle as he read 'Alexander, The Virtues Of War'. Sarah occasionally moaned, so he held her hand, it being the only way to comfort her. Once, he heard a loud boom in the distance. He peered out the bedroom window, but saw nothing unusual, so resumed reading.

Eventually, John fell asleep sitting next to the bed. When he awoke, the candle had burned out. John glanced at his wristwatch—four a.m. His head pounded as if he had a marching band inside. Perhaps that was because he'd slept awkwardly with his head at an odd angle. When he stood, the room spun around, forcing him to brace against the wall to avoid falling down. A wave of nausea caused him to clamp his jaw shut.

"Oh, shit!"

The illness developed at speed, with the fever arriving within half an hour. Soon enough, John experienced painful swellings under his arms and in his neck—in fact, just about everything hurt. He tried to vomit, but nothing came and the effort exhausted him. His mouth was dry with an unpleasant metallic taste. John went to pee and even that stung. His whole body seemed to be falling apart.

John had a stock of high-dose ibuprofen for his back pain, so he swallowed two. An hour later, he took two more. By then, he barely had the strength to stand and shook uncontrollably. John was torn between looking after Sarah and the desperate need to lie down.

There was no point trying to fool himself. He had the plague. The disease was killing most people. But not all, surely? No disease ever killed absolutely everyone. What might he do to improve his chances? Ibuprofen and paracetamol would help to reduce inflammation and fever. He must stay hydrated and he needed energy. He remembered sachets of energy gel left over from his last marathon. They were past their 'use by' date but, what the hell. Now, where would they be ?

As he pulled the contents out of one drawer after another, he attempted to stay calm. To focus on what was essential. However small his chances were, they would only be worse if he gave in to terror, and that knowledge steadied him. For somebody who cared little for his life, he was eager to cheat death.

After ten minutes, John dumped an armful of pills, energy sachets and a bottle of water on the nightstand in the guest bedroom. He slumped on the bed, too exhausted to stand any more.

John set his phone alarm for thirty minutes, enough time to take a nap before checking on his Mother again. He swallowed pills and two energy gel sachets with as much water as he could stomach, then lay down and closed his eyes.

\* \* \*

John's phone alarm began playing 'Mad World' thirty minutes later. The volume gradually increased until, on some level, it penetrated his consciousness.

John knew he had to do something. Something important. He couldn't think straight. Some idiot was smashing a sledgehammer on the inside of his skull. The music became louder still, then changed to an annoying bugle sounding 'Reveille'.

Without opening his eyes, his arm flailed about, trying to silence the irritating noise, and he knocked the phone off the nightstand onto the floor. John turned over and groaned as every part of his body objected to the movement. That damn bugle continued to sound, but was too far away to reach. He pulled a pillow over his head. The alarm rang for another minute before giving up.

Silence returned to the house.

If only he could remember what he should be doing. Sod it. It can't be that important. It would have to wait until he felt better. He just needed a couple of hours' rest.

John drifted back into a fitful sleep with beads of sweat running off his forehead and soaking his pillow.

Unbeknown to John, dawn was breaking outside and birds were singing to welcome a new day.

A new day for a very different world.

## Chapter Twenty-Seven

# Cal Meets the C.U.G.

TIMELINE: 1 YEAR AND 6 MONTHS AFTER THE YELLOW DEATH

"I would suggest that barbarism be considered as a permanent and universal human characteristic which becomes more or less pronounced according to the play of circumstances."
                          Simone Weil (1909–1943)

Cal was vaguely aware of a strange sound interrupting his sleep. By the time he recognised the threat, it was too late. Several minutes too late. A knife blade sliced through their small tent from one end to another in a single smooth movement. Rough hands snatched and dragged him from his sleeping bag.

He fumbled for his pistol, but could not find it. Out in the open air, the night was pitch black and freezing. The campfire still burned brightly, so they must only have been sleeping a short time. Men yelled at each other. Flashlight beams scythed through the night air. Gathering his wits, he struggled, only to be rewarded with a fist punch to his face, leaving his head spinning and the coppery taste of blood. Through the daze, he heard Juliet cry out, "Get off! Let go of me, you bastards."

A gruff voice barked, "Shut up, you little bitch," followed by a slap and scream.

Cal scanned the area. Torch beams and vehicle headlights flashed across the campsite. Three men kicked in the door of the motorhome before bursting inside. Cries of surprise and pain mixed with crashing crockery followed.

Clearly, a large and disciplined force had ambushed them.

Minutes later, Cal, Juliet, Susan and Ken, were on their knees in front of the campfire, hands tied behind them with plastic ties cutting into their flesh. Cal made an effort to keep calm. He ignored the throbbing of his nose, stayed silent and observed the proceedings, desperately trying to gather as much information as possible. Several times, Ken protested and each time they hit or kicked him, yet his outrage knew no bounds, nor common sense. Cal wanted to tell him to shut the fuck up. Couldn't he see he would make it worse for all of them?

Cal understood they should not resist, to appear defeated and broken. Only if they convinced their attackers they were no threat might there be any chance of getting them off guard. Even that was a long shot. Cal had already identified eight attackers armed with military weapons.

Perhaps if he could just free his hands. Then, if he could grab a weapon, then rapidly shoot everyone standing, then perhaps in the darkness and confusion, he might just get away with it. Cal realised that sequence of events would be miraculous. But, in that moment, it was all he had.

Cal tested his bonds, putting all his strength into stretching the cable ties whilst ignoring the pain as they cut further into his skin. No movement. Could he somehow trick them into releasing his hands?

Two of the attackers stood behind them, whilst the others searched the camp and their vehicles. Cal glanced to his right and saw Juliet slumped with her head bowed. Darkness hid any injuries she suffered, but he noticed she was shaking. The searchers were jubilant, whooping, and shouting out what they found. One man squealed with delight as he went through Susan's underwear collection, holding an item up close to his face, "Hmm. Smells good."

"Fuck's sake, Boysy, you're disgusting. Hey, look here, vodka and...twelve-year-old malt whisky!"

They uncovered the weapons in Cal's Land Rover.

"Jesus Christ, look at this, sir. This car's a bloody mobile armoury. Guns, missiles, explosives, grenades. Fuck me."

"Holy crap, what the fuck's this?" Another voice shouted.

"I don't know, but be careful what you touch, you'll blow us to shit."

"Wow, take a look at this—Claymore mines—I've seen these on telly."

Cal watched the silhouette of a man striding to the men who were searching his Land Rover. This man spoke with authority. "All right, men! Steady yourselves. I want every item here listed on the inventory. Stop playing with that thing, Barnes."

"Yes, sir. Sorry, sir."

The man in charge walked over to the four kneeling prisoners. Cal kept his gaze on the leader's feet, not wanting to provoke him. He noticed the man's combat boots were so polished they reflected the flames from the fire.

Ken spoke up again, his words distorted by swollen lips. "Who are you people, what do you want with us?"

The man slowly turned to face Ken. "My name is Captain Simon Davidson. I represent the Christian Unified Government. This is an authorised search and seizure operation to locate contraband and looted goods. Now, if you speak out of turn again, I shall have you shot in the kneecaps. Do I make myself clear?"

"Yes," Ken mumbled.

"And you will address me as sir." He motioned to a guard, who promptly hit Ken on the back of the head with his rifle butt.

*For fuck's sake, Ken, just shut up.*

☣☣☣☣

The soldiers took their time over a detailed search of the campsite. They rifled through their possessions, with not a care about the damage and disruption they caused. Anything of interest was added to a list. The four prisoners remained kneeling. Like the others, Cal wore night clothes and soon felt the chill night air. The muscles in his legs ached and his nose continued to throb, but he kept his silence and was relieved that even Ken knew better than to complain.

Captain Davidson strutted around casually. "It's getting late. We'll camp here for the night while we interrogate the prisoners. Set up my tent over there."

After what seemed like an age, Davidson approached the kneeling captives. He sat on a folding chair on the opposite side of the campfire. His soldiers had added logs, so the flames blazed brightly. Most soldiers wore head torches. They moved two vehicles so their headlights illuminated the campsite. The vehicle lights shone into Cal's eyes, making him squint and throwing Davidson into a silhouette. Davidson asked their names and dates of birth, one by one, while a soldier stood by the side, recording all the details. Cal gave his name as John Jones.

Another soldier brought a cup of tea for Davidson, who took it without comment. It reminded Cal of how dry his own throat was.

"Who's in charge? Who speaks for your group?" Davidson said.

Cal and Juliet both spoke together. "I do."

"Typical bloody civvies. Don't even have a leader." He glared at Cal. "I'm treating you as in charge of this little band of...thieves."

Cal bristled, but said nothing.

"You have a lot of modern weapons here. Where did you get them all?"

"Various army bases, sir."

"I see, and what about the food and supplies in your vehicles?"

"We just took those from shops and houses we came across, sir."

"Sergeant, did you hear that?"

"I sure did, sir. He just admitted looting. Plain as day."

Cal saw where this was heading. They were about to be pronounced guilty of trumped-up crimes. He decided he had nothing to lose in trying to plead their case. "With respect, sir, it wasn't looting. Nobody owned that stuff, no one who was alive, anyway."

Davidson motioned with his hand and something hard struck the back of Cal's head.

"You will only speak to answer direct questions. Do you understand?"

"Yes, sir."

"You people have contravened so many laws it's difficult to decide where to start. I presume you have no travel permit?"

"I didn't even know they existed, sir," Cal said. His head still throbbed.

"Too bad. Ignorance is no defence in law. Sergeant, have you made out a charge list yet?"

"Yes, sir!"

"Let me see it."

Davidson read the clipboard the sergeant passed and wrote something on it. "Okay," he said. "The list of charges are; travelling without an authorised permit; failing to register with the C.U.G; multiple counts of looting; possession of firearms without a permit; travelling with weapons and resisting arrest. I'm sure if we looked a little deeper we'd find more transgressions, but we already have sufficient. Mr Jones, as leader of your group, do you have anything to say before I pass sentence?"

"Listen, man—" Ken started to say, but the soldier behind him struck him viciously on the side of his head. Ken fell forward in a heap and lay motionless.

"Ken! Ken!" Susan screamed, then tried to stand up. Strong arms grabbed her shoulder and held her in place.

Davidson chuckled. "Some people never learn." He took a sip from his mug. "Benson! How do you manage to make such fucking lousy tea? Do you piss in it or something?"

"Er, yes sir. I mean, no, sir. I think it's the powdered milk, sir. It ain't no good."

Davidson sipped his tea again, screwed up his face and tipped the rest away. He looked back at Cal. "Well? Do you have anything to say or not?"

The breeze blew smoke from the campfire into Cal's face, making his eyes sting, but he could do nothing to relieve it. "As you say, sir, I'm in charge of this group. We weren't aware we were breaking any rules. If we were, then I'm sorry and I take full responsibility. As for the ordnance, it's all mine, that's why it's all in my Land Rover. I'm an officer in the British Army, trained and allowed to use such weapons. Sir."

This ploy was a long shot, but he hoped the excuse for having the weapons would carry some weight.

Ken groaned and moved.

Davidson leaned back and lit a cigarette. "Well said, Mr Jones—taking responsibility for your actions. Good on you. Usually, by this time, people are whining, grovelling, and begging for mercy. Disgusting. It's a pity we didn't meet under different circumstances."

He took a drag of his cigarette and slowly blew out the smoke. Clearly in no hurry.

"Tell me, John Jones, if that's really your name. You say you were a soldier, eh? What rank, serial number and unit?"

"Captain. 24424202. Sixth Battalion, The Rifles, sir. Finest regiment in the Army."

Davidson nodded. "I see. Tell me, when you were in the army, were you permitted to help yourself to whatever weapons took your fancy?"

Cal's heart sank. "Well, no, of course not, sir."

"No, I'm sure you bloody weren't. You carried only what you were allowed and signed for, didn't you?"

"Yes, sir."

"So, where's your authorisation for that mountain of guns and explosives?"

Cal realised Davidson was not about to be placated. He had doubted his excuse would work, but he had to try—it was all he had.

"Hmm. Suddenly very quiet, aren't you?" Davidson said, smirking. "Sergeant, mark the records that the defendants were found guilty on all charges."

"Sir!"

"Very good. Under the current state of emergency, these crimes more than justify the death penalty. However, in mitigation, I accept that you probably weren't aware of the offences you were committing—communications not being what they were. Furthermore, and, fortunately for you, although you resisted arrest, my men weren't harmed. Thus, I'm inclined to be lenient. Of course, your contraband property will be confiscated. Since you do not possess receipts for anything you have, we'll take everything. That includes the Land Rover. You can keep that monstrosity of a motorhome."

The men chuckled.

"In addition, as punishment for your offences, one of your women is to serve under the C.U.G. for a period of at least six months."

One man gave a wolf whistle. Davidson continued. "You can collect her from C.U.G. headquarters at Drewsteignton at the end of the sentence."

He looked Cal in the eyes, leaned forward, and smiled. "Since you lead this group, you may choose which woman we'll take with us."

"For the love of God. No, please, you can't."

Davidson handed the clipboard back to the sergeant, who was also grinning. The serious business was over, and everything was under control. Now they could enjoy themselves.

"Oh come on now, Mr Jones, or should that be Captain Jones? It's not so bad. If she behaves herself, you'll get her back, more or less intact, and who knows what tricks she'll have learnt in the meantime."

The men guffawed and jeered. One shouted, "I'll teach her a few tricks."

Cal's face twisted with hate and frustration. He futilely pulled at the binding on his wrists. The plastic cable dug deeper into his flesh, but he ignored the pain.

Davidson seemed to enjoy the distress Cal was suffering.

"Come along Jones. If you can't decide, we'll take both of them."

Cal was paralysed with indecision. How could he possibly choose? But if he said nothing, Davidson might take out his spite on both Juliet and Susan.

During the conversation, Ken had gradually been regaining consciousness. Without warning, he sprang up from the ground. With a wild banshee scream, he ran headlong straight through the fire and rammed his head into Davidson's face, throwing them both over backwards.

A scrum ensued while the soldiers pulled Ken away—kicking, screaming, and biting—before they viciously kicked and beat him unconscious.

Davidson staggered to his feet, gasping and holding his face, which streamed with blood. In the dim light, a shiny jet-black waterfall ran from his nose.

"Hold 'em here," he shouted, spitting blood. He lurched away towards the C.U.G. vehicles, with the sergeant following dutifully behind him.

☣☣☣☣

Captain Davidson returned to the campfire a few minutes later, holding a handkerchief up to his face. The front of his jacket was blood-stained.

"Jenkins!" he bellowed, wincing at the pain his shouting caused to his injured nose. The soldier who had been watching over Ken jumped to attention.

"You were supposed to be guarding that man. How did he manage to jump up and attack me?"

"Sir, I don't know, sir. I thought he was unconscious. He was too quick for me, sir!"

"You mean you were too bloody slow! You weren't paying fucking attention, were you!"

"Sir, no sir!"

"Good, I'm glad that's cleared up."

Davidson pulled out his pistol and shot Jenkins in the face. The bullet exploded from the back of his head and he staggered back several steps before falling backwards to the ground, making a dull thud. The other soldiers cursed.

"Let's be clear. The C.U.G. does not tolerate failure or incompetence. Because that man didn't do his job properly, I have a fuckin' broken nose. Learn from this, all of you."

He pointed at Ken, still in an unconscious heap. "This black bastard is to be executed if he ever wakes up. Slowly and painfully, is that understood?"

The group grunted approvingly, glad their officer's wrath was being directed at the prisoners. Susan's whimpering turned into uncontrolled sobbing.

Davidson turned towards Cal. "Well, Jones. That idiot has done you a small favour. You no longer have to choose between your women. Both of them are to serve the C.U.G. for five years!" He pointed to Juliet. "Sergeant, I'll have the blonde one tonight. Take her to my tent and make sure she's well restrained. I'm not in the mood for a wrestling match. The men can amuse themselves with the other bitch."

"Yes, Sir!"

The soldiers whooped and cheered, clearly looking forward to unexpected entertainment. The fate of their comrade was already history.

"Wait!" Juliet said. Everyone stopped and looked at her. "I want to propose a deal."

Davidson laughed. "A deal. The lady wants to deal with us lads."

They snickered.

"This should be interesting."

Davidson turned his folding chair the right way up and sat opposite Juliet.

"Well go ahead, I'm listening."

She took a deep breath. "I have access to several supply caches. They're mostly irreplaceable medical supplies—drugs, antibiotics, that sort of thing. Only I know where they're located, not even my friends could find them. I can take you there. Keep me if you wish, but let my friends go and I'll show you where they are."

Cal groaned inside.

*No. No. No. You don't know what you're doing. You can't bargain with these monsters.*

Davidson smiled. "Hmm. An interesting offer indeed. So it appears your looting has been more extensive than we first thought. No matter."

He stood up. "Sergeant. Tie the two men to that tree." He pointed at a huge oak tree a few yards away. Several soldiers rushed forward, eager to please their officer. They dragged Ken and Cal to the tree and bound them on opposite sides, spread-eagled, with their backs to the bark. Then they pulled Cal's arms behind him and around the tree trunk. Each of Cal's hands was tied to one of Ken's hands. The trunk was so large, Cal's hands barely reached Ken, who stayed unconscious through the process.

As they were being moved, Cal noticed Ken was a terrible mess. His face had been pulped, and one eye was horrifically swollen.

Davidson strutted up and down impatiently as he waited.

"The two men are secure, sir," one soldier declared.

"Good. Now this is where things become really interesting." He turned to the guard standing directly behind Juliet. "Taylor. Make sure the blonde bitch keeps kneeling. Hold her head back tightly, so she doesn't miss any of this."

"Yes, sir!" Taylor knelt right behind Juliet, putting his arm around her neck and taking a good handful of her hair at the back. She cried out.

"Bring the other one over here. Hold her down on the floor and spread her legs nice and wide." Two soldiers came forward and picked up Susan.

"Oh God! No! Please, I've not done anything." Susan screamed. The guards dragged her as she kicked and struggled violently, but their grip was relentless. The troops pushed her down in front of Davidson, and two more men joined in to pin her to the ground. Davidson stared down at her and smiled. The thugs tugged Susan's legs apart and ripped her pyjama trousers off to leave her half-naked.

Davidson strolled to the fire and pulled out a burning stick. He put a cigarette between his lips and lit it with the stick before flicking the stick to kill the flame, leaving the end glowing red hot. Davidson inhaled the cigarette deeply as he looked at Juliet.

"Did you really believe I'd let you bargain your way out with looted goods you've no right to have in the first place?"

Without hesitation, he pressed the glowing stick against the inside of Susan's thigh. She became rigid and gave a piercing scream which went on and on.

Juliet shouted, "Noooo!" and then started sobbing.

Davidson slowly dragged the stick down Susan's thigh, before removing it. Susan wept hysterically.

Cal's mind raced for a way out of this nightmare. Again and again, he pulled at his bonds, to no effect. The smell of burnt flesh reached him and he clamped his throat to hold back the bile.

"Hmm," Davidson said. "This stick has lost most of its heat. I'll need to get a fresh one."

"No, no, no! Stop!" Juliet said. "I'll tell you everything, everything."

"Well, go on then," Davidson said.

"Okay, okay. In our Land Rover. Inside the jacket of the book called 'Herbal Remedies Revisited', there's a map. It shows the location of all the medical caches. There's a code. All the marked sites have an eight-figure number, but only those numbers that include my day and month of birth are real locations."

Davidson nodded. "Excellent. That wasn't so difficult now, was it? Sergeant, find the map."

The Sergeant began rummaging through the pile of books in the Rover and a few moments later shouted. "I've found it, sir. Just like she said."

He ran over to Davidson, opened the map, then showed it to him. Davidson scanned over it.

"Very good indeed. I'm impressed." He walked back to the fire and picked another burning stick out of it.

"No, please," Juliet screamed. "I promise I've told you everything."

"Oh, I'm sure you have," Davidson said. "But you need to understand the consequences of resisting." He pressed the smouldering stick against Susan's other thigh.

☣☣☣☣

By chance, they tied Ken to the tree facing towards the campsite. Cal was on the opposite side, unable to see the horrors unfolding—but he heard them.

After Davidson scorched both of Susan's thighs, he lost interest in her. The soldiers continued to hold her down and took turns to use her while Juliet was forced to watch. Susan screamed continuously, while Juliet pleaded and sobbed. Juliet begged them to leave Susan alone and take her instead. One thug guffawed. "Don't be in such a hurry, darling. Your turn will come soon enough."

Ken moaned. Cal stretched his arm backwards so he could grab Ken's hand and shake it. "Ken, Ken, wake up. You've got to wake up."

"Urrr," Ken coughed several times and spat. "What happened?" He opened his remaining good eye to witness the events in the camp. "Oh shit, no man. No, no, no, no, no. This can't be happening."

"It is happening. We have to stay in control. Keep focused. Look out for an opportunity. Wait 'till they make a mistake."

"Oh, man, are you crazy? We're royally fucked. What are you expecting them to do—accidentally untie us? We're dead meat. All we can hope is that it's quick."

Ken was unaware that Davidson specifically ordered his soldiers to give him a slow and painful death. Cal decided to leave Ken in ignorance.

"I can't see anything from this side. Tell me what's happening."

"You don't want to know."

"Yes, I do! I need to know *everything*. Any information might help us."

"Wake up and smell the coffee, man. There ain't no getting out of here. We're fucked."

"Will you stop moaning and just tell me what's going on, for Christ's sake."

Ken described the macabre scene he was witnessing. He was barely coherent, wailing and groaning pitifully. When the gang rape of Susan ended, her hands were tied behind her and they left her in a naked, sobbing heap.

The sergeant pulled Juliet to her feet and marched her off to Davidson's tent, with the men following in a jeering group. The sounds of voices near the tent reached Cal, but he could not make out the words. Juliet gave a long scream which pierced the night like a dagger. Cheering and laughing followed.

Cal strained against his bonds with every fibre of his being until his veins were ready to burst. When nothing moved, he gave a banshee cry into the woods and collapsed.

Ken spoke up. "Cal. Are you still there?"

"No. I thought I'd go off and take a walk. Of course, I'm still here. You twat!"

"I'm sorry, man. You've been right all along. We should've been more careful."

"Yes, Ken. We should've been more fucking careful."

*And I should have insisted on it.*

A few moments later, a small group of soldiers sauntered towards the oak tree, laughing and joking with each other.

Ken piped up. "Cal. It's time. They're comin' for us. They got fucking big knives. I think they're gonna skin us alive. Oh, God, no."

The men stopped in front of the tree, facing Ken. Once again, Cal could only hear them behind him.

Cal recognised the sergeant's voice. "Okay, men. These are the rules. First man chucks his knife. He says before he throws what he's aiming for. He sets the standard. Second person follows. If he gets closer, then he's still in the game. If not, then he's out. Next person throws and so on. Simple. If the blade hits the fella, it don't count. The prize for each round is a smoke from everyone playing. But if you hit the fella, you lose a smoke, it goes into the pot. Savvy? Remember, you're trying to get as close as you can without cutting the fella. We'll start off with the darkie over here. Questions?"

A voice with a Scottish accent spoke up. "I think we should win an extra smoke if we slice his knob off."

Raucous laughter followed.

So, the soldiers began their macabre knife throwing game, hurling their blades at Ken, aiming to strike close without hitting him. They were drunk and clearly not skilled. Ken screamed many times. With each throw, Cal listened out for either the thud of metal striking timber or the scream of metal sinking into flesh. Frequently, Ken was struck by the knife handle, or blade edge, causing only bruising, or a surface gash.

The game continued for an eternity. The men passed around the bottle of booze. As each round passed, the competitors became increasingly drunk and riotous.

Again, the sound of screaming came from Davidson's tent. Cal used all his strength to fight his bonds, but they held firm. He was utterly defeated.

Eventually, Ken became quiet and stopped reacting to the impacts. One man came forward to check on him. "Aw shit, he's a gonner. Looks like he bled out and we ain't finished our game yet."

"Not to worry. We've got a spare target, remember?"

"Stuff that. I'm fucked and losing too many ciggies. I'm going to turn in."

"You're fucked? Not as much as that bitch over there."

Roars of laughter followed.

"Speaking of which, I think I'll give her another seeing to before bed. Helps me get to sleep."

"Good call, I'll join you," said another.

The sergeant shouted after them, "When you've finished, tie her to a tree or something. I don't want her crawling off in the night."

Cal heard two men walking to the campsite, casually discussing what to try next with Susan. The three remaining soldiers came round the tree and stood in front of him.

"Okay, looks like only the hardcore knife throwers left to settle this contest," the sergeant said, then belched.

Cal watched the proceedings closely and tried to stay calm. He did not know how to survive this situation, but he needed to try. He could do nothing to help Juliet and Susan if he let them kill him.

So, it began again. The soldiers always declared where they were aiming. Cal observed each throw carefully and tried to move his body away at the last moment. Sometimes it worked, sometimes not. Between throws of the knife, the men passed a bottle of whisky to each other.

The knives struck him several times—both arms, a shoulder, a shin. One throw bounced off his chest, leaving a long, shallow gash. He wore a white T-shirt, which soon became drenched in blood.

He must stay alive. It was late into the night and his tormentors were so drunk they staggered about like Bambi on ice. They would get tired and give up the game soon. If he could only hang on for a bit longer.

Now the target was Cal's right thigh. The first throw was accurate and stuck in the tree between his legs, only a few inches from his groin. The other two players would aim closer. On the next throw, Cal tried to gain an inch in height, but the knife still hit him, handle first, before bouncing away. He breathed out, relieved. The men jeered.

"Fuck me, Charlie," said the sergeant. "I hope you never have to do this in a proper fight."

The third man took up position for his turn. He swayed from side to side and blinked several times to focus his vision.

Cal waited until the knife was flying before making the same little jump to gain height. He cried out at the sharp piercing pain and looked down. The blade stuck firmly in his thigh. The men cheered. When the thrower reclaimed his weapon, Cal screamed as it withdrew. If an artery had been opened, he was dead. Cal sensed precious, warm liquid trickling down his leg.

"Jesus, look at the state of that, just like a stuck pig!" one man said.

The next round started. The first pitch landed millimetres from his arm. The next missed the tree entirely, and the knife flew into the bushes. The owner went searching and a few seconds later moaned, "Oh, for fuck's sake. I've stood in some fucker's shit. Jeez, it stinks real bad, it's all over my sodding foot. Bleeding hell, I'll never find my knife in the dark. I'm off to bed. See you two in the morning." With that, he staggered off.

The sergeant used Ken's shirt to wipe the blood off his knife blade. "Time for us to turn in, I think. Davidson will probably be bollocking us to get up early tomorrow. Let's call it a day."

"Right, sarge. Perhaps there's time to visit the lady of the camp once more?"

The sergeant laughed. "I'm bushed, but help yourself."

The two men walked off. Moments later, Susan cried out. Later still, the only sounds were her sobbing and the crackling of the fire.

Now he was alone, Cal remembered earlier in the evening, how Ken had gone for a dump in the bushes. Cal often complained about Ken shitting too near their campsites, yet his pile of crap stopped the knife game. It saved his life—at least for the time being. Saved because Ken was too lazy to walk a few yards from camp. Cal was an expert in military strategy and tactics, yet all his knowledge proved useless. A heap of Ken's excrement saved him.

Cal's thigh badly throbbed, and he could not tell how much blood was draining out. He felt chilled to the bone. That might be due to a loss of blood, or simply because he was tied to a tree wearing only shorts and a T-shirt.

He was alone. This might be the only chance to escape. Once again, he tugged at his bonds with what was left of his strength. Over and over, he wriggled and pulled in different directions. Being spread-eagled against the tree trunk made it difficult to get any leverage and he soon became fatigued without making any difference. Just his luck. Those bastards were good at tying knots.

The next few hours were hellish, as he hung from the tree—cold, exhausted, with pain from a dozen wounds and pitifully miserable. Ken's body hung inches from him The thought of Juliet being violated a short distance away tormented him. Every minute stretched like an hour.

Sleep was impossible. If he relaxed his legs, the ropes yanked at his arms and dug into his shoulders, so he was forced to support his own weight.

Cal replayed the evening over in his head, wondering if he might have done something to avert this disaster. Should he have acted differently? From the outset, he behaved submissive and cooperative—never antagonising the aggressors and waiting for a chance which never came.

On the surface, his behaviour was like the TA training weekend, ten years ago, when he had broken down under interrogation. Yet this was different. Back then, he genuinely crumbled. This time, he was putting on a show. Tonight, his actions were based on rational decisions.

It also felt different from when he escaped Gibson's convoy. Back then, he had panicked and lost the initiative. So what had made the difference tonight?

Perhaps his experiences since the Yellow Death—especially with Gibson's convoy—had made him a little more mature and wiser. But there was something more. That something was Juliet. Everything he did tonight was intended to increase her chance of survival, even at the cost of his own life. Juliet had got under his skin like nobody else.

To think that only a few hours ago he was threatening to leave her. Stupid. He would never have walked away from her, even if it meant living with the Ken and Susan carnival until the end of time.

If only he could be with her and tell her it had all been a stupid mistake and he would stay with her forever. Too bloody late. Why was he always too bloody late?

So, he had managed to stay rational and avoid panicking this time. Where had it got him?

Ken had been the opposite of rational. From the start, he acted aggressively and challenging. Even after being beaten unconscious, he came back and attacked Davidson. Ken was a lazy pain in the arse, yet, when it came down to it, he had guts.

Brave Ken. Indefatigable Ken.

But Ken was dead and nothing he had done made any difference to their fate, either. Or had it? Perhaps Ken made things worse. He had irritated the soldiers from the outset, making them more hostile. Ken prompted Davidson to take both women and give them harsher sentences. He had also bought himself a death sentence.

Reckless Ken. Stupid Ken.

Cal believed his own actions had been the right course. He had stayed quiet and subservient, but not out of fear this time—he had made an informed choice under extreme pressure to maximise the chances of saving Juliet.

But did it make any difference in the end? Cal believed whatever he had done tonight would have resulted in the same conclusion. The soldiers were always going to kill him and Ken so they could take Juliet and Susan. That was what people like them did. The mistake had been to allow the soldiers to ambush them in the first place.

How long would it be before he joined Ken? He might bleed to death quickly, or die slowly of hypothermia, or dehydration, whilst tied to this tree. Or maybe they would shoot him tomorrow morning. There was no way out. He acted so differently to Ken tonight, yet both of them would suffer the same fate and die back to back against this tree.

A gentle rain began to fall, and soon large drops fell from the leaves onto his head and shoulders, soaking his clothes. Never had he felt so cold. Part of him welcomed death, but whilst there was still an infinitesimal chance he might save Juliet, he must cling on to life.

# Chapter Twenty-Eight

# JOHN & CAL

TIMELINE: AT THE TIME OF THE YELLOW DEATH

"There will come a time when you believe everything is finished. That will be the beginning."
Louis L'Amour (1908–1988)

John was aware of nothing but pain, nausea, and discomfort for a long time. Occasionally, he would surface through the layers of delirium. Sometimes it would be light outside his bedroom window and other times dark.

By his bed, a two-litre bottle of water rested on the nightstand. Once in a while, when he became semi-conscious, his desperate thirst was enough to make him suffer the pain of moving an arm to take a drink. His throat was sore, and it hurt to swallow, but it hurt to do anything. That water bottle may have saved his life. The plague killed billions, but dehydration proved to be the final straw for many. Victims would lay alone in bed, lacking the strength to walk to a faucet, with nobody to help.

That bottle also brought him back to the real world. John reached out for it one more time and knocked it off the stand. It made a hollow, bonging sound as it hit the wooden floorboards. John half-opened his eyes. They were caked with sleep, so he blinked several times. The room appeared in brilliant clarity. The sun shone outside the window and bees buzzed around the honeysuckle growing up the wall.

The stench was appalling. A mixture of rancid sweat, urine, and faeces. It shocked him to realise he was the source of the foul odour. The bedclothes stuck to him and were stiff in places, like cardboard. He lifted the top sheet and looked down at his body. He had soiled himself. Badly. His delirious tossing and turning had efficiently spread the substance throughout the bed and over his legs before drying hard.

Only then did it occur to John he had survived the Yellow Death. So what if he felt ghastly? He ached all over, was desperately thirsty and pitifully weak—but he was alive. The fever had passed. Millions, perhaps billions, died, yet he lived. John lay for several minutes revelling in the simple truth of not being dead and wondering why him.

Why not him? A few people would survive, they always did. Natural immunity, a freak genetic mutation? It might even be as simple as being young and fit, with plenty of drinking water. Who cares?

He rolled out of bed after carefully peeling the sheets away from the skin of his legs. He crawled across the landing to the bathroom and drank from the tap. And drank. And drank some more. The tepid water tasted metallic. It tasted wonderful. He was alive.

Fortunately, the shower still worked, although with reduced pressure. The cold water tank was situated in the attic, which overheated on sunny days. Thus, John revelled in a waterfall of lukewarm water. He was alive.

He spent some time removing the caked-on faeces from his legs. The substance proved surprisingly persistent and John had so little strength. John remembered houses used to be built from a mixture of straw and dung, and he could see why.

When he was eventually clean, he crawled from the shower exhausted, and lay naked on the bathroom floor, bathing in the sunlight's warmth streaming through the window. He was alive!

When he closed his eyes, the backs of his lids glowed orange from the sunlight. Such a wonderful colour. Why had he never noticed it before?

Sleep came soon and, when John awoke again, some of his strength had returned.

He wrapped a towel around himself for modesty, realising how ridiculous that was in the circumstances. John went downstairs to the kitchen, gripping the handrail tightly. Unable to face the thought of eating, he stumbled from his mother's cottage across the lawn to his chalet. His reflection in the mirror came as a shock. A cadaverous face with eyes like dark hollows stared back at him. Stubble and yellow teeth completed the picture of decay. All in all, he looked a mess.

Slowly and deliberately, he shaved, combed his hair, and then dressed in a clean army uniform. Every action appeared new and fresh, as if he had just been born as a fully grown man.

Something wonderful occurred to him. No pain in his back. John made a few experimental movements. A little stiffness remained, but he had woken up without pain being his first sensation. Maybe the days of lying in bed, together with the cortisone injections, had promoted healing. Perhaps the Yellow Death had kick-started his immune system. That would be ironic. Still, he knew better than to push his luck, so he spent the next twenty minutes methodically working through his back exercises to loosen up properly.

The power was still out. The phone still silent. The internet still dead. He tried searching for radio stations using the portable radio, but only static greeted him. Pretty much what he expected. John was alive, but civilisation was as dead as the dinosaurs.

He looked in the mirror again and breathed deeply. Much better. Still gaunt, but no longer looking like he was dressed for Halloween.

John walked back to Sarah's cottage, steeling himself for what had to be done next. The garden was vividly coloured, and he revelled in the sun on his face and the twittering orchestra from the avian community.

The inside of the cottage felt dark and foreboding in comparison. An earthy, musty smell struck him. The trudge up the stairs was strenuous, and he gripped the bannister for support. Reaching the top left him breathless and dizzy. A moment to recover himself, before he finally turned the door handle to Sarah's bedroom and pushed the door open, remaining standing on the landing. The odour of decay brought him to his senses, and he stepped into the room.

Sarah lay in bed on her side, curled up like a foetus. Flies buzzed around.

John stood over her. Sarah's body had shrivelled and shrunk. It was as if his mother had moved on, leaving only a husk. John wrapped the bed sheet around her and bent to pick her up, instinctively positioning himself to reduce the strain on his back. She was lighter than a child but, in his weakened state, he could not lift her body. Regrettably, he was forced to drag her corpse across the landing and down the stairs, struggling to give it some dignity.

When he reached the garden, he slumped on the ground to regain his strength.

Sarah would want to be laid to rest here. This was her real home, and she loved the garden more than anything.

The flower borders were a glorious blaze of colour and light and life. John normally never noticed them. He considered gardening as no more than an endless chore. Sarah had always been weeding, pruning, thinning out, replanting, fertilising, or dead-heading. Gardening was never done, never finished. Always a long list of jobs to be tackled. A hell of a lot of work for what purpose? Yet, when he scanned the garden now, he noticed the artistry. The myriad shades and colours complimented one another, whilst the eye naturally darted here and there.

Somehow, his dance with the Grim Reaper generated a new appreciation of life—how long would it last?

At this moment, the garden radiated beauty in a kaleidoscope of colours. Manicured to perfection. But how would it appear in six months, without its human servant constantly tending to it's needs? John felt an urge to capture the vision before the inevitable decline. But what would be the point? His phone—with it's gazillion pixel camera—was now technology from a dead civilisation. Dead Man's Technology.

Only hours after waking, John understood this was a different world. Adapt or die.

He dug the grave—slowly. His progress limited by weakness and the need to stop every few minutes to gather his breath.

As John shovelled out the earth, he thought about his father. Dad was almost certainly dead like everyone else, but what if he wasn't? John could not recollect when they last spoke and had no idea where his father would be. It might equally be Afghanistan or Aldershot. Did it matter? His father had shown no interest in his life to date, so why should that change?

John decided not to waste time searching. His father had been dead to him long before the Yellow Death.

After digging down seventy centimetres, John hit a layer of hard clay and stone. On a normal day, he would fetch a pick-axe and force his way deeper into the regolith, but today he lacked both the will and the strength. "Sorry Mum, this will have to do."

An hour later, he stood over the grave, out of breath, with limbs aching from the effort. The grave was a simple mound of earth. John felt only a strange numbness. He owed her more than this. She bore him and brought him up almost single-handed. Sarah devoted her life to helping him overcome autism. She bought this cottage with him in mind, so he could live on his own. His mother deserved more than this. Why did he not shed a tear?

Yet John never cried. It seemed such emotional intensity was beyond him.

He experienced a strange sense of loss at the thought of never seeing his mother again. Sarah had been such a major part of his life. The one constant. The person who was always there for him—even when he didn't want her to be. He regretted letting her down in her hour of need. He wished he had shown more gratitude for all her support over the years. Also, he felt sadness her life had been cut short—she so much wanted grandchildren. If only he could be with her for another ten minutes. That was all it would take to say thank you for everything she did for him. Too late for that. Always too late.

Despite all these negative feelings, John also had a strange sense of release and freedom, as if some invisible chains had vanished. No more was he 'Sarah's John', who lived at the bottom of the garden like a gnome. All the bonds to his previous life were shattered. Now he was truly independent of his mother and did not need to consider how his actions would affect her, or anyone else.

He tried to suppress the emotion. Billions had died in a gruesome manner, including everyone he ever knew. No way should he feel anything positive about this horror show. Why was he not traumatised? Why was he not in shock, like a normal person?

Perhaps because he wasn't a 'normal' person.

Maybe it was because he lacked any real friends or social contacts. His relationship with his father was non-existent and he had no siblings, uncles, or aunts. He could think of nothing from the old world he much cared for, or would particularly miss. He could shed the old world as easily as removing a worn-out, dirty coat—except for his mother.

John wanted to speak poignant words over her grave, but even had he known a prayer, he would not have recited it. He no more believed in God than he did Father Christmas. John knew no poetry or meaningful prose.

"Goodbye Mum. Your garden looks beautiful. I wish you were here to see it. Thanks for everything. I'll try to make you proud of me. I promise I'll make something good out of my life."

☣☣☣☣

After John finished burying his mother, he went back into her cottage to rest and eat. The feat of digging his mother's grave left him drained. Although the sun shone full in the sky, he remained chilled to the bone. The house was cold, so he opened the French doors, letting in the warmth and releasing the stench of death.

Nature had woken up, unconcerned with the human misery. Songbirds sang, pigeons strutted on the lawn and cooed, distant sheep bleated. The bees provided their background buzz as they busied themselves with the roses on the trellis next to the door.

John did not realise he was hungry until he put food in his mouth and then he stuffed himself silly. Nothing fancy. The food in the freezer and fridge had gone bad. A layer of green mould covered the loaf in the bread bin. So, he opened a few cans and ate out of them, moaning with pleasure as syrupy tinned peaches slid down his throat.

He boiled a saucepan of water and made an enormous pot of tea. Fortunately, his mother kept cartons of long-life milk in the larder "for emergencies". He thought this probably qualified as an emergency.

He sat looking out at the garden and savoured his brew. A mug of tea never tasted so good. Breathing in the steam felt comforting and familiar.

The world had changed. Almost everyone had died. The UK population reduced from tens of millions to perhaps tens of thousands—or less. All the beloved technology gone. No more social media. That was one thing he wouldn't miss. His skills as a website developer were entirely useless. Not much call for writing HTML code in a pre-industrial society. Good. Coding bored him stiff anyway—something else he was glad to see the back of.

So, if he couldn't write code for websites, what would he do? People defined themselves by their jobs. They didn't say 'my job is a builder', or 'my job is a solicitor'. They'd say 'I'm a builder', or 'I'm a solicitor'. It was the first question to ask a stranger. If somebody said they were retired, the next question would be, "What did you do before you retired?" A person's occupation defined their status and value.

How would he respond to a stranger asking about his job?

Cal chuckled. He could say whatever he wanted. The rules had all changed. All the records and central databases were as dead as the civilisation which created them. He might say he was an astronaut, or a brain surgeon. Nobody could prove different. He didn't fancy telling people he was a website developer. That was boring and identified him as a geek. Besides, it also labelled him as useless. Who needed a website developer after the apocalypse?

Which persona should he adopt to impress others? What might he pass himself off as? The answer was obvious—a soldier. After all, there was some truth to the story, since he'd served in the T.A. He loved the idea of being a soldier hero.

So, from today, he would tell everyone he was a full-time soldier. An officer, no less. In reality, the army had rejected John's officer application because he was a nerd with autism. They didn't have the foresight to see his talents. That was their mistake. Now he would declare himself to be an officer. A Captain. A Captain with combat experience in Afghanistan, Syria and who knows where else? He would think up the details later. Making up a cover story would be fun. Perhaps he should have medals for bravery? No. No. No. That crossed a line. It felt wrong to falsely claim to have won a medal.

This was great. His imagination was turbo charged. He would completely reinvent himself. No more would he be a dorky developer with a dodgy back, living in his mother's garden. He was a captain in the British Army.

What else to upgrade? How about his name? His first name was okay, but so common, and he yearned for something distinctive. People changed their names all the time. Now was the perfect time to adopt a new name. In the T.A. they called him 'Cal'. He liked the name. Simple, easy to say and to recognise. That would do nicely. From now on, he wouldn't answer to 'John Callaghan-Bryant'. He would be 'Cal'. Cal the soldier.

Fantastic! He had been reborn—or reinvented. What was he going to do next? The first priority would be to arm himself. Law and order were out of the window and everyone had to look out for themselves. He would visit the nearest army base and get tooled up.

After that, he needed a suitable vehicle. Cal, the kick-ass soldier, would not drive about in a Volkswagen Golf. He should have a rugged SUV. Now he could take any one he wanted. Bloody brilliant. He would need to fit a tow bar and roof rack, but that should not be beyond his capabilities—at his disposal were unlimited tools and materials.

The third item on his list would be to kit himself out with camping equipment. He would live on the road, carrying everything he needed with him. A small tent, sleeping bag, mat, stove, torches—he would make a list—only the best quality goods would do, since the price was irrelevant.

Those tasks would keep him busy for a few days, but what about long-term plans? He suspected the world would degenerate into brutality. Without Government or police, there would be nothing to stop the worst elements of society from running amok. Even assuming most people were good most of the time, there would be a minority taking advantage of the situation.

The strong do eat, the weak are meat. Owning anything meant nothing unless you had the power to stop others from stealing it from you.

In the land of the blind, the one-eyed man is king. In post-Yellow Death Britain, the man with the gun was king. Those with weapons would be the rulers. John knew about weapons. He should collect and hoard as much modern weaponry and ammunition as possible.

By having a store of armaments, he would make sure they ended up in the right hands. He would give them to people who needed to defend themselves and keep them away from thugs who wanted to prey on the innocent. Maybe he would be some sort of modern-day Robin Hood? That was so much cooler than being a web developer.

So, he had his purpose, at least for a while. Of course, it would also be sensible to store food and other irreplaceable essentials. Even if he restricted his searches to just Devon, that was 3,000 square miles of land with 8,000 miles of roads. Enough to keep him busy for months.

After that, he would need to settle down somewhere. He would choose a community showing promise which shared his values. They would welcome him with open arms if he brought supplies of weapons and provisions. This was fantastic. He had a plan and a purpose—for the first time in his life.

John—now Cal—put his cup down. He had drunk three mugs of tea and finally, his thirst was quenched. Time to get moving. He was on a mission. By tonight, he would be armed and driving his brand-new SUV. He would do what he wanted when he wanted. Nobody would give him orders, look down on him, or make fun of him ever again.

## Chapter Twenty-Nine

# Kim & The Yellow Death

TIMELINE: At the time of the Yellow Death

"Must not all things at the last be swallowed up in death?"

Plato (427–347 BCE)

Kim continued to deteriorate until she was forced to retreat to her bed. She displayed all the Yellow Death symptoms being reported on the news—fever, shivering, headaches, nausea, stomach cramps, vomiting and diarrhoea. Painful swellings developed in her neck and armpits. Her hair and clothes stuck to her skin with sweat.

Over the next three days, Rachel did everything possible to help Kim get through the fever, including making her drink plenty of water and take the precious antibiotics. Even in her agony, Kim asked about Katy, and Rachel assured her Katy was fine and being taken care of. Rachel said she thought it best to keep Katy away from Kim. Katy would be distressed to see her mother so ill and might become infected with close contact.

That's what Rachel told Kim during one of Kim's brief periods of lucidity. In truth, Katy lay deathly ill in her bedroom. She developed symptoms shortly after Kim had taken to her bed. The disease progressed rapidly in the little girl, exactly as Rachel had been told to expect.

Rachel remembered the words her scientist friend spoke. "There's no good news, Rachel. The information coming from around the world indicates almost everyone is dying. We've no resistance and nothing seems to have much effect. These drugs may help a little. They appear to increase the survival rate from bugger all to a few percent. But..." he had fixed his gaze on her. "Use them wisely. All the reports suggest nobody past their sixties survives, even with the medicine. This damned disease kills elderly people fast and without exception. I'm sorry, but these won't do you any good."

Rachel was not surprised. Even common diseases, such as flu, took the heaviest toll on the aged. "What about the young? Will these pills work on children?"

He frowned. "We don't know for sure. There's been little time for testing and so many are dying whatever we do. What we suspect is these antibiotics give us a slight advantage. For a healthy adult, they may tilt the balance between life and death. But a small child is unlikely to have the stamina to fight this disease even with antibiotics. Probably. It's all guesswork. I wish I could tell you something more definite."

"So, you can't rule out the chance that the pills might help a child?"

He shrugged. "We lack reliable evidence either way. If we only had a few months to do some trials."

Those words created a dilemma for Rachel. She needed to choose between Kim and Katy. Daughter or granddaughter. It sounded like Kim would stand the greatest chance of survival if she took the pills. Even if Katy miraculously survived because of the drugs, she would wake up to find her mother dead. How might a three-year-old survive alone in a post-apocalyptic world? Katy could not even open a can of soup, or get out of the house. If Kim didn't survive, then neither could Katy. Thus, cold hard logic dictated Kim should be the one to take the new medicine.

However, if Kim knew the truth, she would never agree. She would insist Katy be given the pills. In that event, both would almost certainly die.

So Rachel made her choice. She lied to Kim and told her Katy could not have the antibiotics. She hoped if Kim survived, she would be able to live with that choice and forgive her.

☣☣☣☣

Rachel woke with a start. The book she had been cradling slid from her lap onto the floor. The thud had woken her. The room was dark. She felt cold and stiff.

Katy lay in her bed next to her. It took a few seconds to orientate herself and remember where she was. She had fallen asleep reading a bedtime story. *'Giraffes Can't Dance'* was one of Katy's favourite story books. Rachel must have read it to her hundreds of times.

Although the curtains were closed, Rachel could hear the steady thrum of rain on the windowpanes. In the dim light of the candle, she noted the time—four a.m.

"Oh, my goodness. Time for Kim's last antibiotic tablet."

For three days, Rachel had conscientiously nursed her daughter and granddaughter. At times, she virtually had to force the antibiotics down Kim's throat as she struggled to swallow.

Rachel reached out to hold her granddaughter's hand and recoiled in shock. The flesh was frigid. She stood up and bent over Katy. The life had left her small body some time ago.

"Oh no. My poor, sweet, innocent, little girl. You never stood a chance."

Rachel remained rigid for a few moments, gazing at her granddaughter's still face. Katy was at peace and could have been sleeping. *Thank God her eyes are closed.* Rachel sat down and quietly wept until she had no more tears, before wiping her eyes with a handkerchief.

Rachel picked up Panda, Katy's favourite cuddly toy, put him next to her body and put Katy's arm over the toy. She tidied Katy's hair and wiped a dribble of dried spittle from her cheek. Finally, she lifted the sheet and covered her. This was how she wanted Kim to find her.

The dying candle sputtered out, and Rachel was grateful for the cloak of darkness.

"Goodbye, my darling. You were too good for this world. I hope we meet again in a better one."

Rachel crept into Kim's room, bracing herself for another shock. It took all of her courage to switch on the torch and shine the beam on Kim's bed. Kim lay on her back, hair stuck to her forehead with dried sweat. At some point, she had thrown the bedsheets off herself.

*Thank God she's still breathing.*

Rachel gathered up the sheets again and wrapped them carefully around Kim. She poured a glass of Lucozade energy drink and lifted Kim into a half-sitting position. Kim groaned, cradled her armpits, and half opened her eyes.

"Here, sip this," Rachel said.

Kim took several sips. Rachel held up the antibiotic pill, so Kim could see it.

"No," Kim said, her voice only a croak. "Throat hurts...can't swallow."

"Yes, you damn well can, Kim Sullivan," Rachel said with a firm voice. She put her fingers in Kim's mouth and deposited the tablet on the back of her tongue.

"Drink," she said.

"Want...sleep, feel awful."

"You can sleep as soon as you've swallowed your pill."

Kim took another sip of Lucozade, then swallowed, half choking, but the pill stayed down. Rachel lowered her again, then started to leave the room.

"Katy?" Kim moaned.

Rachel did not turn around. "Katy's fine. She's fast asleep in her bedroom. Now you get some sleep too. You need to get your strength back. You must get better to look after Katy."

☣☣☣☣

Rachel came downstairs. The headache had started a short time ago, and she felt feverish with a gut ache. She was surprised at how long her aged body had resisted the disease, but was grateful for the delay. Katy had not died alone and, perhaps it was her imagination, but Kim slept more comfortably. Rachel had given Kim the full course of antibiotics and kept her hydrated and clean. Kim's life was in the hands of God now. There was still hope.

Rachel had already tidied the house and thrown away food spoiling in the fridge. She had written a brief note for Kim. Perhaps if Kim lived through this nightmare, she would understand the impossible decision and forgive her.

*Please, God, let Kim have the strength to carry on. Don't let it all end here.*

She had done all she could and knew soon she, too, would be incapacitated. This was her time now.

Rachel walked into the living room, put the candle on the coffee table and drew back the curtains to let in the early dawn light. Rain rattled against the windows. She slumped on the couch and pulled a blanket over her knees. Beside her sat a bottle of *Glenfiddich* twelve-year-old single malt whiskey, a bottle of sleeping pills, a photograph of the family and her favourite book: *A Tale of Two Cities*, by Charles Dickens.

After pouring a good measure of whisky, she put it under her nose and savoured the peaty, oaky aroma. She carefully placed two pills on her tongue, before washing them down with a gulp of whisky. The golden liquid made her cough, but the burning in her throat felt good. She repeated the process another three times, then filled her glass one final time. Settling back on the couch, she opened the book at the first page and started reading:

It was the best of times,
It was the worst of times,
It was the age of wisdom,
It was the age of foolishness,
It was the epoch of belief,
It was the epoch of incredulity,
It was the season of light,
It was the season of darkness,
It was the spring of hope,
It was the winter of despair…

# AFTERWORD

THIS IS THE CONCLUSION OF BOOK ONE OF THE YELLOW DEATH CHRONICLES. THE STORY CONTINUES WITH YELLOW DEATH: AFTERMATH.

If you have enjoyed this story, please leave a review on Amazon and other bookish websites. You can hardly imagine how important it is for independent authors like myself to receive ratings from readers. Not only does it mean that Amazon is more likely to recommend the book to other readers, but it really means a lot to me personally to know what you think.

QR code to leave a review on Amazon.com

QR code to leave a review on Amazon.co.uk

If you wish to sign up for my irregular newsletter, you will receive a free novella with story background and deleted scenes. Please visit www.peterhallauthor.com or scan the QR code below:

And remember: When faced with two decisions, always favour the boldest. That proverb was written down and handed to me by Chay Blythe—the round-the-world yachtsman—when I was a small boy. It made a big impression and I deeply regret losing the postcard it was written on.

# Acknowledgements

What started as a solitary project became a family collaboration and is all the better for it. Suzanne, David, Seb, and Jenny worked through various drafts and provided much useful feedback.

Special mention to my beta readers whose input added the final polish: Suzanne Hall, Valjandra Davis, Peter Sevenoaks, and Meredith Hurst.

I'm also grateful for the help and support from these Facebook groups:

> SPF Community
> SPF Genius
> On Writing
> South West Authors and Writers (UK)

My Website: www.peterhallauthor.com

I love to hear from my readers and will reply to all emails and enquiries. The best way to submit these is to send an email to peter@peterhallauthor.com.

Printed in Great Britain
by Amazon